THE
UNCOMMON APPEAL
OF CLOUDS

ALEXANDER McCALL SMITH

ISIS
LARGE
PRINT

First published in Great Britain 2012
by
Little, Brown Book Group
an imprint of Headline Publishing Group

First Isis Edition
published 2016
by arrangement with
Little, Brown Book Group
An Hachette UK Company

A catalogue record for this book is available
from the British Library.

ISBN 978–1–78541–146–5 (hb)
ISBN 978–1–78541–152–6 (pb)

THE UNCOMMON APPEAL OF CLOUDS

As a philosopher, mother, employer and resident of Edinburgh — the birthplace of moral philosophy — Isabel Dalhousie is aware that to be human is to be responsible. But morals, it turns out, are rather like clouds: complex, changeable and tricky to get a grip on. As she enters into ransom negotiations over a stolen painting on behalf of wealthy philanthropist Duncan Munrowe, a case where heroes and villains should be obvious turns murky. The list of those who desire the painting — or the money — is long, and hasty judgement must be avoided. Isabel has tact, a lively intelligence and a sharp eye, and she'll need them all if she is to see the culprit clearly.

This book is for Edward and Maryla Green

CHAPTER
ONE

"Mozart," said Isabel Dalhousie. And then she added, "Srinivasa Ramanujan."

From his side of the kitchen table, Jamie, her husband of one year, lover of more than four, looked up quizzically. "Mozart, of course, but Srini . . ." He attempted the name, but decided he could not manage it and trailed off into a liquid melt of *vees* and *sibilants*. Indian names, mellifluous sounding though so many of them may be, can defeat even those with a musical ear. Jamie was accustomed to the stocky sound of Scottish names, redolent as they were of an altogether more forbidding and windswept landscape — those Macdonalds and Macgregors, Macleans and Mackays.

"Srinivasa Ramanujan," Isabel repeated. "He was, like Mozart, a child prodigy. A genius."

"I used to be so discouraged by Mozart," said Jamie. "I suspect he has that effect on any child who's interested in music. You hear about how he was composing complicated pieces at the age of five, or whatever, and you think *I'm already twelve* — *which is ancient by comparison* — *and I haven't written anything*. And it makes you ask yourself whether there's much point in making all that effort." He paused. "But what about this Srinivasa?"

1

"He was a brilliant mathematician back in his day," said Isabel. She made a gesture that indicated the earlier part of the twentieth century — or at least did so to her; to Jamie it was no more than a vague movement of the hand. "He died when he was barely into his forties."

"Like Mozart. What age was he when he died? Thirty-five, wasn't he?"

Isabel nodded. "Which prompts the usual thoughts of what might have been."

"Of music lost," said Jamie. He had noticed that people invariably said something like that when the shortness of Mozart's life was mentioned. What he could have done if he had lived another ten years, another twenty . . . the symphonies, the operas . . .

Isabel reached for her teacup. "Yes. And in the case of Ramanujan, of problems unsolved. But that's not what interests me. I've been thinking of the parents and of their role in their children's lives. Mozart's father spent a very large part of his time on his children's musical education. Teaching him to compose, taking him on those long tours. A pushy father, if ever there was one."

"And Srinivasa . . . what about his parents?"

Isabel smiled. "He had a mother to contend with. She doted on him. She said that he was the special gift of the household's private god. She was a mathematician too."

"So the best chance of being a prodigy is to have an obsessive parent?"

Isabel agreed, but only to an extent. She believed in nurture, but she gave more weight to nature. "You have

2

to have the right genes in the first place. Mozart's sister had the same upbringing as he did, with the same musical attention. She became a very competent performer but she was not a musical genius."

Jamie looked up at the ceiling. "Imagine being Mozart's sister . . ."

"Yes, imagine. That bit — the genius bit — has to be there somewhere in the brain. It's probably a matter of brain design, of neuro-anatomy. Mozart had it; his sister clearly didn't."

Jamie called that the *wiring*. Badness, he thought, was usually a question of faulty wiring; Isabel was not so sure. "I read about a rather interesting case of mathematical genius," she said. "Nabokov."

"The author? The one who wrote *Lolita*?"

"Yes," said Isabel. "Nabokov was a mathematical prodigy as a child. He could do elaborate calculations in his head, within seconds."

Jamie was interested. Musicians were often competent or even more than competent mathematicians — the *wiring*, perhaps, was similar. At school his best subject, after music, had been mathematics, and yet he had always had to approach it slowly, even ploddingly. "How do they do it? I just can't imagine how it's possible. Do they have to think it through, or does the answer come to them automatically, just like that?"

Isabel said that she thought they had their tricks — systems that allowed them to make seemingly instantaneous calculations, just as people with exceptional memories had their mnemonics. "Some of it, though, comes to them instantly because they just *know* it." She took a sip of her iced tea, and looked at Jamie. "You wouldn't have to think, would you, if I asked you what number multiplied by itself gives you nine." She smiled encouragingly. "Would you?"

"Three."

"You didn't have to work that out?"

Jamie replied that the answer had simply been there. He had, in fact, seen the figure 3.

"Then perhaps it's the same for them," said Isabel. "The work is done at a subconscious level — the conscious mind doesn't even know it's being done." She returned to Nabokov. "He was capable of amazing calculations and then suddenly he became ill with a very high fever. When he recovered his mathematical ability had gone. Just like that."

"The fever affected the brain?"

"Yes. Burned out the wiring, as you might say."

"How strange."

"Yes. Very."

They looked at one another wordlessly. Each knew that the other was thinking of their young son, Charlie, now an energetic three-and-three-quarter-year-old; energetic, but currently asleep in his bedroom on that summer morning that was already growing hot. An uncharacteristic heat wave had descended on Edinburgh and the east of Scotland. It brought with it not only a summer languor, but the scent of the country into the town — cut hay, baked hillsides, heather that was soon to flower purple, the sea at Cramond . . .

Isabel broke the silence. "So what exactly did he say?"

4

Jamie's reply was hesitant. "I think it was something like this. You know those bricks of his — the yellow ones?"

Isabel did. They had on them bright pictures of ducks engaged in various pursuits — driving a train, drinking tea, flying in small biplanes — and Charlie adored them, even to the extent of secreting one of them under his pillow at night. One could love anything as a child, she thought; a teddy bear, a security blanket, a yellow brick . . .

"There were twenty bricks," Jamie went on. "We counted them. And he counted with me, all the way up to twenty — which is impressive enough, if you ask me. But then I said, 'Let's take half of them away.' I don't know why I said it — I hadn't imagined that he'd be able to cope with the concept of halves. But you know what he said? He said, 'Ten.' Just like that. He said, 'Ten.'"

There was more. "Then I said, 'All right, let's put eight bricks here and take half of those away.' And he said, 'Four.' He didn't even seem to think about it."

Isabel was listening intently. Had Charlie ever done anything similar for her? She did not think so. He had asked some perceptive questions, though, and one or two of them had startled her. The other day, apropos of nothing, he had suddenly said, "Brother Fox know something? Know not a dog?" She had been momentarily taken aback but had replied, "I think he knows that." Then she had quizzed him as to why he had asked her this, but his attention had been caught by something else and he had simply said, "Foxes and dogs," before moving on to another, quite different subject. For Isabel's part, she had been left with a question that had become increasingly intriguing the more she thought about it. Brother Fox presumably instinctively understood that dogs were not part of his world, but did that mean that he had some concept of *foxdom*? Probably not.

"So then I tried something different," Jamie continued. "I took nine bricks and asked him to put them in three piles that were all the same. And you know what he said? He said, 'Three.' He said, 'Three bricks, here, here, here.' "

Isabel looked thoughtful. "Division. It sounds impressive, but is it all that unusual?"

Jamie shrugged. "I asked them at the nursery school. They said children of four should be able to add and count up to five. They said nothing about division, or multiplication. Just counting."

"Or the piano," added Isabel.

"Or that. I told them that he can do a C major scale and they said something about his hands still being quite small and it must be difficult for that reason. They didn't seem all that interested."

Isabel imagined that there were numerous parents who believed their children to have prodigious skills and boasted to teachers about it. She did not want to be one of them; and yet if the child was really talented, then shouldn't the nursery at least know?

From upstairs there came the sound of a high-pitched voice — something between a chuckle and a shout. Charlie was awake.

6

"I'll go," said Jamie.

Isabel nodded. "We'll need to talk about it. About what we do — if anything."

He gave her a searching look. "Do about what? About his being good at numbers? You think we should ignore it rather than encourage it?"

"I'm just not sure that it's in his interests. Would he be any happier if we encouraged him to be a mathematical prodigy?" And there was something else that worried her: being a pushy mother. All mothers were pushy to an extent: one did not have to look far in the natural world to see mothers being pushy for their offspring — any self-respecting lioness would make sure her cubs got their fair share — but there were limits . . . "I don't think we should push him too much."

Jamie frowned. He encountered pushy parents in his work, and one in particular came to mind. She had written to him recently asking whether her son's innate musical ability was being adequately recognised and whether he was ready for a public performance. Jamie did not want the stage of the Usher Hall for Charlie, although if it came to that he and Isabel would of course be in the front row. And Charlie would come onstage and need a box to stand on to climb on to the piano stool; or perhaps have his teddy bear carefully seated on the stool next to him while the conductor raised his baton to bring the accompanying orchestra to order. The frown became a smile. "Can one ignore something like that? Wouldn't that be to waste it?"

Isabel did not have time to answer. Another cry came from Charlie, more urgent now, followed by a rattling of the bars at the top of his bed. Jamie began to leave the kitchen but turned at the door and said, "Mozart was quite happy being Mozart, you know. He liked billiards. He kept a canary — and a horse. He enjoyed practical jokes."

Isabel reflected on this while Jamie was upstairs. To play billiards, to keep a canary and a horse, and to enjoy practical jokes — were very ordinary things like that the recipe for an enjoyable life?

That conversation with Jamie about mathematical ability took place on one of Isabel's working days. Jamie, who was a musician, kept irregular hours, and frequently had days when not only did he not have any rehearsal or performance commitments, but he also had no teaching. He taught bassoon at the Edinburgh Academy and had a number of private pupils too, but he managed to cram all his teaching into two mornings and one afternoon a week, which left three weekdays for other things. Those days might easily have filled up with session work or preparation for concerts but times were hard and there seemed less and less of that work around. "Perhaps the music's stopped," he remarked to Isabel. She had assured him that music seemed to continue in the face of every difficulty, just as philosophy did. "We imagine our crises are unlike all other crises," she said. "But they aren't. There's always been uncertainty. There's always been danger. It's the human condition — the normal one, perhaps."

On Jamie's free days, he took over responsibility for Charlie, allowing Isabel to attend to her job as editor,

8

and owner too, of the *Review of Applied Ethics*. Charlie now went to a small nursery school round the corner, and Jamie would take him there at eight-thirty in the morning, deposit him in the classroom with his neatly packed tiffin box, and then return for him five hours later. After lunch, while Isabel worked in her study on the latest issue of the *Review*, Jamie would often supervise Charlie's afternoon rest, read to him, play the piano with him, or take him for a walk by the canal or, as a special treat, to Blackford Pond. That pond, inhabited by a tribe of over-fed and demanding ducks, could keep Charlie amused for hours, and Jamie knew every inch of its muddy shore quite as well as an experienced mariner knows the bays and inlets of his native waters. He had also come to know the personality of the various ducks and could identify where each stood in order of precedence. Size, it seemed, was the sole determinant of that.

Even though she had made an early start while it was still comparatively cool, already the weather was making it difficult for Isabel to work. She had opened her study windows, but there was only an intermittent breeze and the air inside was heavy. Her study had a particular smell to it — the smell of paper, she had decided — and for some reason this oppressed her. Perhaps it was not a day on which to sequester oneself inside; perhaps it was simply not a day on which to do philosophy. Her friend, Julian Baggini, who, like her, edited a philosophical paper, seemed to be able to do his thinking in all sorts of circumstances — in the car, in a train, in the bath — but it was different for Isabel.

9

It was true that thoughts came to her at the oddest of moments, but what she called *organised thinking* needed the time and place to be right; and the thinking she was trying to do that day — assessing submissions for a future issue of the *Review* — was definitely organised thinking.

She got up from her desk, putting aside the paper she had been trying to read. There was nothing wrong with the paper itself, which was a discussion of responsibility to future generations; there was no reason why it should not see the light of day. The author was a post-doctoral fellow at the University of Toronto and needed publications for the next stage of her career. Isabel knew just how competitive the academic world could be and just how easily people could fall at any of the fences that stood between them and a career as a philosopher. She was aware that the author would be waiting anxiously for her verdict, and that a positive answer would lead to the popping of champagne corks, real or metaphorical, in some apartment in Toronto. All that was required was a one-word email: *Yes*. One word, three letters, that would bring such joy to somebody she had never met and probably never would. And by the same token, *No* would have the opposite effect.

She had found it difficult to concentrate on the author's argument. We obviously can owe duties to people we do not know. *Yes, of course we can*. So what is the difference between people who do not yet exist (future generations) and people we do not know? Well, thought Isabel, one set of people exists and the other does not. So, the author continued, the essence of the problem is whether one can harm the non-existent. *Or is it?* Isabel asked herself. Surely the non-existence of the victim at the time of the harmful act is not the real issue: the real issue is future harm to people *who will exist.*

Eating fish, the author wrote, *is a good example.* We know that if we eat fish now, fish stocks will be depleted and there will not be enough for the people who follow us. So does our current hunger — or current taste for fish — justify using up fish stocks that would otherwise be enjoyed by people as yet unborn? *Do we owe any fish to those who follow us?* the paper asked.

Do we owe any fish to those who follow us? The sentence struck Isabel as vaguely comic, as if it might have been lifted from some music-hall song; it was redolent, perhaps, of "Yes, we have no bananas".

She put the paper down and moved across the room to the open window. From where she was standing, she could see her neighbour's contract gardener digging in a flower-bed. He was a hard-working man who had once told her that he looked after twenty gardens and was thinking of taking on several more. He had been a coal miner before the mines closed — digging, in one form or another, had been his life. And thinking of that made Isabel wonder whether the work she did — thinking about responsibility to future generations and such problems — could really be described as work. Work usually made something happen in the world, and she was not sure whether she did that at all. There was a physical product — several hundred copies of a journal once every three months — but did that actually change anything?

She looked at her watch. She was due to relieve Jamie of Charlie duties in two hours' time but if she stopped work now she would have time to go to her niece Cat's delicatessen and buy something for lunch. Cat had a supplier who delivered freshly made onion tarts in the morning, which people picked up during their lunchbreak or on their way home from work. If she left now, she would be able to have her choice of the tarts, and still have time to finish reading the responsibility-to-future-generations paper — and make a decision too. It would be yes, of course; she already felt that.

She closed her study windows, collected her shopping bag from the kitchen cupboard and let herself out of the house. It was even warmer outside than indoors, though tucked inside the shopping bag was her light jacket; the weather in Edinburgh was notoriously fickle, and even a day like this could suddenly turn hostile. There would be room for the onion tart too, and for some salad things — the bag was capacious.

She made her way into Bruntsfield. Halfway along the road, she saw a large For Sale notice on the railings of one of the houses. She stopped and looked up at the windows of the property. It was a large Victorian house that had been divided into flats, and it was one of these that was now on the market. She paused; she had been expecting its sale, as the owner, a quiet man whom people rarely saw, had died six months before. He had lived by himself and it was thought that he had met somebody one evening who had stabbed him to death in his own hallway.

Isabel stared up at the windows. Places where unhappy events have taken place are no different from anywhere else. The physical world — the world of stone and brick — is indifferent to our suffering, to our dramas, she thought. Even a battlefield can be peaceful, can be a place for flowers to grow, for children to play; the memories, the sadness, are within us, not part of the world about us. And yet this house, as she gazed at it, seemed bereft, seemed tragic and loveless, a reminder of the dark thing that had happened there.

"Isabel?"

She gave a start.

"Sorry to give you a fright."

She turned and saw Martha Drummond. In Isabel's life, Martha was one of those people who occupied that awkward territory between acquaintanceship and friendship; she saw her relatively infrequently and they were not on dropping-in terms. If she had been pressed, Isabel would probably have confessed that she found Martha slightly irritating, and felt bad about this feeling. It was hard to put her finger on it: Martha meant well — whatever that meant — but had the habit of making intrusive remarks. There were some people, in Isabel's view, who lacked social judgement, not picking up quite the same social cues as others did. The expression "They don't quite get it" expressed the notion exactly. They didn't.

Martha lived several streets away, in a house surrounded by a large rhododendron-filled garden. And the rhododendrons were a case in point: a few months ago, when Isabel had bumped into Martha in the supermarket, there had been an exchange that had left Isabel thinking distinctly uncharitable thoughts. Martha had let drop the fact that she had recently walked past Isabel's garden and noticed her rhododendrons. "They don't seem to be doing all that well," she said casually. "My own rhododendrons are much more — how shall I put it? — luxuriant."

Isabel had stared at her mutely. "There's nothing wrong with my rhododendrons," she had eventually said. It was extremely tactless, she thought, to criticise another person's rhododendrons and, anyway, such criticism in this context was objectively wrong.

"They don't look very healthy to me," Martha persisted. "Perhaps you've got the wrong sort of soil."

Isabel smarted. That was another serious accusation: to suggest to somebody that they have the wrong sort of soil.

"There's nothing wrong with my soil," she said coolly. "Or with my rhododendrons, for that matter."

It had been a ridiculous exchange but it was typical of the direction in which a conversation with Martha could go. And it was for that reason that Isabel found it difficult to consider Martha as a friend, although she knew that friendship did not depend on seeing eye-to-eye.

Martha, who was in her early forties and divorced, shared her rhododendron-surrounded house with her elderly mother who, in her heyday, had been one of Scotland's best-known artists. Isabel liked her work,

14

and had one of her smaller paintings in a corner of her study.

"Not the best of Mother's works," Martha had said when Isabel had shown it to her. "In fact, barely recognisable as one of her works at all."

That had led to another pointless exchange. "Others might not agree with you," Isabel suggested through clenched teeth.

"But others are not the painter's own daughter," retorted Martha. "I imagine that people don't dismiss too readily the opinions of Paloma Picasso."

Isabel had quickly planned her reply to that. A painter's family, she would suggest, were probably the last people to be asked for a judgement on their relative's work — they were simply too close to it, too emotionally involved to be able to give an objective view. But she stopped herself, mainly because it would not be true. Members of the family were often the best of judges, just as her friend, Guy Peploe — to think of only one example — was the best judge of the paintings of his grandfather, S. J. Peploe. So she had said nothing.

Now, standing in front of the For Sale notice, Martha asked after Charlie. "Where's your little boy?"

"Jamie's taken him to nursery," Isabel explained. She pointed to the notice. "I was thinking about this . . ."

Martha sighed. "Very sad. Did you know him?"

"I think I saw him," said Isabel. "But no, I didn't know him."

They were both silent for a few moments. Then Martha asked Isabel whether she was going to Cat's delicatessen. "I thought you might be," she said. "Something easy for lunch?"

Isabel smiled, and nodded.

"I'm headed there too," said Martha. "I can't be bothered to cook in this heat. And Mother eats like a bird. A couple of lettuce leaves and a slice — a very thin slice — of smoked salmon, and she'll be complaining about being bloated."

"How convenient for you," said Isabel.

"I'm very lucky with my aged parent," said Martha cheerfully. "But listen, I need to talk to you about something. About somebody I know who's in difficulty."

Isabel looked up at the sky. People asked her to do things for them. She had no idea why they did, but they did. What did they think she was? A private detective? An agony aunt? Or simply a friend? And because of her particular sense of moral obligation, she felt that she had to do something, and that led to Jamie's accusing her of not minding her own business. But I cannot do otherwise, she thought. I am no saint; I am no heroine; but how can anybody say no to a request for help?

"Do you mind?" asked Martha. "We could have a cup of coffee and I could tell you about it." She looked at Isabel enquiringly. "But only if you don't mind."

Isabel shook her head. "I don't mind," she said.

"Good," said Martha. "Because I promised my friend I would speak to you and he was very relieved. He said 'Thank God'."

They began to make their way together down the road. As they walked, Martha told Isabel about her latest letter from her former husband. "Do you know, he said that if he could turn the clock back, he would. Can you credit it?"

"He wants to come back to you?" asked Isabel.

"So it would seem."

"And how do you feel about that?"

"It's the last thing I want," she said. "I've gone right off men."

"Altogether?"

"Yes." She paused. "Except for your Jamie. I would willingly have him on my mantelpiece. Just to look at him, of course."

Isabel smiled. "Not possible," she said. "Sorry."

"If I had somebody who looked like that," mused Martha, "I would spend all day just gazing at him, drinking it in. Do you do that sometimes, Isabel? Do you just sit there looking at Jamie and . . . and purring?"

CHAPTER
TWO

Cat's delicatessen was unusually busy when they arrived and it was a good ten minutes before Eddie, who was single-handed behind the counter that morning, managed to serve them. Eddie had recently returned from a trip across the United States he had made with his uncle and his uncle's girlfriend. The trip had been extended to include a four-month stay in Canada, during which Eddie had worked — underpaid, and illegally — as a waiter in a ski resort in Alberta. North America had changed him profoundly, boosting his confidence and pasting a healthy tan over his normally pallid Scottish skin. The tan was now fading, but the same could not be said of the traces of an affected American accent that Eddie had somehow miraculously picked up on his travels. His conversation was now littered with "sure things" and "you bets", so much so that Isabel had found it difficult to conceal her amusement. Eddie had noticed this, and had looked injured. Isabel was mortified; she was fond of Eddie and had always done her best to encourage him. Now she had hurt him.

If offence had been taken, it was not long-lasting. Eddie greeted Isabel cheerfully and went to some trouble to select for her the best of the onion tarts.

"I know you're going to get the best tart," Martha said over Isabel's shoulder. "But could I at least have the second best?"

Isabel drew in her breath. There was so much she could have said, including an observation that people got the onion tarts they deserved in this life; but that would have been childish. Martha simply did not know that virtually everything she said was inappropriate, and so there was no point in remonstrating with her. Isabel remembered the discussion with Jamie about the *wiring*. This was much the same issue. Those important brain circuits, the ones that enabled most of us to avoid saying the wrong thing, were simply not there in Martha's case; or fired in the wrong order; or were short-circuiting. In other words, Martha Drummond was an electrical problem. And understanding people as electrical problems undoubtedly helped one to tolerate them.

Once they had purchased their tarts, alongside one or two other things needed for their respective meals, Isabel and Martha sat down at one of the tables Cat kept for the serving of coffee. The customers were thinner on the ground in the pre-lunchtime lull, and Eddie had time to prepare and bring to their table two large, steaming cappuccinos.

"Here we are, ma'am," he said as he placed Martha's cup in front of her. The intonation was contrived American, overlaid with a heavy dose of Scotland.

Martha looked at him. "You from Glasgow?" she asked.

Eddie looked down at the floor, humiliated.

Martha smiled at Isabel, and winked conspiratorially.

"Eddie has just spent quite a bit of time in America," said Isabel quickly.

"Yes," said Martha, still smiling. "I suppose it must rub off eventually."

Eddie went back to the counter in silence.

"That wasn't necessary," Isabel said quietly. "That young man has had a lot to put up with."

Martha looked towards Eddie on the other side of the counter. "Seems robust enough to me. And I was only joking."

Isabel wanted Martha to know the implications of her casual tactlessness. "Something bad happened to him some time ago. Something traumatic."

Martha looked interested. "What? What happened?"

"I'm not absolutely sure."

Martha shrugged. "Dreadful things have happened to just about everyone," she said. "It's called growing up. You know the statistics . . ."

Isabel decided to change the subject. She was not sure that she wanted to spend too much time with Martha — time that could be better spent making up the salad that would go with the onion tart. "You wanted to talk to me about somebody?" she said.

Martha looked at Isabel over the rim of her coffee cup. "I did. Of course I don't want to impose . . ."

Isabel cut her short. "Don't worry."

Martha lowered her cup. "You're very good, you know. Everybody knows that you help people in all sorts of ways. Where does it come from?"

Isabel squirmed with embarrassment. "I'm no better than anybody else," she said. "I have all the usual faults and flaws."

"And you're modest too," said Martha.

Isabel said nothing, waiting for Martha to continue.

"So," said Martha. "This problem: do you know somebody called Duncan Munrowe?"

She did not give Isabel time to answer. "You might have read about him. He crops up in the *Scotsman* from time to time. He does a lot for charity." Martha paused, but only briefly. "He's the sort of person everybody hears about but doesn't really meet very much. That's not to say that he hasn't got any friends. He has quite a few actually."

Isabel waited until it looked as if she would be allowed to speak. "I've heard of him. I get him mixed up, though, with those other Duncan Munroes."

"They're Munro with an *o*. He's Munrowe with a *w* and an *e* at the end. Not to be confused with all those Munros that are mountains over three thousand feet."

"I see," said Isabel. She decided to be brief; sometimes people like Martha, who spoke at excessive length, eventually exhausted themselves. The problem then was that they lacked the energy to listen to what you had to say.

Martha continued. "These Munrowes — Duncan's lot — are originally from Wigtown or somewhere near there. I've always thought of that part of Scotland as being virtually Ireland, it's that close." She looked at Isabel with sudden interest. "Have you got any Irish blood in you?"

"On my mother's side there was some, I think. Irish and Acadian. They drifted down to the South generations ago. The Acadian part of the family was from Nova Scotia, I believe." She thought: my sainted American mother, who would have been patient even with somebody like Martha. And I must try.

"You've probably got a temper then," said Martha, almost to herself.

Isabel sipped at her coffee. Martha was impossible — risible, really.

"Not that I'm one to talk," Martha went on. "There are some things that make me see red. I have to watch myself."

"We all do," said Isabel. *Watching yourself*, she thought. It was the essence of the moral life. Watch yourself; evaluate. The examined life; the watched life. "Duncan Munrowe? You were telling me about him."

It was as if Isabel had introduced an entirely new topic of conversation. "Oh yes," said Martha. "Duncan would very much like to meet you."

"Why?"

"Because something has happened up at his place." Although there was nobody near them, Martha lowered her voice. "Duncan's family used to be pretty well-off. They had rubber plantations in Malaya. And they were something to do with Hong Kong — I have no idea what, but they were. So when they came back to Scotland there was plenty of money."

Isabel remarked that this was not an unusual story. The Scots had profited greatly from the British Empire; they did not always like to admit it, but they had. There were numerous families that had done well out of things like jute in Calcutta or wool in Australia and had returned to Scotland to buy landed estates. It sounded as if the Munrowes were in this category.

Martha leaned forward. "They were discreet about it, but one of them, Duncan's grandfather, had a very good eye. He was rather like that shipping man in Glasgow — what was he called?"

"Burrell?"

"That's him. He put that great collection together, didn't he? Well, Duncan Munrowe's grandfather had the same sense not only of what was what in the art world, but also of what *would be* what. He anticipated fashions."

This began to sound familiar to Isabel. "And he lent paintings to the Scottish National Gallery?"

Martha nodded. "Yes. You might have seen some of the Munrowe collection there. It's not quite as impressive as the Sutherland collection, but it's still pretty good. He was particularly strong on the Post-Impressionists. Bonnard and so on. He picked those up by the dozen in Paris, as you could in those days."

Isabel had seen them. She remembered the wording on the labels: *On loan from the Munrowe Collection.* The galleries, with their tiny acquisitions budget, increasingly relied on such generosity. She tried to bring to mind particular Munrowe paintings, but could not. There were the Titians, and that whole roomful of Poussins, but they belonged to the Sutherlands. Was there a Bonnard of a woman sewing, or was that Vuillard? And was it part of the Munrowe collection?

"They still have some of the paintings in the house," Martha continued. "They live near Doune. It's a rather shy house. I call it shy because it's tucked away and you'd not know it was there until you turn a corner and there it is next to some woods. And a hill. It has a hill directly behind it — straight up. It's an odd place to put a house, but there we are."

Isabel was keen to hear what had taken place. "You said something happened. What was it?"

"They have all these paintings in the house, as I've said. Maybe they're not quite as good as the ones in the Gallery, but they're still pretty special. There's a whole room of seventeenth-century French and Italian paintings, and the dining room has got a Toulouse-Lautrec in it — not a big one — and a Vuillard, I think."

"They're very fortunate," said Isabel. "Imagine being able to look at paintings like that over your boiled egg in the morning."

Martha laughed. "There's a small Degas drawing in one of the loos."

"Loos, too, can be made beautiful."

Martha frowned. "Have you heard of the open gardens weekend that they have round here?"

"Yes. It arranges for private gardens —"

"To be open to the public on a particular day. Exactly. And Munrowe House — that's the name of their place; somewhat unimaginative, but accurate, I suppose — was opened to the public. The house too."

Isabel could tell what was coming. "And some of the paintings were . . ."

24

"Stolen. Not some, just one. But, as it happened, it was the most valuable painting in the whole house. Duncan had been thinking of transferring it to the Gallery, where it would be safer, but he hadn't got round to it."

"What was it?"

"A Poussin. One of the relatively few in private hands in this country. And a rather nice one. It was worth about three million, they thought. Possibly more."

Isabel asked what the subject was, and Martha explained. It was a painting known as *Time Reconsidered* and bore some relationship to the artist's great *A Dance to the Music of Time*. Martha began to describe that painting but Isabel told her that she had visited the Wallace Collection in London and knew the picture well.

"It was insured, of course," Martha said.

Isabel said that she was relieved to hear that. An insurance payment was not always full compensation for loss, but it undoubtedly dulled the pain. "I assume that what he really wants is to get the painting back."

"Yes. He does. They picked the one thing he didn't want to lose."

Eddie appeared at the table to collect their empty cups. He took Martha's wordlessly, but at the same time gave Isabel a look of gentle reproach. Isabel mentally sent him a message: *Yes, I know what she's like, but we can't . . .*

"Anything else?" he asked Isabel.

Isabel shook her head and Eddie went back to the counter.

"There's something lost about that boy," Martha said. "Odd."

Isabel did not engage. "Duncan Munrowe?"

"Oh yes, Duncan. It's the reward, you see."

Isabel looked puzzled. "The reward?"

"I gather that many of these art thefts are really ransom attempts," Martha explained. "They can't sell these very well-known paintings — or at least not on the ordinary market — and so they use them to extort money from the insurance companies."

Isabel had read about this. "That must be difficult," she said. "If you pay the Dane to go away, he always comes back. So perhaps you should make a point of never paying ransom."

Martha frowned at the mention of Danes.

"Danegeld," said Isabel. "It's what people used to pay the Vikings to stop them destroying things. You paid your Danegeld and the Vikings went away. Until next time."

Martha shrugged. "I suppose there is a general issue about paying ransom. But that's not the problem here — or at least it's not the problem that's worrying Duncan. His difficulty is the attitude of the insurers. They've suggested one thing and he's wanted to do the other. They've argued about figures too. The insurers say that the market is depressed at the moment and this means they need pay less. They also don't want to pay a ransom until it's clear that the painting won't be recovered."

"Insurers are like that," remarked Isabel. "As a general rule, if they can avoid paying, that's what they'll do."

"And yet we can't be late with our premiums," said Martha sharply.

Isabel agreed. People were always very keen to have their bills paid promptly but were not so willing to reciprocate.

"So that's where you come in," Martha announced.

Isabel frowned. "I don't see . . ."

"Duncan wondered whether you might help him deal with this. In particular, he wants help in dealing with any approach from the people who have the painting. They'll be in touch, he thinks. They might even have already contacted him — I'm not sure about that."

Isabel's surprise was immediately apparent. "But what possible assistance can I give? I know nothing about this sort of thing. Nothing at all."

Martha laid a hand on Isabel's forearm. "But everybody knows how helpful you are. That's why I recommended you when he asked me about you."

"You recommended me?"

"Yes. Poor Duncan: he so wanted somebody to talk to about it — to advise him. Somebody had mentioned your name. I said that you had quite a reputation for helping people in a tight spot and that he could talk to you. I hope you don't mind."

Of course Isabel minded; it was very easy, she thought, to offer the services of others. But then she remembered her sainted American mother and asked herself how she would have reacted to such a request. She knew the answer. "Never turn your back on another," her mother had said to her when she was a girl. "The person you're turning your back on might die that night." It was not, Isabel realised, the sort of thing one should say to children, who could feel unreasonably anxious about death anyway. And if somebody died, the child could well blame himself or herself; children often did that, the psychologists told us; they felt guilty about things that happened, even if they had nothing at all to do with them. *I turned my back on her, and she went and died!* But it was advice that had stuck, and came back to Isabel now, years later, in this difficult encounter. She stared at Martha. "I will, if you want me to," she said. She almost added, "Though I can't say I'm overly enthusiastic," but decided against it. There was no need to be churlish.

Martha looked at her gratefully. "Even if you just talk to him," she said. "Listen to his tale of woe. Even that would help."

"I'll try," said Isabel.

"Tomorrow?" asked Martha. "Duncan's coming into town. Could you see him then? Lunch — just the three of us. Unless you'd rather I didn't come."

Isabel hesitated. There were times when one had to act self-defensively, even if it caused disappointment. It went against the grain, but one had to.

"Just him and me, I think," she said. She tried to speak gently, but even then felt she had to explain. "It's sometimes easier for people to talk if there's nobody else there."

"Do you think so?" said Martha.

"I do," said Isabel.

Martha shrugged. "Odd," she said.

It was true, thought Isabel, that none of us ever imagined that people might *not* wish to be in our company. We assumed that people found us good company, would like to be with us. But they might not. They might find us opinionated or dull or irritating — as poor Martha undoubtedly was; all of which qualities we would be the last to discern in ourselves.

Isabel swallowed. It was so easy to forget the needs of others, and to allow irritation, boredom, or sheer indifference to get the better of us. She would not do that; she would make an effort. It was very easy to build people up, to make them feel better about themselves: a few words of praise, an appreciative comment or two, and people felt better. Martha clearly took pains to look her best; perhaps a remark about that would help the situation.

"I must say," Isabel began, and then searched desperately for a suitable comment. "I must say that you're looking really . . . really attractive. That top suits you, I think. Your colour."

She drew in her breath. The top was beige: she had just suggested that Martha's colour was beige.

"Beige?"

"No," said Isabel quickly. "I wouldn't call it beige. I'd say *oatmeal*. I've got a carpet that colour in the upstairs bedroom and . . ." She trailed off as it struck her that she had now compared Martha's top to a carpet.

Martha stared at her for a moment before smiling wryly. "It's kind of you to say that, Isabel, but I'm sure you don't really mean it."

"I did mean it," Isabel lied. And she thought, more than a little ashamedly: Kant would never, *never* have given that answer. He would never have paid an insincere compliment in the first place. Kant would not have noticed the way a woman was dressed; Hume might have, and Voltaire certainly would. *What the Great Philosophers Would Say about your Wardrobe*: that would be an amusing book to write — and it might even prove rather popular, as Robert Pirsig's *Zen and the Art of Motorcycle Maintenance* had become.

She became aware that Martha was shaking an admonitory finger at her. "Not really, but thanks anyway. It's good to be told nice things, even if they aren't true." She paused. "And it's very kind of you to say it, especially when you're so . . . Well, you're much more glamorous than I am. And your life . . . your whole life is so much more — how shall I put it? Intense? And . . ."

"Please," said Isabel, reaching out to touch her gently. "That's a generous thing to say, but you're wrong, you know. My life isn't really any different from anybody else's."

Martha shook her head. "But it is! You've got money. You live in that fantastic house. You've got that man of yours. Everything. You've got everything."

Isabel looked down at the floor. It made her feel uncomfortable to hear her blessings enumerated — nobody welcomed that, least of all those who, like Isabel, were aware enough to know that all the good things that we have in life are on temporary loan, at best, and can be taken away from us in an instant. The borderline between good fortune and disaster, between plenitude and paucity, between the warm hearth of love and the cold chamber of loneliness, was a narrow one. We could cross over from one to the other at any moment, as when we stumbled or fell, or simply walked over to the other side because we were paying insufficient attention to where we were. It was well to remember one's good luck, but it was not always helpful to be reminded of it by one who was not equally blessed. Or to be reminded of it in public, when Nemesis, whose radar is said never to be switched off, picks up the echo and begins to take an interest.

CHAPTER
THREE

Martha left the delicatessen, telling Isabel that she had other shops to visit before returning home to her lunch of onion tart. Isabel said goodbye to her but remained at the table; she had decided that she would read the newspaper, even if the only paper she could see on the rack was what looked like a three-day-old copy of the *Corriere della Sera*. Cat had the Italian newspapers passed on to her by a friend who bought them religiously to keep her language up to scratch. Isabel was the only beneficiary of this generosity; she had never seen anyone else reading the papers, although she had observed some customers examining them in puzzlement, trying to stretch their restaurant Italian or to make sense of the reports from the pictures. But their presence seemed just right: it went so well with the smell of coffee and the sight of the salamis that Cat hung above the counter, almost over the heads of customers; the salami of Damocles, she thought . . .

The *Corriere* would give her half an hour in the opaque realms of Italian politics; a world of Byzantine intrigues and endless feuds; operatic in its intensity. She scanned the front page and noticed a trailer for an interview on an inside page. A well-known politician, now disgraced, was speaking about his fall from power. It was a bad decision, he said, to replace him; the country needed him more than ever and the attempts to prosecute him were symptomatic of the ingratitude for which the country was becoming so famous. Isabel smiled. She never ceased to be amazed by the antics of politicians. It was as if politics was all about *them*, and not about ordinary members of the public who were, after all, the people whom politicians were meant to serve. People like me, she thought — sitting here drinking coffee, waiting to be served by politicians . . . She closed her eyes and imagined the Prime Minister, in a waiter's apron, serving coffee. Martha, curiously, came into the picture, shaking her head and saying disapprovingly, "They'll do *anything* for votes, won't they?"

She opened her eyes a few seconds later to see Eddie standing in front of her holding a replacement cup of coffee.

"I assumed you wanted a refill," he said. He spoke normally now, the attempt to affect an American accent being abandoned.

Isabel smiled at him and took the proffered cup. Eddie hesitated, glancing around the shop to see if there was anybody needing attention. But, seeing that there was nobody waiting to be served, he sat down on the chair recently vacated by Martha. "That woman you were with looks familiar, who is she?" he asked, nodding his head in the direction of the door.

"She's called Martha Drummond."

Eddie made a face. "I didn't like her. Sorry, I know she's your friend, but she behaved like a real cow just now."

"That's possibly a bit unfair," Isabel said. "She's not all that bad."

"I can tell you don't think that," said Eddie. "Your eyes looked different when you said it."

I'm a bad liar, thought Isabel. That was twice in the last few minutes that she had been accused of insincerity. "All right," she confessed. "I'll admit it: she gets on my nerves a bit. A lot, sometimes. I feel guilty about my attitude towards her. I'm not proud of it. But you know how it is? We all have people in our lives we don't really choose as friends but with whom we're, well, lumbered, I suppose. Heart-sink friends. Have you heard that expression?"

Eddie had, and yes, he knew a few people like that. There had been a boy in his year at school, he said, who smelled of fish but who always wanted to sit next to him in class. "He had this condition, you see. It wasn't that he didn't wash — he did — it's just that he smelled of fish. It was a medical condition, see."

Isabel said she had heard of it.

"One of the teachers told us about it," Eddie went on. "Apparently people who have it can't break down some sort of chemical and that's what makes them smell. It's not their fault."

He looked at Isabel as if to challenge her to refute the proposition that smell has nothing to do with fault. And that was right, she thought, though only in respect of smells we could not help; those we could help were

34

our responsibility; soap was readily available, and water too. A paper in the *Review*, perhaps? Responsibility for the body? Do we have a moral obligation to look — and smell — as good as we can manage? In one view, this could be a Kantian duty to the self, but in another it could be part of our duty not to offend those around us — one of those items of good social manners that strayed into the scope of morality proper. Of course, that had all sorts of ramifications. What about wearing clothes that offended other people — clothes that revealed bad colour coordination, for example? Was that wrong? Surely not, although wearing scanty clothing in sensitive settings was another matter. When important women went to see the Pope, they dressed conservatively out of respect for . . . for what? Now it became even more complicated: the following of a dress code that treated women as potential temptresses revealed an acceptance of a whole attitude towards women that some did not condone. So had the Pope any *right*, Isabel wondered, to expect women to dress in a particular way when they called on him? That raised the question of whether the hosts could dictate the dress of their guests — and they could, Isabel considered, because people were always telling their invitees what to wear: *black tie, casual-smart* and all the rest of the signals were everyday examples of precisely that. So the Pope had the right, if he wished, to expect a certain sort of dress on the part of his visitors. And so did everybody else, it seemed. She smiled; that sorted *that* out.

Eddie could tell that Isabel's mind was elsewhere. It was chronic, he thought. She's always thinking about all sorts of really *stupid* things. He continued, "The teacher said that we needed to know about it because she didn't want people saying anything to him. He was called Julian, which was bad luck too, because that's not a name that many people have where I come from."

"I'm sure you were kind to him," Isabel said. "It must be a pretty difficult condition."

Eddie hesitated. "Some people tried to be kind," he said. "Not everybody, though. There was this boy called Derek who was a real thug. People hated him. He used to call out 'Look out, rotten fish!' whenever Julian came near."

"Children are like that," Isabel said. "We were tremendously cruel. All of us." She took a sip of her coffee. "What happened to Julian?"

Eddie stared at her. It seemed that he had not been prepared for the question or had not understood it.

"I mean, what did he go on to do after he left school? Do you ever see him these days?"

Eddie frowned, and looked away. Isabel waited.

"He topped himself," he said quietly.

Isabel sat quite still. Perhaps she had misunderstood. "You mean he —"

Eddie interrupted her. "Yes. He put himself in the bath and then he got one of those electric fires and dropped it in. That was it."

Isabel said nothing.

"I felt bad."

"I'm sure you'd done your best. You said he liked you. That must have been because you'd been good to him."

"Not good enough," muttered Eddie.

She decided not to argue with him. "I'm really sorry to hear that story," she said.

"He had an older brother," said Eddie. "He's a DJ in a club on Lothian Road, I still see him now and then. He's got long greasy hair. It's quite disgusting, actually. He's called Daniel. He doesn't really know who I am, but we still say hello to one another in the street. He has a girlfriend who rides a big Harley-Davidson."

Isabel listened to these almost random facts. They were the ordinary details of life, all of them quite unexceptional: the disgusting greasy hair, the club on Lothian Road — except perhaps for the Harley-Davidson-riding girlfriend — and yet it was these same mundane facts that were the background for the poignant story of Julian.

For a few moments they were both silent. Then Eddie shrugged. "These things happen," he said.

Isabel inclined her head.

"And we shouldn't think about them too much, should we?" Eddie went on.

No, agreed Isabel, we should not; and Eddie, she thought, had had enough difficulty in his life without dwelling on additional tragedies. She made an effort to brighten up. "I've been reading about an Italian politician," she said, pointing to the newspaper.

Eddie glanced at the photograph accompanying the interview. "Oh, him. He's the one who liked parties."

"He was very outgoing," Isabel agreed.

Eddie looked more closely at the picture. "Has he had cosmetic surgery?" he asked inconsequentially. "By the way, I've got some photographs I want to show you some time. I took them in Alaska — on the trip. You wouldn't believe it. The mountains. They make ours look tiny."

Our tiny mountains, thought Isabel. We are a small country with tiny mountains.

"I'd love to see them, Eddie. Maybe you could bring them round some time. Jamie would like to see them too. Have supper with us."

Eddie liked Jamie, she knew, because Jamie had always been kind to him. Eddie was used to being looked through — a shy young man behind the counter. Jamie smiled at him.

"All right. I'll bring them round. And . . ."

He looked at Isabel hesitantly.

"Yes?"

"Could I bring somebody with me?"

Isabel nodded. "Of course you can. Who is it?"

Eddie blushed. "There's a girl I've met."

Isabel waited for him to continue.

"She's called Diane. I've been seeing her for six weeks now." He moved his right hand to rest it on the table. She saw that his nails were dirty. Cat had spoken to him about washing his hands thoroughly before handling food and had equipped the small washroom at the back of the shop with a stiff nailbrush, which Eddie had evidently not used, or used to inadequate effect.

38

"It's serious, Isabel. We're going to live together now."

Isabel caught her breath. In her mind, Eddie was still very young, even if he was twenty-one.

"That's quite an important step," she said.

"I know that," said Eddie. "But it's what we want to do. If it works out, we're going to get engaged."

Isabel's smile was very tentative. "That's . . . well, that's also a big step, isn't it, at your age?"

Eddie looked at her searchingly. "What age were you when you first fell in love?"

She had to think. Most of us first experienced love in our teenage years, sometimes when we were barely into our teens. The passionate friendships of those years were really love affairs even if they remained innocent. And they often focused on friends of the same sex — a rite of passage to heterosexuality, for some people, not all, of course. If people were honest with themselves they would remember such friendships, but then people were far from honest when it came to things like that.

She had fallen in love with a boy when she was sixteen. That had been her eye-opener. She had felt elated, excited, and miserable in roughly equal measure. She had never dreamed that love could be painful, but it was. She had loved him so much that it hurt, and when it ended, as was inevitable, the pain had been even more intense — for three weeks. Then she had suddenly woken up one morning and realised that he was just a boy and that she no longer wanted to spend the entire day thinking about him. That was her cure.

"I loved somebody when I was sixteen, seventeen," she said. "And then again a few years later I fell badly for somebody whom I eventually married. It was a bad mistake on my part. I think I told you once, didn't I?"

Eddie remembered. "Yes. What was he called again?"

Isabel had to make an effort: the uttering of names can be potent — and painful. "John Liamor. He was not a good man, I'm afraid to say."

"Then you're best off without him," said Eddie. "He's history. Forget him."

"I did," said Isabel, and felt, as she uttered the words, a pang of regret. "I had to teach myself not to think about him. It wasn't easy."

"Then let's talk about something else: Diane."

Isabel smiled at him. "You're obviously head over heels in love with her. You're lucky." She paused. Eddie's face had broken into a grin of sheer pleasure.

"Yes," Isabel continued. "You're really lucky, Eddie. Love transforms everything, doesn't it?"

She assumed that he might be embarrassed by this talk of love, as any young man might be. But Eddie seemed to relish it. "Everything's really great, Isabel. I feel really great."

She leaned forward, across the table, and kissed him gently on the cheek. He was surprised, and she heard his breath come sharply; but again he did not seem embarrassed.

"I'm happy for you, Eddie," she said. "Stay head over heels in love. Buy her flowers. Give her lots and lots of kisses. Worship her. Diane, Diana: they're the same goddess, you know. Diana, the Huntress."

40

Eddie looked at her wide-eyed. "She's a nurse."

Isabel laughed. "Don't be too literal," she said. "Being in love allows a certain poetic hyperbole."

Eddie remained wide-eyed.

"What I mean by all that," said Isabel, "is: go for it."

The translation was effective. Eddie beamed. "Thanks, Isabel."

With Charlie still at nursery school, Isabel and Jamie ate their lunch on the lawn, shaded by the large oak tree that dominated one side of Isabel's garden. They sat on green canvas deckchairs that were nearing the end of their life but were still the most comfortable garden furniture that Isabel had ever known. The fabric, rotted in places by summer after summer of not being put away promptly enough when rain began to fall, had now ripped in several places, and it was only a matter of time, Isabel thought, before it would give way altogether and deposit the person sitting on the chair unceremoniously on the grass. She would not mind if that happened to her, or to Jamie — it seemed as if deckchairs were designed to humiliate their owners, to trap their fingers, to dump them on the ground — but she did not want it to happen to a visitor.

Now, sitting in the shade on that particularly hot day, Isabel struggled to eat a slice of onion tart without distributing flaky crumbs of pastry or fragments of onion all over her clothes. Jamie did not have that problem. He had disposed of his shirt and had only an old pair of jeans to worry about. She glanced at him, and then glanced away. There was no spare flesh on him, she thought; just muscle. She had always felt that somehow it was unfair: Jamie never went to the gym. So did one get like that, she wondered, just from playing the bassoon? She glanced at him again; his skin was brown from exposure to the summer sun, and he was perfect. She wanted to touch him. But did not, and instead looked up at the sky, which was empty.

"Do you believe in angels?"

He had not been paying attention; a bee had landed on his foot and he had leaned forward to flick it off.

"Do I believe in eagles? Of course I do. Who doesn't? You can see them flying about in the Highlands."

"Angels."

"Oh, that's another matter."

Isabel looked back up at the sky. "There is no evidence for the existence of angels, and I suppose we must reluctantly conclude that they don't exist. It's a pity, I think, because I can just imagine them floating across a sky like this one."

Jamie looked up.

"What's that poem you quoted to me once?" he asked. "Something about Italy."

Isabel closed her eyes. " 'Angels in Italy'. Al Alvarez wrote it. He's in Italy, in the country . . ."

"Tuscany, of course."

"Of course. And suddenly he sees angels. He says something about how they make no sound, although their wings move. That's how it starts."

Jamie was intrigued. "Their wings make no sound? That's what he says?"

42

"Yes," said Isabel. "And then he goes on to say that people down below are doing all sorts of ordinary things — like cutting wood with a buzz-saw. And the leaves on the vine rattle like dice. All while the angels are crossing the sky, until the clouds take them."

Jamie whispered again, savouring the words. "Until the clouds take them."

Isabel was silent for a moment. Then she turned to face Jamie. He was watching her. His eyes were kind. She reached out and laid a hand against his cheek and then let it slip down to his shoulder. His skin was smooth. If he had wings they would sprout here, perhaps, right here; great wings; angel, angel.

For a few minutes nothing was said. She felt Jamie's shoulder move slightly as he breathed; she felt, she thought, his heartbeat. She willed him not to say anything, not to disturb the moment. They looked at each other. His lips moved almost imperceptibly into the slightest, the faintest of smiles.

And then it seemed right to speak. "I saw Eddie this morning," she said.

He sounded drowsy. "Oh yes?"

"He wants to get engaged to a girl he's met."

Jamie smiled. "Good. Poor Eddie."

"He's still very young."

Jamie thought that did not matter. "He thinks he's old enough to set up home with her. That's what he wants."

"Perhaps." She paused. She had taken her hand away from his shoulder now. There had been a moment, an extraordinarily intense moment, but it had passed and they had begun to talk about Eddie. What had happened?

The deckchair canvas protested — a tiny, ripping sound as a bit more gave way. And then it came to her: Auden's poem. She had been thinking about "Angels in Italy" while all the time she might have been remembering Auden's "A Summer Night". Was that not about sitting outside, at night, in a deckchair in the company of friends; and with Vega "conspicuous overhead"? Auden had later described how during those few minutes sitting under the stars with his friends he had experienced a mystical understanding of *agape*, that non-sexual love of others. He had been vouchsafed a glimpse of *agape* and it had stayed with him for some time before it had faded. Had she felt something similar?

"And I met somebody else," Isabel said. "Martha Drummond."

Jamie raised an eyebrow. "That rather odd woman? The one who lives round the corner?"

"Yes, her."

He shrugged. "And?"

"We had coffee at Cat's. She said that there was somebody who wanted to speak to me about something."

Jamie said nothing.

"Do you remember reading about the theft of a painting from a house in Stirlingshire? A painting by Poussin?"

Jamie said that he had a vague recollection of it. "It was quite valuable, wasn't it?"

44

"Yes. Not as valuable as that da Vinci that was stolen from Drumlanrig Castle — the one they eventually found in the safe of a Glasgow firm of lawyers. But it was still worth a few million."

Jamie began to lift himself out of his deckchair. The flimsy contraption started to wobble and then, with a sudden loud ripping sound, the canvas gave way. This had the effect of making him fall, causing the restraining bar on the chair to slip from its home and the whole chair to fold in upon itself.

Jamie gave a howl of pain. His left hand had been unfortunately placed and had become trapped in the collapsing frame.

"Jamie!" She struggled to get out of her chair. There was another ripping sound, but the canvas held and Isabel was on her feet. Jamie had extricated himself from the chair mechanism and was nursing his hand.

"Painful," he said.

"Are you all right?"

He nodded. "I knew that would happen."

They both laughed. "Why does anyone sit in dangerous chairs?" Isabel asked.

"Why does anybody do anything dangerous?" Jamie asked, examining his hand for signs of damage.

"I don't know," said Isabel. "Boredom, perhaps. Danger gives a bit of spice to our lives."

He turned to her, resuming the conversation that had been interrupted by the failure of the deckchair. "You were saying, this person — whoever it is — wants to speak to you. It's going to be about the theft of the Poussin, isn't it?"

She looked down at the ground. "Yes."

He sighed. "You've done something like this before. That artist you traced. When we went to Jura. Remember?"

"Yes. But this is different."

He reached out to take her hand. "Do you think it's a good idea? Do you really think so?"

She began to lead him back to the house. "Yes, I know. I know what you mean. It's vaguely ridiculous that here am I, the editor of a philosophical review of all things, and I keep getting involved in the messes that people get themselves into."

Jamie agreed. "Yes, it is ridiculous. And yet it seems to go on happening."

Isabel sighed. "I don't exactly advertise."

"Well, you know my views," said Jamie. "I don't think it's a terribly good idea."

"No, it may not be a good idea, but some of the things we have to do are not particularly good ideas — but we have to do them anyway."

"You don't have to do this. Nobody says you have to do this."

"No. But this poor man, this Munrowe man — apparently he's pretty cut up about it. And all he wants to do is talk. I can't really refuse to talk to him."

They made their way into the house. Isabel slipped an arm around his shoulder and asked him if he was cross with her.

He hesitated. "No, I'm not cross. If anything, I suppose I should be proud of you — which I am. I'm very proud of you." He paused. "But please be careful over this one. This isn't just some minor issue you're helping with — this is really serious."

Isabel sought to reassure him. "I'm only going to be speaking to him. That's all."

It was as if he had not heard. "And the point about serious matters like this is that people get hurt."

"I shall be very careful. I promise you."

They went inside. She bathed Jamie's hand, as the clash with the deckchair had broken the skin slightly. She patted it dry with a clean towel and then kissed it. He looked at the clock; Charlie would have to be fetched in half an hour or so. He put his arms about Isabel and embraced her, pulling her to him. Her hands were on his shoulder blades. It was warm in the house and the sound of a mower drifted in from over the road through an open window, bringing with it the smell of cut grass.

CHAPTER
FOUR

The arrangement, made by Martha Drummond, and relayed to Isabel later that afternoon in a telephone call from Martha, was that Duncan Munrowe would come, as Isabel had suggested, to the German bakery in Bruntsfield at one o'clock the following day. Isabel's housekeeper Grace had been on holiday but would be back in the morning and would be able to collect Charlie from nursery school in place of Jamie, who was recording in Glasgow.

Grace had been in Stranraer, where she had a cousin who was married to a farmer. Each year she went to visit this cousin for a week, and inevitably came back sleep-deprived and vaguely grumpy as a result. "He snores something terrible," she explained to Isabel. "I'm short of a week's sleep. He goes to bed at ten every night — regular as clockwork. By ten-fifteen the snoring starts, and it goes on all night. You hear it throughout the house and it makes the walls shake. I'm not exaggerating — all night. Snoring and snorting."

"Poor man," said Isabel.

"Poor man? Poor us. My cousin hardly sleeps, she says, and no sooner do I drop off than I'm woken up by the sound of his snoring down the corridor."

"It sounds as if he might have sleep apnoea," suggested Isabel. "My father had it. You stop breathing every so often and wake up. People who have sleep apnoea are usually chronically sleep-deprived." She thought of the cumbersome mask her father had sometimes used to deal with the problem. "He could be helped."

"Not him," said Grace. "He's stubborn. He doesn't think there's anything wrong."

This discussion of sleep led to the matter of Charlie's afternoon nap. In Grace's absence, Charlie had taken to resisting this period of rest, and yet he was clearly tired.

"His mind seems very active," said Isabel. "He wants to keep going."

She paused, remembering her conversation with Jamie about Charlie's mathematical ability. "He seems to be very keen on counting things at the moment," she went on. "Have you noticed that?"

Grace did not seem surprised. "Yes, of course I have. I've been teaching him, you see."

Isabel frowned. "Teaching him mathematics?"

Grace nodded. "Yes. I'd noticed that he was quite good at counting and so I've been giving him lessons. I've taught him how to divide things, and some basic multiplication. I found a book in the library that tells you how to do this. It's by a Korean woman who's had two of her children win prizes in the Maths Olympiad. She explains how it's done."

Isabel was not sure what to say. So that was how Charlie had been able to come up with what seemed to be naturally brilliant answers: he had been taught. For a few moments she was silent. She trusted Grace with so much of Charlie's life and she was not sure why she should feel concerned about her teaching him mathematics. At the back of her mind was a feeling that one had to be careful with method when it came to mathematics: she seemed to remember being told that if you developed the wrong way of doing mathematics when you were young, you could be lumbered with it for the rest of your life. It was the same with many activities — from typing to playing the violin: it was sometimes far harder to unlearn bad habits than to learn them in the first place. But the issue would have to be handled delicately; Grace was touchy and could take offence at the slightest reproach, even if unintended.

"I suppose he must have natural ability," said Isabel mildly.

Grace looked thoughtful. "Probably no more than any other child of his age. It's the teaching, I think. The book is really good. It says any child can be really good at calculating if you follow their method."

Isabel looked doubtful. "Surely not every single child. Genes must play some sort of role," she said. "Mathematical ability and musicality often go together. Jamie's a musician, after all, and maybe Charlie gets it from him."

Grace shook her head. "It's the book, I think."

Isabel decided not to argue. This was not the time to voice her reservations — especially when Grace was feeling sleep-deprived as a result of the snoring Wigtownshire farmer. "Oh, well," she said.

"Yes," said Grace. "I'm going to teach him to count money next. There's a chapter on that in the book. It's called 'The Baby Accountant'."

Isabel bit her lip. She was grateful to Grace for all she did for Charlie, but did she really want him to be a baby accountant? Charlie should develop at his own pace, she thought. He should get every help, naturally, but Isabel was definite that she did not want to be a pushy parent who made her child jump through all sorts of hoops. Surely Grace did not want that for Charlie either. Surely not.

"Miss Dalhousie?"

He was already sitting at a table when Isabel arrived at Falko's Konditorei, the German bakery and coffee shop along the street from Cat's delicatessen. There were only a few other people in the café, but even had there been a much larger crowd Isabel would have had no difficulty in picking out Duncan Munrowe. It was largely a matter of dress — a jacket in a quiet browny-green; a dark-blue tie, discreetly checked; brown brogues: the uniform of the moneyed countryman — nothing ostentatious, nothing loud. And that was just the clothing; the physiognomy, too, revealed his origins: regular features, chiselled, showing a certain intelligence, even if not the face of an intellectual or aesthete. It was a handsome face, she thought, and the man's overall bearing was impressive.

"Isabel, please."

"Of course. And I'm Duncan: Duncan Munrowe."

They shook hands. The handshake, too, conformed to type.

Duncan Munrowe thanked her for agreeing to see him. "It's an awful cheek on my part," he said. "We haven't met and here I am inviting you to listen to my problems."

Isabel laughed. "I don't mind." And she decided that she did not; her immediate impression of him was positive. This man, she decided, was exactly what he purported to be: a country gentleman, for want of a better term; nothing more, nor less, than that. He was at the opposite end of the spectrum from . . . She hesitated: who *was* at the other end of the spectrum? It came to her: Professor Lettuce and Christopher Dove. Scheming philosophers. Waspish backbiters.

"Well, you're very kind," Duncan said. "But I must admit I feel a trifle embarrassed."

She assured him that this was unnecessary. As she did so, she considered his voice. There was a hint of a Scottish burr, but only a hint. That would have been taken out of the Munrowe voice two or three generations ago through being educated at schools that modelled themselves on the English public-school system, even if they were in Scotland. Or they would have been sent off to the South, to Harrow or Eton, or the like, where the conditioning of the English upper class would have been all-encompassing and where young Scots became indistinguishable in voice and outlook from their English contemporaries. That practice was changing, but there were still many people who lived in its shadow.

52

They placed their order with the waitress. Isabel glanced about her; it was not crowded and the nearest table, from which their conversation might easily be heard, was empty.

"I suppose it would help," Duncan began, "if I told you a little bit about our collection. I've heard, by the way, that you're interested in art."

"Oh?" She wondered how he knew this. It would be Martha, of course, who had seen her mother's painting and had perhaps noticed some of the other pictures. And Martha would probably have overstated Isabel's knowledge of the subject, which was, by her own admission, modest.

"Yes," he said. "Guy's mentioned you — I know him too. I've bought the odd thing from his gallery, but I must admit I haven't really added very much to the family collection."

That explained it. Isabel regularly discussed art with Guy Peploe who ran the Scottish Gallery in Dundas Street.

"As you may know," Duncan continued, "quite a bit of our collection is in the Scottish National Gallery on the Mound. Which is where it should be, in my view. Private collectors are just custodians, I think. They look after works of art but they don't really own them. Not in any absolute sense."

It was an admirable sentiment, and Isabel found herself warming all the more to Duncan. This was not one of those well-heeled people who are smug about their possessions. "Do you think that many others share your view? Other collectors, that is."

Duncan shrugged. "Some do, as you'll see if you look at any of the big collections. Look at the Burrell in Glasgow — Burrell gave everything he had to the city — the whole shooting match. And there are lots of other examples. The Met in New York is full of collections that have been given or bequeathed. The Wallace Collection in London. That odd place outside Philadelphia that used to let you look at it only when there was a full moon or whatever. The name escapes me, but he handed over the lot, didn't he? Or sort of handed it over."

"The Barnes," said Isabel.

"That's it. He gave the lot, didn't he?"

"Yes. And will you?" asked Isabel.

For a moment a shadow passed over his face, and she realised that her question, which had just slipped out, was intrusive, even rude. You did not ask people just how charitable they intended to be.

"I'm sorry. I shouldn't have asked you. It's none of my business."

He smiled. "Not at all. It's a reasonable question, and I'd raised the subject anyway. No, I'm not going to give everything away. I'm going to pass some on to the next generation."

"Fair enough."

"But the more important things will go to the Scottish National Gallery." He stopped, and looked at her, lowering his voice. His tone, now, bore a note of apology. "The Poussin, for example."

"The one that was stolen?"

54

"Yes, although I suppose that's very much in doubt now." He paused again. "And that makes me feel extremely regretful. After all, I promised it to them."

Isabel felt that he hardly needed to reproach himself over that, and told him as much. He listened attentively, but she could see that her words did not persuade him. It was something to do with honour, she thought; this man was out of his time, barely at home in an age as casual as ours. There were people like that.

"Tell me about the painting," she said. "I looked it up but one can never really tell from a photograph."

He responded enthusiastically to her comment. "I couldn't agree more about photographs. You don't get any sense of the presence of the painting — the atmosphere it creates just by being there in the room. For that, you have to see it in the flesh, so to speak."

He sat back in his chair. The waitress had arrived with their order — an open sandwich for Isabel and a slice of quiche and a salad for Duncan.

He seemed suddenly to have remembered something. "Have you noticed something about Caravaggio?"

She was not sure how to answer. One could hardly be unaware of Caravaggio, but to notice something . . . His use of light?

"It's just this business about seeing a painting in a room, in front of you. Caravaggio is so powerful he sterilises any other paintings on the wall in the same room. It just doesn't work. He overpowers them."

"Poussin doesn't?"

"The opposite. Poussin is a tremendously courteous painter. He doesn't shout at you. Far from it."

They began their lunch. She saw that he ate delicately, and slowly, which surprised her. She had imagined that he would have a hearty appetite; country people usually did. But then she remembered that Duncan Munrowe was very far from being a typical country landowner.

"The Poussin we have lost," he went on, "is a late one. Like many of his paintings of that period it has what the experts call a 'cool palette'. In other words, it's not very bright. Those lovely, rather faded colours."

"Like *A Dance to the Music of Time*?"

He nodded. "Yes. Or that other one — you know, the one where the giant is carrying the man on his shoulders, the one in the Louvre?"

Isabel did know it. "One of my absolute favourites," she said. "The man standing on the giant's shoulders is just so utterly extraordinary. But it's not in the Louvre — it's in New York, in the Met."

He blushed. "Of course. I forget what's where. For me, the Louvre's . . ."

Isabel knew what she thought of when she thought of the Louvre. There was a certain inevitability to it. "The *Mona Lisa*?"

He shook his head. "No. I'm afraid that painting does very little for me — I suppose because it's become so well known. And the room it's in is always full to the brim with parties of teenagers on their Paris trip. You can hardly breathe."

"So you search out Poussin?" she prompted.

"Yes," said Duncan. "And also that wonderful Ghirlandaio — the one in which the young boy is

56

looking up in wonderment at his grandfather with the very bulbous nose. Youth and old age. It's such a lovely painting and the look in the old man's eyes is just extraordinary. How do you capture a look of such fondness? How do you get that in paint? Yet he does. It's a magnificent painting."

"Which is what great painting is about," said Isabel. "Capturing those profound human emotions."

Duncan agreed. "That's right. And it makes one ask if we have any great artists among us at present. Who are they? Who's doing that sort of thing now?"

"David Hockney can," said Isabel. "Look at the emotion in those paintings of young men, and some of the portraits too."

"And Lucian Freud?"

"Yes, him too."

He looked thoughtful. "But great painters seem to be thin on the ground, do you think?"

"Perhaps." She steered the conversation back to the Poussin. "So, what happened?"

"The theft?"

"Yes."

He put down his knife and fork. "You may know that we open the garden — and the house — to the public on a couple of days each summer. It's a great way of sharing. We've always done it at Munrowe House."

"And that's when it was stolen?"

"So it seems. We were quite busy — there were almost two hundred people who came and had a look round. Maybe more."

She asked whether they were free to wander around the house as well. Was nothing done about watching them?

He looked at her ruefully. "Of course we had arrangements. There were five or six volunteers — friends of ours, or people who work on the estate next door. We tried to make sure that there was somebody in each of the rooms that was open to the public. There were six of those — the main drawing room, the dining room, the library and so on. But the system didn't work, I'm afraid, and there were spells in between shifts when there was nobody in a room."

Isabel was curious as to how a painting could have been carried out in broad daylight, with people milling around.

"I'm afraid that was very simple," said Duncan. "The Poussin was in the drawing room, and that room has a French window that opens on to the garden. But the bit of the garden in question is secluded and there's a sort of hedged corridor that goes round to the back of the house. It would have been very easy to take the painting out by that route and then bundle it into a car parked near the kitchen. Very simple, I'm afraid. We didn't check beforehand to see whether that door was locked — and it wasn't."

He sighed. "The insurance people hit the roof when they came round. I pointed out to them that if it had been as obvious as all that, then why had they not raised it with me when their man came round last year to look at the alarm system. They wanted to check that we had proper alarms and they had a good walk round the house. They said things seemed fine then."

"And how did they respond to that?"

"Silence. They answer the questions they want to answer and ignore the others. They've been very tight-lipped about this." He paused. "I'm afraid I've been seriously distressed by these people. Seriously . . ." his voice faltered.

Isabel reached across to touch him gently on the forearm. He looked down at her hand, surprised, but did not draw back. She left her hand where it rested for only a moment or two, but it was enough to establish a connection of sympathy.

"It's obviously been pretty upsetting for you," she said. "The loss of the painting in itself must be bad enough, but to have it compounded by a row over insurance must make it all so much worse."

He gave her an appreciative look. "Yes, I'm afraid you're right. I should perhaps have been a bit more robust about it all, but I'm afraid I just found the whole thing . . . well, a bit tawdry. I feel dirtied by it. It's odd, I know, but that's the way I feel."

"But that's the way that anybody who's been burgled feels," Isabel said. "It's a violation. Your space has been invaded. It's a shock. And then along come insurance people who make you feel guilty about it, although you're the victim. It's entirely understandable."

They were silent for a while. Then Duncan said, "That's why I asked to speak to you. I wanted to have somebody on my side, if I could put it that way. Lawyers are all very well, and I could have asked

Douglas Connel — he's very helpful, but he's doing a lot of other things for me at present and I felt it would be burdening him unduly."

"I know Douglas," said Isabel. "I'm sure he wouldn't mind."

"Maybe not. But I also thought that for this it might be better to have somebody who isn't a lawyer." He looked at her cautiously. "And there's a reason for that."

Isabel waited for him to explain. He picked up a paper napkin and folded it carefully, and then refolded it.

"We've had an approach, or rather, the insurance people have had an approach. It's tentative at the moment, but it looks as if something might be happening."

"An approach from the thieves?"

"Possibly."

"And are they going to talk to them?"

"I imagine so. The insurance company wants to avoid paying the claim if at all possible. If they can get the painting back from the thieves for less than the claim, then that suits them just fine."

"I see."

"Remember those Turners that were stolen in Germany?"

Isabel remembered it, but only vaguely.

"They got them back through negotiation with the thieves," Duncan said. "In our case, though, there's something unusual going on."

She waited. The waitress had come to clear their plates.

"They want to talk to me," he said quietly. "They've made the initial approach to the insurance company, but they seem to have gone off them for some reason. Maybe it's something the insurers said. Perhaps they rather scared the thieves off. Anyway, they're now talking directly to me."

She asked what the insurance company thought of that. They were surprised, he said, and unsure what lay behind it. They felt it might be unwise for him to talk directly to the thieves and they were also at pains to stress that Duncan had no power to negotiate in relation to the return of the painting. That was their affair as insurers and the thieves would have to go to them for that. After a while, though, they had changed their tune when it came to initial talks, especially after the thieves had gone quiet for a few weeks. Duncan could talk directly to anybody, as long as he kept them informed and did not try to commit them to any payment.

"So what would you like me to do?" Isabel asked.

Duncan stared at her uncertainly.

"I'm perfectly happy to help," she prompted. "You needn't feel awkward about asking."

"I have to meet them," he said. "They've told me they're going to be in touch about a meeting. I don't yet know where it's going to be."

"How did they contact you?"

"Initially by letter. Anonymous, naturally. Printed on a plain sheet of paper and postmarked Glasgow. It told me nothing."

"You showed it to the insurance people?"

He nodded. "They photographed it. I'm not sure if they showed it to the police. The police have been informed, of course, but seem to be taking a bit of a back seat at present. It seems the insurance company doesn't think it helps to involve them too closely at this stage, as far as I can tell."

"You said — initially. Have they been in touch again?"

He shifted in his seat uneasily. "They telephoned me. At three in the morning."

She waited for him to continue.

"They asked me if I had received their letter. That's how I knew it was the same people. The insurance people say that you get all sorts of cranks phoning up pretending to be the thieves, trying to get in on things. At least we know this is the same group."

It occurred to Isabel that they might still be impostors who had nothing to do with the theft. How could he tell?

"The letter had a photograph with it. It was a close-up of a section of the painting under strong light. It couldn't have been taken when it was in our possession, on the wall — the lighting was quite different."

Their coffee had arrived. Duncan took a sip, looking at Isabel over the rim of his cup. "They said they'd phone to make the arrangements quite soon. They said it wouldn't be them I would be meeting — it would be somebody acting for them. I thought I might tell them that I'll be accompanied by a friend. I'll stress that you have nothing to do with the insurance company."

He waited expectantly. "All right?"

Isabel nodded. "All right."

He looked relieved. "Thank you. And I'm sorry that this has all been about me and I haven't asked you anything about yourself. I know that you edit a journal — Martha told me that — and I know that you have a reputation as being somebody who sorts out people's difficulties. But apart from that?"

"I live in Merchiston," Isabel said. "Just round the corner from here. I run the journal from the house. And I'm married to a musician. He plays the bassoon."

Duncan listened politely. "I see."

"And I have a three-and-three-quarter-year-old son called Charlie. And that, I suppose, is it. And you? Do you have family?"

"I have two children by my first wife," said Duncan. "My daughter is thirty and I have a son of twenty-seven. Both live in Edinburgh — my daughter lives in Nelson Street. I'm going down there immediately after this. We see each other regularly."

"And your wife?" Isabel asked.

"Frederika. Freddie for short. I remarried about ten years ago. I had lost my first wife to cancer a few years earlier. The children were still at school. Alex — that's Alexandra — was just about to leave and Patrick had a couple more years to go. It was very difficult for him. Had he been a little older, he would have coped better, I think."

Had his words been written, the last sentence would have been underlined in red, thought Isabel.

"It's always difficult," said Isabel. "I lost my mother at quite an early age. I was twelve."

"Yes, it's not easy. Alex says that her memories sometimes get jumbled up — even though she was almost eighteen when her mother died."

"They will," said Isabel. "I remember my mother, but the memories are sometimes fuzzy, like a film that's not quite in focus. I remind myself by looking at photographs and by thinking about her."

Isabel thought for a moment: *If she could only walk in through that door. If she could only do that . . .*

They were both silent. Then Duncan glanced at his watch before looking out of the window, as if expecting somebody. His appointment in Nelson Street, Isabel imagined; his daughter opening the door to him, a kiss on the cheek, the exchange of small talk, a cup of tea — how precious. She noticed the watch, which was thin, and made of rose gold. It was discreet, understated. It was exactly right for him.

"Alex has been very upset by the whole business," he said. "She was particularly attached to that painting — she always has been. I keep off the subject because it's just too painful for her."

Isabel thought this quite understandable. She was reminded of a picture of her own that she could not bear to lose — a drawing by James Cowie of a boy, one of his Hospitalfield portraits. Cowie drew the young people whom he taught; they were delicate portraits, entirely natural, catching what the language of James VI's time referred to as "man's innocency". *Innocency*: what a wonderful word, and different, in some indefinable way, from *innocence*. The difference, she thought, lay in the poetry.

"And I must confess it's painful for me too," Duncan suddenly added. "I suppose I'm mourning that picture. Or that's what it feels like."

He reached for the raincoat he had draped over a chair. "I'll tell Martha about our meeting," he said. "She'll be pleased."

Isabel inclined her head. "Good."

Duncan rose to his feet. "Dear Martha."

Isabel was not sure what to say. So she said, "Of course."

It was the best thing to come out with in any circumstances in which one was at a loss for anything more. "Of course" fitted most occasions, as it meant that whatever the other person had said was perfectly understandable, and indeed correct; which is what most of us want to hear.

"Although she can occasionally go on a bit," he added.

Isabel noticed that there were the traces of a smile about his lips.

"Of course," she said. "But we all can, can't we?"

"Of course," he said.

They went to the counter, where he paid the bill. "I'll be in touch, if I may, when we hear from . . . from these people."

"Please do."

"And we'd very much like you to come out to the house. Come and have dinner and stay the night. You and your husband. And little . . ."

65

"Charlie."

"Yes, Charlie too. Would you like to do that?"

She said she would. She was intrigued. But it was more than that. She had taken a liking to this man — to the subtle and sensitive mind that she had detected beneath the unlikely exterior. And she felt sympathy for him. He had lost a painting that he loved and that he had been, generously, intending to give to the nation. The thieves, then, had not just stolen from a private individual, they had stolen from the whole nation. If she could help to deal with that — even if she had no real idea what she could possibly do — then she would do it.

They said goodbye on the pavement outside. He turned and walked back into Bruntsfield, on his way to visit his daughter in Nelson Street. Isabel watched him go and reflected on how a casual observer, driving past, perhaps, and seeing him in the street, might come to entirely the wrong conclusion: might see a rather formal, even slightly military figure, might take him to be exactly what in one sense he was — a country gentleman — and would not imagine for a moment that this was a man who knew, and cared about, art; who could mourn the loss of a picture. But then we can misjudge one another so easily, she thought; so easily.

CHAPTER
FIVE

The following day, which was a Saturday, Jamie was playing in a concert in St Cecilia's Hall and Isabel had a ticket. Grace had agreed to look after Charlie and arrived early so that she could do his dinner and give him his bath too. Isabel would have preferred to do that herself, but she knew how much Grace enjoyed her time with Charlie and so she did not begrudge it.

"And perhaps give him a quick mathematics lesson," she said.

She spoke jokingly, but Grace was immediately defensive.

"I only do that when he's fresh and in a mood to absorb things," she said reproachfully. "The end of the day is no time for that sort of thing."

Isabel made a conciliatory gesture. "Absolutely not." She thought of something else to say. "Could you put some of that oil in his bath? His skin seemed a little dry the other day."

Grace looked sideways at Isabel. "But I always do. You have to be careful about that."

If she always did it, then the implication was that Isabel was at fault. "I am careful," she said, meeting Grace's gaze.

They heard Charlie playing in the morning room with Jamie, and Grace went through to greet them. Isabel retreated into her study. *You have to be careful.* Of course she was careful about dry skin — as if she did not know about it. It was too much — did Grace think that she knew more about looking after children than Isabel did? It was ridiculous. She looked up at the ceiling. No, it was not really ridiculous: what was ridiculous was her own attitude to Grace's entirely understandable lack of tact. All that Grace wanted to show her was that she knew what she was doing, and the reason why she felt she had to do this was because she thought that she — Isabel — would not think that she knew . . . Isabel laughed, and the tension, the resentment, disappeared.

"What are you laughing at?"

It was Jamie, who had followed her into her study and was standing behind her. Isabel crossed the room to close the door behind him — Grace had acute hearing.

"It's something Grace said," she explained. "She reminded me that you have to be careful about children getting dry skin."

"Charlie's skin isn't dry."

"No, but sometimes it can get a bit on the dry side. If you don't use that baby oil stuff."

"But I always do."

She smiled. "Not you too! I didn't say that you didn't use it. I'm not accusing you."

"But Grace is? Grace is accusing you of letting his skin get dry?"

Isabel laughed again. "No, this is becoming absurd. She just wanted me to know that she knew about it. I got all huffy and came in here thinking what a cheek she had and then realised that I had no reason to think that. And shouldn't. So I stopped. And that's when you came in."

Jamie shrugged. "An argument about nothing."

Isabel agreed, but pointed out that a great deal of life was all about small things like that: arguments about baby oil, about eggs, about who's put something in the wrong place. She had not yet mentioned the Korean mathematics book, but now she did.

"I meant to tell you. She's giving him mathematics lessons."

Jamie's face fell. "You mean . . ."

"Yes, she's taught him how to divide."

"But I thought it was his natural ability . . ."

Isabel smiled. "It is. No amount of tuition would enable an untalented three-year-old to divide. No, he's obviously got ability."

Jamie sat down. He looks cross, thought Isabel. First, the dry-skin affair, and now mathematics.

"She should have asked us," Jamie said eventually. "I mean, things like that — educational matters — are parental affairs, wouldn't you say? I wouldn't try to teach some other person's child how to do mental arithmetic. Would you?"

Isabel sat on the arm of his chair. It was the most comfortable chair in the house and it occupied pride of place in her study, where it had always been. Jamie liked it and would sometimes sit reading in it while

Isabel worked; she liked having him there, but his presence did not help her to work. Isabel had always found it difficult to concentrate with other people in the room; they distracted her, as she found herself wondering what they were thinking. It would be fascinating to have some sort of printout of the thoughts of other people — a stream-of-consciousness report. It would read, she suspected, like a badly constructed novel, by an author who had no sense of the flow of narrative. *Look at her. Where did she get that? I had something like that back when I was living in that flat. Who lives there now? Did I turn the iron off? I'm feeling a bit hot. What did the weather forecast say? Bill hasn't telephoned. He said he would.* And so on, for page after page.

She addressed his question. "It's different with Grace. She has a lot of responsibility for Charlie. She's not quite family, but she's close enough. And that makes her an important part of his life."

He looked up at her. "I suppose so. But still . . ."

"Yes," she said. "But still."

"I'd like to see the book."

She suggested he ask her.

He got up out of the chair. "We still need to think about all that. We need to ask ourselves whether we really want him to have lessons at this point. I'm not sure that I want to turn him into a performing monkey."

Neither did Isabel.

"And there's another thing," said Jamie. "You have to be careful how you teach things. Music teachers are very careful about teaching very young children. You can get it all wrong and then they grow up with bad habits. Or you can ruin their lips — you don't let small children play brass, for example."

"We need to talk to her," she said. "Both of us. But not now."

"When?"

She sighed. "After the weekend." She wanted to enjoy the concert and did not want to go out after a row with Grace. But there was more to it: she also wanted to make it easy for Grace; she did not believe in painting people into a corner and making them lose face. So she would have to work out a method of doing it that would mean that Grace would believe it was her decision. It would not be easy, and Isabel had to admit that she had no idea how she could possibly do this.

They walked to St Cecilia's Hall. The weather had held and the evening air was balmy. In the Meadows, the large slice of park that separated Edinburgh's Old Town from the Victorian suburbs to the south, spontaneous games had sprung up: rounders played by a mixture of parents and eight-year-olds; a small game of cricket with only five or six fielders and a tennis ball. Isabel looked up at the branches of the trees that formed a canopy above the footpath they were following. The trees were in full leaf, but sky still showed through gaps in the foliage, a fading blue with drifting lace-like clouds. It made her dizzy to look at clouds when they were moving, as these were, and Isabel reached for Jamie's arm so that they might stop for a moment.

"Look at those clouds," she said. "They're very high. Cirrus, I think."

Jamie looked up too. "I don't know the names. Does it help if you know the names?"

She shrugged. "In the same way as it helps to know the names of trees. Or flowers. People tend to know about trees and flowers, but not about clouds. Strange, isn't it?"

"Maybe it's because they're always there," said Jamie. "We take for granted things that are always there."

As they continued on their way, Isabel felt a deep sense of contentment. There were other cities where, on an equally fine evening, much the same scenes as these would be played out. There were cities of equal or similar beauty: Venice, Vienna, St Petersburg. But this place, this city, this particular sky was *hers*, the place where the accident of birth had placed her. And she knew it so well; knew each turn of its winding streets; each cliff-face of ascending stone; each sweep of skyline.

As they made their way down Forest Road, and passed Sandy Bell's Bar, she remembered how, some years ago, she had been there with that man who had had the heart transplant. And before that, she had been there to listen to the music, and had heard Hamish Henderson sing "Freedom Come All Ye" and his heartbreaking "Banks of Sicily"; and a young Irishman launch into "Sam Hall". He had had such expressive eyes, and had sung as if he meant every word — "My name it is Sam Hall, and I *curse* you, one and all".

72

And in Candlemaker Row she remembered how she had walked down there not all that long ago with Jamie after a concert in Greyfriars Church, and they had talked about the Covenanters, or she had thought about them — she could not quite remember which. She slipped her hand into his.

"Nervous?"

He shook his head. "I like what we're playing tonight. And it's not very demanding for me — the benefits of being down on the bass line."

When they arrived, Jamie went into the green room with his fellow musicians, leaving Isabel to choose a seat in the upstairs room. The concert was part of a series organised by the Early Scottish Music Society, and there was to be a drinks reception afterwards, for which preparations were already being made. Jamie had suggested that they stay for this, as it was an opportunity for the performers, who otherwise would not have time to socialise, to get to know one another. Isabel was happy to agree; she had friends who had season tickets to these concerts and they might be there.

The concert began. A couple of pieces were familiar to Isabel — the rest were new, but there were full programme notes that explained who the composers were and put their music in context. She did not go out at the interval, but remained where she was, reading the notes for the second half. Jamie caught her eye and smiled; she returned the smile. She felt so proud of him.

At the end of the concert, the audience went downstairs, where most stayed for the reception. A group of young women in black skirts and white tops circulated among the guests, offering glasses of wine and small, rather greasy snacks. Isabel took a sausage on a stick and nibbled at it: it was not at all warm and seemed to be packed with cold fat. She steeled herself to swallow it. The Scottish diet was famously unhealthy, and it seemed that the same applied to Scottish canapés.

There was no sign of her friends, and she found herself in conversation with a couple she had not met before. Looking for something to talk about, she asked them where they lived. Their eyes lit up: they had recently moved to a new house and were full of the details. "It has a large conservatory," the woman said. "With a vine — an established vine."

"And there's a terrific garden," said the husband.

"Yes, terrific," agreed his wife. "The people before us were demon gardeners. Demons."

Isabel sipped at her wine, discreetly eyeing the prospects for escape. Jamie was on the other side of the room, with the musicians. They were enjoying themselves, and a peal of laughter sounded across the room to make the point. She pointed to him. "My husband."

The woman looked across the room. "On the right?"

Isabel shook her head. "On the left. And I must have a word with him, if you'll excuse me."

Isabel could tell that the woman was interested. The musician on the right was a short man with a thickset neck, much older than Jamie. She has assumed, thought Isabel, that that is the sort of husband I should have. And now she had seen Jamie and was thinking: how did *she* get *him*? People are transparent, Isabel thought; so often we can tell exactly what they're thinking although they may not have said a thing. And I am equally transparent: this woman knows that I'm not really interested in our conversation and that I don't really have to have a word with Jamie; not an urgent word; not anything that couldn't wait until they've finished telling me about their garden.

The woman's interest in Jamie changed now to offence that Isabel wanted to get away from her. "Please," she said. "Don't let us hold you up."

Isabel blushed, and moved away. She did not like to give offence, but sometimes it was difficult not to do so. Sometimes the ordinary contingencies of social life meant that offence was inevitable: the turning down of an invitation that one could not accept because one had another engagement — that could give offence, no matter how genuine the excuse: *she doesn't want to come; she says that she's got something else on . . . that's what she says.* Or at a cocktail party — those occasions that Isabel sometimes called "trials by cocktail" — you had to move on; you couldn't stay and talk to the same person for hours; and yet how to detach yourself? What formula could one use for getting away? Could you simply say, "I've enjoyed our chat," and walk away? That was somewhat abrupt. "I must fill up my glass." "But it's quite full already." "Oh, is it? I hadn't noticed." Perhaps one might try: "I need some fresh air. I must get to a window." "Oh, so do I! I'll come with you." As a last resort, a quick glance at one's watch, and then, "I really have to go. What a pity." "Oh, so do —" "No. Actually I'll stay — you go. Goodbye."

Isabel moved towards the other side of the room. She sensed that the woman was watching her; she felt her eyes upon her, and thought she should be seen to be walking in that direction. Then she hesitated: why? Why should she worry about what somebody whom she had just met, and whom she would probably never meet again, should think about her? She had done nothing wrong; she had been perfectly polite when they had been going on about their garden. She had done nothing for which she should reproach herself.

She stopped. There was a young man standing in front of her. He had just finished talking to a woman in a purple dress, a large woman who was a regular attendee at Edinburgh concerts and who was considered vividly eccentric by many; an enthusiastic exponent of a wide range of subjects, on which she entertained strong and unconventional opinions. The young man looked bemused, which often happened when people spoke to that particular woman for the first time. She was now making off towards her husband, who was standing near the door; a rather insignificant-looking man who had the appearance of being permanently overwhelmed; shell-shocked, perhaps, after years of marriage to that woman. The Scots expression *hauden doon* — held down — was made for people like him, thought Isabel.

Isabel caught the young man's eye. She had the feeling he wanted to speak to her.

"Enjoyed the concert?" she asked.

He looked at her gratefully; in a room full of people talking, we do not wish to be by ourselves. "Yes. A lot. I love early music and we don't get enough of it, I think."

"I like it too."

He transferred his glass from right hand to left to be able to shake hands. "I'm Patrick Munrowe."

It took a moment for the name to register. But then, in an instant, she saw the resemblance. Of course he was Patrick Munrowe; there was Duncan's forehead, and the same eyes; the same presence.

The coincidence struck her sharply. "Your father's Duncan Munrowe?"

He nodded, somewhat surprised. She looked at him appraisingly. He was slightly taller than his father with the same good looks, but had an air of vulnerability about him; the air that some men have of being slightly lost.

"I had lunch with him yesterday, you see."

He looked thoughtful. "Here? In Edinburgh?"

"Yes, he was in town."

"I see. I didn't know."

There was nothing in his tone to suggest that he was aggrieved to hear that his father had been in Edinburgh and had not told him, and yet Duncan had made a point of saying that he always saw his daughter when he came to town. If the daughter, then why not the son?

"I think it was a pretty brief visit," she said hurriedly. "It was business."

He started to enquire. "You're a . . .?" He did not finish the sentence.

"It was about the loss of the painting."

"So you're with the insurance company?"

"No." She was not sure how to proceed, being uncertain as to whether the approach from Duncan was meant to be confidential. She had already given it away, if it was. "No. I've got nothing to do with that side of it. I was asked by Martha Drummond to speak to him about it."

The mention of Martha's name had an immediate effect: he looked incredulous. "Her?"

"Yes. I believe that she's a friend of your father's."

"I suppose so. It's just that, well, frankly I find that woman rather difficult to take. Sorry."

"She may not be everybody's cup of tea."

He took a sip of his wine. "Has he asked you to help him?"

Isabel felt that she could hardly decline to talk about it now. "He has. I'm not sure what I can do — if anything. But I think your father needed a sounding board, so to speak."

He nodded. "Fair enough. He was very upset by it, you know."

"I know."

"And it wasn't because of the money side of it. Pop is very unworldly. He's one of the least materialistic people I know."

Isabel said that she had formed the impression that it was the painting that counted rather than its monetary value.

"Dead right," said Patrick. "With him, it's a question of . . . well, there's no other word for it but honour. It's a question of honour that he promised the painting to the Scottish National Gallery. That's what's really hurt him — the possibility that the painting might never be recovered or could be damaged."

"I can understand that."

He looked at her with interest. "May I ask what you do? Are you a psychologist?"

"No. I'm a philosopher."

He seemed impressed. "There aren't many people who can answer that question that way. That's what you actually do — philosophy?"

She explained about the *Review* and about the sort of articles she published. And then she turned the question back on him. "And you?"

His reply was delivered in a tone of self-deprecation. "Nothing nearly as interesting, I'm afraid. I work for a company that advises on investment in pharmaceutical companies. I've been doing it for the grand total of six years so far."

She wondered about his age. Duncan had told her, but she had forgotten. Twenty-something — twenty-seven? So he must have gone straight from university into the job. And that left another forty years to do it. Forty years of working on drug companies. Forty years.

"I'm not sure that I'd say that was uninteresting. Drugs don't strike me as boring. And isn't what you do a form of intelligence gathering?"

He smiled, "I suppose you could look at it that way. We look at pharmaceutical companies with a view to putting the investors' money in them. I suppose that's intelligence gathering. I look at smaller companies — the ones who think they might just invent the cure for something big."

"And do they?"

"Sometimes, but very rarely. I've recently been looking at one that is trying to find an Alzheimer's drug. There have been one or two possibilities, but at the end of the day they've fizzled out. Then somebody comes up with something that makes everybody's efforts look a bit expensive. Such as eating oily fish. Apparently that stops your brain shrinking and protects you against Alzheimer's. But there's no profit in that."

Isabel laughed. "Sardines? A tin of sardines a day?"

"Exactly. And if you're worried about strokes, then . . ."

They were interrupted by Jamie, who had left the group of musicians. He took Isabel's hand and squeezed it lightly.

"Lovely concert," said Isabel. And to Patrick, "This is Jamie."

Patrick smiled at Jamie. "Yes," he said. "You played the bassoon, didn't you?"

"I did."

"I played a curtal once," said Patrick. "At school. We had a music teacher who loved old instruments. He arranged for us to play sackbuts and sordunes and whatever."

Isabel asked what the curtal was.

"The precursor of the bassoon," Jamie told her.

"And the racket," prompted Patrick. "Don't forget the racket."

"That's another early instrument," said Jamie. "It looks like a little pot. You blow down a crook into the little pot and a deep sound comes out. It's a sort of bassoon for people who were waiting for the bassoon to be invented."

Patrick laughed. She saw that his eyes had lit up during this conversation. "Imagine people wanting to play instruments that haven't yet been invented. One might say, 'I really want to play the saxophone but Adolf Sax hasn't invented it yet.'"

Isabel smiled. She liked a conversation that went in odd directions; she liked the idea of playfulness in speech. People could be so depressingly literal.

Jamie now turned to her. "I think perhaps we should go home. Grace doesn't want to stay over tonight, she wants to get home."

Isabel explained to Patrick, "Grace is our babysitter."

She saw Patrick's eyes move quickly to Jamie and then back to her. It was quick, but she noticed. There was a look of disappointment on his face; it was unmistakable.

"I must be on my way too," Patrick said quietly.

Isabel felt a sudden sympathy for him. "Where do you live?"

"I live in the New Town," he said. "St Bernard's Crescent."

"I like it there," said Isabel.

"Yes," he said flatly. "So . . ."

"Well, I'm sure we'll meet again," said Isabel. "Your father has invited me to the house."

"You'll like it there too."

He smiled and began to turn away. Isabel took Jamie's arm and led him through the crowd, towards the door. Outside, in the darkness, she looked up at the towering stone buildings that lined the narrow thoroughfare of the Cowgate. A soft rain was falling, a spitting.

"Your bassoon?" she asked. "You've left your bassoon behind."

"They're looking after all our instruments. They have a van that will bring everything back tomorrow."

They began to make their way back towards the Grassmarket, undecided as to whether to walk home or catch a taxi.

"That was Patrick Munrowe," said Isabel. "His father is the man whose painting was stolen."

Jamie seemed distracted by something. "That second piece we played," he said. "I'm not sure it was a success. The flute —"

"What did you think of him?" pressed Isabel.

"Of Patrick?"

"Yes."

"I was interested to hear that he had played the curtal. He knew what he was talking about."

"And?"

"Well, I don't know."

"Gay?" asked Isabel.

"Maybe," said Jamie. "Did you think so?"

"Yes," she said. "He was very disappointed when we mentioned Grace and getting back for the babysitter. Did you notice it?"

Jamie had not. "That second piece," he said. "We sounded much better at rehearsal."

"It was because he hadn't realised that you and I were together. That was why."

Jamie was silent. Isabel's deduction embarrassed him. "You mean . . . Well, how can you tell? And anyway, what does it matter?"

"Oh, it doesn't matter at all. But I think there's an issue between him and his father. It may have nothing to do with that, or it may. I can't tell."

"Gaydar can be misleading, you know," said Jamie. "It needs to be calibrated."

"Like sympathy," said Isabel. "And all our emotions and feelings. Shame. Anger. Love. Pain. Calibration is required if we are to use them sensitively."

"How do you calibrate pain?" asked Jamie.

"By cutting out the background pain of the world," answered Isabel. "By cutting all that out, not registering it, and responding only to those painful things that we can do something about. Because otherwise . . ."

Jamie had seen a taxi approaching; the thin band of yellow light above the vehicle's windscreen weaving its way towards them. He stepped out into the road and raised an arm.

"Because otherwise what?"

"Because otherwise we couldn't get on with our day-to-day lives. The pain of the world would burden us too much."

"True," said Jamie.

CHAPTER
SIX

There was an unspoken understanding between Isabel and her niece Cat that when Cat went away on holiday or was otherwise unable to get in to the delicatessen, then Isabel would take over, even with very little notice. It would have been more sensible for Eddie to do this, but Eddie, for all his willingness to embark on a long tour of North America with his uncle — and uncle's girlfriend — and to follow this with a spell working at a ski resort in Alberta, still lacked the confidence to be left in sole charge of the delicatessen. Isabel wondered whether this might be changed by his having reached the milestone of his twenty-first birthday and having met his new girlfriend Diane — or the Huntress, as she had unfortunately become lodged in Isabel's mind, though not a reference to any man-hunting on her part — Eddie was not the most obvious prey for a dedicated man-hunter — but to the occupation of the Greek goddess of that name. Eddie was still unwilling to accept full responsibility and had shown signs of alarm when Cat telephoned the following Monday morning to inform him that she had come down with a norovirus and would be off work for at least three days, possibly more. Cat had reassured him that Isabel would

84

help out and that he would not be left to manage by himself; she had then phoned Isabel and broken the news to her.

"I hate asking you," she said. "But I really can't go in. I don't want to go into details —"

"Then don't," said Isabel quickly.

"But I'm bringing up the most amazing amount of fluid," Cat persisted. "I have no idea where it's all coming from. And the diarrhoea, I'm not exaggerating, I promise you —"

"I'll be there," Isabel interjected. "How many days?"

When Cat warned her that it could be the whole week, Isabel's heart sank. There were spells in her life — often as long as a month — when the affairs of the *Review of Applied Ethics* could safely be put to one side, or benignly neglected as Isabel put it, but this was not one of them. The proofs of the next issue had arrived and an entire article was being withdrawn on the grounds that the author had placed it elsewhere without telling Isabel. He had been keen, she believed, to have a backup home for it if another possibility of publication — in a rather more prestigious journal — came to nothing. The prestigious journal had accepted the paper and the author had either forgotten to inform Isabel timeously or had become too embarrassed to do so, eventually leaving it to a secretary in his department to let her know what was happening. Isabel had mentally composed a stinging rebuke, and had gone so far as to type it out as an email, but had eventually decided not to send it. The delete button, that saviour of how many relationships, had again done its work: the swingeing censure had been replaced by a mild, rather sad reproach: *It would have been helpful to know about this before I sent everything off to the printer; but no matter, I'm very pleased that you've found such a good home for your very fine piece. And their circulation is admittedly so much larger than ours, and looks as if it will remain so, no matter how hard we try.* The "no matter how hard we try" was later removed; reproach should not too quickly become self-pity.

All this, though, meant that she had to find an article to take its place, contact the author and have all the editing done within the next three days. That was feasible, even if she were to be busy in the delicatessen, but it would mean that she would have to work in the evenings as well as all day — something she did not particularly enjoy. She was, after all, a mother with an affectionate and demanding three-and-three-quarter-year-old to look after. She wanted to spend as much time with Charlie as she could, and now she would be unable to get away from the delicatessen until six-thirty every evening, by which time the bath would be over and the bedtime story would be about to begin.

But she could not let Cat down, and, after a quick consultation with Grace, who had just come in at the door, and a rushed telephone conversation with Jamie, who was on his way down to the Academy to start one of his teaching days, she finished her breakfast quickly and started out of the house.

Eddie greeted her warmly. He always arrived at the delicatessen early and he had coped perfectly well with the rush of people who called in on their way to work.

That rush had now abated, and there were only one or two customers browsing the shelves when Isabel arrived.

"It's been all go," said Eddie, wiping his hands on his apron. "I've taken over two hundred and fifty pounds in . . ." He looked up at the clock above the refrigerated display. "In forty minutes. How about that?"

"Very good," said Isabel, reaching for a fresh apron from the hook on the wall. "You spoke to Cat, I take it?"

"I did," said Eddie. "She's got projectile vomiting, you know."

Isabel looked away. Any sort of vomiting was bad enough, but projectile vomiting . . .

"I've never had projectile vomiting," Eddie went on. "I was really sick for a day or two on the trip, though. We were in a place in Idaho and I was really hungry. We'd booked into a motel just outside town and my uncle and his girlfriend had gone to a bar. I stayed in the motel. Then I found that I got really hungry, and so I went to this hot-dog place and ordered a really big hot dog. You should have seen it, Isabel, it was humungous. And it tasted really good."

Isabel busied herself with sweeping excess grounds off the work surface around the coffee machine. "But it wasn't?"

"No," said Eddie. "I think it had E. coli in it. Or something like that. I was seriously sick. Not projectile vomiting, but I felt really bad. The man in the motel said it was E. coli. He said that there was a lot of E. coli about and some of those hot-dog places make their hot dogs out of dead horse meat. Yuck. That's what he told me. He said the horses die and if they go like that, rather than being sent to the slaughterhouse, they shouldn't be eaten. But apparently the mafia have a racket in horse meat and they sell it to these hot-dog places and pretend that it comes from cows."

"Well, you survived," said Isabel. "And I'm sure Cat will too. So let's get things organised."

Eddie worked calmly and efficiently, and yet Isabel suspected that if she were not there he would be jittery and anxious. "Could you manage by yourself, do you think?" she asked him during a lull at the counter.

He looked at her with alarm. "Why?"

"I just wondered."

"Do you have to do something else?" His voice was taut with anxiety.

"It's all right, Eddie," she said calmly. "I'll stay. I'm not going anywhere."

He visibly relaxed. "Good," he said. "I know I should be able to handle things by myself, but I get this tight feeling — right here . . ." He pointed to his chest. "And it makes it hard for me to do anything. I know it's stupid, really stupid. But . . ."

She put a hand on his shoulder. "Eddie, you're doing just fine. You're fine."

He looked down for a moment, and then raised his eyes to meet hers. Something passed between them — a moment of understanding, she thought. He had never told her what had happened to him — she had an idea — but now it seemed to her that he had somehow acknowledged that she knew, and that fact made it much easier for him. He was getting better, she was sure of it; time's healing effect — the old saw, the folk wisdom — was absolutely true. It was something to do with memory: things forgotten lost their power.

She changed the subject. "How's Diane?"

Eddie smiled. "You could meet her," he said. "She's around today. I could phone her and ask her to drop in." He looked at Isabel enquiringly. "That's if you want to. Only if you want to."

"Of course I want to meet her, Eddie. Phone her. Tell her to come after lunch some time when we're not so busy."

He reached for his mobile phone and made the call.

"She can come," he said. "She wants to meet you too."

"Good."

Eddie looked anxious. "I hope you like her, Isabel."

"I will."

He hesitated. "She's older than me, Isabel."

Isabel paused. "Much older?" she asked, trying to keep her tone natural. What if Diane were fifty?

"A bit," said Eddie. "Twenty-six."

Inwardly, Isabel breathed a sigh of relief. "Well, that's nothing, Eddie. I'm older than Jamie. It's nothing to worry about."

Eddie looked shifty. "There's something else," he said.

"Yes."

"I may have told her that I'm a bit older than I really am." He began to mumble. "I told her I'm twenty-four."

Isabel frowned. "That's a bit stupid, Eddie. What on earth possessed you to do that?"

The censure was unplanned; and she herself was surprised by its forcefulness. Almost immediately, she repented. Isabel was sensitive about telling other people what to do in a moralistic sense — that was most definitely *not* the role of the moral philosopher. Philosophy was there to guide people to the right and the good — not to wag a disapproving finger at them.

She tried to make up for her mistake. "I'm sorry, Eddie. I shouldn't have said it was stupid. It's just that . . ." She saw his face crumple. "It's just that it's best to be honest in a relationship. And I'm sure that you yourself want to be honest, don't you?"

"Of course."

She reached out to take his hand. He resisted for a moment, and then allowed her. "All of us are dishonest in some respects — from time to time. Hands up all those who've never been dishonest about something. See, my hand didn't go up."

He smiled weakly. "You don't lie to people. I know you don't."

"I try not to. But sometimes I'm tempted to. Lying can be so much easier."

"Easier?"

"Yes, in the short term. But any advantage it confers doesn't usually last very long."

He thought about this for a moment. "What shall I do?"

Isabel squeezed his hand. "That's for you to decide."

"I should tell her?"

"You could."

He nodded. "I will."

Isabel smiled at him encouragingly. "I suspect that you'll find she won't mind. If she loves you . . ." She was not sure whether she should have said that.

Eddie looked at her. "How can I know that? How can I know that she loves me?"

Isabel let go of his hand. "That sort of thing is usually obvious. If she wants to live with you, then I'd have thought that she probably does."

Eddie bit his lip. "I could ask her, I suppose."

"You could."

He hesitated for a moment before continuing. "How do you know that Jamie loves you?"

"He married me," said Isabel. "He stood in the Canongate Kirk and made a declaration to that effect. In public."

"That's what I want to do," said Eddie. "I want to stand up in front of a whole lot of people and tell Diane that I love her. And I want to do that soon."

"I understand," said Isabel. "That's how one feels when one is in love. But perhaps you shouldn't do anything too sudden."

"Why not?"

She did not want to pour cold water on his enthusiasm. "Because one of the things about falling in love is that you can fall out of it again. So you have to be sure."

He was adamant. "I am. I am sure."

Lunchtime was particularly busy that day. Both Eddie and Isabel were kept at it solidly from twelve-thirty until shortly after two, when the shop suddenly emptied.

"You go and sit down," said Eddie. "Diane will be here in ten minutes."

Isabel went to one of the tables and flopped down on a seat. One of the customers had left a newspaper behind, a copy of the *Financial Times*, and she paged through this idly as she waited for Eddie to bring the restorative cup of tea he had promised her. She was not particularly interested in the doings of the markets, but the paper had good arts coverage too, and she found herself absorbed in a review of a recent staging in London of a new opera on the life of a Colombian drug baron. Opera could be as recondite, as obscure, as it liked, she mused, because people expected it. And the plot really did not matter too much either way — Philip Glass's *Einstein on the Beach* had no plot at all, as far as Isabel could ascertain, and there were operas with plots so complex that lengthy explanations were required before one could work out what was going on. And a silly plot — of which there were numerous examples — was not necessarily a drawback. Isabel had always considered that *Cosi fan tutte* was all about nothing very much, and yet it was one of the most beautiful of Mozart's operas.

She read the critic's review. "Why are we fascinated by the life of large-scale wrongdoers?" he asked. "Why do we find the tawdry doings of the wicked anything but banal?"

Isabel stopped reading for a moment. The tawdry doings of the wicked: it was a beguilingly succinct

92

dismissal of evil. And it was quite right, she thought, to deny any possible romance to wrongful deeds. Most major criminals, in or out of uniform, in or out of political office, in or out of the corporate boardroom, were simple bullies, prepared to use force to achieve their goals — and a Colombian drug lord would be a bully par excellence. Should we even bother to look at the life of a bully? What was there to say about it?

"This man," the critic continued, "is vile. He has used murder to progress through the criminal *cursus honorum*. He has profited from the endless misery of the illicit drug trade. He has grown rich on death. And yet here is a sophisticated London audience, a group of middle-class music-lovers, thrilling to the biography of this foul creature. And when he dies, as he does in the final scene, the music that accompanies his death is every bit as tragic as that which sees Mimi out in *La bohème*! Can that be right, or is there something here that needs to be considered by a social psychologist?"

Isabel looked up. Eddie was leading a young woman to her table. She thought: *the Huntress*, and then corrected herself. Not the Huntress; not the Huntress. Diane, plain and simple; Diane.

"This is Diane."

Isabel folded the paper and stood up to greet her visitor.

Eddie, who was clearly nervous, announced that he would bring two cups of tea. "Diane doesn't drink very much coffee, do you, Diane?"

"No," said Diane. "I don't."

"Too much coffee is bad for you," said Eddie.

"Everything in moderation," continued Isabel.

"In what?" asked Eddie nervously.

They were still standing, and Isabel gestured for Diane to sit down. "In moderation," she said to Eddie.

He nodded and went off behind the counter. Isabel noticed that Diane's eyes followed him. Yes, she thought, she loves him. I've seen the answer Eddie wanted.

"I'm really pleased that I'm getting the chance to meet you," said Isabel. "I'm very fond of Eddie."

She discreetly studied Diane as she spoke. Twenty-six was about right, she thought. And she's rather attractive in a slightly bony sort of way. Too thin? One had to be aware of that because so many people were anorexic now. Eddie himself was thin, though, and he definitely did not have an eating disorder, whatever other problems he might have. He ate rather a lot, in fact; he was always nibbling on the shavings from blocks of Parmesan or on scraps of ham or salami.

"He's very fond of you too," said Diane.

They were both silent for a moment. "What do you do?" asked Isabel.

"I'm a nurse," said Diane. "But now I'm studying to be a physiotherapist. I've got two years to go."

"They'll go very quickly," said Isabel.

"I think so," said Diane.

There was a further silence.

"Eddie tells me that you and he are planning to share," said Isabel. *To share* sounded better than *to live together*, she felt. It was not suggestive of anything beyond simple cohabitation, and sounded less prying as a result.

Diane said that this was their plan. "But . . ." Her voice trailed off.

Isabel waited.

"But I don't really see how we can."

"Why?"

"Money," she said simply. "We can't afford it. A flat costs at least eight hundred a month for a one-bedroom place. Usually more. Often a thousand."

"It's expensive," agreed Isabel. She was out of touch; she had thought three or four hundred was about right.

"And there's something else," Diane went on. "My parents are dead against it."

Isabel raised an eyebrow. "But you're twenty . . ."

"Twenty-six," supplied Diane. "Yes. And Eddie's . . ."

Isabel held her breath.

"Twenty-one," said Diane.

Isabel stared at her. She was taken aback, but now she made up her mind very quickly: this was her chance to defuse the situation for Eddie. "Eddie sometimes likes to think he's twenty-four," she said. "I suppose it's because he'd like to be twenty-four and sometimes we —"

"Sometimes we make things up," said Diane. She explained. "I know somebody who was in his year at school. That's how I realised." She shrugged. "I understand. I really do. I remember wanting to be older than I was. I really did. So, don't worry."

"He wants to tell you, you know," whispered Isabel. "Make it easy for him."

"I will," said Diane. "Of course I will."

Isabel felt a surge of affection rise within her. She liked this young woman. She was just right for Eddie. She loved him and she was straightforward and sensible. She was exactly what Eddie needed.

"Your parents?" prompted Isabel.

Diane looked apologetic. "I live with them at the moment," she said. "They live here in Edinburgh, in Murrayfield. They've got this large house, you see, and it's much cheaper for me to stay there than to rent a flat, or even a room in a flat, while I'm a student."

"Naturally," said Isabel. "And lots of people do that, don't they?"

Diane confirmed this. "But it's a bit more complicated in my case," she said. "They give me money. I've taken out a large student loan but it's never enough, even if you're careful. So they give me money each month."

"Many parents do that. And the child can pay it back later on."

Diane nodded. "But the complication is this: they don't like Eddie. They just don't."

"Have they seen much of him?"

"They've met him twice. It wasn't a success."

Isabel sighed. "Eddie might not come across all that well on a first or second meeting. He's shy. He becomes anxious."

Diane said that she knew that, but the problem with her parents was deeper-rooted. "They think he's not good enough for me. It's as simple as that. And . . ."

Isabel waited for her to continue.

"And they think that it's not going to last. They think that I'll grow out of him; that I'll realise we don't have very much in common; that I'll decide Eddie doesn't quite fit in." She paused. "They're snobs, you see."

Isabel was not sure what to say. It certainly sounded to her as though Diane's parents were behaving snobbishly, and yet she could hardly admit that she agreed with her and her parents really were snobs. One may speak disparagingly of one's own parents, but one did not like to hear others expressing the same sentiments.

"They've said that if I go and live with Eddie, then I won't get any more money. They spelled that out."

Isabel waited a few moments before saying anything. Then she said, "I'm very sorry to hear it."

"No," said Diane. "But you see the problem now?"

"I do," said Isabel.

"So we can't live together," said Diane. "It's just not on. Eddie thinks it is, and I'd love him to be right. But he isn't. It's just not possible. I'm too much in debt as it is. End of story."

CHAPTER
SEVEN

Cat's recovery was quicker than expected. On the following day she telephoned the delicatessen to tell Isabel that she was now up and about and that it looked as if the vomiting had stopped. She felt well enough to come in to work but thought it wiser to remain off for a further day in case she was still infectious. Isabel encouraged her in this. "The last thing you want is to pass these things on," she said. "One wouldn't wish projectile vomiting on anyone."

After Isabel had rung off, Eddie, who had overheard Isabel's side of the conversation, called out to her, "What did you say about projectile vomiting? Is she still doing it?"

"Why the big interest in it?" asked Isabel. Vomiting was vomiting, she thought, projectile or otherwise.

Eddie defended himself. "Well, it is pretty interesting, isn't it? I wonder how far she was projecting? Two or three feet, do you think?"

Isabel assumed an expression of disgust. "Really, Eddie, I don't share your fascination with the subject."

"Well, you mentioned it first," he said. "You were talking to her about it. You raised the subject."

"I just said that it's not something you would want to pass on to others. That's all. And it isn't, is it?"

"Of course not." He looked thoughtful. "I suppose with projectile vomiting you could really pass it on, couldn't you. If you hit anybody, even if they were standing a couple of feet away, thinking they were safe . . ."

"Eddie! You're disgusting."

"I was just thinking aloud."

"Well, please don't. You can keep those sorts of thoughts to yourself."

He was silent for a few moments. Isabel had noticed that Eddie's mood was very changeable that morning; perhaps he was anxious about Diane. She eyed him carefully. Now, something had come over him; maybe something triggered by this odd discussion. She had seen him do this before — slip into a sombre mood — although she thought that it happened much less frequently these days.

He lowered his voice; there was a customer within earshot, browsing the shelves. "What if you thought that you might . . . might have something because of something that happened . . . What should you do?"

Isabel looked at him with concern, causing him to glance away sharply.

"I'm not quite sure what you mean," she said carefully. "Do you mean, what if you think you've got some sort of infection: should you go to a doctor? Is that what you're asking me?"

He hesitated. He was fiddling with the strings of his blue-striped butcher's apron. The strings were frayed and he was tugging at them nervously. She noticed again his less than clean fingernails. He was just a boy; just a boy with the unwashed hands that boys have. And suddenly, with no warning at all, he had become a frightened boy.

He spoke slowly, stumbling over the phrases. "Yes. That's right. Except it may not be your fault that you might have something that . . . something that you wouldn't want to have. And then you suddenly think, maybe I shouldn't take the risk of passing it on to anybody. Say, a heavy cold, or something like that. Something like what Cat's had. That stuff. Or even . . . or even something worse than that. But it wasn't your fault, you see."

She waited, but he seemed to have finished what he wanted to say.

"Something worse?" Isabel asked quietly.

Eddie nodded mutely. He had been standing on the other side of the counter, and Isabel now crossed over to him. Taking his hand, she led him through the door into Cat's office. He did not resist. His hand, she thought, felt so soft. Over by the shelves, the customer turned and looked briefly in their direction, but then turned away.

"Eddie, I think I know what you're talking about. I think I do — but I'm not sure."

"I . . ."

"No, listen to me, Eddie. You don't have to tell me. I don't want you to feel that you must. There are things that happen to people that are very cruel, and people

100

don't have to talk about them if they don't want to. You know that, don't you?"

His gaze was fixed on the floor, his head bowed. But he nodded — almost imperceptibly.

"So all I'm going to say to you is this: I know that something bad happened to you, and I'm so, so sorry, Eddie. And if you think that because of this thing that happened you may need to have a check-up, then that's exactly the right thing to do. I'm sure that you'll be all right because it must have been quite some time ago, mustn't it, and you seem fine, don't you? But you can set your mind at rest."

He said nothing. He was weeping.

Isabel put her arm around his shoulder. She drew him to her. His frame was shaking with sobs. "Do you want me to go with you? I can go with you to the doctor."

He reached in his pocket for a handkerchief that was not there. Isabel took a tissue from the box on Cat's desk and handed it to him.

"Yes, please."

Isabel put her hand against his cheek. She reached for another tissue and dabbed at his tears.

"Dear Eddie," she whispered. "You've been very brave. And you're not alone, you know. You've got me, Cat, Diane. You've got all of us. Your friends."

"I feel stupid," he said. "And I feel dirty too."

She was shocked by his words. "Eddie, every one of us, every single one feels stupid about something. And maybe dirty too. And often it's not a big thing and it's not our fault either. All right, Eddie? All right?"

"I still feel stupid."

Isabel felt a rush of sympathy for the young man. "I know somebody who can help," she said. "They help people who have these worries. It's a charity. I've supported them in the past. You can talk to them and they'll arrange everything for you. And I'll come too, if you like."

His voice was small. "Please."

There was a knocking sound from outside. The customer who had been browsing was now standing at the counter knocking peremptorily on the glass, demanding service.

"I'm tempted to make her wait," said Isabel under her breath. "Impatient woman."

Eddie gave a wry smile. "She's a real cow, that woman. She comes in quite regularly. She thinks she owns the place."

Isabel touched him lightly on the shoulder. "Everything fine now?"

He nodded.

When Isabel returned home that evening, exhausted by what had turned into a busy early evening in the delicatessen, Jamie had already bathed Charlie and dressed him in his pyjamas. The small boy, beaming with pleasure at the return of his mother, launched himself into Isabel's arms, burying his face in her hair.

"Clever Mummy," he said.

She looked at him with delight. "How very kind, Charlie. But I'm not all that clever, darling. Just average."

Jamie smiled. "Yes, you are. Not average, I mean. Yes, you're clever."

Isabel ruffled Charlie's hair. "*You're* the clever one, I think. You're the one who can tell me what two and three make."

"Five," said Charlie immediately.

Isabel looked at Jamie, who made an "I told you so" gesture.

"That's absolutely right," she said. "Two and three do indeed make five."

"Olive," said Charlie. That had been his first word, and he still referred to it frequently.

"Olive?"

"More olives," said Charlie. "More olives now."

Isabel looked at Jamie. "Have you been giving him olives?" she asked. She had been trying to cut down on the number of olives Charlie ate because there was too much salt in the brine in which they were stored. She did not think that too much salt would do him any good.

Jamie shook his head. "No," he said. "Grace . . ."

"Grace!" shouted Charlie. "Grace got olives."

Isabel sighed. It would be another thing they would have to discuss with Grace: olives and mathematics — both, in their way, problematic.

Jamie looked at his watch. He had a rehearsal that evening and would have to leave shortly if he were to be in time.

"Oh," he said, "that man you were talking about — Duncan Munrowe — called this afternoon. He said could you phone him back this evening. He asked me not to forget to pass on the message. He asked me twice. I got the message . . . about the message."

He handed her a slip of paper on which a telephone number had been pencilled.

"Did he say anything else?" asked Isabel.

Jamie thought for a moment. "He said something about there having been a development." He looked at her almost reproachfully. "Yes, that's what he said. He said there had been a development."

Isabel waited until Jamie had gone off to his rehearsal and she had settled Charlie before she telephoned Duncan Munrowe. Charlie was clingy — he often was when she had spent an entire day out of the house — and she allowed him a small extension on his day, sitting on the edge of his bed, his tiny hand now moving, now restful in hers, as she told him a story of her own making. She had turned out the light, but in spite of the curtains the room was not completely dark. At midsummer, in Scotland, the night is never truly dark, and Charlie's bedtime came well before sunset. Even later, approaching midnight, the sky only dims, fades into something between the clarity of day and the opacity of night, a long-drawn-out crepuscule.

A week or two earlier she had started to tell Charlie a story that had immediately thrilled him and that he had insisted on hearing again. It had become a serial, the episodic life of a man made out of mud, who loved the rain but at the same time had to avoid it — for obvious reasons. "He'd melt, you see," she said. And Charlie had nodded wisely; he knew that from sand-play at the nursery.

"Some of his friends had melted," said Isabel. "And he missed them."

She did not know why she had said that; it was the wrong note to introduce into a bedtime story; an adult note of loss that would only sadden a child. And yet every child had to confront the notion of loss at some time, and perhaps this moment came earlier than we liked to imagine.

"He could make his friends again," she added. "He could find some mud and make his friends again."

"No," said Charlie. "Friends all gone."

But now the man made out of mud was happy, as he had discovered a pond where mud ducks lived and he was throwing bread made out of mud to these mud ducks. Not a sophisticated story line, thought Isabel, but Charlie was rapt; this was social realism to him because he knew a real pond where there were real ducks to which he threw bread with his father.

The story over, and Charlie on the verge of sleep, Isabel leaned forward and planted a kiss on his brow. She felt a wisp of his hair against her lips; it was so fine, and smelled of soap and the fresh linen of his pillow, and something else that she could only label love, or happiness, or something like that. Then she crept out of the room and made her way into her study where she had placed Jamie's note on her desk.

She dialled the number. It took a long time for the telephone to be answered but Isabel was prepared for this; people who lived in the country often seemed to take much longer to answer than those in towns. Their houses were bigger. She had never seen Munrowe

105

House but she could imagine that it had lengthy corridors and inconveniently placed telephones. She imagined a bell ringing in one of those corridors, and Duncan looking up from what he was doing and trudging off to answer it.

"Munrowe House," he announced politely.

It sounded quite appropriate to Isabel, but she could not help but wonder: at what point should one give the name of one's house on the telephone? It would sound ridiculous to answer 36 Oak Avenue, or Flat 28, or something of that sort.

"Munrowe House," Duncan repeated.

She thought: *the house speaks*, and smiled. "It's Isabel Dalhousie."

He thanked her for calling back. "I didn't want to burden your . . ."

"Husband. It was my husband."

"Yes, I didn't want to burden your husband with the details, but the other side has been in touch again."

She found the expression rather strange. "The other side" was how lawyers spoke in litigation. Or spies, she imagined. But the thieves really were the other side, she thought. Criminals of any sort put themselves on the other side from the rest of us who were not criminals, or were only occasionally criminal. Isabel had received a parking ticket recently and had reflected on the fact that she was required to pay a fine. Did that make her a criminal, even if only briefly and in a very attenuated way? Surely not. Yet it was still an offence that she had committed — the wording of the penalty notice made that quite clear.

"What did they say?" she asked.

"They want a meeting. They've given me a time."

"I see."

She could hear Duncan's breathing at the other end of the line. She could sense his anxiety.

"Have you spoken to the insurance people?"

He said that he had. "They wanted to come but I told them that the other side said that they wanted to see only me." He paused. "And I'm going to interpret that as meaning you and me. They'll just have to accept that."

She wanted to repeat what she had said before — that she did not see what she could possibly bring to such a meeting, but she had agreed to be there and she would not renege on it.

"They haven't given me much warning," Duncan went on. "They want to meet tomorrow. Do you think you could possibly make it?"

Cat would be back and Isabel would not be needed at the delicatessen. But there were those journal proofs, which even now stared reproachfully at her from their position at the top of her in-tray. She sighed, and failed, through sheer tiredness, to mask the sound.

"I know it's no notice at all," said Duncan apologetically. "It's not my idea . . ."

Isabel reassured him. "No, don't apologise. I'll be all right. Where is the meeting going to be?"

She was not prepared for his answer.

"Here. At the house."

He detected her surprise. "I know," he said. "It sounds very brazen, but I gather this is not the thieves themselves we'll be meeting, but a lawyer acting for them, or for an intermediary."

"Their lawyer!"

Duncan explained that the insurers had told him at the outset that anybody who did get in touch would probably not be the original thief, or even the people in possession of the painting. "They said that it could be lawyers," he said. "And they were right."

"Do lawyers write anonymous letters? You said the original letter was anonymous." She imagined an anonymous letter from a firm of lawyers. It would be signed *Anon* or *From a Friend*, as anonymous letters tended to be, but it would then say: *For and on behalf of Messrs . . .* and give the name of a firm.

"No, it's not anonymous," said Duncan. "It's not from the person who wrote the original letter. This one is on headed notepaper."

"Let me get this straight," Isabel said. "This is a lawyer acting for somebody who isn't the thief but who knows the thief? Is that right?"

"Yes."

"So we're two links away from the thief? There's the thief, then there's a second person, and then there's the lawyer, who's acting on behalf of the second person."

Duncan was patient. "Yes, that's more or less it. The insurers said that this is the way it often happens. The second person — the intermediary — goes to a lawyer and says, 'I hear there's a reward for the return of such a painting. Well, I know where it is and will you arrange for me to get the reward if I tell you where the painting

108

is?' That's one of the ways it can happen. There are, of course, others."

She asked about these other ways.

"If there's no reward, the intermediary can just ask for money from the owner — which means ultimately from the insurer, as the insurer may already have paid up. Or he can go straight to the insurer and ask for money for the safe return of the painting."

Isabel thought about this. "That sounds like paying ransom," she said.

Duncan agreed. "And nobody likes to do that."

"Well, we can talk further about it," said Isabel. "Shall I come up a bit before the meeting?"

"Yes. Could you make it before ten in the morning?"

She thought of her car. She had not used it for weeks and she hoped that it would start. Jamie had been pressing her to get a new one, but she was attached to her green Swedish car and was unwilling to replace it. Swedish cars were under threat and might disappear — overtaken by a torrent of anodyne cars from somewhere on the other side of the world, produced in great numbers in factories run and staffed by robots; those strange, impersonal factories in which there appeared to be no people, just machines with extended mechanical arms that moved according to some pre-programmed choreography. She did not want that. She wanted a car with idiosyncratic lines; a car that looked at home on winding Scottish roads, that could complement a backdrop of granite and heather. As long as it started. That was important too.

She paused. Was there anything wrong in wanting to have things about you that were made in places you knew, or liked? Was it a form of nationalism — a jingoistic position that was prepared to expect other people to import one's goods but not to buy theirs? For a long time — since the Industrial Revolution really — the West had expected the East to buy the things we made, but now the tables had been turned and they were making things more quickly and cheaply than we were. Was it unfair, then, to turn round and decline their goods in favour of our own? Or could one prefer one's own goods because they were made by people for whom one had, by virtue of shared citizenship, some form of responsibility? *Charity begins at home.* Was that a narrow, selfish adage or was it simply an inescapable, bedrock fact of life in human society? Does the one in need on your doorstep have a greater claim than the one in need in a distant country — if the level of need in each case is exactly the same? It was an old, old problem — the sort of thing that students of philosophy discussed over endless cups of coffee in their first year of study, little imagining that they would still be pondering the very same question twenty years later. And twenty years later, were the answers any clearer? Isabel thought they probably were not. But then one thing you did learn with the passage of time was not to ask too many questions. That was the difference, she decided, between being twenty and being forty. That, and other things, of course.

CHAPTER
EIGHT

The car started uncomplainingly, only protesting slightly as it moved the first few inches of the forty-mile journey to Munrowe House. It was the brakes, Isabel realised: two weeks without movement in the damp climate of Scotland meant that tiny filaments of rust would have built up between the brake pads and brake drum, the beginning of a slow bonding that could turn into a more permanent embrace if the car was unused for six months — or so her mechanic, the obliging Mr Cooper at the small garage on the canal, had told her. "Cars are like people," he had said. "We rust up if we don't exercise; well, so do they." He had gone on to warn her of the consequences of fluids being left in an engine that was idle for months on end; of how they would eventually eat away at the pipes in which they were trapped, making irreparable holes in cooling systems, causing radiators to fall from their mounts. All of that could happen so easily, he said, and he had then fixed her with a baleful stare, as might a doctor who knew that his advice on diet or exercise would go unheeded.

Each time the car started after a spell of disuse, Isabel vowed to treat it better in the future and to give it the weekly ten-mile run that Mr Cooper recommended; but knew that she would not, and that one day his predictions would come true. For now, though, the Swedish car sounded contented enough, and smelled just right too: that odd odour it had — a mixture of old leather, rubber and machine; a mustiness that would be dispelled by the winding down of a window and the resulting rush of morning air.

It was shortly after eight o'clock when she left the house, which meant that she would have an hour for the journey and an hour to talk to Duncan before the arrival at ten of the lawyer — the thief's lawyer, as she thought of him. That took some getting used to — the notion that those who flouted the law could use the law, even through an intermediary, to pursue their objectives. But lawyers did precisely that; that was the whole reason for their existence: they put forward a point of view even if that position was manifestly unworthy or perverse. Lawyers stood up in criminal courts everywhere, everyday, and argued on behalf of defendants who had hurt others in all those ways in which others can be hurt. She understood that well enough: everybody had this right and at least some of those accused were innocent. Yet this was something different: here a lawyer seemed to be assisting somebody to benefit from a crime rather than defending somebody who had already committed the crime. It somehow *felt* different . . .

The traffic was light. Isabel drove out by way of Colinton, past the Victorian military barracks at Redford, and then on to the road that skirted the city and the lower slopes of the Pentland Hills. The sky was empty to the south, over the soft folds of the Pentlands, but to the north there was a bank of cirrocumulus, a mackerel sky, or *Schaefchenvolken* — "sheep cloud" — as she remembered her father calling it. For some reason he had used German when talking about clouds and sea conditions; an odd habit that she had accepted as just being one of the things he did. "The weather," he had once said to her, smiling, "is German. I don't know why; it just is. Sorry."

And there were those *Schaefchenwolken*, high above Fife and stretching out over the North Sea. That meant a depression was on the way, and rain might arrive in a few hours, even if for the moment the weather was fine. Isabel sat back in her seat and relaxed her grip on the wheel, allowing her mind to wander. There was a lot to think about: the conversation that she knew she would have to have with Grace about mathematics; the anxieties that poor Eddie had revealed the day before and that would require what was bound to be an emotionally trying trip to the doctor. She reflected on this and decided that Eddie had no reason to worry: they must have talked to him about it when whatever had happened happened. And then it occurred to her that he might not have reported it. That was always possible; people were too ashamed, they suffered in silence. And if that were the case, then Eddie would have received no help, no support at all. Did Cat know? Was she aware of what he might have been going through all these years?

And then there was Cat herself to worry about. There had been no word of a boyfriend for some time now, which might be good news, or might just as likely be bad. If there were no boyfriend, then it could be a sign that Cat was taking a romantic sabbatical — a nice notion, that, thought Isabel. "I'm sorry, I can't get emotionally involved with you — I'm on sabbatical from that sort of thing." It would be like a strict diet: no chocolates, no lovers. And people might speak with the same enthusiasm about the benefits: "Do you know, I've felt so much better, so much lighter, since I gave up men. I have so much more energy, and my clothes seem to fit me again."

On the other hand, Cat's silence on this topic might mean that there was an unsuitable man in the background, concealed lest Isabel slip into disapproving-relative mode. That had happened before, when Isabel had only found out about a boyfriend of Cat's by accident. That awful tightrope walker, for example: Cat had initially not been open about him — understand-ably so. If I were going out with a diminutive tightrope walker who wore elevator shoes, then I might be reticent, too . . . Isabel stopped herself. It was wrong to write him off because he was very short — that had no bearing on merit. Gandhi had been very short, as had Beethoven. But Bruno, as the tightrope walker was called, was unlike Gandhi or Beethoven: he had no merits at all — at least as far as she could make out; he was domineering and, she suspected, violent too. She shuddered. What would have happened if Cat had married him and she, Isabel, had had to welcome him

114

into the family? She would have done her best, but surely her true feelings would have shown and Cat, sensing this, would have challenged her. "You don't like him do you, Isabel? You don't like him because he's a tightrope walker." "Listen, Cat, that's got nothing to do with it. It's him; it's what he is within himself that's the problem."

By the time Isabel drew level with Stirling, the mackerel sky had drifted away. She glanced at the shape of Stirling Castle against its backdrop of green hills, with the Wallace Monument rising spikily behind it. Isabel smiled. Scottish rugby crowds still sang about William Wallace, seven hundred years after he had defeated the English army of cruel Edward, "and sent him packing", as the song had it, "tae think again". Well, he had, she supposed, but why did we still need to sing about it? She automatically answered her own question: *because we may not have very much else, apart from our past.* It was not the answer she had expected to arrive at, and she thought it was probably wrong, and defeatist. We did have a great deal else. We had this land that was unfolding before her now as she turned off towards Doune; these fields and these soft hills and this sky and this light and these rivers that were pure and fresh, and this music that could send shivers of pleasure up the spine and make one so proud of Scotland and of belonging. We had all that.

Duncan Munrowe came out of his front door to greet her. "Your car," he said, "is lovely."

"It doesn't always start."

He smiled, and touched the roof of the car as if to confirm that it was real. "The best cars don't," he said. "I'd never want a car that had so little personality that it always started."

This brief exchange confirmed what she had felt over that lunch in Edinburgh. Her host was slightly eccentric. Out of touch with the modern world. His own man.

She looked up at the front of the house. It was fairly modest in its proportions — a comfortable country house of the sort that in the very early eighteenth century, when she suspected it was built, would have housed a minor country gentleman — one who did not actually have to farm, but had the farming done for him. And it still housed exactly such a man, she thought, as she glanced discreetly at Duncan and took in his outfit: the moleskin trousers, the waistcoat, the Harris tweed jacket. One would not drive a tractor or unload bales of hay in those clothes. One might watch other people do it instead. And that, she thought, was a good enough definition of the *rentier* class as any. And of me, too, she found herself thinking, guiltily. The land and gas company in Louisiana that enabled her to live as she did was based on the physical work of others — people whom she did not know. Her maternal great-grandfather had been responsible for that, and the trickle-down effect had seen to the rest. He would never have imagined that she, his descendant, living in twenty-first-century Scotland, and editing a philosophical review, of all things, would be reaping the benefits of the financial plotting and scheming at which family

116

history held him to have been such a master. At least it was not plantation money — or slave money, to give it the name that more accurately reflected its origins. They had not been involved in that, as far as Isabel knew, for had they been, she could never have accepted the legacy, even generations later. Or at least she hoped she would not have accepted it, although there was plenty of slave money in Britain. There had been the great plantations in the West Indies, and the descendants of the people who benefited from those — the sugar families and others — must still be there, still enjoying, although attenuated by the years that had passed, their sticky, suffering-based fortunes. She hoped she would never have accepted it, or its equivalent, although honesty required one to remind oneself that when there were bills to be paid, an offer of money was harder to reject than when there were no such bills. Other people's money, we tell ourselves, is always less deserved than our own.

At school she had known a girl who came from a family that had done very well out of coal mining two generations earlier. They had been good people, and charitably inclined, but Isabel had once said to this girl, with all the thoughtlessness of her sixteen years, "Think of all the miners who got sick and died." And the girl had stared at her mutely, and turned white, and then cried. Something had been said by the girl's father to Isabel's father — they knew one another through membership of a golf club — and Isabel's father, who never spoke harshly, had said to her, "Don't blame other people for things that happened before they were

117

born. And don't blame them for things that seemed right at the time, even if we come to see that they aren't right any more. And finally, remember that our people — that's your mother's people and my people — were probably not angels, because *nobody* was an angel in those days, except those people at the bottom of everything, who had no alternative." He had held her gaze, and she had shrivelled inside with embarrassment and guilt. It had been so easy to strike a position of moral superiority — it always is — but she had not intended to hurt her friend. Her father had paused for a moment, and judged the lesson to have been learned. "Remember that, darling, and say sorry for what you said. That's all you have to do."

Was Duncan speaking to her? She had been thinking about unearned money and her father and coal mining, and as often happened when she was thinking, time became slightly distorted and seemed to pass without her realising it.

"Sorry, what was that?"

"Nothing," he said. "I didn't say anything."

She looked again at the front of the house. "Early eighteenth century?"

He smiled. "Very close. 1698, There's a date carved into one of the lintels on the other side." He gestured towards the door. "Do come in. I'll show you round, if you like. My wife, I'm afraid, is in London. We have a small flat down there and she likes going to the opera."

"So do I," said Isabel. "If I lived in London, I'd live at the ENO and Covent Garden. Or New York. Imagine living in Manhattan and being able to walk — to walk! — to the Met."

"I'm told you're half American," he said.

They were entering the hall — a comfortable, simply furnished room from which a stone staircase ascended at the far end.

"Yes," said Isabel. "On my mother's side." And then she wondered: who told him? Did Martha know about her mother? Possibly. Or had he been asking people about her? She looked up at the ceiling, which had a surprisingly elaborate cornice: plaster thistles, twined about one another, were interspersed with roses. It was in good condition and although it was predominantly white, here and there were traces of other colours: the thistles green in their foliage and receptacles, with faded purple just to be made out on some of the flower heads. The roses, though, were untouched, and were the white of the surrounding plaster, which was significant.

"Roses," she said.

Duncan followed her glance. "Yes. Roses." He paused and said, "Long before our time. My grandfather bought this place in the nineteen twenties. The roses, we think, date back to the early seventeen hundreds. And, yes, they are —"

"Jacobite."

He nodded. "The family who lived here then were fairly strongly of that persuasion." He looked up at the cornice. "The Jacobite white rose. We believe that one of them helped Prince Charlie on his way to

Edinburgh. Fed his troops or something like that. Probably gave him money."

"And suffered the consequences when Charlie came unstuck?"

He looked down again. There was sympathy in his eyes. "They lost the place, but stayed alive. Others were less lucky."

She reflected on how human sympathy could be felt for ancient misfortune. The Jacobite uprising — that lost cause that almost succeeded — had been in 1745; over two hundred and fifty years separated us from them, and Duncan felt sympathy for those amongst the ranks of the losers who had occupied his house. One could feel sorry for any suffering, Isabel supposed, even if it was a long time ago, but surely there were limits — a point at which hearing of suffering no longer engaged our emotions. The Christians facing the lions in Rome? The victims of the Assyrians who enjoyed massacring the inhabitants of besieged towns? The distance in time was too great; suffering, to move us, must be warmer than that.

Suddenly she said, "It helps if you know the name."

He looked at her in puzzlement. "I'm sorry . . . I'm not quite with you."

She explained. "I was thinking about suffering and the passage of time. We can feel more sympathy for the victims whose names we know."

He looked at her with interest. "Yes, I suppose that's right."

"Aberdeen man lost at sea," she muttered.

"What? Aberdeen . . ."

"It's how an Aberdeen newspaper was said to have reported the sinking of the *Titanic*. I suspect it's apocryphal, but it makes the point, doesn't it?"

He laughed. "Local papers always see the world in that way. That's what they're about." He gestured for her to follow him and led the way into a room off the back of the hall. "The library," he said. "Rather a lot of unread books."

Her eyes went to the shelves that stretched up to within a few inches of the ceiling. All four walls were covered; piles of books stood here and there, teetering, vulnerable, she judged, to the slightest footfall. "But who doesn't have a lot of unread books? It's nice, though, just to know that they're there."

He picked up a book that had been placed on the edge of a nearby shelf. "I suspect you've read much more than I have. Scott. You know, I've only read one of his novels? Just one. *Rob Roy*."

"Scott was very prolix. You can't read everything. I've never got beyond the beginning of Proust. I love him, but I can't seem to get beyond about page three."

They were comfortable in each other's company, and this confession seemed to accentuate the ease of their relationship. The confession itself was not entirely true; Isabel had read more Proust than that, but other people undoubtedly found it reassuring to think that one had only read a few pages. Certainly those who claimed to have read Proust in his entirety got scant sympathy from others. And yet, she suddenly wondered, should you actually lie about how much Proust you've read? Some politicians, she reminded herself, did that — or the equivalent — when they claimed to be down-to-earth, no-nonsense types, just like the voters, when all the time they were secretly delighting in Proust . . .

"We should take a look at some of the paintings," Duncan said. "That's more to the point."

Isabel put Proust out of her mind and followed him into a large drawing room. In some respects it was typical of drawing rooms in such houses — furnished with armchairs and sofas in good but faded fabric, a sofa table with a silver tray on which stood a couple of decanters, a fireplace — Robert Adam or a follower, she thought — and this was where the similarity with a hundred such rooms in Scottish country houses ended: the paintings. One wall was completely covered, floor to ceiling, hung with large works which even as she entered and saw them side on, Isabel could more or less identify: a small Renoir of a woman, ruddy-cheeked as all of his women, in a hat; a de Hooch interior, with a Dutch girl and light slanting in from a window — almost a Vermeer, but not quite; what looked like a Bonnard — and must have been, Isabel decided.

She caught her breath. "I hadn't expected . . ."

"We're very lucky," he said.

Isabel moved into the middle of the room to get a better view of the paintings. "There's everything you'd want," she said.

"That's what people tell me," said Duncan. "And that's where the Poussin was. Over there." He directed Isabel's attention to the wall above the fireplace.

If she had expected a glaring hole, she was disappointed. An ornate candlestick, in candelabra style with crystal drops, had been placed at either end of the mantelpiece and had made up for any visual emptiness that the removal of the Poussin might have caused. She could just discern, though, a rectangular shape — a section of wallpaper that had been protected from fading by the picture that had once hung there.

"I can see where it was," she said quietly. "It must break your heart."

He looked at her in gratitude — as if she were the first person to acknowledge his loss. Others must have said something, she thought; he must have been comforted. Unless there were those around him who *wanted* him to lose his Poussin . . . A jealous neighbour, one with no paintings of his own, might have smarted at the thought of the great works nearby. Farmers could be envious of each other, she had heard; could resent another's better crops, better animals. *Thou shalt not covet thy neighbour's ox, nor ass.* The Commandment was unambiguous, and also mentioned wives and houses. *Nor his Poussin, if he hath one . . .*

Duncan was saying something about one of the other paintings. ". . . it's thought to be the first of a number of paintings that Lotto did for . . ." Yes, how interesting. Of course. And what better way of dealing with sheer envy than stealing the thing of which you feel so envious. *It's mine now, it's mine!* A secret pleasure, and not enough for some, no doubt, but there were many for whom covert satisfaction would be quite enough and sweeter, too, than any public triumph.

"There are others upstairs. Rather more, I'm afraid." He looked at his watch. "I should show you the letter."

123

Isabel dragged herself away from the paintings. "I'd like to see it."

"We can look at it in the kitchen," he said. "I have coffee brewing, if you'd like a cup."

They left the hall to follow a short corridor into a kitchen dominated by a large cooking range and a scrubbed pine table. Three cups were neatly lined up on the table, alongside a jug of milk and a bowl of sugar lumps.

Duncan handed her a piece of paper as she sat down. "This is it," he said.

"Thank you."

He remained silent as she turned her attention to the paper. It was a printed letter, headed with the name of a firm of solicitors in Perth. Isabel thought it looked slightly crudely printed — thanks to modern printers, anybody could make a letterhead these days, and put anything they chose on it. At the foot of the letter were two names — the names of the partners, both women.

It did not take long for Isabel to read. The letter was signed by a Heather Darnt, one of the partners listed. It established that the firm was acting for a client who was aware of the whereabouts of the painting. *We stress that our client is not the party responsible for the theft.* Why not say *the thief*? thought Isabel.

Our client is keen to facilitate the return of this painting, the letter went on. *He does this in the hope that he can in this way prevent damage being done to an important piece of artistic heritage. That is his only motivation.*

That, and money? Isabel asked herself.

CHAPTER
NINE

Isabel looked at her watch. She had imagined that they would have plenty of opportunity to talk before the lawyer arrived, but the time seemed to have disappeared. There was a lot she wanted to discuss with Duncan, but now there was only half an hour before they would be joined by the lawyer. There would be discussion of the recovery of the painting: proposals, no doubt, and figures. She was struck by the naked effrontery of it — an effrontery that was there, she supposed, in all deliberate crime. By his acts, the criminal effectively said to the victim: *You don't matter*. And that, Isabel thought, was the most fundamentally wrong of all attitudes, whether it lay behind acts of great cruelty or the mundane crime of bag-snatching. *You don't matter*. How could anybody look another person in the eye and say that? Quite easily, it seemed — there were enough instances of it, every day, every moment of every day, in just about every context of human life.

When Isabel had read the letter, Duncan suggested that they move through to the drawing room, taking their coffee with them. Once there, they seated themselves on a settee, Duncan at one end, Isabel at the other. Isabel noticed how comfortable the settee was, with its plumped-up feather cushions. Penury was a matter of hard chairs and mean cushions; prosperity — old money — was a matter of feathers: an absurd reductionist view of it, but at times quite strikingly true.

"They could have taken anything else," Duncan remarked. "They could have taken any of the others and I wouldn't have felt it." He pointed to the wall behind them. "That Gimignani behind us," he said, "I wouldn't have blinked an eyelid if they'd carted that off. Or the Ramsays or the Raeburns. You can replace those — not with exactly the same painting, but something that does pretty much the same job."

"They knew its value," said Isabel.

He nodded miserably. "I know," he said. "But somehow it made it personal. As if they wanted to hurt me."

"I doubt that," said Isabel. "If they wanted to hurt you, they could have done something really unpleasant. Set fire to something perhaps. There are plenty of ways of hurting somebody in such a manner that you can get away with it."

"I suppose so."

She watched him. He belonged to a sector of society that did not like to show its feelings. Displays of emotion, in their view, were vulgar — showy. And yet there was no doubt in her mind now as to how he was feeling.

"I assume that the existence of the painting was well enough known," said Isabel.

Duncan thought for a moment. "If you did your research," he said. "It's in some of the books on Poussin — not in others. Under the photograph it usually just says *Private Collection*, but there's a literature on this. If you trace the painting's progress through the salerooms, you can find out when it was bought by my grandfather. And you'll see his name down as the purchaser. Those were more trusting days."

Isabel was interested in his mention of the literature. "People have written about it?"

"Yes. There was a small literature on it before Blunt made his attribution. Prior to that, it was thought to be by a seventeenth-century Veronese painter. Then Blunt looked at it and gave it the nod. His word counted for more than anything else at the time."

"Anthony Blunt?"

Duncan smiled. "The very same. Better known as a spy than as the authority on Poussin, I suspect." He paused, and glanced quickly at his watch. He was anxious — she could see that.

"When did he see it?

"In the mid-seventies. A guest recognised it — a distant cousin of my father's who happened to be an art historian. He had been at the Courtauld during Blunt's reign there and he knew him well enough to phone him up and tell him about it. He said that he was sure enough to encourage Blunt to come up to look at it — my father was unwilling to let it leave the house. He was very attached to that painting."

"So Blunt came up?"

"Yes, he did. He was very grand, apparently. Very tall and with a certain haughty detachment. He could look right through you, my father said. I remember his saying that Blunt's look was like ice."

Isabel had read something to that effect. And yet Blunt was human; others had spoken of his generosity, his kindness, his warmth. "Perhaps he wanted to keep people at a distance. Shyness sometimes has the same effect, and then we reach the conclusion that somebody is cold, when in fact they're just reserved."

Duncan agreed. "Yes, people are very quick to dismiss others they've never met. Blunt kept his distance, I imagine, and I don't see what's wrong with that. I can't understand why people expect everyone to open up immediately to everyone they meet." He looked at her, as if assessing whether they could speak at this greater level of intimacy. "Reticence can be a virtue, don't you think?"

Isabel was not sure. "Keeping yourself to yourself? Possibly . . ."

Duncan continued. "Not wearing your heart on your sleeve. Not displaying your private life for all to see."

"As on those television programmes? Where people expose their relationship problems to the public gaze?"

He nodded. "Exactly. We live in an age where the assumption is made that you can — perhaps should — talk about every aspect of your life, even to complete strangers."

"Some would simply call that honesty," Isabel suggested. And she thought of a line from Auden where he talked about being *honest like children*. It was from

128

the Freud poem; Auden said that Freud taught us the benefit of such honesty. Children were honest — often disarmingly so — but could an adult be the same?

Duncan shifted slightly further down the settee, away from her — as if distancing himself — putting into practice the reticence to which he had just referred. "Sorry," he said. "I'm not being rude — or unduly reticent. It's just that the sun was getting in my eyes."

A beam of morning sun, warm and discrete, a shaft of yellow, was coming in through a window on the side of the room; it was this that he had shifted to avoid. *A yellow knife*, thought Isabel; *a yellow knife through the air of the room*.

"Yes, we have to be honest," he said. "But honesty is not incompatible with a certain reserve, or reticence — call it what you will. Call it privacy, perhaps. It makes sense, I should have thought, to talk about a sense of privacy. People have every right to some degree of privacy and perhaps that's what reserved people feel. They value their privacy."

Isabel had nothing against that. She, too, believed that there were areas of our lives that we were entitled to guard against the eyes of others. People may have nothing to hide in their living rooms, but they were entitled to curtains that would keep others from looking in.

"What you say is interesting," she said. "And I think I agree with you — for the most part."

He smiled. "Good. I imagined that we might agree on quite a number of subjects."

That, she realised, was a statement of friendship. "So did I," she said.

She gazed thoughtfully at the place where the Poussin had been. Sir Anthony Blunt had been gay.

She dropped the question into the conversation without really considering it; it seemed to be the next place for their discussion to go. "Do you think that people need to state their sexuality? Do they need to tell people?"

He did not answer immediately, and she glanced at him. He had folded his arms across his chest, a gesture that Isabel always interpreted as protective. Had she unthinkingly presumed too much by asking the question? Had she strayed into the very territory of the private they had been discussing?

His tone now was distant. "No," he said. "It's their own business. What does it matter to the rest of us if somebody is . . . that way? I don't see it as any business of mine, frankly."

She noted his use of the term *that* way. It was old-fashioned, but she felt that it also disclosed a certain distaste. Not to use an accepted term raised the distinct possibility that one did not like that expression, or did not share the assumptions that went with it. *Gay* was a word that gay people themselves had endorsed and was different, therefore, from the mean-spirited language that others had used in the past.

The topic was obviously not one he wanted to discuss, and so she moved away from it, not wishing to intrude further.

"So you say Blunt accepted the painting?" she asked.

Duncan seemed relieved that they had come back to art. "Yes. I was in my late teens then and not all that interested in the paintings. I knew what they were, but I had yet to develop much knowledge of art. That came a bit later."

"Were you here when Blunt came?"

"No, I was away at boarding school. I heard about it from my father."

"You heard about the icy look?"

"Yes, although I wouldn't want to make too much of that — as I've said. I was more interested in the fact that he came up after he had been revealed as a Soviet spy. I'd read about all that in the newspapers, of course. They had a field day, as you can imagine."

"Indeed they did," said Isabel. "After all, who could invent a better story for them? Soviet agents. The rarefied world of art connoisseurship. The fact that he was some sort of cousin of the Queen's. There was something for everybody in it." She had been about to add sex to the list, but stopped herself in time.

"They loved it. They bayed for his blood, but, as you know, he had been given immunity by the Government in return for spilling the beans. They couldn't prosecute him or no government immunity would be worth the paper it's written on in the future."

Isabel agreed. *Pacta sunt servanda* — agreements should be honoured. It was one of the most basic of the rules we needed to function as a society. *Keep your promises.*

"He was a broken man afterwards," said Duncan. "I read a biography a few years ago that described it rather well. He continued to live in London but was careful about going out. He went to the cinema in Notting Hill once and was recognised. The audience slow-handclapped him until he left. Can you imagine it?"

Isabel was busy doing just that. She saw the cinema and Blunt coming in — that tall, aesthetically distinguished figure who must have found it very difficult to appear anonymous. She saw him sitting down in his seat, perhaps with a friend or two — some people, at least, stuck by him — some of his old friends and students from the Courtauld who either forgave him or thought there was nothing to forgive. She saw another member of the audience a few rows forward turn his neck and stare and then whisper to those around him. And then she saw more heads craning to see whether it really was him and then, perhaps more as a joke than anything else, or an act of bravado, a man somewhere started to clap slowly. And then the psychology of the crowd took over, and people felt the bravery of the group. The slow-handclapping swelled — a crowd will always pick up a stone — and Blunt, at first confused, begins to realise it is him they want to leave. Me? A glance exchanged with his companions, and then a retreat that not even a proud and unrepentant man — if he really was like that — could find anything but humiliating. *Their bad manners*, a companion whispers, but Blunt, too shocked, is unable to speak.

"He never apologised," said Isabel. "Or did he?"

132

"He said that he regretted it," said Duncan. "That's not the same thing as saying sorry."

"But perhaps he didn't feel sorry," said Isabel. "He was recruited in the nineteen thirties, wasn't he? A lot of people believed then that communism — and the Soviet Union — were the only forces really standing up to fascism. So maybe he felt that what he did was right."

Duncan did not disagree. "Yes, it was ideological — to begin with. Then when Stalin came along it was too late. Blunt wanted out, but it was difficult."

"So he thought he had done the right thing?"

"Undoubtedly."

Isabel gave this some thought. "But he was wrong, wasn't he? And the whole point of his offence was that he betrayed his country."

Duncan's smile was challenging. "Is that always wrong?"

She thought that if he were expecting a simple answer, she was not going to give him one. "That depends on what one's country is up to, doesn't it? We don't think that people who betray their own country when it happens to be a tyranny are doing wrong, do we? Russians who betrayed the Soviet Union were welcomed here with open arms, I seem to remember."

"So no real betrayal?" he said. "Because they were acting in the real interests of their country anyway — those interests being obscured by the tyranny in power?"

"Something like that. There's a difference between loyalty to a government and loyalty to a country."

He pressed further. "Which would cover Blunt? And Philby? And Maclean and Burgess?"

"We didn't have a tyranny in power. That's the difference."

She could see that he was not prepared to make that distinction. "I'm not happy about that," he said. "Let's say that there was a coup in this country — in Britain — and we had an unelected government. We could still owe a duty of loyalty to our fellow citizens not to betray the state of which we were all members."

Isabel looked up at the ceiling. There was a crack in the plaster, stretching from one side to the other, a zigzag, a San Andreas fault. "Tribal feeling?"

She had not intended to sound flippant, and she was not ready for the look of sheer anger that passed across his face. "I'm sorry," she said. "I didn't mean to make light of it."

He clearly felt guilty for showing his anger. According to the code by which he lived, a gentleman did not do that. That's what he was thinking, she decided; that's why he was reproaching himself.

He made a reassuring gesture. "I know that." He paused. "You know, it's very stimulating for me to have this conversation. Living out here, I don't get enough of that sort of thing. My neighbours . . ." He sighed. "They don't talk about these things — their interests are mostly horses and cattle. I couldn't discuss loyalty with them — not at all: they'd find it too awkward."

"That's understandable," said Isabel. "Most people don't question themselves about such matters."

134

"Maybe they should," Duncan mused. "Maybe we're all too used to spending our time in a state of . . ." He frowned as he tried to find the right term. "In a state of deadened acceptance rather than . . ." Again he struggled. "Engagement. Yes, that's it — engagement."

"Maybe."

He brushed some imaginary lint off his trousers; we clean things that are already clean. His shoes, Isabel noticed, were highly polished — so highly so that they caught the light from the window, as a mirror might. Why, she wondered, would one spend so much time — and it must have taken a lot of time to get that shine — in buffing leather? People dressed for certain things, of course, for a special meeting or task — what had Michael Longley written about Emily Dickinson? She dressed each morning with care for the act of poetry . . .

They were interrupted by a car drawing up outside the house, the sound of crunching gravel drifting in from outside; it was like a wave breaking on the shore, thought Isabel — it had the same quality. Duncan rose to his feet quickly.

"We can finish our conversation later," he said. "We've touched on things that we need to talk about a bit more."

She said that she agreed. Loyalty, Anthony Blunt, Poussin, living with passion rather than with dull acceptance — there was a lot to be said about all of these subjects. Whole books had been written on them; whole libraries — or sections of libraries in the case of two of them. And nobody ever claimed to reach a definitive conclusion, nor felt they had put the matter to bed. "You could talk about these things for ever, don't you think . . ." she began, but was cut off. Duncan was moving towards the door, distracted to the point of ignoring her; he suddenly appeared rude, which was most unusual for him, she thought, but he did not mean it. He's afraid . . . That explained it. He was afraid of this lawyer and what she represented, or rather the person she represented, the thief, he who had come into this room and taken the beloved painting, disregarding the consequences of his action, the distress caused by the act of misappropriation. She returned to her earlier thoughts on the shocking attitude of the criminal towards his victim — it was the moral primal scene, to borrow the language of Freudians: the realisation that people could treat others as if they did not matter. And yet they did — they behaved exactly like that — all the time, and with conviction. Whole nations said it to other whole nations. *You do not matter. You do not count.*

CHAPTER
TEN

Isabel was not prepared. After Duncan had left the room to meet the lawyer, she had risen from the settee to stretch her legs. Moving to one of the windows, she was looking out of it, over a box hedge and lawn to trees beyond: sycamores, with some birch. The branches of the birch, silver and green, swayed against the sky, brushing it, but only just, as the breeze was a slight one. She thought of Poussin and his skies; that blue, that bright blue that was none the less cold, framed, as it so often was in his paintings, by clouds. He had understood clouds — appreciated them, and now . . .

"We can talk in here."

She turned round. Duncan was showing a woman into the room, and he was looking in Isabel's direction. The first thing that Isabel noticed was that Heather Darnt, a woman she judged to be in her early forties, was wearing jeans. The denim was dark, but it was definitely denim, and it was tight, disappearing into high black boots. Above the jeans was a white cotton formal shirt and an inappropriately large Orthodox cross necklace. But when Isabel's eyes went to the face, she saw a spreading port-wine birthmark across the lawyer's left temple. It was not small, but no attempt had been made to conceal it — indeed, as she approached to shake hands, Isabel saw that her choice of lipstick, liberally applied, was in an exactly matching shade of port wine.

They shook hands. Isabel found, to her surprise, that she was trembling. She tried to smile, but it was hard; she did not feel like smiling.

"Miss Darnt has driven over from Perth," said Duncan.

It was insignificant information, but it was something to say. "Oh yes," said Isabel. "Perth . . . that's where you practise?"

It was small talk, and she felt foolish making it, but she was distracted by everything: by the jeans — unexpected of a lawyer making a business call; by the birthmark to which one could not be indifferent; by the Orthodox cross; by the fact that this woman was acting for figures from the shadowy world of art theft.

Duncan gestured for them to sit down.

"Yes," said the lawyer, in answer to Isabel's question, "I practise in Perth."

Isabel wanted to say: *and do you always do this sort of thing?* Instead, she said, "I've been told about the theft." She found herself emphasising the word *theft*, as if to shame the other woman.

Her eyes drifted up to the birthmark. She found it hard to look away, but when she did, and glanced at Duncan, sitting at the other end of the sofa from Heather Darnt, she saw that he was staring at it too.

138

The lawyer had brought a small bag with her, a cross between a briefcase and a handbag, and she now leaned forward to extract a manila file from this. As she did so, she said, "These are present from birth. They result from dilated capillaries."

Isabel drew in her breath inadvertently. "I'm sorry." She felt ashamed and embarrassed. Duncan, she noticed, was blushing.

The lawyer did not look at either of them, but concentrated on the file before her. "It's all right. No harm done."

Isabel persisted. "It was very rude of me."

Heather Darnt looked up at her, and Isabel felt her eyes again move helplessly to the birthmark. Now the lawyer looked amused. "You don't have to apologise. I'm used to it."

"The painting . . ." began Duncan, in an obvious attempt to move the conversation on.

"Yes," said the lawyer. "The Poussin."

She pronounced it *Powsinn*, and Isabel noticed a flicker of amusement cross Duncan's face. And so did the lawyer.

"Clearly, I mispronounce it," she said calmly. "I very evidently don't have your advantages."

Isabel winced. "We all know what we're referring to. It doesn't matter how one pronounces it."

The lawyer looked at her with amusement. "Sometimes pronunciation matters a lot."

Isabel looked away. There were some encounters that started off on the wrong foot and never recovered. This was one of them.

"The painting," said Duncan. And then, correcting himself, "My painting."

Heather Darnt busied herself with removing a paperclip from the top of a sheet of paper, and then slipping it back into position. Isabel watched her: she's the nervous one, she thought. I have no cause to be anxious, nor does Duncan; but *she* does.

"Where is the painting?" Isabel asked suddenly. "Have you seen it?"

The lawyer did not look at her as she answered. "I believe that the painting is in Scotland. I don't know exactly where in Scotland, but it's still here." She paused. "Have I seen it? The answer to that is no."

"So how do you know that it's in the country? How do you know that it hasn't been destroyed?"

The lawyer seemed to weigh these questions carefully. When she answered, she spoke slowly and guardedly. "I have taken what has been said to me on trust."

Duncan's expression changed. He now looked angry, thought Isabel. "On trust from thieves?"

Heather Darnt continued to move the papers in her hands, folding one and tucking it behind another. "It can be seen," she said. "We can make arrangements for you to see it. The insurance company, I think, will want that to happen. It's standard practice when there's a reward."

Isabel looked enquiringly at Duncan. They had not discussed a possible reward. "Who's offering a reward?" she asked. "Are you?"

140

"No, certainly not me," he answered. "The insurance company."

Heather Darnt seemed surprised that Isabel was unaware of this. "It's very common," she said. "That's how paintings are recovered. By means of the reward."

Isabel wanted to make sure she understood. "And these people you're acting for," she asked, "they're after the reward?"

The lawyer answered the question with a nod.

Isabel asked another question. "Who are they? The thieves themselves?"

The lawyer shook her head. "No. They're people who are in touch with the people holding the painting."

Isabel considered this. "What exactly does 'in touch' mean?"

Heather Darnt gave her a look that was on the verge of pitying. "What it usually means. In touch. Speaking to one another."

"Seeing one another face to face?"

The lawyer shrugged. "Maybe. Maybe not. I can't speak for them."

But that, thought Isabel, is exactly what a lawyer does, and if I were to be as sarcastic — and as rude — as you are being, that is what I might point out to you.

She was blunt. "May I ask who's paying you?" And quickly answered her own question. "I imagine it's these people who know the thieves — the thieves' friends."

The lawyer said nothing. An eye twitched slightly, but otherwise she remained impassive.

"But the money really comes from the ransom, doesn't it?" Isabel continued. "A slice of that ransom comes to you through the intermediary." She paused. "You profit from the theft."

Duncan looked at Isabel nervously. He was about to say something when the lawyer spoke.

"Any lawyer who does anything profits from the needs of another — or from misfortune." She spoke slowly and quietly, as if explaining a simple truth to a young person who was having difficulty grasping it. "How do you think criminal lawyers are paid? Where do their fees come from?"

Duncan interrupted. "I don't think this is a particularly constructive line of discussion," he said. He gave Isabel a warning glance. "I'd like to talk about how we are to see the painting. How is that going to be arranged?"

The lawyer turned her attention from Isabel to Duncan. It was a deliberate — and very obvious — piece of body language. Isabel was now facing a half-turned-away shoulder and would have had to address that if she had had anything more to say.

"We will arrange a place," said Heather Darnt. "We'll give you a time when you'll get a telephone call telling you where to go. It'll be somewhere in Edinburgh."

We, thought Isabel.

"And you'll bring the painting to . . ."

"Not me. Them. They'll bring the painting."

Duncan glanced at Isabel, then looked back at the lawyer.

142

"Of course," went on the lawyer, "if there is any question of the authorities being present, then they — the current holders of the painting — will be aware of that and the whole discussion will be off. They have indicated that if there is any involvement of anybody other than yourself and the insurance company, then the painting will be destroyed. It will be safer for them to do that than to risk . . . other consequences."

Duncan gasped. "They'll destroy a Poussin . . . just like that? For nothing?"

The lawyer spread her hands in a gesture of resignation. "These people are not aesthetes, Mr Munrowe. They are —"

"Art thieves," interjected Isabel.

The lawyer began to turn back to face Isabel, but clearly thought better of it. "The world is as it is," she said quietly, addressing her response to Duncan but evidently intending it for Isabel. "People may think that we live in a world where moral boundaries are very clearly delineated, but lawyers know otherwise. Nothing is that straightforward, is it? For the most part, great concentrations of wealth are in the hands they are in because somebody, a few generations back, was rapacious." She paused. "I don't wish to be rude, Mr Munrowe, but I'd like to point out that the fact that there are certain very well-off families in Scotland — people living in big houses in the country and all the rest — merely reflects the successful thefts of the past. The Highland Clearances made some people very rich indeed. That was based on burning people out of their homes — yes, burning them. Or profiting from the back-breaking labour of men down the pits or in the steel works. The big Glasgow ship-owners — who built the ships? Who was blinded by the flying rivets? Who died at thirty-eight, forty? Not the shipowners."

Isabel lowered her eyes. All of this was true, but she was not sure that it justified the stealing of a Poussin that was destined for the National Gallery of Scotland.

Duncan could not conceal his embarrassment. "You clearly feel very strongly," he said. "And I understand your argument."

"Do you?" said Heather Darnt sarcastically. "Do you indeed? Well, that's good."

Duncan rose to his feet. "I think we've covered everything," he said decisively. "Although I imagine the insurance company will have something to say about its conditions. They'll want to satisfy themselves that the painting is undamaged, and so on. But that, I suppose, can be sorted out later — after I've met with these . . . these people." He paused, looking down at Heather Darnt with an expression that revealed his distaste. "Will you let me know when I'm to be in Edinburgh to expect — and act on — that telephone call?"

The lawyer stood up. She did not look at Isabel. "I'll phone you later today and tell you what day it will be. Expect a call from me at about four this afternoon — maybe a little later."

Now she turned to Isabel. "It was good to meet you," she said.

Isabel tried to raise a smile. The niceties had to be maintained, even in extremis — sometimes they were

144

all that stood between us and the collapse of civil discourse. "Yes," she said. "I enjoyed our meeting."

How easy it was to lie, she thought, not only about Proust, but about other, more important things. It was the simplest thing in the world to utter words that bore no relation to one's true feelings or intent. That was something that was well known to tyrants and their spokesmen. They could stand there and say "The people are on our side" in the face of all the evidence to the contrary. And they did say that, even as the mob reached their palace gates; even as their henchmen defected and forswore the cause; even as the bombs rained down on their last redoubts. *The people are on our side.*

Heather Darnt was trying a similar tactic. She was asserting the rightfulness of what she was doing, whereas it was, for all her attempted justification, manifestly wrong; perhaps she had succeeded in convincing herself — people did that, repeated an excuse or a rationale until they believed it. But surely she should have refused to act for a client who was obviously in league with the thieves; surely she, or any other reputable lawyer, should have refused to have anything to do with the negotiation of a ransom. And as Isabel thought this, it occurred to her that the insurance company should do the same and refuse to pay ransom. If they paid, then the principle would be established that you could demand a ransom with impunity — and expect to be paid it. Their solution was to call it a reward, but what, Isabel wondered, was the distinction?

Heather Darnt was shown out to her car and drove off down the drive. When Duncan came back in, he looked slightly apologetic. "What an unpleasant woman," he began, and then checked himself. "I'm sorry, I shouldn't really —"

Isabel cut him short. "Shouldn't? Why not? You're absolutely right: she *is* unpleasant. And . . ."

He looked at her expectantly.

"And, frankly, I don't see the distinction between her and the thieves. She's obviously in pretty deeply with them. Of course, there's all those references to clients and intermediaries and so on, but do you know what I think?"

He was watching her closely. "Tell me."

She had not formulated this until a few moments ago, but now it seemed to her to be so obvious: "She's one of them — one of the thieves."

As she spoke, Isabel found herself thinking of the power of words. A single word, a phrase, a sentence or two could have such extraordinary power; could end a world, break a heart, or, as in this case, consign another to moral purdah.

"I think you may be right," he said. "I did not like her."

Isabel shrugged. "But that, I suppose, is neither here nor there. If we want the painting back, then I suppose we do what we have to do: pay the ransom."

"Well, it's the insurance company that will be paying. But, yes, that's what it amounts to." He paused, as if engaged in the process of weighing choices. "What

146

should our priority be? Money, or a beautiful painting?"

Isabel thought: *this is why I'm here; this is why he wants to involve me*. It was all very well being the editor of a journal of applied ethics; you could deliberate to your heart's content on the rightness or wrongness of actions, but none of it was real; not until somebody actually came up to you, as Duncan now was doing, and said: "Tell me what to do."

"It amounts to paying ransom," she said quietly, almost to herself. "No matter how you dress it up."

"I know," he said. "And surely that's wrong."

She made a gesture of hopelessness. "Put yourself in the position of a person who has to pay ransom to get a relative back from a kidnapper. Think of those people — and there are quite a few of them right now — who have relatives being held by pirates in Somalia." It sounded ridiculous to be talking about pirates in the twenty-first century, but that was exactly what they were. There were still pirates in the world, just as there were still slaves. We imagined that our world had gone beyond all that, but it had not.

"Oh, I'd pay," said Duncan. "Who wouldn't?"

"Governments," answered Isabel. "Governments won't negotiate with terrorists, will they?"

Duncan said that he understood why they took that position. "If they did," he said, "then it would just get worse and worse."

Isabel nodded. "And art thieves? If we negotiate with them? If we pay the ransom they demand, then they'll simply be encouraged."

He was silent for a while. "Maybe I shouldn't," he said.

She had not intended him to reach this conclusion quite so quickly. And she was not entirely sure that this was the position at which she would herself arrive.

"I wouldn't necessarily reach that conclusion," she said.

He looked at her with interest. "But you implied . . ."

"I was voicing a general doubt," she said. "Individual situations may differ. Everything depends . . ." She looked at her hands. *I am not being helpful*, she said to herself. *He wants guidance, and I am giving him doubt.*

"You should save the Poussin," she said decisively. "If that's what you want, then there's no reason why you shouldn't participate in the business of arranging the ransom. Artistic value trumps the general social interest in this case, I think."

He seemed relieved. "I hoped that you'd say that."

She smiled at him. "I can see what that painting means to you. I understand."

"I'm glad you do. Sometimes I wonder if it's just me — whether I've become excessively attached to it, but then, when I think it through, I come to the conclusion that great art really is as important as we say it is. It's nothing to do with material value — money just complicates the matter. It's what art stands for."

She inclined her head. "Of course."

The decision made, they were both relieved to be able to allow their conversation to become more general, more relaxed. Duncan wanted to talk about Poussin, and Isabel sensed that this was helpful for him.

"There's something that particularly interests me about Poussin," he said. "He was a landscape painter as much as he was a figurative painter, you know."

She did know that. "Yes. I saw that exhibition *Poussin and Nature* a few years back. He had a lot to say about the natural world."

"Exactly," said Duncan. "He may paint something dramatic, something fairly intense in human terms, and yet there it is, shown in a natural setting."

"And a calm one at that," said Isabel.

"Yes. Classical landscapes always have that air of peacefulness about them. Do you know the Poussin in the National Gallery in London? The one of the man killed by a snake?"

She remembered being in a roomful of Poussins in the National Gallery, but it had been a long time ago.

"It's a very powerful painting," Duncan continued. "That poor man lying on the ground with the snake coiled around him. And the man who has discovered him running up the path to report the matter — too late."

Suddenly she recalled it. "There's a boat, isn't there? Men fishing somewhere nearby."

"Yes. Poussin makes the point, doesn't he? Normal life goes on in spite of tragedies occurring all around it."

She smiled in recognition. Auden had said exactly that. "About suffering, they were never wrong, / The Old Masters: how well they understood / Its human position . . ."

"That's vaguely familiar," he said.

149

"It's Auden's poem about Brueghel's *Fall of Icarus*," she said. "You may know the painting — there's a ploughman tilling a field in the foreground and a ship sailing out of the bay below. Icarus can be seen falling into the water — his legs disappearing — but everybody gets on with their business in spite of the tragedy. The ship has somewhere to sail, the man has his field to plough. If they notice, they don't pay much attention."

Duncan was silent for a moment. "I suppose that's true. I suppose that even as we sit here talking somebody, somewhere in the world, is facing imminent execution — about to be shot or given a lethal injection — something brutal, some piece of licensed awfulness like that. And we sit here and talk about art and its meaning and think of a dinner that awaits us this evening, or a conversation with friends, or anything, really."

Isabel looked at him, and he held her gaze for a few moments before looking down. It was as if he had unwittingly shown to her something of himself that he would rather not have revealed — for all his earlier talk of an appropriate reticence. She felt an urge to reach out and touch him, to reassure him that he could be honest with her, that there was no need for him to shelter behind the identity that he otherwise presented to the world — that of the countryman, the gentleman farmer. But she did not: there were limits to the intimacy that had suddenly grown up between them and she knew that if she infringed these limits, he might retreat again. So she was silent, and looked at her watch. He nodded. "I understand," he said. "You must get back to Edinburgh."

"Will you let me know when they get in touch?" she said.

"I will." He hesitated before continuing. "I take it that you're happy to come and see the painting?"

"I want to do that," she said.

"I'm glad. I'll feel less exposed with you there."

He saw her to her car.

"I'll say it again, that really is a very good car. I love Swedish cars," he said. "In fact, I love everything Swedish."

She knew what he meant. There were many in Scotland who felt that their country had somehow been misplaced — that it should have been closer to Scandinavia.

"Perhaps one day," she said.

He laughed. "Scotland will become more Swedish?"

She made a gesture of mock despair. That would never happen. We would have to change everything, she mused — ourselves, the way we thought, our attitudes, and our clothes.

Jamie cooked dinner that evening using a recipe for a vegetable paella that he had read in the *Scotsman* weekend magazine, cut out and then stuffed into a pocket of his jacket. He was an enthusiastic cook but a sporadic one, and would often only announce to Isabel in the late afternoon that he would cook that evening — if she wanted him to. By then she would have made her plans for their meal, but would readily shelve them in order to have the evening off. There would be Charlie's supper to prepare, but that was simplicity itself: his tastes ran to macaroni cheese, spaghetti, and a curious mixture of cauliflower and olives that he had named *cauliolives* and always devoured with gusto. Oddly for a child, he seemed to have little interest in sweet things, apart from ice cream: macaroons, irresistible to other children, would be left untouched, and marzipan, if ever he encountered it, spat out in disgust.

While Jamie cooked, Isabel read Charlie his bedtime story. He had discovered A. A. Milne — or that writer had been discovered for him — and loved to hear the poems in *Now We Are Six*, especially the lines about King John, who was not a good man — who was not spoken to for days and days and days, but was miraculously given the present he so yearned for. "Good boys get presents," said Charlie, looking up at his mother with a mixture of challenge and hope.

"They do, Charlie," said Isabel. "And give them too."

He had nodded wisely; he understood, she suspected, about reciprocity — or at least had some glimpse of what it meant, but probably only in the crudest, most elementary terms. Plenty of people gave gifts to get gifts back, and Charlie at present was among them. That would change, of course — unless he remained one of those who never grew into altruism. And they existed. Her mother's cousin, Mimi McKnight in Dallas, had told her once about one of the Mobile aunts, an ancient Southern lady, all powder and eau de cologne, who had been famous for being incapable of giving anybody anything at all, not even on

152

important birthdays, when a homemade card was all that she would rise to. On her death, a sealed will was discovered in a drawer, stating that there was nothing to leave and therefore there would be no legacies. It was not true; she was comfortably off, but could not bring herself to acknowledge that fact, nor the claims that any of her family might have on her.

"What lies behind an attitude like that?" Isabel had asked.

Mimi had thought for a moment and then said, "Ask Dr Freud."

"Fear?" suggested Isabel. "Fear of having nothing left?"

"Possibly," said Mimi. "Or a stony heart."

Now, with the last of the Milne recited — for a second time — she switched out Charlie's light and kissed him goodnight. He was drowsy and already half asleep, but he puckered his lips slightly as she planted the kiss on his forehead. She could have wept; she could have wept for the love of him, as any mother might while watching over her child. There was no human emotion stronger than this, she felt; biology dictated it and the heart willingly became party to the bond. That was what Renaissance artists meant when they painted those beautiful, entrancing madonnas: their work was commissioned by religious piety, but the spirit that moved the artist was nothing to do with that but everything to do with maternal tenderness and love, with what she felt now . . .

Jamie had laid the table in the kitchen and poured Isabel a glass of New Zealand white wine; the chilled

153

glass was covered in a mist of condensation, small rivulets beginning to move down towards the stem. She took the glass in her hand and held it up to the evening light from the window. Outside, viewed through the wine, Scotland was blurred and made golden-yellow. Up above, there were clouds, and beyond them was a slice of blue that made her think again of Poussin and of his skies; it was the same shade of blue that the artist had habitually used in his paintings, a blue that spoke of the cold that was there in any real sky, at that altitude.

Jamie was busying himself with the chopping of parsley.

"I'm using curly parsley rather than the flat-leaf sort," he said. "Do you think it matters?"

"That's fine," said Isabel. "Flat-leaf parsley has a stronger flavour. Curly will probably go more easily with the other things you're using."

Jamie finished chopping the parsley and moved on to garlic. "Double quantities," he said, smiling at Isabel. "To protect us against any vampires that may be lurking around Edinburgh." He held up a half-chopped bulb of garlic and then crossed the room towards her, holding it out in front of him for her to sniff.

She took the hand in which he held the garlic. She steadied it and then sniffed at the half-sliced bulb. It bled — the garlic bled — a clear liquid.

"Lovely," she said. "Sinful."

He stood before her. She looked into his eyes.

"I love it," he said. "It goes with everything, doesn't it?"

154

"Except kisses," she said.

He lowered his hand. "No? So one should kiss people *before* eating garlic?"

"If that's what one wants to do," she said. And I do, she thought. I want to kiss you. I want to kiss you.

He leaned forward and kissed her on the lips. Then again. And once more.

"I have to cook," he said, drawing back.

"Yes, indeed." She took a sip of her wine. "I had an uncomfortable meeting today," she said.

"Oh? Tell me about it."

She answered his invitation with a question. "Do you know that feeling when you meet somebody who's ill-disposed to you — right from the beginning, before you've even had the chance to offend them?"

Jamie had encountered that. "Yes, I know it. There's a conductor who hates me. I could tell straight away. The moment he lifted his baton at the first rehearsal, he hated me."

"Why?"

He shrugged. "Maybe he doesn't like bassoons," he said.

Isabel thought: no, it was not that. It would have been something quite different; something to do with the way that Jamie looked, something to do with who he was. Envy? Jamie was young and older people can hate the young just because they are young and because they are going to have the world for a long time yet.

Jamie tipped a pile of chopped vegetables into a large cast-iron frying pan and moved it on to the plate of the

155

cooker. The oil in the pan sizzled. "Who was this person anyway?" he asked.

"She's a lawyer from Perth," said Isabel. "A woman called Heather Darnt."

"Never heard of her," said Jamie. "But I don't like her either."

Isabel smiled. "Thanks for the solidarity. She's horrible." She realised that to describe somebody as horrible sounded very childish. She had a friend — someone she had known at school — who used expressions like that, who spoke the same way as she did when they were both fifteen. People could be *horrible*, or *horrid*, or, by contrast, *fab*, or *cool*. These adjectives were interspersed with Scots terms, words that were vividly expressive, as Scots can so often be. The overall effect was one of decisive partisanship.

"Or maybe not exactly horrible," she continued. "Just rude. Cold. Rather sinister."

Jamie nodded. "The sort of person you can picture commanding a firing squad?" There are more people like that than you imagine."

"I know."

"And so what did she say?"

Isabel told him about their conversation and the promise that the painting would be available for inspection. He listened intently, stirring the vegetables in the frying pan as Isabel spoke. When she had finished, he turned and fixed her with a stare.

"You're not going to go?" he asked. "You aren't going to go and meet these people, are you?"

"Duncan wants me to," Isabel replied. "And I've agreed."

For a moment Jamie said nothing, and turned back to his cooking. "I know I can never persuade you not to do things," he said over his shoulder. "So I won't try. But just be careful with this one."

"It'll be in full public view, I imagine," said Isabel. "They won't want to give us an actual address to go to."

"Why not?"

"Because we could pass that on to the authorities, and they could turn up and recover the painting."

"So how will you do it?

She did not know the answer to that. "I imagine that it will be in a bar or a café, or somewhere like that. We'll be told to meet them somewhere at the last moment."

Jamie looked doubtful. "Why somewhere public? But won't it look very odd if you start examining a painting in the middle of a bar?"

"I imagine they won't want somewhere private because they'll want to be able to melt away into a crowd, or into the traffic perhaps. So it's likely to be somewhere public, but where . . ." She looked at him helplessly. "I don't know exactly. In fact, I don't know at all. I'm not very good at these things."

He smiled at her. "I could say, then, that perhaps you shouldn't take them on. But I won't say that. I really won't."

"What will you say instead?"

He hesitated for a moment. "That I'm really happy that you're the way you are. That I'm glad that you're not somebody who can ignore the troubles of others. That you're the most perfect woman I've ever met in my life and that I love you more than the . . . more than the Atlantic Ocean."

She put down her glass. "What you've said is more than enough for any woman," she said. "To be loved more than the Atlantic Ocean . . ."

"It's true," said Jamie. "I know it sounds odd . . ."

The Atlantic stood for so much — for breadth and openness and empty, watery wastes — and was not the most obvious metaphor for love; but she knew why he should have thought of the sea in trying to say what he wanted to say: Burns had talked of the duration of his love, which would last, he said, *Till a' the seas gang dry*, and so she said, "I understand. It doesn't sound odd at all — not to me."

CHAPTER
ELEVEN

It was Alex Munrowe, Duncan's daughter, who contacted Isabel with the suggestion that they meet, rather than the other way round. Isabel had thought of getting in touch with her: having met Patrick, the son, her curiosity about the family had been aroused. Duncan had said very little about his daughter, other than to mention that she lived in Nelson Street and to let drop the information that he saw her regularly when he came down to Edinburgh. There was nothing unusual about that, even if it suggested that Duncan might have a preference for the company of his daughter. He would not be the only father to feel that way; many fathers had closer relations with their daughters than with their sons. The evolutionary biologists might have something to say about that, thought Isabel, and if they did not, then the Freudians certainly would. But in this case it was no real concern of hers; she had not been asked to involve herself in the internal dynamics of the Munrowe family, and it was only curiosity that drove her to speculate about Alex.

The telephone call came on the day following Isabel's trip to Munrowe House and her uncomfortable meeting with Heather Darnt. After introducing herself,

159

Alex apologised for telephoning Isabel at home. *But there's nowhere else to telephone me*, she thought.

"My father gave me your number," Alex continued. "He said you wouldn't mind my getting in touch."

Isabel assured her that she did not mind in the least. "In fact, I was hoping to meet you at some point. Your father told me all about you." She said that without thinking; Duncan had mentioned her, but had hardly said very much at all.

There was a silence at the other end of the line and Isabel wondered whether she had inadvertently given offence. But she had not. Alex confessed that she had been finishing off a piece of toast and had been licking butter off her fingers. "I know that sounds rude," she said. "But I have to go out shortly and there are two calls I have to make."

"It's not rude at all," said Isabel. "There may be some occasions when you certainly shouldn't phone somebody, but while eating toast is not one of them."

There was a further silence before Alex cleared her throat; a crumb had gone down the wrong way, Isabel decided.

"My father is very grateful to you. So am I."

Isabel felt embarrassed. "I've done nothing."

"You're being a support for him," said Alex. "Martha Drummond said you would be, and she was right."

"Well," said Isabel, "I'm sorry that he's had this happen to him."

"It's awful," agreed Alex. "Of all the pictures they could have taken, to take that one . . . It's just so cruel."

160

"Yes," said Isabel. "It is." She waited for Alex to reveal why she had called.

"Could we meet?" asked Alex. "So that I can put a face to the name."

Isabel agreed, and a time was agreed for later that day; she was going over to that side of town, and she could drop in at about four in the afternoon, if that suited Alex.

It did. "Sponge cake? Sandwiches? Coffee? Tea?"

"Sandwiches, if you're making them," said Isabel.

"Cucumber?"

Isabel laughed. "You guessed."

"Nobody dislikes cucumber sandwiches. Or nobody I've met."

Isabel suddenly wondered: are there cultures where the cucumber, for some reason, was spurned? People had such strange ideas about food: apples had, in some places, once been regarded as sinful — Eve's fault — and potatoes had been seen as encouraging laziness. Cucumbers, surely, had escaped censure, and, rather, had attracted admiration, even though it was not always complimentary to be described as being "as cool as a cucumber". The French might describe a lover as a *little cabbage*, but not, she thought, as a *little cucumber*. Certainly not. She smiled.

"Are you still there?"

"Yes," said Isabel. "Sorry. I was thinking." She did not say that she was thinking about cucumbers.

Alex gave her address, and they rang off. Grace had just arrived and Isabel could hear her in the kitchen emptying the bin in a way that told her that something had incurred her housekeeper's displeasure. When things were knocked together or banged, it was a clear sign that some incident, probably something in the newspaper, had served to irritate Grace.

Isabel left her study and entered the kitchen. Grace had just tipped the contents of the bin underneath the sink into a large black plastic sack. She looked up as Isabel entered.

"Have you seen the *Scotsman* today?" Grace asked.

I was right, thought Isabel.

"There's an article about a wee boy in Fife who's a real expert in physics. He's just nine and he's outstripping the seventeen-year-olds. They won't let him go to physics classes at the secondary school."

Isabel was not prepared for this. She had been putting off a discussion about Charlie and mathematics, but this report seemed to be leading in that direction.

"Who's preventing him going there?" she asked.

"The education committee." Grace spat the words out with maximum distaste. "Those councillors. What have they ever done? That's what I ask? They've all made a career of being politicians and they've never done anything in their lives. And then when a boy of real talent comes along, they say things like, 'Our resources must be fairly shared — we can't encourage one child at the expense of another.' Can you believe it? That's what they said."

Isabel moved towards the kettle. A cup of coffee could often calm Grace down, and she decided that this was an occasion for just such a tactic.

162

But Grace continued. "It's the same with Charlie, isn't it?"

Isabel was noncommittal. "I'm not sure —"

Grace cut her short. "Yes, it is." She looked reproachfully at Isabel. "He's doing very well, you know."

Isabel frowned. "We're very grateful to you, Grace. We're very grateful to you for everything you do. But in this particular instance, I think that there may be a case for speaking to an expert . . ." And here she looked at Grace before going on, "I freely admit I'm out of my depth here. I don't know how to teach mathematics — how to get the right approach. We could ask an expert — maybe somebody at one of the schools, at Watson's perhaps." She paused. "Don't you think that's a good idea?"

"We already have an expert," said Grace. "The book I've been using to help Charlie is written by a world expert. She's in California."

"The fact that somebody is in California doesn't necessarily mean that she's . . ." Isabel searched for the right word. "Reliable. In fact, California is the sort of place where all sorts of fads take hold. It's famous for that. It's a big place for fads."

Grace came back immediately. "Not this book. The book I've been using is definitely not faddish. It's been proved."

Isabel sighed. "I think we need to talk about it," she said mildly. "If children learn mathematics the wrong way, they can develop bad habits. Then you can't get them to do it the right way ever again."

Grace narrowed her eyes. "I'm not making any mistakes," she said. She turned away. "And if you don't trust me with Charlie, then quite honestly I don't really see how I can continue to work here. I'm sorry, but what other conclusion can I reach?"

Isabel gasped. "Oh, Grace, I didn't mean to upset you. I really didn't. Of course I trust you with Charlie. We both do."

"Then why did you say that?"

Isabel spoke softly. "I didn't say what you think I said. All that I said was that mathematics is the sort of thing that perhaps an expert . . ."

"An expert? That is, anybody but me. That's what that means, doesn't it?"

Isabel shook her head. "No, not at all. I'm not an expert either. Nor is Jamie."

"And you haven't even read the book," said Grace. "You've accused me of making all sorts of mistakes and you haven't even read the book." She turned away and began to undo the strings of her apron, which dropped to the floor as she loosened it. She did not bend down to pick it up, but patted her hair as if to compose herself for her next move. "I'm sorry that it's ending in this way," she said.

"Look," said Isabel. "I'm really sorry if I've offended you. I didn't mean to. You must know that, Grace. It's just that neither Jamie nor I want to push Charlie too much. We want him to have time to be a little boy. There'll be time for mathematics later on."

Grace was not listening. "I was merely doing what needed to be done," she said. "No more than that."

164

"Well, then, let's talk about it. Let's sit down and work it out."

Grace moved away. "No. It's too late for that. I'm going now," she said.

"Grace —"

The kitchen door slammed. Isabel sat down and put her head in her hands. Grace had resigned twice before, and on both occasions had been persuaded to return. In neither of the previous cases did Isabel feel it had been her fault — and she was right: she was an infinitely considerate employer. She imagined that once again Grace would be prevailed upon to change her mind, but it would involve prolonged explanations and assurances. And neither of the previous resignations had been so firm and so reproachful, which did not bode well for a rapid resolution. Jamie would have to be involved, Isabel decided. Grace normally ate out of his hand and he had been responsible for bringing the last resignation to an end. He would be an ambassador, sent on a mission of reconciliation and peace-keeping, the bearer of a diplomatic note and a peace-offering.

That was what Grace would expect, and it was what she would get, although for a brief moment Isabel allowed herself to speculate on what would happen if she were simply to accept Grace's resignation. Would Grace then apologise and ask for her job back, or would she stand on her dignity? It was inconceivable that she should go. She had been there for ever, it seemed, and the house would not be the same without her. Isabel owned the house, it was true, but that did not make her feel that she, alone, had the right to be

165

there. The right to be in a place came in different forms: the legal title was one such form, but only one, and could sometimes be considerably weaker than moral rights of another form altogether. Those with legal title often misunderstood that; they thought that a piece of paper — a legal device — spoke more eloquently than any human link, any claim of long presence or association. But they were wrong, even if they had the crude mechanisms of enforcement on their side.

No, Jamie would be sent on his peace mission and, with any luck, Grace would soon be back at work as normal. Charlie might ask where she was but Isabel was prepared for that. She had resolved never to lie to her young son, and she would not start now. So if he asked where she was, Isabel thought that she might simply say that Grace was reviewing her position. She had no idea how that would sound to a three-year-old, perhaps rather as if Grace had gone off to watch a film. Then she realised that this was meretricious. She would say to Charlie that Grace had gone home because she was cross. She hoped that she would not be cross the next morning, but she could not be sure. That would be both truthful and comprehensible, and Charlie, she was sure, would accept it. Children understood that adults could become angry — curiously so, and for no apparent reason, just as the weather could change and a smiling day might suddenly frown.

The contretemps with Grace left her feeling slightly raw, despite Jamie's later assurances that she could likely be persuaded to withdraw her resignation. "And

166

she won't make a fuss about the mathematics," he said. "You'll see — she'll have picked up your concerns about that and won't make a fuss."

Isabel hoped that he was right, but as she made her way down to her meeting with Alex Munrowe, she decided that if Grace was determined to persevere with her mathematics teaching, then they would simply have to have another talk. She did not relish the prospect of specifically overruling Grace on the matter, but she had her duty as a mother to consider. And it was not unreasonable, she thought, to insist on something when it came to the education of her son; surely Grace would understand that and would see it from Isabel's point of view. That was what she hoped, but there remained a nagging doubt. Grace could be stubborn and it was just possible that this question of mathematics was going to be a battlefield that neither of them wanted but neither felt she could avoid.

Alex's flat in Nelson Street was on the second floor of a four-storey tenement, built in the early years of the nineteenth century when the Edinburgh New Town spread confidently down the hill towards the Firth of Forth. Nelson Street was a short street by the standards of its neighbours, a brief, sloping link between two sets of elegant private gardens. Unlike most New Town streets, which ran in a straight line or, at most, followed a leisurely curve, Nelson Street had a zigzag where it was interrupted at a right angle by another street; Alex lived in the *zag*, just before it opened out on to the broad square of Drummond Place. Her flat was served

167

by a common stair that ascended from behind a classical panelled door. This staircase, chilly in spite of its being summer, still retained its original heavy mahogany handrail and ornate ironwork banisters: craftsmanship that had been built to last, and had done just that. The stone stairs themselves were worn by centuries of feet, creating in the middle of each step a small curved indentation — not enough to make the stairs hazardous but deep enough to remind the visitor that he or she was not the first to walk that way.

The door off the landing had two names on it, each separately engraved on a small brass plate. Isabel noticed that the screws holding these plates were countersunk so as not to protrude even by the smallest fraction of an inch above the surface; it was an odd detail for her to notice, and not, she decided, one loaded with meaning — except that, perhaps, it was because we were so used to cheapness in our surroundings, to sloppiness, that craftsmanlike standards stood out and reminded us of what had once been taken for granted.

She tugged at another brass fitting — a lever with a small model of a human fist at the end — and heard the tinkling of a bell somewhere inside the flat. After a few seconds there came the sound of footsteps and then the turning of the latch. The door opened to a woman who looked about thirty, attractive in spite of an unusually high forehead — or because of it — and possessed of the same reserved look that she had noticed in Duncan Munrowe.

168

They shook hands and Isabel followed Alex into a drawing room at the end of a short corridor.

"We can sit in here," said Alex. "Facing west, we get a bit of afternoon light. In the morning, the kitchen gets it — it's on the other side."

"My orientation too," said Isabel.

"Martha Drummond says you live near her. It's rather nice up there, isn't it?"

Isabel nodded. "Do you know Martha well?"

Alex hesitated. "I do. Yes, quite well."

There was something in her tone that suggested that Martha might have been a heart-sink friend for Alex, much as she was for Isabel.

"There's a Stirlingshire connection," Alex went on. "Martha's father was a close friend of my grandfather's. The two families go back a long time — generations before that they knew one another too. You know how Scotland is."

Isabel smiled. Of course she knew how Scotland was.

Alex gestured to a sofa. "Please . . ."

Isabel sat down and looked about her. The room was a typical drawing room of the sort that was to be found in virtually all the flats in that part of Edinburgh. Being Georgian, the proportions were almost perfect — if not actually perfect — with the length of each wall being more or less 1.6180339887 times the height of the ceiling: the golden section. Isabel had always thought that it was a tragedy that the Victorians had abandoned this ratio and favoured high ceilings. The result had been rooms that were rather like cubes; rooms that we could not feel fully comfortable in because we were

169

intuitively predisposed to relate warmly to *phi* (1.61 etc.). She imagined, for a moment, going into a room one liked and exclaiming, "*Phi!*" People might say, "Don't you mean *phew?*" and one would reply, "No, *phi!*" She smiled at the thought.

Alex was staring at her. "What's the joke?"

Isabel shook her head. "Just a ridiculous notion about the golden section." She could not retell it, but said instead, "I do love these Georgian rooms."

Alex looked about her, as if noticing the decor for the first time.

"The curtains came from my father's house," she said. "He sent us off to university with curtains. I thought it rather odd at the time. Most of the other students arrived with stereos and laptops and so on. My brother and I arrived with curtains."

Isabel laughed. "Well, I went off for my first year at Cambridge with one of those machines that makes tea for you while you're still lying in bed. I remember that people laughed at me, but they saw the point in due course and one or two of them actually asked me where I had got it."

Her eyes wandered from the curtains to the mantelpiece, which was of old pine, with an elaborate moulded frieze along its length. This frieze was dominated by the figure of a woman leaning on an upright anchor; around her feet, and off to each side, were shells stacked in profusion, with crabs and twists of rope. A pair of delicately painted Chinese ginger jars, *famille rose*, stood on the mantelshelf, and on the wall above was a large painting in an elaborate gilded frame.

170

Isabel drew in her breath. "That's not another Poussin, is it?"

"Yes," said Alex, and then, almost immediately, and smiling in response to Isabel's look of astonishment, she qualified her answer. "And no. Gaspard Poussin, or Gaspard Dughet to give him his original name. He was Poussin's brother-in-law — and his pupil. He changed his name to Poussin after he married Poussin's sister."

Isabel got up from the sofa and examined the painting more closely.

Alex joined her. Isabel noticed that she had been eating garlic.

"It's a beautiful painting," Isabel said.

"I'm glad you like it," said Alex. "He painted just like his master when it came to the overall composition. You see that hill village there? Very typical of Poussin. And that lake in the foreground — again, you see a lot of that in Poussin — Nicolas Poussin, that is. And those trees: those aren't bad at all — they could be the real thing, I suppose. Except this painting is not immensely valuable. It was in the house, upstairs; my father gave it to me as a housewarming present when I bought this place."

Isabel leaned forward to peer more closely at a figure that the artist had placed under a tree. "A shepherd?"

"Probably. Dughet liked shepherds. But I suppose if you looked at any stretch of countryside in the seventeenth century it would have been well peopled by shepherds. Not today, of course."

"And beside the lake? Over there?"

"That's somebody sleeping. I don't think there's anything untoward going on. If that were Nicolas, then he might have had that figure constricted by a snake. He was fascinated by snakes. You know that —"

"Painting in the National Gallery in London? *Man Killed by a Snake.* Yes. Your father talked to me about it."

"Did he? Well, he taught me all about it when I was ten. He took me all the way to London to visit the National Gallery and stand in front of the Poussins. And the Rembrandts. I remember wanting to go outside and feed the pigeons in Trafalgar Square, but I couldn't do that for hours because we had a whole list of paintings to see."

Isabel laughed. "It could have put you off for life."

"Yes, but it didn't. I think it had the opposite effect, actually. It made me love art. I just love it."

Duncan had not told Isabel what his daughter did, and Isabel had not found out. Alex was seeing her on a weekday at four in the afternoon — this suggested that she did not have to observe regular office hours. She said that she had bought the flat, and so she must have had some money, presumably money from somewhere in the family. But what about the other person who lived here? She recalled the other name on the brass plate: a husband? A live-in boyfriend? Did she support him, or did he support her? She glanced at Alex's left hand; there was a small diamond ring on the fourth finger that caught the light, now, as Isabel looked — a tiny spark of white fire.

Alex had noticed the direction of Isabel's gaze and interpreted it accurately, but if she resented the curiosity, she did not show it. "I live with my fiancé," she said. "He's called Iain. Iain Douglas. He's a doctor — an orthopaedic surgeon."

Isabel looked away, feeling embarrassed at having been caught in the act of curiosity. But of course people thought about these things — we summed up others all the time; it was getting caught at it that was difficult. She remembered once having been in a queue for tickets at the Festival Theatre and she had seen a fashionably dressed woman standing nearby looking at her cardigan with what seemed to be unambiguous pity. Their eyes had met, and the other woman had looked away guiltily, pretending to interest herself in a poster for a forthcoming performance of *Macbeth* in Turkish. Isabel had wanted to go up to her and say, "Yes, I know, it's a bit shabby, but honestly, don't worry, I've got better clothes at home." She felt that they might then have coffee together, drawn to one another by this sudden moment of fellow feeling and sympathy. And she might have said to the woman that she should not worry about how she — or others — dressed, and that there was liberation on offer for those who were trapped by fashion. But that would be going too far, and could be hurtful, even if it were true. While the full truth should sometimes be told, it should not *always* be told.

She returned to the sofa while Alex, saying that she was going to fetch the tea, left the room. On her own, Isabel could not help but look at the spines of the books on the bookshelf that took up half a wall. The lower shelves were filled with books too large to be housed further up: most of them, she noticed, on art. There was a large book on Vermeer and a three-volume set on Vuillard. *Netherlandish Art 1660 to 1700. From van Eyck to Dürer.* Her gaze moved upwards. *The Making of Classical Edinburgh. The Island of Jura. Cabinetmaking for Pleasure and Profit . . .*

Alex had re-entered the room, carrying a tray on which there was a teapot, a small jug and two cups.

"Most of those are mine," she said. "Iain has very little time for reading these days."

Isabel blushed. It was the second exposure of her curiosity. But again she thought: one's *entitled* to look at the books on a person's shelves — that's what bookshelves are for: display.

"Did you study art?" she asked, as Alex put the tray down on a table behind the sofa.

"Yes. History of Art at St Andrews."

"And do anything with it?"

Alex gave her a look that struck Isabel as being slightly defensive. "What can you do with a degree like that? Become a curator, I suppose, if you're lucky enough to get one of the tiny handful of jobs going. Work in a commercial gallery carrying paintings up and down stairs?"

Isabel knew what she meant. It was the same with a degree in philosophy. A tiny number of those who studied philosophy managed to earn their living teaching or writing about the subject, or even thinking about it; the rest had to turn to something else. She had

174

been extremely lucky in that respect, and, even then, that she was still running the *Review of Applied Ethics* was entirely owing to the fact that she had been in a position to buy it. Had she not been able to do that, the *Review* would be in the hands of Professor Lettuce by now, ably assisted by his partner-in-crime, Professor Christopher Dove.

It was pure privilege that determined where so many of us ended up in life, Isabel reflected; it was nothing to do with merit, it was privilege. Or, putting it another way, it was a matter of accident, or luck. To be born in circumstances where one had enough to eat was the first resounding piece of luck, and good luck could be piled upon you from that point onwards. To be given a good education, not to be struck down by debilitating illness, not to have, like Heather Darnt, a disfiguring birthmark that must, with all the courage in the world, make one's teenage years an agony of embarrassment and exclusion — all of that was pure luck and nothing to do with desert. That was so, unless one believed in karma or some other notion of the acquisition of merit in a previous life. There were plenty of people who believed that — millions upon millions of adherents of Hinduism did — and it was not luck in their eyes. In such a view, Professor Lettuce had something to worry about; he may have got sufficiently far in the cycle of reincarnation as to be a professor of philosophy, but he was certainly going no further in the next life. He would be descending rather than ascending, Isabel thought, and was surely in danger of coming back as a toad or some other lowly creature. Or perhaps bad

175

professors came back as research assistants, stuck on the lowest rung of the academic ladder and obliged to endure the humiliations of that uncertain and unrewarding position. Or as a lettuce, if it was possible to come back as a vegetable . . .

Alex was looking at her.

"I'm sorry," said Isabel. "I have a tendency to drift off a bit."

"I asked you what you thought of that woman."

"Which woman?"

"The lawyer."

Isabel did not hesitate. "I'm afraid I didn't like her. I think she's in league with the thieves."

She was aware of the fact that she should not have said that; it was a direct imputation of criminality, and she had no evidence to substantiate the allegation.

Alex laughed. "Oh, come now! She's a lawyer. Lawyers represent people — even thieves — but that doesn't mean they're in league with them."

Isabel looked sheepish. "Yes, you're right. I shouldn't have said that."

Alex had now poured Isabel a cup of tea and was handing it to her. Isabel noticed that there were no cucumber sandwiches on the tray. She felt a momentary disappointment; sandwiches had definitely been mentioned on the telephone. Indeed, there had been an undertaking to serve cucumber sandwiches and, once again, *pacta sunt servanda* . . . She was never sure about the positioning of the *sunt*: she was inclined to put it at the end, as in *Carthago delenda est!*, which Cato was said to have proclaimed; but it was also

176

possible to leave the *sunt* out altogether and say, more succinctly and equally gerundively, *pacta servanda*. Could one say, she wondered, *cucumis ministranda est* — cucumber must be served?

Alex sat down. "So what's going to happen?" she asked.

"I gather that the insurance company has offered a reward. That's what usually happens."

Alex nodded. "I heard that." She paused. "And that'll be paid to the lawyer?"

"Yes. And she will pass it on once the painting has been recovered."

"So she acts as the holder, so to speak?"

Isabel said that she would. "I suppose they just have to trust her not to disappear with the money. Lawyers tend not to disappear."

Alex raised an eyebrow. "There must be crooked lawyers. Every profession has its rotten apples." She took a sip of her tea. Her eyes were on Isabel, who felt that she had to say something; the silence that had descended was slightly uncomfortable.

"With your interest in art," Isabel began, "you must have been particularly upset by all this."

"Absolutely," said Alex. "I was. I loved that painting, you know. I adored it. So the really important thing is to get it back."

"Especially since it's going to go to the nation eventually," said Isabel. "That makes it even more important."

Alex was about to say something, but seemed to check herself. She looked at Isabel's cup and offered her more tea. "Tell me," she said as she began to pour. "Tell me: have you got any idea who's behind this?"

Isabel sighed. "None at all. You see, I know absolutely nothing about the world of art theft."

Alex digested this silently. Then she said, "But Martha said that you were somebody with a reputation for sorting out extremely difficult situations. She said that you had helped people find out all sorts of things."

Isabel shook her head. "Would that that were true. I suppose I've been able to help a few people who have found themselves in a bit of a mess, but nothing more than that. I have no qualifications for any of it."

"Perhaps being a philosopher is the best qualification of all," suggested Alex.

"For what? For tracking down art thieves? Surely not."

Alex persisted. "For understanding things that are difficult to understand."

"To an extent," said Isabel. "But not this sort of thing."

"So you have no idea?" asked Alex, again.

"No," said Isabel. "Sorry."

Alex shifted in her seat. She leaned back, closed her eyes, and then opened them again, to fix Isabel with a playful but still serious stare. "So what if I were to suggest to you that it's my brother?" she asked.

CHAPTER
TWELVE

"How exactly did she put it?" asked Jamie.

They were sitting at the kitchen table, their evening meal over, the dishes stacked in the dishwasher, their two wine glasses, which Isabel preferred to wash by hand, now rinsed and standing inverted on the drying rack. It was half past nine, and at fifty-five degrees and fifty-six minutes' latitude, where Edinburgh lay, the sky still had plenty of light in it; Isabel loved these white nights of summer.

"How did she put it? Well, at first I thought it was a joke — but then I realised that it wasn't quite that."

"Not quite?"

"No. I think that she . . . well, she sort of meant it. I know that sounds pretty vague, but that's how I felt."

Jamie looked puzzled. "I'm not sure what 'sort of meaning' something amounts to."

"It means that you mean it, but aren't really sure." Isabel paused; she was not sure Alex had meant it when she suggested that her brother might be behind the theft of the painting. Perhaps she had intended to raise it as a possibility — something that she thought might be true but for which she had no evidence. And, as it happened, Alex had initially not taken the matter further, but had merely shrugged and raised an eyebrow when Isabel had asked her why she thought her brother might have stolen the painting. After a while, though, she had said, "He's greedy, my brother."

"Any more greedy than the rest of us?" asked Isabel.

Alex laughed. "If you mean more than me, yes, much more. He likes money. He likes the way it smells. He likes the power it gives you." She warmed to her theme. "He works in the pharmaceutical industry, you know. Oh, he likes to portray it as all being very high-minded, but it's all about money and profits — just like any other industry."

Isabel found herself defending Patrick. "Don't most people enjoy such things? Maybe those of us who feel ourselves free from all that — and I assume you, like me, are one — would have to admit that we're still susceptible."

Alex had looked at her slightly askance. "Not many. My brother, you see, needs money because of his habits. They're expensive — some of them very expensive. And I suspect that he'd do anything for money."

Isabel had expected her to continue on this theme, but she steered the conversation in another direction. About twenty minutes later, when Alex brought the visit to an end, Isabel felt that she had learned very little about the other woman, who had seemed more interested in finding out about her than revealing anything about herself. She had elicited at least some information, though: she had discovered that Alex was engaged; that she was interested in art; and that she had what seemed like an unusually strong dislike of her

180

brother. Isabel already knew that there was a close relationship between Alex and her father, and she could imagine why this should be: Alex's manner, her air of slight reserve, something that might easily be mistaken for shyness, mirrored that of Duncan Munrowe: he would see himself in her, no doubt, more so, perhaps, than he might in his son — if what Alex had said about Patrick's venality were true.

"It sounds to me," Jamie said, "as if this is a classic case of sibling jealousy. And if it is, then I wouldn't pay any attention to what they say about each other." He leaned back in his chair. "Why would he steal one of his father's paintings? Presumably he'll get his share of everything when he and his sister eventually inherit. Why steal now?"

"He may need the money now rather than later. She mentioned expensive habits."

Jamie shook his head. "Again, we don't know whether that's true or not. Other people's habits are expensive — our own, never." He paused. "And anyway, what are you going to do with the information, even if you decide to take it seriously? Are you going to tell the father that his son's a thief? You want to be supportive towards him — I don't think that telling him that will be all that helpful, frankly."

She agreed. "You're right. It's probably best for me to put it out of my mind."

"Good."

She hesitated. "Although it's difficult, isn't it, to forget something you've been told? Mud sticks. We used to say that as children."

Jamie smiled. "Yes. It does." He looked at her affectionately. "What else did you say?"

"As a child?"

"Yes."

She looked out of the window. A branch from the tree that grew outside the kitchen moved against the sky, gently, almost imperceptibly. The things that we said as children stayed with us, like certain religious beliefs which we might have grown out of even if the faith that underlay them might still be there. One might stop believing in angels, for instance, and yet feel their presence, or think one does; one might stop believing in hell and still feel nagging concern over the possibility of punishment. As a child she had picked up the superstitious belief that one should never store shoes above one's head — to do so resulted in headaches that could last for two weeks or more. Even now, her shoes were stored only at foot level.

"Isabel?"

She gave a start. "What did we say? Well, we said something about where you put your shoes."

"I didn't," said Jamie. "But I did say something about frogs giving you warts."

"But of course they do," said Isabel. She smiled; there is a particular delight in discovering that those whom one loves share similar memories of childhood. "You should never pick up a frog. And then there was something about bread."

"Oh yes?"

"We said that if you cut bread crooked, you've told a lie."

182

He laughed. "But I always do. You've seen my toast."

"There must be exceptions," said Isabel. "Every rule has its exceptions."

Jamie remembered something. "And what about getting a cut in the skin between one's thumb and forefinger — in that bit of webbed skin? What about that?"

"Oh, that," said Isabel. "Everybody knows the consequences of that: lockjaw."

"Yes," said Jamie. "And you died, just as you were likely to die of blood poisoning if somebody stabbed you with the nib of a pen."

"We ignore these things at our peril," said Isabel gravely.

Jamie thought of Charlie. He cast his eyes up at the ceiling; it was how they referred to their child when they were in the kitchen and he was in his room directly above. "Do you think he'll pick these things up?"

"I'm sure he will," said Isabel. "But I hope that he doesn't have the fears we had — the real fears. Remember your boyhood. You must have been frightened of some things."

He had been. He had been frightened that his father would die; he had been frightened that a boy called James MacArthur would punch him and break his nose, as he had threatened to do on a number of occasions; he had been frightened that somebody would come into his room at night when he was asleep and put a pillow over his head — a fear that came from hearing of what the wicked uncle did to the Princes in the Tower. Much later, as a teenager, he had been

183

frightened that he would never find a girlfriend, and that he would die without ever discovering sex.

"All of those things?" said Isabel sympathetically.

"Yes. And what about you?"

She thought. "As a very small girl I was frightened that the cat we had would be run over. I was frightened that my pants would fall off in gym."

Jamie let out a hoot of laughter. "What a terrific fear! That your pants will fall off!"

"It was very real," said Isabel. "And it happened to a girl in my class. Toffee Macleod. Her pants fell off. I wouldn't be surprised if she never fully recovered."

"Toffee Macleod? What a name. What happened to her?"

"She went to Australia and married a pilot. That's as much as I know."

"Nobody in Australia would have known," said Jamie. "She left her shame behind in Scotland."

Isabel was about to say something more about Toffee — to tell the story of how she was the first girl in the class to be asked to the cinema by a boy (not a boy and his parents, but a boy acting under his own auspices). But then the telephone rang and she knew, by some inexplicable sixth sense, that it would be Duncan. It was. Contact had been made, he said, and they should go to Rutland Square the following morning at nine-thirty. They should be on foot and they should walk round the square until they were contacted further.

Jamie, who had been able to overhear this conversation, said nothing, but looked disapproving.

184

Once Isabel had put down the phone, he said quietly, "Rutland Square?"

"Yes," said Isabel. "Apparently so."

"Why there?"

She had no idea. "The picture won't be there. We'll get instructions."

"Promise me one thing," said Jamie. "Promise me you'll phone and let me know where they've told you to go."

"I promise."

She suddenly remembered the cucumber sandwiches. "She promised cucumber sandwiches," she said. "But they never appeared."

"She must have forgotten."

Isabel had to concede that was possible. "It's a ridiculous thing to resent something like that," she said. "I know I shouldn't, and so I shan't." There were so many bigger moral problems connected with food — our duty to help the hungry, the implications of genetic manipulation of crops, and so on; these dwarfed all those smaller food issues that were really not much more than questions of etiquette. And that reminded her — "Jamie?"

"Yes?"

"What do you think of this? Somebody told me the other day that they had invited friends round to dinner and they had agreed that the couple who had been invited would bring a course. It was that sort of casual, kitchen-supper arrangement in which everybody contributes."

"So?"

"Well, the guests — a husband and wife — brought a casserole dish of stew. The hosts provided the starter and the pudding."

"All right."

"Everything went very well," Isabel continued. "The guests, though, had brought too much stew. There were only four people at the table and their stew would have fed six. So there were two portions left over. The hostess noticed and thought, *Good, that'll do for our dinner tomorrow. I won't have to cook.*"

Jamie listened. "Stew improves, doesn't it? I think it tastes better the next day."

"So do I," said Isabel. "Perhaps one should always eat leftovers. One would cook everything a day in advance and not touch it until the next day. But that's not the point of this story. The point is this: at the end of the meal the guests took the leftovers away with them."

Jamie looked pensive. "It was their casserole dish. That's reasonable enough."

Isabel had thought of that. "Yes, they had to take it back. But the stew had been taken from their casserole dish before the dinner and put into the host's serving dish."

Jamie frowned. "So they put it back into their casserole?"

"Yes. At the end. They all cleared up and she — the guest — spooned the stew back into its original casserole, which she then took away with her."

Jamie did not hesitate to condemn that. "Way out of line," he said. "The stew belonged to the hostess from

186

when it was transferred to her serving dish." He paused. "But it was also mean."

"That's what I think," said Isabel. "The whole case becomes complicated because of the casserole dish. It would be simpler if it had been breakfast they were having and the guests had brought, say, eight croissants — two each — and people didn't finish them."

"Four left?" suggested Jamie.

"Yes. Four. Let's say they'll be sitting on a table still in their brown-paper packet."

"That's where they should remain," said Jamie firmly.

"I agree," said Isabel. "It's a gift, isn't it?"

"Yes, of course. And you don't take gifts back, do you?"

Jamie wondered whether that was an absolute rule. Could there not be circumstances in which it became apparent that a gift was not appreciated or not being used? Surely you could ask for it back in such a case? Isabel thought you could not. "You have to put up with it," she said. "You might hint. You might say something like: 'Remember that china tea service we gave you for your wedding? We love that pattern and it's such a pity they're not making it any more. I'd do anything — anything! — to get my hands on more like it.'" She smiled. "And then you might add: 'You're so wise, keeping it in a cupboard, unused.'"

"Not very subtle," said Jamie.

"No. Perhaps not. But there are times when subtlety just won't work, don't you think?"

"Perhaps you should have been less subtle yourself," he said. "Perhaps you should have mentioned cucumbers."

"Just dropped them into the conversation? Perhaps as an expletive. *Oh, cucumber!* Expletives don't have to have a meaning. 'Cucumber' would do fine — like that marvellous Italian expression, *caspita!* It doesn't mean anything at all. It's the equivalent of saying 'heavens'."

"But 'heavens' does mean something," Jamie objected.

Isabel said nothing.

"And 'cucumber' means something too," Jamie continued.

Isabel rose to her feet and crossed the room to the fridge in the corner. "I know we've just had dinner," she said. "But all this talk of cucumber is just too much. I'm going to make myself a cucumber sandwich." She turned and looked over her shoulder at Jamie. "Want one?"

He did, and a minute or two later they were seated at the table again, a small plate of thinly cut cucumber sandwiches in front of them. "Heaven," said Isabel, as she began to eat. "Singular. Heaven."

As Isabel let Duncan into the house the following morning she could see that he was nervous.

"I'm sorry that I'm so early," he said. "I was worried what would happen if there was a delay on the roads."

She reassured him that it made no difference to her, as long as he would not mind entertaining himself for half an hour or so. "I have to take my son to nursery school."

188

He made an apologetic gesture. "Of course, of course. I'll be fine."

She left him in the sitting room with a copy of that morning's newspaper. She had started the crossword over her breakfast cup of coffee and had not got very far. She enquired whether he did crosswords. He did. "Eight down," she said. " 'A dirty child will not like this command.' Four words. It begins with an o."

He took the paper from her. His hand, she saw, was shaking. He glanced at the crossword and then looked up. "Order of the Bath," he said.

Isabel laughed. "Yes! Why didn't I think of that?"

"I'm sure that you would have," he said.

"It's such an odd name for a chivalric order," mused Isabel. "I gather it was something to do with the fact that medieval knights were washed to purify them. Rather like baptism."

Duncan made a polite expression of interest, but she could tell that his mind was elsewhere.

"Not that people bathed very much in those days," said Isabel. "Do you know that a Venetian ambassador expressed surprise that Queen Elizabeth I took a bath every month — even when she didn't need one."

He did not laugh.

"You're nervous," she said.

He looked down at his feet. "Very."

"I don't think there's any danger," she said. "All these people want is money. I don't think they're violent criminals or anything like that."

"It's not that I'm worried about," Duncan said. "It's my painting I'm worried about. It could get damaged if they're carting it around. These people will know nothing about how to treat a painting." As he spoke, his anxiety gave way to anger. "It means nothing to them. It's just a way of extorting money. They don't care about anything else."

Isabel put a hand on his forearm. "There's every chance we'll get this back," she said. "They have no interest in damaging it."

She wondered why she was trying to persuade him out of his anger. People had a right to be angry when they were the victims of ill-treatment. We automatically tended to calm them down, but perhaps we should let anger run its course. It had its function, she imagined, which was . . . What exactly *was* the role of anger? Self-protection? Did anger serve the purpose of encouraging us to avoid harmful situations in the future? Did it show us who our enemies were?

She looked at her watch. Jamie had been dressing Charlie upstairs and she needed to relieve him: he had to be at the Academy in forty minutes for his pupils, and he was planning to call on Grace later. She left Duncan with the newspaper, inviting him to tackle the crossword if he wished. Upstairs, Charlie was now ready. "Tiffin box," he said. "Don't forget tiffin box."

She led him downstairs, collected the tiffin box from the kitchen, and made her way out of the front door, Charlie walking beside her, his hand in hers. He was wearing a pair of red shoes of which he was inordinately proud. "Red shoes go fast," he announced.

"That's right, they do, darling," said Isabel.

She squeezed the tiny hand that was holding on to hers, and the tiny hand squeezed back. She imagined what it must be like to have Charlie's mind — to believe that red shoes are faster than other shoes; to believe, as he did, that ducks could drive fire engines and that pigs built houses of bricks and straw. There were plenty of people who weren't three-and-three-quarters who believed equally implausible things . . . and went to war over them.

They made slow progress, as Charlie's steps, in spite of his red shoes, were small. A few yards away from the house Isabel noticed a car that had been parked in one of the parking bays pull out into the road. She had not been paying particular attention to it, but she glimpsed the driver briefly before he made off. He was vaguely familiar; somebody from a neighbouring street whom she had seen walking in to Bruntsfield or in the delicatessen, perhaps? Or had she met him somewhere else? Her gaze followed the retreating car: she could just make out the back of the driver's head now; nothing more than that. And then it dawned on her. It was Patrick, or somebody who looked very much like him.

She stopped in her tracks.

"Why we stopping?" asked Charlie.

"Because I've just seen something, Charlie. I've just seen something odd."

They resumed the journey, but as they did so, Isabel went over in her mind the possible explanations for Patrick's presence. Coincidence led the list. Patrick might have a friend in the area and might be visiting him; there was no law against visiting your friends first thing in the morning. Or he had spent the night at a friend's house and was now going back to his flat. Or it was not Patrick at all.

Those were the innocent explanations. The less innocent included the possibility that Patrick was watching his father, or, and this made Isabel's heart skip a beat, that he was watching *her*. If Patrick were in some way mixed up in the theft of the painting, then he could be expected to have a close interest in the outcome of today's meeting. The thieves would be concerned about the police coming to the meeting, and so they would naturally want to be warned when Duncan came into town to pick up Isabel. That could explain Patrick's presence — if, indeed, it was Patrick whom she had seen.

After she had dropped Charlie off at the nursery, Isabel returned to the house, where she found Duncan immersed in the crossword.

"It took my mind off things," he said. "Not that I've made much progress with it — apart from this." He passed her the newspaper and she looked at the clues he had filled in. Order of the Bath had helped him to get *The sea sounds like a man* (brinc) and *A plucked instrument says Italian yes to group of notes; it has a keyboard* (harpsichord).

"Very clever," she said.

"Not really."

She looked at her watch. They could walk to Rutland Square if they had time — it was only twenty minutes from Isabel's house to the west end of Princes Street, and Rutland Square was only minutes from there. But it was now nine o'clock and they could not afford to be late. Isabel telephoned for a taxi and suggested that they wait for it at the gate. "They don't take long," she said. Duncan nodded; he was still distracted, she noticed, and she thought that she could make out beads of sweat across his brow.

"It's going to be all right," she said, as she locked the front door behind him.

He swallowed. "Yes, thank you. Thank you."

They stood under the large tree at the front of the house. Somewhere in the foliage a bird moved; that tree was popular with doves. Charlie was fascinated by them. "Doves got bedrooms?" he had asked.

She looked up the street, attentive now to any cars that were parked nearby. For the first time, she felt what she realised was fear. The people they were about to meet did not belong to her world; they came from a world in which the rights of others did not matter. She had assured Duncan that they would not be violent, but how did she know that? The answer was that she did not.

In the taxi, Duncan sat quietly, not attempting to make conversation but staring out of the window at the houses and at the cluster of shops at the top of the road that led down to the canal. They passed a church on which a large banner had been hung. We *must love one another*, it said. We must, she thought. And Auden came to mind, again, as he did in the most unexpected circumstances. It was "1st September 1939", the poem that people in New York read and sent to one another after that fateful September day in 2001. They found comfort in it because it was about the ending of a world and the despair that this will bring. He had originally written: "We must love one another or die", and had changed it to: "We must love one another *and* die". Auden disowned the poem, considering it mendacious; but it had a grave beauty about it. Things that are not sincere can be as striking as those that are, and insincerity, thought Isabel, can — curiously — end up being sincere.

She turned to Duncan. The taxi had stopped at the lights outside the King's Theatre; the traffic was moving slowly. "Your son," she said. "Your son, Patrick. I thought I saw him."

He looked puzzled. "You met him?"

"I did. At a concert. I thought I'd told you that when I came out to Doune."

"Did you? Perhaps you did. I can't remember, I'm afraid."

"I thought I saw him," she said.

He frowned.

"I mean, I thought I saw him this morning. In a car. On my street."

He took a handkerchief out of his pocket and dabbed at his brow. "You probably did."

Now it was Isabel's turn to look puzzled.

"He drove me to your place," said Duncan. "I called on him this morning. I wanted to leave my car near his flat. You can park up there. Your area has these regulations."

Isabel felt relieved. The innocent explanation meant that she had not been imagining things — it had been him — and at the same time served to defuse the awkward possibility that Patrick was somehow involved in the theft of the painting.

"He knows what's happening this morning?" she asked.

"Yes," said Duncan. "I told him." He looked down at his hands. "My son and I are, regrettably, not close."

She said that she was sorry to hear that.

"Thank you. I'm afraid that he's something of a disappointment to me."

He looked at her as he spoke, and she felt that he was asking something of her. Did he want reassurance? Did he want some sort of comfort?

"I suspected that," she said.

"Why?" There was a note of surprise in his voice.

She chose her words carefully. "I formed the impression that you might . . ." She faltered. What did she want to say? That he and Patrick inhabited different worlds?

"Go on," he said. "Please go on. Tell me what you think."

She had not imagined that she would discuss it with him, but now he was asking. "I can understand how it's sometimes difficult," she said.

"It is," he said. "It is difficult."

"I have a friend whose son is gay," said Isabel. "She found it hard at first, but she realised that what really counted was his happiness, and he was happy. She . . ." She trailed off. Duncan was staring at her in incomprehension.

195

"I really don't know what you mean," he said.

She struggled to find words. It had suddenly dawned on her that either he did not know or that she had been mistaken in her conclusion that Patrick was gay. Perhaps the assumption was misplaced — one cannot read the lives of others on a cursory meeting.

Duncan now looked confused. "My son . . ." he began, and then, looking down at the floor of the cab, he lapsed into silence.

"I'm sorry," said Isabel. "I really don't know your son."

He did not meet her eyes. "There is a political difference between us," he said. "My own views are liberal — middle-of-the-roadish. I'm not particularly political, I suppose. But he . . . he's an extremist, I'm sorry to say. He's in with a very leftish bunch — not the Labour Party or any of the other mainstream options of the Left, but the real hard left — a small outfit in Glasgow. He gives them money. Castro is his hero, as far as I can make out. I try to point out to him that Castro took many prisoners of conscience over the years, but he won't hear any of it. He even laments the passing of the Soviet Union. He forgets about the Gulag, the KGB, the millions who perished under Stalin."

Isabel listened. Had the traffic not been so slow, they would have been at their destination by now; as it was, they were stuck in a line of cars outside the Usher Hall. "People change," she said. "The scales may fall from his eyes. And . . ." She hesitated, unsure whether to broaden the discussion, but decided to do so. "And if you look behind the party allegiance you may find some

196

fine sentiments. The Left generally want people to have good lives, don't you think? They want people to have their material needs satisfied, to be lifted out of poverty. Perhaps your son —"

He interrupted her. "We all want that." He sounded vehement. "Who doesn't want hospitals and schools and all the rest? It's how we achieve the material satisfaction that's the issue. He thinks you can have it by taking everybody's property away from them and having state ownership of everything. He really thinks that."

"No," said Isabel. "That wouldn't work."

He looked at her now. "I'm a farmer, and I know that if you take land out of the hands of individual farmers and collectivise it, you destroy agriculture. Every single historical example has shown that to be the case. Yet Patrick, my own son, told me that I had no right to the five hundred acres I farm. He said that if I leave the farm to him he'll treat it as a collective." He snorted. "Collective agriculture? How long would that work? A month?"

The traffic had started to move again and they were approaching the end of Lothian Road. To their left was the Caledonian Hotel, a great edifice of red sandstone, while on the other side of the road St John's Church marked the end of Princes Street Gardens. The church was displaying a line of flags on its forecourt: the Scottish flag, the Saltire, fluttered above flags of the various European countries and a flag on which the word *Peace* was sewn in great black letters. *We must love one another and die*, thought Isabel.

The taxi turned and began to make its way down the short road that led to Rutland Square. "You could drop us right here," Isabel called out to the driver.

Duncan reached for his coat. "We can talk about Patrick some other time," he said; he spoke in the tone of one wanting to shelve an awkward topic.

Isabel knew Rutland Square for two reasons. Her friend, Lesley Kerr, had her legal office in one corner of the square, and she had occasionally called there to collect her for lunch. And on the other side, in a three-storeyed Georgian building looking out over the gardens that made up the centre of the square, was the Scottish Arts Club. Isabel went to dinners there from time to time, and parties too — the club had long had a reputation as the most hospitable of Edinburgh clubs with its talks on the arts, its Sheeps Heid dinners, its Burns Nights. Isabel sometimes had lunch there with another friend, Lucy Mackay, an artist known for her portraits and wispy, whimsical watercolours. That was her Rutland Square, a place with predominantly positive associations but which Isabel was now visiting in a very different context.

Duncan paid off the taxi and the cab shot off to its next assignment. Duncan, whose nervousness had now returned, looked about him uneasily. "What now? We walk around?"

Isabel took his arm. "Yes. To all intents and purposes we are just two people out for a walk." She pointed to a man walking two black Labradors on their leashes. "Like him."

They began to walk round the square. Isabel glanced discreetly at her watch; in spite of the traffic delays they were still at least ten minutes early.

"They could be watching us," said Duncan.

"They probably are," said Isabel.

They continued their walk in silence. There was not a great deal happening in the square, which was tucked away from the busy thoroughfares of Princes Street and Lothian Road. Now, in midsummer, the trees made an island of green, their leaves sibilant in the warm morning breeze. "The winds must come from somewhere when they blow" . . . it was among the most beautiful of lines. WHA again, even here, she thought, when I'm about to enter the murky, unpleasant world of theft.

They reached the western end of the square and began to make their way in the direction of the Scottish Arts Club. The lights were on in the drawing room; somebody was reading a paper, enjoying a cup of coffee. And on the other side of the club, in a house now converted to offices, she saw a man and a woman talking in front of a window — the ordinary world of legitimate business: a world in which people did not hold one another to ransom; a world in which rules, like hidden, powerful electrical fields, governed the affairs of men.

She was suddenly aware of Duncan's hand on her arm. He was whispering something that she found it hard to catch.

She whispered back, although there was nobody about to hear them. "Yes? What is it?"

"There's somebody parked up ahead. He's looking at us."

She switched her gaze to the vehicles parked up against the garden railings. She saw a large grey car that had been carelessly parked and was protruding into the road; an old Morgan, lovingly tended, its silver trimmings worn almost to the base metal below from the rubbing of generations of polishing cloth; both were empty. But then, behind the Morgan, parked hard up against it so that the bumpers must almost have been touching, was a black van with a long crack in the windscreen. There was a man at the wheel.

"I think that must be them," said Duncan out of the side of his mouth.

"We'll find out soon enough," said Isabel. She was not sure; there were building works going on in one of the buildings in the square and the man could have had something to do with those — there were other builders' vans in the square, disgorging planks of wood and other mysteries of their craft.

Isabel slowed her pace. She found it hard to pretend to be casual in the face of observation, particularly from somebody who was probably either a builder or a thief. Some builders took it as their right to watch women with an appraising look that was frequently nakedly intrusive; they still wolf-whistled and called out — as Italian men used to do before they suddenly grew up. Why did men think they could behave that way? What satisfaction did they get from wolf-whistling? It was about power, thought Isabel. It was about being able to assert themselves publicly and to objectify women. It

200

was a direct denial of the idea that men and women should treat one another with courtesy and consideration; it was a nod to the days of strutting men and meek, passive women.

Thinking of builders helped to take her mind off being watched, with the result that when the window of the van was suddenly — and noisily — wound down, she was not paying full attention to it.

"Over here."

The tone of the voice was peremptory; the vowels were those of the east of Scotland. Isabel looked. He was staring at them through the open window of the van: a man in his early thirties, or thereabouts, with lank, mousy hair and a chin that was covered in heavy stubble.

She stepped off the pavement and began to cross the road towards the van with Duncan following behind. "Quick," the man called out. "Get a move on."

Isabel, offended by his rudeness, regarded him with disdain as they approached the van. She saw that there were two earrings in his right ear — two small studs, one of which was red. It was a code, she imagined. What had Eddie once said to her about men and earrings? Left: right; right: wrong.

He stared at them through the open window. "Get in the back," he said. "The door's open."

She smelled something on the man's breath: stale alcohol. She saw that his eyes were bloodshot and that the skin around them seemed to be puffed-up. He was not sober, she thought, but then some men like this never were.

"Why?" she asked.

"Do you want to see the thing?" His voice had become a sneer.

She felt her heart beating within her. She would remain calm; she was determined to deny him the satisfaction of seeing her riled.

Isabel kept her voice level as she replied, "Yes. That's why we're here."

Duncan now stepped forward. "Is my painting in the back?" he asked.

The driver stared at him for a moment or two before answering. "No, it isn't, Pop. I'm taking you to see it. But only if youses shift yoursels and get in." He used the demotic plural of *you*, a common feature of speech in Scotland. Isabel had always rather liked it, just as she liked the complimentary Texan plural *you-all* that her mother had told her about. "It assumes that nobody would be unfortunate enough to be on their own," she used to explain. "Hence *you-all*."

There was something in the driver's answer that made Duncan start. She looked at him and he shook his head, as if to put her off saying anything now.

"I think we should probably do this," Duncan said to her. "Do you mind?"

Isabel weighed the possibilities. It was no small step to get into the back of a strange van, especially one driven by so patently unpleasant a person as this; but what was the alternative? If they declined, then the whole arrangement for the recovery of the Poussin — and the painting — could be in jeopardy.

She nodded to Duncan, and they walked round to the back of the van. Duncan opened the doors hesitantly.

"I'm not sure," he said. He stopped. A man dressed entirely in black, his face half covered by a football scarf, his eyes obscured by sunglasses, was crouching on the floor of the van. Gripped on either side by his gloved hands was the Poussin.

Isabel gasped. Her hand went to her mouth.

"See this," said the man, jerking the painting towards them but still keeping his tight grip on it. "See?"

Isabel noticed the sky, saw the intense Poussin blue, saw the clouds; that was her abiding impression — the clouds. Absurdly, she wanted to say something about the painting, even now, in this threatening, tense situation — she wanted to say something about the beauty of the painting. *We don't react in the right way,* she thought; *we think the wrong things, as I am doing now.* She had read of people who found themselves facing death and who subsequently survived and of how they had spent what could have been their last precious seconds thinking about some matter of no real consequence — whether they had paid the newsagent's bill or licensed the car or something like that. It was the same with last words, which were no doubt mostly banal and often inappropriate, although some, at least, managed a memorable final statement, as did Charles II. He had apologised for taking so long to go: *You must pardon me, gentlemen, for being a most unconscionable time a-dying.*

There came a growl from the front, as the engine started. The man holding the painting looked over his shoulder through a small window that gave on to the cab. Then he looked back and jerked his head. "That's it," he said. "Out."

He laid the Poussin down on the floor and reached forward to close the doors. Isabel backed off, but Duncan did not. She looked at him in alarm, concerned that he might try to snatch the painting.

"My painting . . ." he stuttered.

The man pushed him out of the way, not roughly but firmly. "Sorry," he said. "Show's over."

The door slammed shut and the van pulled out sharply on to the road. They watched as it sped away; it barely slowed down to negotiate the difficult bend that would allow it access to the back lane behind the square.

Isabel turned to Duncan. She saw that he was about to cry, and intuitively she reached out to embrace him, to comfort him.

"I'm very sorry," he said, struggling to compose himself. "I find this very upsetting."

"Of course it is. And there's nothing to be embarrassed about."

She patted his shoulder, as she might pat Charlie when he hurt himself and ran to her for the embrace that could so miraculously relieve the pain. It was understandable that one might cry in the face of something like this, not only out of frustration at seeing a beloved object treated in this way, but for what the whole unpleasant little episode represented. So one might cry for everything that was wrong with the world, for all the injustice and crudity and cruelty, for all the things that are stolen from people.

CHAPTER
THIRTEEN

Eddie cried, too, later that morning. It was in very different circumstances — not publicly, in Rutland Square, but in a small clinic room, with the antiseptic smell so characteristic of such places, the smell of cleanliness. On the wall behind Eddie's head, tacked on to a noticeboard, was a poster with dietary recommendations: *Five pieces of fruit and vegetables a day for a healthy life.* Isabel, seated beside Eddie, wondered briefly: do they mean five pieces of fruit and five pieces of vegetable, or five in total? It was five in total, she knew, because that was the message that had been drummed into people's heads over the last few years — except for some heads, particularly in those Scottish cities where the diet tended to greasy food and no vegetables at all and, according to legend, deep-fried chocolate bars. Jamie confirmed that he had seen them served and had even tasted one after an evening at the Glasgow Concert Hall; not that they sold them there, he hastily added, but they had found somewhere nearby that did. "When in Rome," he said, smiling. In Rome, of course, they did nothing so foolish as eating deep-fried chocolate bars, but courted disaster in their own ways, as all people do. We each have our own way of behaving self-destructively, thought Isabel; we each have our folly, and for the Italians it was . . . What was it? Their Mediterranean diet was famously healthy, with all its tomatoes and fish and olive oil, and although they liked wine, there was evidence, much proclaimed by topers, that two glasses of wine a day was positively beneficial. They took siestas — if they could — and that was also good for health. So what did they do that was self-destructive? They drove too fast; that was all she could think of.

She held Eddie's hand as the nurse behind the desk referred to the file in front of her.

"Everything's fine," said the nurse. "All the tests are clear."

Isabel thought at first that Eddie had not understood. He gasped as the nurse spoke, and half turned to Isabel. Then he started to sob.

"It's fine, Eddie," Isabel said. "Listen to what she said. It's fine."

Eddie turned back to face the nurse.

"Yes, it's all right," repeated the nurse. "Negative. Everything's fine."

"It takes a little time to sink in," said Isabel, pressing Eddie's hand gently.

"So . . ." Eddie began, but stopped.

"So, you're fine." Isabel pressed his hand again. She looked at the nurse, who nodded.

The nurse began to say something about counselling and being careful; Isabel looked away, as she did not feel that it was appropriate for her to listen at that point. But it did not last long. Eddie said, "Yes, I know, I know," and the nurse did not persist.

They went outside, into the sun.

"That's that," said Isabel. "Happier?"

Eddie nodded. "Very," he said.

Isabel looked at the sky. On the same day, within little more than a few hours, she had seen two men cry, and had comforted both. She could not help but reflect on the differences between these men: Duncan, middle-aged and wealthy, the product of an expensive education and a family that was perfectly assured of its place in the world; Eddie, whose life had been far harder in every respect, whose horizons had been so much more limited, but who had a future before him. Would Duncan exchange lives with Eddie if, by some miracle, he were given the chance? It was a peculiar thought experiment that Isabel liked to engage in occasionally. Would one choose youth — and years — rather than comfort and the security of being oneself? Would the elderly millionaire change places with the indigent twenty-one-year-old?

They decided to walk back to their side of town. Isabel had a book to collect from a bookshop on South Bridge and Eddie said that he would accompany her. "I just want to walk," he said. "I don't think I could focus on anything right now. I actually want to fly, you know, but I can't, and so I'll walk."

She smiled at him.

Eddie continued: "I was worried for so long. I put things out of my mind and then every so often it would come back to me and I would go all cold."

"Anybody would," said Isabel.

They made their way along Hanover Street and then up the Playfair Steps at the back of the National Gallery. Below them, the railway lines caught the afternoon sun until they were swallowed by the tunnel under the Gallery.

"When I was very young," said Isabel, "I thought that the tunnel down there was Glasgow. I was told that the trains went to Glasgow and I saw them disappear into that tunnel. I thought that it must be Glasgow."

Eddie laughed. "When I was seven, something like that, I used to go through to Glasgow to see an uncle," he said. "But he was never in. We went several times but I don't think he was ever there."

"What do they say? It's better to travel hopefully than to arrive?"

"Do they?"

"Yes," she said. "They do."

They climbed the remaining steps in silence. Isabel thought about Eddie's saying that he wanted to fly. We all did. Who had not imagined themselves flying; who had not dreamed that they could fly? The dream interpreters spoiled those dreams of flying, which they said were not about flying at all. But they were; that, or freedom, perhaps, but not about sex, as they insisted. Everything, they said, was about sex except . . . perhaps sex itself. Isabel smiled: a dream about sex was really about flying — what would they say to that?

They paused at the top of the steps and looked back over the New Town, now lying below them. Isabel noticed that although neither of them was breathless from the exertion of climbing the steps, Eddie's face had coloured. She wondered about exercise: he came to the delicatessen each morning by bus; perhaps he should be encouraged to walk to work. But that was none of her business. You did not tell your friends to get fit or lose weight. They made that decision themselves and then you complimented them on the effort.

After collecting the book, Isabel treated Eddie to a cup of coffee in the bookshop coffee bar. Eddie had cream on the top of his, and she found herself pointing to the topping — rich, white, fatal — and saying, "You can't, Eddie!"

He looked at her in surprise. "What's wrong with cream?"

"Everything," she replied, then thought again. "Well, no, not everything, but you see, we have these things called arteries and . . ."

He was grinning at her. "Yes?"

"Another time. I don't want you to think that I'm trying to run your life."

His grin widened. "Unless I wanted you to."

She toyed with the small packet of sugar — destined to be unused — that had come with her coffee. "Which, of course, you don't want."

"Who says?"

The conversation had started lightly but there was now a tinge of seriousness. Isabel frowned as she wondered where it was leading. He was Eddie, the young man who worked in the delicatessen; she was his employer's aunt; he was in his early twenties and she was in her early forties. There were not quite twenty years between them, but the gap was almost that large. He was damaged, and was hesitantly feeling his way towards recovery; she would help in that — of course she would — but it would not be a good idea for him to replace whatever had been missing in his relationship with his parents with some form of substitute provided by her.

He answered his own question quickly. "I say . . ."

She looked away.

"I mean," he continued, "that there's something I really want you to do for me, Isabel. Will you do it?"

She looked back at him. His expression was imploring. Whatever he had in mind was important to him and she could not simply brush him off.

"It depends, Eddie. Obviously it depends. You know that I'm happy to help you but I can't do everything."

"I know that. And this isn't everything. It's dead simple."

"What is it?"

He sniffed.

"Do you need a hanky?"

"No. I'm all right. Sometimes there are things that make me sniff. Something in the air. Pollen maybe. But not here, I suppose."

"You were telling me about this thing you want me to do."

He sniffed again. "You know I've got this girlfriend?"

"Yes, Diane. I met her the other day at the deli, remember?" She paused. "Is everything still all right there?"

"Yeah, yeah. Fine. No problems with that."

She said that she was glad to hear it. And then he went on, "Her parents are the problem. They hate me."

Perhaps it was an exaggeration to say that they hated him, but Diane had told Isabel herself that her parents disapproved of him, considered him beneath them. And for Eddie, the difference between hate and disapproval in such circumstances surely seemed slight.

She tried to reassure him. "Hate is a very strong word, as we know, Eddie. Parents often don't see things the way their children do. They have their own ideas about who are suitable boyfriends or girlfriends for their sons and daughters. They may have ambitions for them —"

He cut her short, his anger now surfacing. "They think I'm no good."

She wondered how to respond to that. He evidently understood exactly how they felt.

"I'm sure they don't think you're . . ." She searched for the right word. "Bad. I'm sure they don't think that. You're not involved in drugs or anything like that."

"I could be, the way they talk about me . . . So, if it's not that, then what is it? Because I'm not from their group or whatever? Is that it?"

She nodded. "To be frank, yes. People are like that."

He shook his head in frustration. "So what do they expect me to do?"

She considered his question. It was, she thought, exactly the right question to ask, as it exposed the moral flaw in Diane's parents' position. You can only blame people for that which they have chosen to do — Aristotle spelled that out clearly enough. And that

212

meant that you should not hold it against somebody for being what he *is*. A person's background, then, was the classic example of something for which he can never be judged adversely.

"They shouldn't expect anything of you, Eddie. There's nothing wrong with being who you are and you have nothing to be ashamed of or to reproach yourself about. Nothing."

"So why do they hate me?"

They wished him to be something different, she said, and that was impossible, and wrong. If they knew him properly, then they would surely realise that there was nothing wrong with him; that he was a perfectly good choice for Diane.

He was alerted by what she said. "If they knew me properly?"

"Yes. I'm sure that if they knew you better they'd see your merits. You're kind to Diane, aren't you? You treat her well?"

"Of course."

"And the two of you are happy together?"

"Yes. Really happy. That's why we want to live together, which they don't want." He paused. "But listen, you said that if they knew more about me they might not be so hostile. That's just what I want you to do for me. I want you to talk to them."

"Diane's parents?"

"Yes. Talk to them. Tell them that I'm OK. Tell them that there's no reason why we shouldn't get this flat. Tell them —"

She stopped him. "I'm not sure, Eddie. I don't think I should interfere."

He looked incredulous. "But Cat says that you're always interfering. She says that you get mixed up in all sorts of things and that you help people. She told me. And everybody knows it. They know that if they need something sorted, they can go to you."

Isabel looked at her watch. "You have to get back to work," she said. "Cat's expecting you."

"But you haven't answered me."

She picked up her coffee cup. The coffee was almost too cold to drink. "Give me some time to think," she said briskly. "I need to think about it."

"Do you think you can? Do you think you can speak to them?"

She put down her cup. "I don't know them," she said. "How can I go and speak to people I don't know?"

"You do that for other people," he muttered.

She knew that what he said was true. She spoke to people for other people. But she also knew Diane's difficulties over setting up home with Eddie were not simply to do with parental opposition.

"I'll think about it," she said, picking up the plastic bag that contained her book. It was a book she had ordered a week ago, Scanlon's *What We Owe to Each Other*. She needed it for an editorial she was writing on contractualism in moral philosophy and . . . she smiled; she needed it for her life.

"What's so funny?" asked Eddie nervously.

She wanted to cheer him up. Half an hour previously he had been talking about wanting to fly; now he seemed morose. "What's so funny? Life," said Isabel. "Come on, Eddie. Let's get going."

She was back at the house in time to collect Charlie from nursery. Jamie was at home, practising, in case Isabel should be late and he would need to do the Charlie collection. Her return liberated him; he had promised to see a friend about a recital they were planning and he needed to get away. He was anxious, though, to hear about Isabel's morning.

"You saw the painting?"

She nodded. "Yes. Can we talk about it later, though? I'll have to go for Charlie."

He looked relieved. "Did you see them — the thieves?"

"Yes." She stopped. Were those men the thieves or the intermediaries? Did it make much difference? "I saw the people who had the painting. I didn't see very much of them, though . . ."

Jamie's eyes widened. "They were masked?"

"Nothing so melodramatic. It all happened rather quickly — and they were wearing scarves. I couldn't really give you a description of them. Thirty-ish? One had earrings. There was a certain amount of tension and aggression but we weren't hurt." She turned. Talking about what had happened made her feel somehow queasy. Was this how people felt after a traumatic experience? Weak at the knees, sick, fearful perhaps? Or even dirtied? She had heard about how people who were the victims of assault could sometimes blame themselves for what happened. Was that happening to her?

To change the subject, Isabel asked about Grace. "Will you tell me about the peace mission? Later?"

Jamie's face fell. "Some messages of peace fall on stony ground."

"Oh."

He nodded. "I'll try again."

She wanted him to do that. The house seemed empty without Grace. And it would be dustier too and Jamie's shirts would be unironed and she would miss hearing about the latest goings-on with the local council and their iniquities, and the failings of the bus service, and the spiritualist meetings . . . There was so much that Grace brought to her life, as any friend or colleague does. That, Isabel thought, was what made the texture of our lives: the doings, the little ways of those about us. We defined ourselves socially as much as we did individually, perhaps even more so, and that, or course, meant duties to others . . . including to people like Eddie. But I can't, she said to herself; I can't go out and interfere in the lives of people I've never met, who would not thank me for giving them my opinion on a matter that is no affair of mine. No, I can't. And yet Eddie has asked me to do this and if he has no claim on me, then who does?

Charlie was brewing a cold and would not settle to any activity that afternoon. By the time that Jamie came home at seven in the evening, Isabel was ready for a

216

glass of wine. Charlie had been put to bed and had dozed off quickly in spite of his runny nose and incipient cough.

"Should I be worried?" she said to Jamie. "I really want a glass of wine, and that makes me wonder whether I should be concerned."

"Anybody can want a glass of wine," Jamie reassured her. "I'd be worried if you wanted a whole bottle."

"Sometimes . . ."

He had never seen her the worse for alcohol. "I don't believe you," he said, handing her a glass. "And here's the remedy from New Zealand."

The wine had a delicious fruitiness. She let it linger in her mouth. "Oh, well," she said. "My day."

Suddenly, and with so little warning that she surprised even herself, she felt tears well up in her eyes.

Jamie put down the glass he had poured for himself. "Isabel . . ."

She fought it for a moment or two, but then yielded. "It's been . . ."

He took the wine glass from her hand. "It must have been."

". . . horrible."

"Yes. I know."

She spoke between sobs, the words jumbled. "Eddie too. Poor Eddie."

A cloud passed over Jamie's face. "Bad news?"

She shook her head. "No. Good news."

He stroked her cheek gently. His hand was wet with her tears. "I'm glad. I thought it could be different."

"He asked me. He asked me to speak to . . . you know, that girlfriend of his has parents who disapprove of him and he wants to live with her . . ."

"You said something about that. But listen, don't worry about all that."

"And those people, those people who stole the painting . . ."

He said nothing.

"It was an attitude of disregard," Isabel went on. "We were nothing to them."

"There are plenty of people like that," said Jamie. "Plenty of people disregard others. Plenty of people hold others in contempt. Turn on the television and see it."

She was beginning to compose herself. She reached for her wine glass; he dropped his hands from her shoulders. "Here's to those nice New Zealanders," she said.

"At least there are plenty of those," said Jamie.

Isabel was thinking. "I've been trying to remember the details of what happened. I've been trying to piece it together."

"Tell me then," said Jamie. "Describe it exactly as it happened, moment by moment. That might help you to remember."

They sat down at the kitchen table. "We were walking in Rutland Square, Duncan and I."

"Yes. Then?"

"Then Duncan drew my attention to a van parked nearby. I saw a man in the driver's seat. He was

218

watching us and he put the window down and called us over."

"What did he say?"

"Something like 'Come here'. No, it was 'Over here'. Just that."

"And what did he look like? Picture him."

"His eyes were puffy and bloodshot. He had a thin face. Earrings. Two rings in one ear. One of the earrings was red. I noticed that and thought it might be a code of some sort."

Jamie shrugged. "Piercings mean nothing. They mean you've been pierced — that's all."

Then Isabel remembered something. It came back to her with clarity. "He called Duncan 'Pop'."

Jamie looked puzzled. "Is that important?"

She did not answer immediately. She was thinking. Pop. Why would that be significant? She felt that it was, but she could not work out why this should be so. It was the sort of thing that somebody like that might call a middle-aged man if he wanted to show contempt; a casual, sarcastic equivalent of "Granddad". And then she remembered. That was what Patrick had called his father; he had said, "Pop is very unworldly."

She explained this to Jamie and asked him what he thought. He looked doubtful. "Anybody might call somebody that," he said. "I don't think that proves anything."

"But it could," Isabel insisted.

"Yes. It could. But that's not the same as saying that it does. Could and does are different."

She conceded that. But now that she thought about it, it was quite possible the painting had been stolen by Patrick. He had the knowledge and obviously he would have the opportunity. But what about motive?

"Imagine for a moment that Patrick did it," she said. "What would his motive have been?"

Jamie returned the question. "Why does anybody steal anything?"

"Money, usually. Either that, or they want the thing itself."

He nodded. "Does he need money?"

"According to his sister, yes. She said something about expensive habits."

Jamie made a gesture that said: Well, there you have it.

"So what do I do?"

Jamie made another gesture. This time it said: Don't ask me. Then he expanded on the theme. "I really can't suggest anything, Isabel. And, frankly, I don't see what you can possibly do. If the insurance company wants the painting back, then they're going to have to pay. It may stick in their throats, but I can't see what else they can do."

"Unless . . ." interjected Isabel.

"Unless what?"

"Unless the person who stole it were to have it made known to him that we know who he is. We might then give him a chance to return it, failing which . . ."

"Yes? Failing which?"

"Failing which, the police are informed."

"On the basis of what evidence? Your hunch?"

He was right. They knew nothing more than they had known a few days ago.

"I think I should see him again," said Isabel. She was speaking half to herself, half to Jamie.

"Who?" he asked.

"Patrick."

Jamie frowned. "And confront him with your suspicions?"

"I shall be more subtle than that," said Isabel.

Jamie looked away. "I doubt if you'll achieve anything," he said.

She suspected that he was right, but she felt that she could still try.

"You know something?" she said. "I sometimes feel that lies are tangible. When they're being told, they seem to hang in the air, almost so that you can touch them. It's very strange."

Jamie looked bemused. "I think it depends on the liar," he said. "A good liar doesn't create that impression; a bad one does."

She knew what he meant. Her metaphor was probably based on no more than a reading of body language — those small clues that people give to what is in their mind. And guilt was a powerful creator of such tell-tale signs: the flushed expression, the avoidance of eye contact, the shifting of limbs: all these revealed inner discomfort springing from simple guilt. A liar could show these signs just as surely as he could show any of those physical signs that triggered a response on a polygraph: the heart rate, respiration, the reactions of the skin. But what if the liar is psychopathic and feels none of that? What if he feels not in the slightest bit guilty? What if he is proud of his lie? Patrick might feel that if he had acted out of a sense of entitlement, or because he believed that he was redistributing what he saw as his father's ill-gotten wealth. The children of the rich can feel strongly about that, Isabel knew; there is no fervour like the fervour of those who have been raised in the bosom of those they despise.

"I'd like to try," she said. "I'll see him and say things that might provoke a reaction — one way or the other."

Jamie was curious. "What things?"

She could not answer because she did not know what she was going to say. Sensing her uncertainty, Jamie laughed. "You're the most unlikely Sherlock Holmes," he said. "But very kissable."

"Don't condescend," she said. "Don't speak down to me."

"But I don't," he protested. "Everything I say to you is said from down here to up there. You're up there. I promise. I promise."

"Let's have another glass of wine," she said.

He reached for the bottle. "A bad day can always end well."

"Yes."

He passed her glass. She took it and smiled at him. She had everything. A few years ago, a day that had brought two men to tears and then had ended with her crying, too, would have been irredeemable. Now it could be salvaged. Completely.

They went through to the music room and he played the piano while she sat on the stool beside him. She put her hand on his knee. He played at random, as he could do for hours, moving from one melody to another. She thought she recognised something from Verdi. "*La traviata?*" He nodded. And then a complete change; a shift of mood and style as he suddenly started to sing "Shoals of Herring", all about a young man on a fishing boat pursuing the herring. Isabel closed her eyes. She imagined Jamie as that young man. Or Charlie, when he was older. Her little boy — a fisherman, battling the North Sea. She thought: I love all these men. I love the men who went to sea and led that hard life. I love them. But how strange to think and say that.

CHAPTER
FOURTEEN

"You want my brother's number?" said Alex Munrowe.

At the other end of the telephone, Isabel detected a note of satisfaction in Alex's voice.

"If you don't mind. I didn't want to disturb your father."

"I don't mind at all," said Alex quickly. "May I ask . . . no, perhaps I shouldn't."

There was an expectant silence. Isabel felt she had to explain. "I feel I should discuss the matter with him. That's why."

Now satisfaction was replaced with concern. "You won't mention the conversation we had the other day, will you?"

Isabel thought: perhaps you shouldn't accuse your brother of theft quite so readily if you don't want it to get back to him. But she did not say that; instead she reassured Alex that she would not dream of mentioning it. "I regard what you said to me as confidential. I promise you that."

"Good. Maybe I shouldn't have been so explicit; it's just that the thought crossed my mind that if there was anybody who could think of doing something like this, it's him."

224

"You don't have a very high opinion of your brother, if you don't mind my saying."

Alex laughed. "He has his good points. And he is my brother, after all. I've never forgotten that. And I'm not sure that he would actually stoop to theft. Yet . . ."

It seemed to Isabel that Alex was blowing hot and cold. If she suspected him of the theft, then she should state her grounds for doing so.

Isabel changed tack. "May I ask you something? If your father discovered that Patrick was behind this, what would the effect be?"

"What do you think?" expostulated Alex. "He'd be devastated. He worships my brother."

Isabel kept her voice level. "Really?"

"Yes. Pop thinks he's marvellous — he always has."

Isabel noticed the use of "Pop". It was natural that siblings would each use the same name for their father, but it meant that if anything were going to be read into its use by the thieves, then this would throw suspicion on both Alex and Patrick — not just on Patrick. But what puzzled Isabel now was the suggestion that relations between Patrick and his father were good; that was the direct opposite of what Duncan had said to her. This raised the possibility that Alex simply did not know what her father's real feelings were, which could be the case, she decided; children thought they knew what their parents felt, but they could be wrong about that — sometimes dramatically so.

She brought the conversation to an end even though she felt that Alex would have liked to prolong it. There was something irritating about her manner, thought

Isabel; it was as if she enjoyed being mischievous. She may have disliked her brother but to suggest, as she had, that he was behind the theft carried with it a feeling of sourness. Disloyalty was like that, Isabel thought: it left a sour taste in the mouth.

By the time she rang off, Isabel had reached a decision. The allegations against Patrick were meretricious and highly unlikely. She would see him, though, because she felt that she had to do something to justify her involvement in this matter. She would talk to him simply to confirm her view that Alex was an idle troublemaker pursuing some sort of petty squabble with her brother — a squabble that probably had its roots in the jealousies of childhood. Somebody had enjoyed more parental attention than somebody else; somebody had been able to run faster or been better at playing the piano; somebody had won more prizes at school . . . there were so many reasons why one sibling might resent another and carry the resentment well into adult life.

She lost no time in dialling the number that Alex had given her. It was a mobile number and when it was answered Isabel could hear the sound of voices in the background. Patrick was in the office, possibly in a meeting.

"Yes," he said, his voice lowered. "I'm with people. Who is it?"

"Isabel Dalhousie. Sorry to bother you. Could I call back?"

There was a brief silence. The voices in the background seemed to fade. Had a door been closed?

"No, it's fine. You can speak now."

"I wondered if we could meet soon. Not for a long meeting. Half an hour maybe."

She heard him breathing. "Yes. If you need to. How soon do you want to meet? Today?"

She had not expected that, and had to think quickly of her schedule for the day. Without Grace, Charlie became more of an issue. Jamie was in, though, and had not said anything about going out.

"If you could manage today," she said, "that would suit me perfectly well."

"Lunchtime?"

That was two hours away.

"That would be fine," she said. "You suggest a place."

He explained that his office was in the financial quarter just behind Lothian Road. There was a restaurant in the Lyceum Theatre, not far away — did she know the place? She did, and they agreed to meet there at one.

"What do you want to talk about?" asked Patrick.

Isabel thought quickly. "Your father. How he's coping with all this."

Patrick made a noncommittal sound. "He's tougher than you think."

"Well," said Isabel. "We can talk about that too. Sometimes it's hard for men to be tough."

She thought this was true: yesterday she had seen two men cry, and for every two men in this world who wept, she suspected, there were twenty who wanted to but couldn't.

★   ★   ★

She ordered a plate of tagliatelle with chopped smoked salmon and a sauce that was creamy, but not too thick. All that one needed, she felt, was a hint of cream. *A hint of cream* . . . it could be the title of a song, something that Jamie could sing perhaps. It would be about how life should be kept simple, but the addition of small treats, small self-indulgences, could make all the difference.

Patrick ordered a salad, and when it came she noticed that he separated out the various ingredients, pushing them to different corners of his plate. Tomatoes went in one place, lettuce leaves in another, spring onions elsewhere. She was fascinated; she had never seen anybody do that before, and she wondered what it said about him. Was he obsessive-compulsive — one of those people who make sure that everything is neatly arranged; who line the cutlery up in scrupulous parallels, who fold the towels in the bathroom into perfect squares?

He saw her watching. "Sorry," he said. "I've always done this."

She looked away guiltily.

"You see," he went on, "I worry that if I don't, then something will go wrong."

"That sounds like a superstition," she said. "I take it you won't walk under ladders?"

He smiled. "Who does?"

Isabel thought: I don't.

"There's nothing wrong with a bit of superstitious behaviour now and then," she said. "In fact . . ."

He looked at her expectantly, his fork poised above a slice of tomato. "Yes?"

"In fact, I've read somewhere that research . . ."

He laughed. "You aren't going to tell me that superstitions actually *work?*"

She remembered her conversations with Jamie about childhood superstitions, about ambulances and touching your collar and your toes. "No," she said. "Not all of them. But some superstitious behaviour, apparently, can have positive results. If you believe that doing something will bring you good luck, then you may do better if you do the thing in question."

"Carry a rabbit's foot?"

"Yes. Or you might wear one of those odd-looking charms that they wear in southern Italy — those things that look like peppers. You know the ones?"

He did. "Swarthy types wear them round their necks on gold chains."

She nodded, picturing hairy chests and open-necked shirts and the charms against the evil eye. "If you have your lucky rabbit's foot in your pocket when you write an exam, then you probably feel calmer. If you feel calmer, then you do better in the exam. *Post hoc, propter hoc.*"

He speared the tomato with his fork and began to eat his salad. "Latin," he mumbled.

Isabel apologised. "I'm sorry," she said. "I didn't mean to sound pretentious. *Afterwards and therefore caused by* . . . it doesn't sound quite as effective in English."

"I had a lot of Latin at school," Patrick said. "I never want to read or hear it again. It represents everything I hated about that school. Everything. Latin allows you to obfuscate. It allows you to dress up a system that puts people down."

"Does it? I thought it could have a certain beauty."

He shrugged. "*Quot homines, tot sententiae.*"

She laughed at this. *There are as many opinions as there are people.* "You brought yourself to utter it."

He saw the humour in the situation. "My Latin teacher liked boys."

"Did he?"

He held her gaze. "Yes."

"I'm sorry." She was not sure what to say. Was this the issue?

"However, he behaved scrupulously correctly. He never touched us."

"Then he was a good man," said Isabel. "He must have resisted a lot of temptation."

Patrick seemed to relax. "You know, I think you and I might be on the same wavelength. People are so quick to condemn. They don't think much of the private battles that others have."

"But I do think of that sort of thing," said Isabel quickly. "I think of it all the time."

He looked at her intensely. "Really?"

"Yes." She paused. "Since this conversation is becoming quite frank, I might as well tell you that I do have an inkling of some of your own battles."

There was nothing in his expression to warn her off, and so she continued. "I don't like to intrude, but I

230

suspect that you have considerable difficulty in being who you are — in the sense of where you come from — and who you are in the sense of what you think."

He smiled. "Maybe."

"Yes. You come from a certain sector of society — a privileged one, if I may describe it as such — and yet you don't identify with all that. In fact, you identify with the opposite. So you reject inherited wealth but at the same time you know you've benefited from it. And your father . . ."

She saw him stiffen slightly, but the moment quickly passed.

"Your father is everything you don't want to be. And yet you're fond of him." She hesitated, but only a second or two. "You want him to love you, but you think he doesn't."

She stopped. Patrick was looking down at the tablecloth; his salad was barely touched. He spoke suddenly. "Pop doesn't like me. That's the problem."

She reached out across the table and touched his arm gently. "I don't think that can be true."

"It is. He doesn't like me because I'm gay. Did you know that? He can't bring himself to accept it."

"Perhaps he needs time."

"He's had a long time. Since I was sixteen and told him."

"He may need longer."

"He hasn't got longer."

She wondered what he meant.

"His heart," he said, pointing to his chest. "He has a condition. He may be all right, but he could drop dead any moment." He paused. "Put it this way: he wouldn't get life insurance."

"I see."

She wanted time to think of the implications of this. If Duncan was unlikely to survive very long, then the issue of the fate of the painting became rather more pressing. So, if somebody wanted to stop the Poussin going to the nation, then he might think it necessary to act sooner rather than later. Her pasta was beginning to get cold. "I should tackle my lunch," she said, twisting a couple of strands of tagliatelle round her fork.

"Of course." He was watching her. He seemed on the point of saying something, faltered, and then spoke. "Why do you suspect me?"

The tagliatelle, made slippery by the sauce, unwound and fell off Isabel's fork. She thought: sensitive conversations and difficult-to-manage food do not go together.

He was staring at her now with a look that seemed to combine challenge and reproach. "I don't know why you think that," she muttered. I'm being disingenuous, she realised; I know why he should think this. This self-reproach shamed her, and, after a brief hesitation, she continued: "Yes, I did think that. I considered the possibility, that is . . . And now, I'm not sure . . ." She trailed off.

She found herself thinking about his political position. If that were as it seemed to be, then he would have no interest in preventing the Poussin from going to the nation — in fact, that was exactly what he would want. Unless that same political position could prompt him to relieve an insurance company of whatever sum might be payable as a reward . . . The doubt resurfaced.

"Well, I can tell you something," he said. "It's not very nice being suspected of stealing from your own father."

"No," she said. "It can't be. And look, I'm sorry: all I said was that I had considered the possibility. That's all. I'm not accusing you of anything."

He sat back in his chair. "My life's a bit of a mess," he said. "I accept that."

She asked him why.

"Emotionally," he said. "I've had bad luck with a relationship. I love somebody, you see, who can't love me back. It can't work."

"I'm sorry about that."

"Thank you. I've loved him for a long time. Fourteen years, in fact, which is almost half my life. Since I was fourteen."

She was silent.

"I've tried to do something about it. I've tried to forget. But I keep thinking of him and all I want is to be with him. That's all. That's it."

She felt a pang of sympathy. She had loved John Liamor and for a few years after that had come to an end she had felt the same way. But she had recovered, as most people in that position do after a while. Time does its work; a scab builds up over the emotional wound and protects it. Only if you scratch does it bleed again. Was he scratching at it? she wondered.

"Do you mind?" he asked.

"Mind? Mind about what?"

"Mind about my speaking of this."

She was quick to reassure him. "Of course not."

He closed his eyes briefly, as if to deal with some pain within him. "I was sent to boarding school. That's what they did — still do — that class. It was thought to be the only education worth having."

"I know," said Isabel. "It's hard to believe that now."

"I went to a place up north. It takes girls too now, but in those days it was just boys. It was, I suppose, quite good academically, but it had this big thing about rugby too. We all had to play. I hated it."

"It's not for everyone," said Isabel. "We had to play lacrosse, which is equally not for everyone."

He smiled. "Those places . . ."

". . . are behind us," said Isabel. She had been happy enough at school, and she felt vaguely disloyal now to be suggesting otherwise. "I wasn't really unhappy," she corrected. "I suppose I resented the restrictions on freedom, but what teenager doesn't?"

Patrick was silent for a moment. Then he continued. "I don't know why I should be telling you this. I don't normally talk about it."

She encouraged him. "If you don't normally talk about it, then perhaps it's something that wants to be talked about."

He looked away. "Yes. This person I fell in love with. He knew. I never told him — never dared — but he knew. And he was very kind. He didn't tell me to get lost or anything, he just gave me his friendship. That was all. He couldn't reciprocate what I felt, but he said to me that I was his best friend. He said that when we

234

were fourteen and I thought about it and thought about it. Not a day went past, not a day, but that I remembered what he said."

He paused. "Do you mind if I go on?"

She shook her head.

"You see, I don't know if other people get this. People don't necessarily empathise. I feel that you do, though. You seem the type to understand, if I may say so. I suppose that's why Alex persuaded my father that you would be the person to help him."

The remark might have passed unnoticed. Isabel's thoughts had begun to drift; she had been thinking about the other boy, trying to envisage him. She saw two boys on a cross-country run, against a backdrop of the Scottish hills, their hair soaked by the rain, shins streaked with mud; and she saw, for some odd reason, a deer that was watching them from the edge of a forest. The deer had a look of frightened interest, the look that would precede its bounding off into the covering darkness of the trees; and one of the boys had a heart that ached, and the other was looking up at the sky, at the veils of gentle rain, like thin muslin curtains across the landscape, and . . .

She gave a start. "Sorry. You said . . ." She collected her thoughts. The deer had bounded off, the boys were gone. "You said that your sister persuaded your father that he should speak to me. Did you say that?"

He was surprised by her interest. "Yes."

"How did you know that?"

He shrugged. "Martha told me. I saw her a couple of days ago. Or rather, she saw me and came and buttonholed me about the Cockburn Association — she's a big supporter and she knows that I approve of them."

"Martha told you," Isabel half muttered.

"Yes. She said that Alex was very keen to get you involved. She was the one who pushed for it once she mentioned your name."

"Who mentioned my name?" asked Isabel.

Patrick looked at his watch. "Martha did," he said. "But look, I have to get back to work. We've got a meeting. Some company's coming to make a presentation to us."

"Wanting money?"

He nodded, and signalled to the waitress for the bill. "Everyone wants money."

Everyone wants money, thought Isabel. Yes.

She suddenly felt emboldened to ask him, "Why do you work with money if you have such a low opinion of the financial world?"

He was clearly surprised by her question, but not offended; he smiled before he answered, "I needed a job. Simple."

"Not because you wanted a job that paid well?"

He shook his head. "I live pretty simply. And the job involves investment in products that make people better. Should that be a problem?" He looked at her, as if working something out. "My sister said something, didn't she?"

Isabel had carefully avoided passing on Alex's comment, but Patrick had divined what lay behind her question. He did not wait for her to confirm or deny it. "She accuses me of being venal, but you know

236

something: when people accuse others of something, it's because they see themselves as being guilty of that precise thing. Yes?"

Isabel agreed. She had often observed as much.

"She's the one who's interested in money," Patrick said. "Her fiancé — I don't know whether you've met him, but he's had two marriages already and three children. He was cleaned out financially — completely cleaned out, and the kids are at fee-paying schools so that's thirty thousand all told a year, out of taxed income. He must be pretty hard up, and Alex earns nothing, or more or less nothing. I suspect she secretly can't wait for my father to go. She'll want to get her hands on anything that's not actually nailed down."

Isabel listened carefully. If she had been looking for a motive for Alex to be behind the theft, then she could not have hoped for a clearer statement of it.

The bill had been brought to the table and Patrick was extracting his wallet.

"Please let me pay," said Isabel.

He put his wallet back. "That's kind of you," he said. "Thank you."

She had one last question, and she put it playfully, as if she were not quite serious about it. "She wouldn't be behind it, would she?"

He frowned. "Why do you say that?"

"Because you've just described to me how she needs money. She might also be unwilling for the Poussin to go to the National Gallery. After all, that's a loss to your father's estate of several million pounds." She watched for the effect of her words.

He shook his head vehemently. "Definitely not. No. She wouldn't. I know her, and she wouldn't."

"Or her fiancé?"

He was equally adamant. "No. Not him. Definitely."

He stood up. "Thank you for what you've been doing for my father," he said. "He and I may not be close, but I love him, you know."

She shook hands, keeping his hand for slightly longer than one would normally do with a handshake.

"I suspect he loves you too."

He looked at her wryly; disbelievingly.

"And there's another thing," she said, lowering her voice. "You told me about your feelings for the person you loved. You told me about your efforts to forget. I had exactly the same problem, you know. I was married to somebody who didn't love me or, if he did, had an odd way of showing it. I got over him eventually, but it took a long, long time. I didn't forget him, though. That's not the way to do it —"

She had not finished, but Patrick was already beginning to move away. He does not want my advice, thought Isabel, because he's not ready to stop loving. Love was a bit like alcohol in that way: the alcoholic would not listen to advice until he was ready to stop drinking. Love was a little bit like that; not always, but it could be.

CHAPTER
FIFTEEN

They lay in bed late the next morning, Charlie sleeping between them. He had awakened early and Jamie had played with him for half an hour or so before bringing him into bed with them. The early start had caught up with the child, and now he had dropped off again, clutching a teddy bear and the already threadbare blanket he liked to drag around with him.

"Look at his eyelids," said Isabel, her voice lowered. "He's dreaming."

Jamie propped himself up on an elbow and gazed at Charlie. "How strange that we made him," he said. "This infinitely complex collection of cells is our son. We made him."

Isabel smiled. "Or facilitated him. The spark comes from somewhere else."

Jamie looked into her eyes. "And becomes Mozart."

"In Mozart's case, it did," said Isabel. She frowned. "We haven't sorted out the mathematics problem."

Jamie shook his head. "I went to see her again, but let's not talk about it just now. She's hard to read. Tell me about yesterday."

He had been back late from a concert in Glasgow and Isabel had already been asleep when he had come into the bedroom shortly before midnight. They had seen one another briefly in the afternoon, when Charlie had been handed over.

She sighed. "I had lunch with Patrick."

Jamie looked blank. "Patrick?"

"Duncan Munrowe's son."

"Oh yes." He remembered now. He stroked Charlie's hand gently. The small fingers moved, gripped the teddy.

Isabel told him about the meeting. "He's certainly not behind it," she concluded. "I don't think he has any reason to be."

"Whereas his sister has?" said Jamie.

Isabel nodded. "Yes, every financial reason. Her fiancé has two expensive divorces behind him. She doesn't work."

"Being hard up doesn't make you a criminal," Jamie pointed out.

"Of course not."

"And you said that Patrick was adamant that it couldn't be her. He must know his own sister."

Isabel thought about this. "Unless he was protecting her." It was an idea to be dismissed as soon as it was raised. "Which I think is unlikely."

She waited for him to say something, but he was silent. Charlie shifted his limbs slightly, but was still fast asleep. Jamie looked at the boy, then at Isabel, and smiled.

"However," Isabel said. "However . . ."

Jamie looked at her expectantly.

240

"However, he said something else which struck me as being very significant."

He raised an eyebrow.

"He said that Martha suggested me in passing but that it was Alex who really pushed for me to be involved. She was the one."

Jamie shrugged. "I don't see what difference it makes," he said. "You. Martha. Duncan. What's the difference?"

Isabel lay back on her pillow and stared at the ceiling. "I think it all adds up. Alex wanted to have suspicion focused on her brother in order to deflect any suspicion that might otherwise be attached to her. So what does she do? She gets somebody else involved — somebody into whose ear she can pour poison."

Charlie stirred now, his eyes opening. He half turned towards Isabel, before turning to Jamie and reaching for his hand. Jamie said: "Look, he's taken my hand." But Isabel's mind was elsewhere. It could be that Patrick had asked Martha to invite her to intervene. Then, to throw suspicion on his sister, he would say that she had recommended Isabel's involvement. And as for his firm rejection of the possibility that Alex was behind the theft, that again could be a deliberate deception. He might think that Isabel thought that he was deliberately covering for his sister, thus increasing the level of suspicion under which Alex laboured.

Or neither of them was involved. Both could be completely innocent. Isabel remembered her university logic classes all those years ago. She had been taught to deal with possibilities in a rational, ordered way. Formal logic dictated that you moved from what you knew to what implications may flow from your knowledge. It required one to weigh evidence and reach conclusions on the basis of those implications. Applied here, the principles of formal logic led to the conclusion that in the absence of any further evidence, responsibility for the theft of the painting could be attributed to neither Alex nor Patrick.

Isabel closed her eyes.

"I'm getting up," said Jamie. "I'm going to give breakfast to this wee man."

"Lots of breakfast," said Charlie. "Lots of egg. Lots of egg. Egg and Marmite toast."

"Egg and Marmite toast," agreed Jamie. "A very good choice." Marmite, that salty yeast paste so adored by Britons and so vigorously disliked by Americans, was not the first choice of the average child, but was craved by Charlie, just as he relished olives and, more recently, garlic.

They left the room and Isabel lay alone in the bed. She stretched out her left leg, lazily, and felt the warmth of the sheet where Jamie had been lying: his heat shadow, as she thought of it; like the heat shadows of those unfortunate residents of Pompeii who were consumed by the lava but who left the outline of their forms on the stone. She had lived with him now for a sufficiently long time to forget, or at least find it hard to remember, what it was like before him, before this young man had moved into her life and into her home, possessing both; so that she dreamed of him and felt his presence about her, a cloak of comfort. And when he

242

was not there, when he was in Glasgow rehearsing or, as occasionally happened, he went abroad for some concert — he had been the previous month to Amsterdam, to play at a music festival — she felt his absence keenly. She always knew where he was, she realised; which made her think of how important it was for us to know what others are doing. When we met friends, for instance, and asked them what they had been doing, we really did want to know. But why? It was, she thought, because of our sense of *being* with others; our need to anchor ourselves in a network of friends and acquaintances. This was our bulwark, our dyke against the sea of loneliness that we were only too aware washed about us.

She got out of bed, showered, and then dressed for the day. She was under the shower for longer than she had intended — it was not good for the skin, she believed, but it was certainly good for thinking, just as walking was. And under the shower that morning it occurred to her that there was a further motive for the theft that she had yet to consider. She had assumed all along that what the thieves really wanted was money — the reward from the insurance company. But what if the real object were the Poussin? What if the person who stole the painting had no intention of collecting the reward but actually wanted the painting for itself? If that were true, then the negotiations for the reward could be just a smokescreen — to make it look like a financially motivated theft.

At first she dismissed the idea. People did not steal well-known paintings in order to hang them on their walls — it was far too risky. Nor, she imagined, were many paintings stolen by apocryphal South American collectors who could display them with impunity in their remote Amazonian villas.

The idea seemed unlikely, and yet, as Isabel thought about it under the stinging water of the shower, she remembered that Alex had said, "I loved that painting . . . I adored it." Was it not possible to love something so much that you would do anything to get it — even if it meant that the pleasure derived from possessing it would be a solitary one? If Alex adored the painting, and felt possessive of it, then she was likely to be strongly opposed to its being given to the National Gallery after her father's death; in which case, the solution was obvious — the painting could simply be removed from Munrowe House and hidden in the flat in Edinburgh until Duncan's death. Alex would hardly be able to hang it on a wall where it might be seen by visitors, but she would at least have it in her possession, which might well be enough for her. It would be important, though, to mask the whole exercise as a theft. That would require elaborate subterfuge — and accomplices too: the solicitor and the men in the van, who might also have been the ones who removed the painting in the first instance. It was possible; yes, it was possible. However, the problem was that for those who live in the normal world — a world in which people did not steal beautiful objects from family members purely for the aesthetic pleasure they might bestow, did not defraud them in that way — such actions seemed vaguely improbable.

244

She stepped out of the shower and wrapped herself in a towel. Jamie had come back upstairs and he now walked into the bedroom. He hesitated at the bathroom door; they still respected each other's privacy in spite of their common life.

"I've finished," she said. "I stood in the shower for ages — thinking."

He raised an eyebrow. "About?"

"About the Poussin."

He nodded. "Well, here's something else for you to think about."

She slipped past him. The bedroom carpet was soft underfoot; her hair was wet upon her shoulders. It was summer, but only a Scottish summer, and goosebumps could still make themselves felt. She turned to face him. He was smiling.

"What am I to think about?"

He spread out the palms of his hands, as an illusionist might do. "Grace — she's back." He seemed pleased with the look of surprise — and gratitude — on Isabel's face.

"Oh."

He came towards her and kissed her lightly on the cheek. She shivered — from the cold, from the contact.

"Apparently everything is normal. She said nothing about having resigned, and she's already cleared the dishwasher. She said something about ironing my shirts."

Isabel smiled. "I'm glad." She looked at Jamie enquiringly. "What shall I say to her? Sorry?"

He shook his head. "You have nothing to apologise for. Just say nothing. It's always better, I think, to say nothing. If things sort themselves out — as they have done here — then why say anything?"

She was not sure he was right that saying nothing was always preferable. Not always: there were occasions when it was clearly unwise to remain silent — when there were misunderstandings, for instance, or suspicions; where a few words could explain something or defuse ill-feeling. There were occasions, too, when those few words might be words of apology — short, potent words that could erase whole landscapes of resentment, undermine entire edifices of anger or hatred. But perhaps he was right; although Isabel would have preferred to resolve her disagreement with Grace by talking things through, Grace had her own way of coping with disagreements, which involved pretending that they had never occurred. And if that worked for her, then Isabel was prepared to let it be.

"All right," she said. "I'll act normally. I'll pretend she didn't resign."

"Good," he said. He reached out to touch her, laying his hand gently on her forearm. His skin was warm against hers, which was chilled by the evaporation of the wet from the shower. She wanted to hold him; she wanted to take him in her arms, but the towel was precarious and there was always an awkwardness between the clothed and unclothed body. So she simply looked at him, and saw the colour of his eyes, and the light within them, and the shape of his brow.

"I'll tell her again how much we appreciate what she does," said Isabel. "We do, don't we?"

"Of course. And I think she knows that."

While Isabel dressed, Jamie went back downstairs and when she made her way into the kitchen he could be heard in the music room beginning a session of practice: scales, arpeggios, the technical limbering-up that even the most experienced professional musician must undertake; musical press-ups, Isabel called it.

She entered the kitchen unannounced. Grace was seated at the table, a piece of paper in front of her, and Charlie was perched on her lap.

"Four," said Charlie. "No, six. Six, Grace! Six!"

"Six," said Grace. "Yes, six." And then she turned round and saw Isabel, and she immediately lifted Charlie off her lap and stood up. Isabel did not see what happened to the piece of paper; it was there and then it was not there, vanishing so quickly that she might have doubted that she had seen it in the first place.

She felt her heart race. Mathematics! Grace had been teaching Charlie mathematics. It was blatant and it dismayed Isabel because she did not relish conflict and she did not want to have to speak to Grace again, not so soon after the row that had led to her resignation. Grace was quite capable of resigning again, and Isabel could not face that. So she turned away and simply said good morning to Grace as if nothing had happened; as if there had been no resignation, no mathematics.

She walked to the window and looked out. There was no reason to look out of that particular window, which had no view to speak of. She was not looking out of it to see what the weather was like, nor was she looking out of it to see whether Brother Fox might be lurking in the rhododendrons which could be seen — just — if one craned one's neck slightly to get a sight of what was happening alongside the house. She realised that she was looking out of the window because she did not have the courage to look in the direction in which she should have been looking. *Blind eye,* she thought. *Turn a blind eye.*

And that thought changed everything. To turn a blind eye was morally reprehensible; it was an affront to the whole concept of seeing — and it was the beginning, in so many cases, of significant failure. No, she would not turn a blind eye. She would not allow herself to be a moral coward.

She turned, her heart hammering within her. "I'm sorry, Grace," she began. "The last thing I want is for you to be upset. But please see it from my point of view. With this mathematics . . ." She paused. The solution had come to her. "Look, I think that it will be fine for Charlie to develop his mathematics. But why don't we wait? How about waiting a couple of years and then, when he's six or so, we can look at it again. Both of us. We can go and talk to somebody about it and do the thing together. I'll read that book of yours then and we might even be able to work from it. How about that?" She paused again. Grace was looking down at the floor. "Are you listening to what I'm saying?" asked Isabel.

Charlie answered. "Charlie listening," he said solemnly.

Isabel bit her lip. She wanted to laugh. *Charlie listening*. Perhaps she might say that in the middle of some discussion with Jamie: *Isabel listening*. It would be so comic, so disconcerting. It would derail anybody.

She could not suppress her amusement, even in this grave moment of challenge. She smiled. And Grace did too.

"Mummy is shouting at Grace," said Grace to Charlie.

"I wasn't exactly shouting," said Isabel.

"Well, I heard you well enough," muttered Grace. "And that sounds fine by me. Now I've got to go upstairs and start the washing."

Isabel felt the tension flood out of her. Her heart returned to its normal beat.

"I really do understand why you wanted to do it," said Isabel. "And we appreciate that — both Jamie and I. We both appreciate it."

Grace acknowledged the thanks. "That's fine," she said. "It's probably a good idea to wait anyway. He'll be even better then."

She stood up, straightening her skirt. Isabel noticed that it looked creased and rather worn in the front, although Grace normally looked smart and attended to that sort of thing. She felt a pang. She paid Grace generously — she always had, as had her father before her — but by the very nature of things she had so much more than the woman who worked for her, and she did not want there to be any sense of a victory having been won.

"Another thing, Grace," she said. "I'm sorry if you've been upset."

"Doesn't matter," said Grace. And then, in a quieter voice, "My fault."

"Not Grace's fault," said Charlie suddenly. He had picked up the tension in the room and he now slipped his hand into Grace's and squeezed it.

"Look," said Isabel. "He loves you."

Grace looked down. She hesitated, and then bent down and kissed Charlie on his brow. She stood up. "Washing," she said, and moved towards the door. Then she added, "One of Jamie's shirts is missing two buttons. Two! I'll replace them this morning."

"Thank you," said Isabel, adding: "Men!"

It was a curious, inconsequential thing to say. Men lost the buttons on their shirts, as did women, but there was no evidence, not one scrap, to show that men lost more buttons than women did. However, Isabel suspected that they did, and this comment, this single word, made her belief quite clear.

"I agree," said Grace. She sighed. "Men."

After that dramatic start, the rest of the morning went smoothly. With the return of Grace and the resolution of the mathematics question — *quod erat demonstrandum*, Isabel could not stop herself from thinking — she was able to concentrate on her work. The *Review* imposed many deadlines, not just those that loomed when it was due to go to press. There were deadlines for the receipt of papers; there were deadlines for the obtaining of reports on articles submitted for peer review; there

250

were minor, self-imposed deadlines for Isabel to answer letters and emails. Those two categories differed, of course. Electronic mail, that pervasive, intrusive means of communication that could penetrate, like the most sophisticated of missiles, the thickest bunkers of privacy, had to be answered within three working days; letters could be left one week before an answer was sent. Or so Isabel had decided, knowing that these periods were arbitrary and, in the case of electronic mail, quite out of kilter with expectations. Many people, she understood, expected emails to be answered within hours, if not minutes, and judged others accordingly. One would-be author of a paper on environmental ethics had actually complained to Isabel one afternoon that she had not answered his email of that morning. *I contacted you some time ago,* he wrote at four o'clock, *and I was wondering whether your reply has been lost. I've looked in my spam folder, but I don't see it.* His original message had arrived at ten that morning, which meant that he considered six hours to be more than enough time for a reply to be formulated, typed and sent.

Isabel had drafted a reply. *Dear Professor Grant, Your message was received this morning. I have read it but have not yet had time to reply. I'm so sorry to test your patience in this way. I know that six hours can seem a very long time, but please be assured that I shall reply to you when I have had time to think a little bit about what you said in your message and to give your remarks the weight they undoubtedly deserve. Yours sincerely, Isabel Dalhousie (Editor).*

She had not sent this message because she had felt, quite rightly, that it was cutting. It was easy to cut; too easy sometimes, and so she had sent back a simple message: *I received your email. I'll get back to you as soon as possible. I. D.* Doing the right thing, she knew, was often not as enjoyable as doing the wrong thing. The wrong thing often made for a better story, but it was still the wrong thing — nothing could change that.

The deadline that morning had nothing to do with letters or emails, nor with anxious printers waiting to press the buttons that would set their presses rolling. Rather, it had to do with the gathering-in of reports on several papers on which an editorial decision had to be taken. Isabel took this process very seriously, being only too aware of the anxious state of those awaiting her response: researchers, post-doctoral fellows, junior lecturers in neglected and unfashionable universities and colleges in obscure places; the unrewarded infantry of the academic profession, who needed publication in order to hang on to their poorly rewarded jobs. And behind these people there were wives and husbands, partners, boyfriends, girlfriends, who were waiting at home and who might ask at the end of the day: "Have you heard from her yet?" The *her* was Isabel. That weighed heavily.

Already she had one letter of rejection to write, and would have to do it that morning. She had received three reports on a paper submitted for a special issue of the *Review* that would be concentrating on the ethical issues surrounding adoption. These issues were manifold and more complex than one might imagine.

There was the right to know parentage, widely accepted now and the subject of a very good paper from someone at Lenoir Rhyne University in Hickory, North Carolina. They would publish that, and she would write a response to this effect later that morning. That was easy.

Then there was a paper on surrogacy and the finality of the mother's consent. Should a surrogate mother be allowed to change her mind after the birth of the "commissioned" child? Could she refuse to hand over the child fathered by one of the prospective parents? Isabel imagined the scene and had made her mind up on that. Of course she could: you could never snatch a child from its natural mother, no matter what pieces of paper had been signed while the child was in utero. No, you could never do that. But, asked the author of the paper, what of the rights of the father, or indeed of the child? Teleologically speaking . . . Isabel sighed. No, one could not obscure the issue by bringing in teleology. Mothers were mothers, and being a mother meant that you had a right against all the world in respect of the baby that had been part of you, within you, for months. No amount of philosophising could change that fundamental, bedrock fact.

This paper was provocative and well-argued, and both reviewers had agreed that it should be published. So that presented no problems; but . . . Isabel picked up the file that she had been subconsciously avoiding since entering her study that morning. The topic was difficult, and one that had been the subject of some debate in the newspapers. That fact alone meant that it deserved a place in the *Review of Applied Ethics* which was, after all, heralded by its very title as being involved in the day-to-day world. "Should children be placed with families of a different ethnic group?" Isabel's initial reaction to the question had been one of puzzlement. Surely there was no reason why this should not be done: loving homes and families had nothing to do with ethnic groups. But then the complications, and the doubts, introduced themselves. What if there were two sets of prospective parents — each belonging to a different group — or, more likely, the choice was between remaining in a children's home or being adopted by parents from a different background? The solution, Isabel thought, would be to ignore ethnicity altogether and concentrate on the home life that the child might expect. Love was love, no matter in what social context it was offered. But not everybody felt that, it seemed, and there were those who argued that taking a child out of its community was to deprive it of a heritage; more than that, it could imply that one group was actually preferable to another.

The paper on this subject was well presented and the argument was cogent. It defended the implicit rejection in many parts of Canada of the adoption of native Canadian children into non-native families. The previous taking of native children out of their communities was a form of cultural genocide, the author argued, and was responsible for cutting off many children from their culture and roots. Isabel was aware of that shameful past and could see the argument against allowing its continuation, even in an attenuated,

254

less culturally arrogant form. She saw that, but the two reviewers did not, and one of these was Professor Lettuce.

Does the author of this paper really suggest, his report asked, *that it would be better for a child to stay in an institution for its entire childhood — as happens, I believe, only too often — rather than be given the chance of a life in a non-native home, with loving parents and all the benefits and chances that go with having loving parents? If he does, then I disagree most profoundly and would recommend strongly against the publication of a paper with such a heartless message at its core.*

The other reviewer had been less bombastic, but had still been against publication. *I'm not impressed with the author's conclusion that the appalling schemes of the past, where native children were snatched from their parents, have much bearing on modern, child-centred adoption regimes. Nobody is taking these children from their mothers or communities. They are taking them from children's homes. Should ideology stand in the way of a child's happiness?*

Isabel read and reread the reports. She found herself inclined to ignore Lettuce simply because he was Lettuce, and she disliked him intensely, and with good reason. Allowing her mind to wander, she thought of Lettuce as a small lettuce being transplanted from a bed of lettuces into a bed of cabbages, and not flourishing at all because the cabbages had thicker leaves and were more vigorous in their growth. She smiled. It was such a childish thought, but so vivid, and

255

so satisfying, and surely one could allow oneself the occasional reverie, the occasional dream of revenge.

She reread the paper itself, and after doing so went to make herself a cup of coffee in the kitchen. She returned with the cup and held the paper lightly in her hand, as if weighing it. Its tone was assertive and there was an air of grievance in it. That had clearly registered badly with the reviewers, but her job as editor was to be dispassionate and also to ensure that the pages of the journal were open to unpopular views. And if there was an air of grievance, it might be that grievance was understandable: injustices had really occurred, even if an effort was now being made to make up for them. Victimhood, however, should not last for ever; the Highland Clearances had been a great wrong to Scotland and to Gaelic culture, but she was not sure that the Scots should continue to regard themselves as victims, even if there were people whose purposes it suited.

She looked at the author's biographical details. He was affiliated to the University of Manitoba and was a graduate of the University of Toronto. There was no further clue to where he came from. He sounded as if he was writing from the perspective of a Canadian aboriginal, or a member of a First Nations group — the terminology, Isabel knew, was sensitive and she was never sure exactly what was considered appropriate and what was not. But he did not say he was a member of such a group. And, anyway, did it make a difference to his argument?

She imagined what the author would say if she rejected the paper. "There! Proves it! Bias. Prejudice. Silencing of the challenging view." No, she would not allow herself to think of that, because it was irrelevant to her decision, or should be. The real test was whether this was a defensible, well-expressed view — and it was both of those. And she was certainly not reaching that decision because she wanted to overrule Professor Lettuce. That would be very satisfactory, but it was a pleasure that should have no bearing on her editorial decision. What the paper presented was uncomfortable, perhaps, and the author's conclusions might seem harsh and unsympathetic, but it was representative of a viewpoint that had found considerable support in Canadian officialdom and could hardly be dismissed on the basis that it caused discomfort. *In*, she thought. *Publish*. Lettuce will be *green* with anger, but that is not why I'm doing it, she hurriedly told herself: the pleasure of flouting Lettuce's opinion was a collateral benefit, nothing more. No, she reminded herself; I must not think that. I must rise above *Schadenfreude* and such pettiness. I must do the right thing because it is the right thing, and for that reason alone. She got to her feet. The window of her study was half open, and she could pick up the scent of summer — the smell of vegetation, of humidity in the air, of a world of humming insects and mulch, of life.

She gazed out of the window. It was close to midday and was not a time when Brother Fox usually showed himself. Foxes liked the watches of the night, or the early hours of a summer morning when the human world was silent. But now he was there, poised halfway between a tunnel of old lavender bushes and the sheltering panoply of a late-flowering rhododendron. The rhododendron provided his heartland, the vulpine headquarters from which he planned his raids. Now he was briefly out in the open and seemed, for a few moments, to be enjoying the sun on his back. He lifted his head and sniffed, and then, quite suddenly, dropped to the ground and rolled over on to his back. Isabel gasped, thinking she had witnessed a death, but it was not that — it was a roll, a brief, hedonistic revelling in the sheer joy of being in the sun, of being warm, and of being alive. Within a few seconds he was back on his feet and had resumed his journey; the dappling shadows had him now; he was gone. She felt disappointed. She wanted him to stay; she wanted him to engage with her. But she knew that he would not. She was nothing to him, even if he understood, as she hoped he did, that she was not an adversary. We are often nothing to the things that fascinate us, or the things we love; she was well aware of that. Charlie, though, did not know that; the world loved him, he believed, because he loved it. Trains loved him, toy cars loved him, long-suffering stuffed toys loved him too, just as he loved them. It was an example of perfect mutuality that would end soon enough — when he discovered that the world did not centre upon him, that it was sometimes cruel, and that love given was not always reciprocated. When would that be? When he was six? Eight? Or did that realisation come much later, in adult life, perhaps, when the first big disappointments struck, when it first dawned upon us that we were not, as we secretly believed in our youth, as deserving of love and success as we had previously imagined? Charlie, dear Charlie, she whispered, may you be protected from that until the last possible moment, and even then may it seem a small cloud on your horizon, a tiny shadow on your landscape. May that be your fate, my darling, my darling boy.

CHAPTER
SIXTEEN

The idea occurred to Isabel later that day, shortly after she had collected Charlie from nursery school. It came as she was walking home — a short journey in her steps but an odyssey in Charlie's — an odyssey that was interrupted by stops to examine objects found or spotted: a piece of paper lying in the gutter, a twig from one of the trees whose boughs overhung the garden walls along the road, a feather from a seagull. The gulls, unwelcome guests in the neighbourhood, occasionally conducted aerial battles, mewing and screeching in outrage over some infringement of territory, some obscure gull slight. Charlie, who for some reason could not manage the word *seagull*, called them *seagirls*, and Isabel now did too, in the way in which we take from our children their special words, their mispronunciations, which strike us as such fitting, attractive neologisms.

"Seagirls cross," said Charlie, looking skywards.

Isabel, however, did not hear this comment, as the idea had dawned on her and it seemed to her that this was the obvious thing to do. It was an unlikely thing to do, of course, and it might not survive close examination, but she could try it. Why not?

"The seagirls . . ." Charlie repeated, looking at his mother for support.

"Yes," said Isabel. "The seagirls." But she did not expand. "Come on, Charlie. Let's hurry."

He tugged at her hand. "The seagirls . . ."

She picked him up. "Let's just go home, Charlie. The seagirls will be all right. I don't think they need us." She paused. "Chocolate pudding."

It never failed: the ultimate, fool-proof bribe. Even so, Charlie sought confirmation. "Chocolate pudding?" he asked.

"Yes," she said. "When we get back."

He was silent for the rest of the journey, thinking, perhaps, of the treat that lay ahead. And when Isabel arrived back at the house, she found that Grace was only too happy to take Charlie into the kitchen and prepare the treat for him. Grace indulged Charlie, and would have willingly provided chocolate pudding in vast quantities, had Isabel permitted it.

She went into her study and took three pieces of writing paper from the stationery drawer. Sitting down at her desk, she pushed aside the small pile of papers on which she had been working that morning — the papers on the ethics of adoption — and began the first of the letters. The wording, she had decided, would be identical: the only difference being the name in the salutation. She wrote first to Duncan: *Dear Duncan, I have found out what has happened. Obviously, I need to talk to you privately about this, as the last thing, I imagine, that you would want would be for it to become a public matter, with all that it would entail for the family. I assure you I shall be discreet. With kind regards, Isabel Dalhousie.*

She looked at the handwritten letter and reached for another sheet of notepaper. *Kind regards* was wrong. Not only did it sound slightly contrived, but she was not sure that regards could be kind: they could be warm regards, they could be best regards, but kindness, surely, was something that would be in the heart of the person sending the regards and it would be unduly self-congratulatory to impute kindness to oneself. Perhaps it would be better to write *With all best wishes*, but then she thought: does this letter really come with all best wishes? It did not. *Yours aye* was an appropriately Scottish ending to a letter, but it meant *Yours ever*, and it implied long and loyal sentiments. These were not there. *Yours* was best, then — the simple contraction of *Yours sincerely* or indeed of *Yours faithfully* or *Yours truly*. What had she been taught at school? Isabel remembered those lessons in that stuffy classroom where Miss . . . what was her name? . . . McLaren or Maclaurin had taught them the etiquette of correspondence. "Don't forget, girls," she had said, "you will be judged by your competence to write a letter. So remember the rules. Never, ever write *Yours sincerely* in a formal or business letter. We are not sincere in such letters, girls; we are, by contrast, faithful." At which Amanda . . . what *was* her name, the first girl in the class to report on experience with a boy? (*experience* being the term used darkly by the teachers to warn of the consequences of such things) — she, that Amanda, had sniggered and whispered, "Speak for

262

yourself!" Amanda . . . Amanda . . . Isabel looked up at the ceiling. Amanda Weir — that was her name. She was two divorces down the line now, Isabel had heard, both because she had gone off with somebody else, and that was presumably because faithfulness had meant so little to her. Amanda Weir had grown into unhappiness because she did not realise that happiness came from sticking at things — things that often seemed mundane, prosaic, boring, unglamorous.

Isabel rewrote the letter in exactly the same terms as her first attempt, inserting only the deliberately perfunctory *Yours, Isabel*. She reread the letter, and then wrote an identical one addressed to Alex and one to Patrick. Next, she addressed the envelopes, wrote *Strictly Personal* on the top left-hand corner of each, and went into the kitchen to inform Grace that she was going out briefly to the postbox. A scene of chocolate chaos greeted her: chocolate smeared around Charlie's mouth, chocolate on his hands and across the front of his shirt. Grace smiled guiltily. "I tried," she said. "I'll put him in the bath afterwards."

Isabel returned the smile. "Such happiness," she muttered.

After she had posted the letters in the small postbox on the corner, Isabel stood for a moment and considered what she had done. She often did this after consigning something important to the post; she stood and reflected. Posting something was a simple act, but it could be the first of a sequence of important events that changed one's world, or somebody else's. The letter of application for a job that might take one far from home; that might result in one's meeting the person with whom one would spend one's life . . . A letter could change so much, could create just as much as it might destroy.

Isabel imagined what the effect might be of the letters she had just put through the mouth of the postbox. What if she changed her mind? Could one ever recall a letter after posting it? It would surely be impossible. Letters lay in the postbox until the next collection — which she noticed was barely an hour away — and then they were removed by the postman when he passed by in his van. One might stand by the postbox and ask him for the letter back but surely he could never accede to such a request. How would he know that the letter was yours? And once a letter was handed over to the postal authorities they were, she presumed, the legal custodian of that letter until it was handed over to the intended recipient. But they did not *own* it, she thought, because the letter and its contents remained your property until it was given to the person named on the envelope. So surely you could ask for the return of your own property? No, she decided, you could not; it was not that simple.

For a few moments Isabel wondered whether she had made a bad mistake. She had claimed that she had found out what happened, but it was simply not true, and if she were to be asked to expand on it, she would have nothing to say. But that was the whole point, she decided: she hoped that *two* of the three would ask her what had happened, while the third would not. And the

264

reason for that was that the third would know and would not need to enquire. Unless, of course, all three asked, which would suggest that all were innocent. Yet the guilty could affect ignorance; there was that to consider, and sometimes the guilty were adept at it — more adept than the innocent might be in the assertion of their innocence.

She moved away from the postbox. It was too late: the stone had been thrown into the pond and all she could do was to return home and wait for the ripples to break — if there were to be any. As Isabel walked back down the road, the seagulls' cries were now a Greek chorus, or so it seemed to her. She looked up at them as they circled overhead. Their earlier dispute resolved, their mewing was now less strident, but some, at least, appeared to be directed at her. *Behold the fowls of the air: for they sow not, neither do they reap, nor gather into barns . . .* And then there were the lilies to be considered; they neither spun nor weaved and yet Solomon in all his glory . . . She stopped herself. The wisdom of Solomon. Would he have written such a letter? Possibly, she thought. Possibly.

Jamie was teaching that afternoon and returned in a bad mood. This was unusual for him, and Isabel knew that it would not last; Jamie's temper was equable, and although he might manage a few minutes of silence, he seemed incapable of sustained grumpiness. Cat was the past master at that: she could sustain a huff for days on end, sometimes to the extent of forgetting — Isabel suspected — the original cause of her annoyance. Isabel had often thought that much the same thing happened in those puzzling animosities between whole nations: although there might be fresh aggravations to keep relations on edge, the original *casus belli* of many of the great historical dislikes were shrouded. The Greeks and Turks disliked one another and each could provide chapter and verse for why this was so, but behind many such recited wrongs there lay ancient animosities based on incidents that really were forgotten. *Greeks and Turks* . . . she remembered now. When she was six, or thereabouts, there had been a boy who lived in the next street whose parents had been friendly with hers. This boy, David, was brought by his mother to play with her and spent long afternoons in her company. His favourite game, which she tended to tire of well before he did, was one of his own invention, or so she believed, and it had been called "Greeks and Turks". The memory of this game always brought a smile to Isabel's lips, as the rules had been so simple. One person was the Greek and the other was the Turk. The Greek chased the Turk and then, on catching him or her, became the Turk, to be chased in turn by the Greek. There were no further implications to the game — it continued until either the Greek or the Turk fell over and grazed a knee — as sometimes happened — or decided that endless running around in pursuit of another was of waning interest. That conclusion was more frequently and more quickly reached by Isabel than by David, and reflected what the young Isabel was to discover as she became older: that boys and men were content to chase things while girls and women saw no point in such behaviour. Jamie's bad mood, such as it was, had been caused by one of his pupils.

"I don't like that boy," he said as he came into Isabel's study. Charlie was having a nap and Isabel was in the middle of a rare tidying session. There was so much paper, so many piles of books, that had she thought about it she too might well have decided to indulge herself in a bad mood. But in general, in the average marriage there is room for only one bad mood at a time and on that afternoon Jamie was there first.

She shifted a pile of papers from one surface to another; the guilt that a pile of papers may induce can be so easily dissipated by a small move, she decided. "What boy? Thomas?"

Thomas was a pupil of whom Jamie had spoken more than once — a boy, he complained, who persistently came to his music lesson without some important part of his bassoon — usually the crook, but often the reed or the sling. Jamie would always have a spare crook that he could lend him, but he disliked providing reeds, which had to be placed in the mouth. He had told Isabel about how he had tackled the subject with Thomas, telling him that one's saliva was, as a general rule, best kept to oneself. Thomas had stared at him uncomprehendingly and had forgotten to bring his reed to the following lesson as well.

"No," said Jamie, flopping down in the armchair beside Isabel's desk, "not Thomas. Barry."

Isabel picked up an unopened letter that had somehow escaped her attention and examined the postmark. "Barry?" The letter was postmarked two weeks earlier, and she winced.

"He's fourteen," said Jamie. "And he has the most ghastly mother. He's ghastly himself, but his mother is really seriously ghastly. And the father's ghastly too. They're nouveau riche and wear really flashy clothes. Barry had this sort of shiny shirt on today and a belt made out of some endangered species. His father came to collect him and he was wearing sunglasses — very designer — and endangered shoes."

Isabel smiled. "They probably weren't actually endangered. Some of these things are imitation crocodile, or lizard, or whatever it is. They're just plastic."

Jamie was having none of this. "No, they're not. Not in this case. You could tell that the father goes for the real thing. He probably shot his shoes himself."

Isabel raised an eyebrow. Jamie was usually tolerant in his views, and rarely vituperative. And surely it could not just be Barry to set him off like this. "Anything else happened?" she asked casually.

He was silent.

"Nothing?" she asked.

Jamie sighed. "There was a letter. It had been delivered to the flat. I told them — I told them two or three times that my mail was to come here, but these people are hopeless, just hopeless. You may as well save your breath."

Isabel said nothing. It was clearly nothing to do with Barry or his father's shoes; it was the letter.

"What was it?" she asked gently.

Jamie spat the word out. "Tax."

"Ah."

"They said that I underpaid last year. They said it was my mistake."

Isabel was about to say "It usually is" but realised that this might not be the moment. So she said instead, "They're *ghastly* . . ." It was, she realised, a curious echo of Jamie's complaint about the unfortunate Barry and his family; a word, as often happens, can be like a musical worm in the mind and invite repetition. But it slipped out. Tax inspectors were not ghastly, she thought; they were simply doing their job, and they did it, she imagined, fairly well — for the most part. They had to contend with all sorts of dishonesty and rudeness on the part of taxpayers, who were, no doubt, quite capable of being particularly ghastly in their dealings with tax officials, and so . . .

"You can say that again," said Jamie. "Why do they have to wait until now to tell me? Why didn't they sort this out earlier? Six months ago?"

Isabel shrugged. "They have a lot of tax to collect. And the public itself can be ghas —" She stopped the word in its tracks. And holding her unopened letter, she was hardly in a position to bemoan the inefficiency of others.

"How much?" she asked.

Jamie closed his eyes. "Eight hundred and fifty pounds."

Isabel looked out of the window. She would have to handle this carefully. "Are you all right for that?" she asked. "I could . . ."

He looked up at her. "I'm all right. It's just that . . . well, I don't want to pay."

"No," she said. "That's understandable."

He sighed. "Oh well."

She could see that the bad mood was already wearing off.

"I've had an interesting day," she volunteered.

"Really?" His tone was almost normal now; the memories of Barry and the tax demand were clearly fading.

"Yes. I had an idea. A rather interesting one, as it happens."

He got to his feet. "I must have a shower. But what was this idea of yours."

"You have your shower," she said. "I could talk to you about it later on. We could go out for dinner."

Her suggestion was well received. "Yes, why not?"

"No reason," said Isabel. "I'll book that place at Holy Corner. The something-or-other bistro. And I'll ask Grace to babysit. She offered earlier today. I think she wants to read to Charlie."

"Not teach him mathematics?"

Isabel laughed. "No, I don't think so."

Jamie nodded. "Good."

Isabel returned to her task of tidying. Jamie's birthday was coming up. She would put a cheque for eight hundred and fifty pounds in an envelope and seal it with a kiss. He would accept it, she felt, because it was his birthday and such things were permitted on birthdays even if pride, however unreasonably, prevented them on other occasions. She would give him anything, she felt. Everything she possessed. But at least eight hundred and fifty pounds was a start.

Jamie stared at her over the dinner table in the Bistro Bia. "So," he said, "you wrote to all three of them and told them that you had worked out . . ."

"Discovered," interjected Isabel.

"Discovered what had happened. And yet you say that this isn't strictly true?" His intonation rose sharply at the end of the sentence, underlining his doubt.

"Not strictly," said Isabel. "Of course I don't want to rely on pedantry, but I could argue that the forming in my mind of a *theory* as to what happened amounts to a discovery. So that means I wasn't really telling a lie."

Jamie looked at her uncertainly. "You don't really mean that, do you?" he said.

Isabel gave a sheepish grin. She had not convinced herself; she had not even tried. "Maybe not. But the point is this — this letter of mine might just flush out the guilty party."

"If one of them *is* the guilty party," said Jamie. "And frankly, it doesn't seem all that likely."

"Maybe not to you," said Isabel. "But if you look at the evidence. One of the men holding the painting called Duncan by the name Alex and Patrick use . . ."

"And the name millions of other people use for their father," said Jamie. He saw her face fall, and he immediately added, almost apologetically, "But carry on anyway."

"Motive," said Isabel.

"Motives aren't evidence."

She bit her lip. "Do you want me to tell you what I think, or not?"

He was placatory now. "I'm trying to play the role that Peter plays when he quizzes you about something." Peter was Peter Stevenson, a friend who often acted as a critical sounding board for Isabel and whose advice she valued.

"But you're not Peter," she blurted out. "You aren't here to test everything I say like . . . like a judge. You asked me what I think and I started to tell you and . . ." She did not finish. Jamie had reached across the table and placed his hand gently on hers.

"You're right. I'm sorry."

She forgave him.

"All right," she said. "Motive: Alex needs money, or rather, her fiancé does. Same thing really. She loves the Poussin. She doesn't want it to be given away. There's also that very odd thing, not motive, I suppose, but back to evidence: the fact that she got me involved and then tried to shift suspicion on to her brother. Patrick may need money — we're not sure. Disagrees with his father on politics and farming and all sorts of things, I imagine, and there's no love lost between him and his sister." She paused. "I suppose his motive is probably the weakest — or at least it's the one we're least sure about. But then . . ."

"Yes? But then?"

"Then there's Duncan himself."

Jamie looked doubtful. "Surely not."

"What if he has financial problems?" asked Isabel.

"He could sell a painting. The Poussin could go down to Christie's and that would be it. Financial problems solved."

Isabel considered this. "Except that he might not feel able to sell something that he has promised to give to the nation." She looked at him enquiringly. "Would you? Would you sell something that you had promised to give to somebody in the future."

Jamie took a sip from his glass of water. "I might — if I needed to."

"But you're not Duncan Munrowe. Remember, he's old-fashioned. He has his reputation to consider."

Jamie smiled. "But you're still suggesting that he might try to defraud an insurance company?"

Isabel shook her head. "No, you're right. I don't really think that he's behind this. It wouldn't be in character, and, for the most part, people act in character, don't they?"

"Almost always," said Jamie.

Isabel thought for a moment about her proposition that people acted in character. It was probably true, but if you were to use character as a means of predicting what people would do, you had to know their character very well. And that was the problem: most people had aspects to their character that they concealed — weaknesses, vices, and so on; not most people, she thought — everybody. Everybody had *some* flaws and these flaws could prompt them to do surprising things.

She looked at Jamie and thought: was Jamie capable of surprising her? Was he capable of doing something low or mean — something that she would think completely out of character?

"Why are you looking at me like that?" he asked.

She looked away quickly. "Was I?"

"Yes," he said. "You were looking at me in a very strange way." He seemed amused rather than unsettled.

"I was wondering whether you could ever do anything that would shock me. I suppose that's what I was thinking."

He gave her an injured look — but he made it clear that he was not serious. "Don't you trust me?"

"Of course I trust you. I was just thinking of cases where wives discover that their husband has been doing something shocking. It was mentioning character that made me think about that sort of thing." She paused. "I don't believe you would ever shock me, though. I really don't believe that."

As she spoke, she thought of all the women who discovered that their husband was having an affair. It was a very common story — banal really, so frequently did it happen. But it was not those cases that involved the real shock: it was when the woman discovered something utterly out of the ordinary; for instance, that their husband had committed a serious crime. What would she do if she found out that Jamie had robbed a bank, or was a secret blackmailer, or had planted a bomb in a public place, or something like that? Isabel wondered. The men who did those things went back, she assumed, to their wives or girlfriends at night. Mafiosi had their families — they tucked their children into bed at night and exhorted them to do well at school. People who plotted the deaths of others bought their wives birthday presents and walked the dog and took the car to the garage. And they had their little tiffs and make-ups and went out for dinner in restaurants just like this one and talked about day-to-day things.

Isabel looked around the restaurant, at the couples at neighbouring tables. Just like us, but were there secrets at every table? There were, she decided. Yes, there were.

"We should talk about something else," said Jamie, picking up the menu that the waitress had placed before him. "Food, maybe." He ran his eye down the list of offerings. "One final thing, though: what do you expect to happen next?"

"I've already told you," she said. "Two of them will be very keen to find out. Two will phone me. One won't. Or . . ." She hesitated. "All of them will get in touch."

Jamie laughed. "Oh well," he said. "Robert Burns."

"What's he got to do with it?"

"*The best laid schemes of mice and men*," said Jamie. "Remember?"

"How could one forget?" said Isabel.

CHAPTER
SEVENTEEN

There was no phone call the next day, although the letters would have been delivered that morning — if the postal system worked as it was meant to do, which it usually did. Isabel spent the first part of the morning at her desk and the rest of the day at the delicatessen, standing in for Cat, who had a trade fair to attend in Glasgow. "All the food people will be there," she had said. "Miles of Italian sausage — miles. Tankers of olive oil. Everything."

"Then you must go," Isabel had replied. "I'll help Eddie. You go to Glasgow."

"Angel," said Cat, blowing Isabel a kiss.

"Well, I'm not sure . . ."

"But you are. You're a rock."

Isabel had wondered whether one could be both an angel and a rock. Angels were somewhat flighty; rocks were more . . . well, more *rocky*. What Cat might have said was that she was a brick; that was a compliment that people paid to those on whom they could rely, but the expression was dying out. Her father had talked about people being bricks — their mechanic, for example, had been a brick because he had been prepared to come and collect the car for its service when her father was too busy at the office to take it to the garage. That was the action of a brick.

She went to the delicatessen shortly after eleven, ready to help Eddie during the busiest period of the day, which was between twelve and two. There was time for a cup of coffee before she got down to work preparing bread rolls for lunchtime, and it was over a cup of coffee that Eddie mentioned Diane.

"Ah, Diane," said Isabel. "How is she?"

"She's going to London."

"Oh. And are you going with her? Have you been to London, Eddie?"

He shook his head. "I've never been there. I've been to America but I've never been to London."

"Well, maybe you should go with her. How long is she going for, the weekend?"

Eddie reached for a jar of pickles. "No, she's going down there to finish her course. She's transferring to another college."

Isabel frowned. "But what about you, Eddie? Are you going too?"

He shook his head. "Not me," he said carelessly. "You wouldn't catch me living in London. Too big."

Isabel digested this. "So?"

"It's not a big problem," said Eddie. "We've finished. It's over."

Isabel put down her coffee cup. "I'm sorry," she said. "I'm really sorry to hear that, Eddie."

He shrugged, and then extracted a pickle from the jar with his fingers.

Isabel shook a finger. "You're not meant to do that, Eddie! Use a fork. You don't put your fingers in jars."

"Sorry." He put the pickle in his mouth. "It's only for me."

"But your fingers have been in the vinegar. You put germs from your hands into the vinegar. Now all those other pickles could be full of your germs."

"OK," he said. "I won't do it again."

She returned to the subject of Diane. "What happened?"

"I thought we should cool it," said Eddie. "So I did. She's cool with that."

Isabel was somewhat surprised by this abrupt change of heart and was about to say something but stopped herself. She had not interfered before in the issue of the two of them living together and would not do so now. He was just too young.

"You'll miss her," said Isabel, largely out of a want of anything else to say.

"Maybe," said Eddie. "Maybe a bit."

Men don't miss women, thought Isabel. More women miss men than men miss women. That was probably right. It was depressingly right.

Work resumed, and it was not until three o'clock that things slackened off sufficiently for Isabel to telephone the house and ask if there had been any calls for her. Grace answered, and said that the glazier had called about a window that needed repairing but there had been nothing else.

She went home at five, leaving Eddie to do the last hour or so by himself. Again there had been no message, and there was no call either that evening. The next morning, though, shortly after eight, the telephone rang. It was Duncan.

"Astonishing news," he blurted out even before giving his name. "The Poussin's back."

Isabel started to say something, but was interrupted.

"This morning," said Duncan. "I went down this morning and it was back in its place. Somebody had put it there last night. Astonishing. But it's safe — that's the important thing."

"Yes," said Isabel. "That's the important thing."

"I've told the insurance people," Duncan continued. "I woke that chap up, I'm afraid. I called him at six."

"I doubt if he minded," said Isabel. "It's rather good news for them."

"Yes," said Duncan. "He sounded pretty chipper. So that's it. Case closed. There's no claim from me, and that makes them extremely happy. Nothing more to be done."

Isabel had her doubts. "Do you think so? Surely the police will want to pursue the matter."

There was silence at the other end of the line.

"Have they said anything?" pressed Isabel.

"I haven't informed them yet," said Duncan. He sounded guarded.

"But you'll have to," said Isabel. She was thinking quickly; he seemed reluctant to inform the police and there had to be a reason for that. *He* was the one; that was the reason. Why else would he not wish to speak to the police? They would have to know eventually, but presumably he felt uneasy about talking to them himself. "After all," she went on, "this is a crime. A very valuable item was stolen. The police aren't going to want to let that go."

Again he was silent. Then: "I don't see what interest the police will have in dealing with something that's no longer a problem. They have better things to do with their time, don't you think?"

She did not get time to answer. Had she been able to say what was on her mind she might have said that the issue was not so much theft as it was insurance fraud.

"Look," Duncan said. "Do you think you could come down here this morning? I know it's an imposition, but it would be much better to speak face to face. There's rather a lot to discuss."

Yes, thought Isabel. There was a great deal to discuss, but she did not see how she could discuss it with him. How could she? Would she accuse him of attempting to defraud his insurers? And if that was what she thought, was she not morally bound to go to the police with her suspicions?

She agreed to go. Jamie offered to accompany her, but she declined his offer. "It will be better for me to go by myself," she said. "I shall be perfectly safe."

She drove up to Doune in the Swedish car, not noticing the skies this time, nor paying much attention to the countryside unfolding on either side of the road. Her mind was occupied with what she might say to Duncan — that is, if she were to say anything, which was far from sure. Her earlier certainty that Duncan was responsible for the theft had been replaced by a measure of doubt. Now she thought: I really don't know. I know very little here and I should simply leave the whole issue where it is. It was no business of hers to bring anybody to justice, nor to interfere in the affairs of a family that she barely knew and that had difficulties enough without her adding fuel to the flames of their dysfunctionality. By the time she arrived at Munrowe House, she had decided that her visit would be a brief one. She would listen to whatever it was that Duncan wished to say and then she would withdraw.

Duncan greeted her on the steps in front of the house. He was smiling broadly, and ushered her in warmly.

"Let's waste no time," he said. "Come into the drawing room. The painting is back where it belongs."

She followed him into the room, which was cold, in spite of the summer weather outside. Old Scottish houses were inevitably cold, she realised; it was the thickness of the stone walls. He saw her shiver. "I make a fire, even in summer," he said.

Isabel did not say anything; her eyes had gone straight to the Poussin.

"Back home," said Duncan.

Isabel walked forward and stood before the painting. She felt as she always did when she stood in front of a great work of art: a sense of marvel that she was so close to an artefact that was once worked upon by an artist of such stature as Poussin. He did this, she mused: he *thought* this painting, he touched this canvas.

She went a step closer. Duncan was now standing beside her. She heard his breathing. She felt his presence.

She turned her head, just slightly, so that she could see Duncan's face. His eyes were bright; there was joy in his expression. This man, it occurred to her, could not have engineered the disappearance of this painting. He could not be dissembling; he simply could not.

She looked at the sky in the painting. She saw the clouds, and behind them the blue of the void. Beyond the range of hills that the artist had painted in the background she could make out a glow in the sky that was the sun, and she remembered being in the Metropolitan Museum in New York and seeing Poussin's picture of Celadion standing on the shoulders of the giant, Orion, and guiding him towards the sun, that his sight might be restored. On the shoulders of great men we go towards the light . . .

"We should take a seat," said Duncan, indicating the sofa. "We can gaze at this lovely sight while we talk."

She sat down at one end of a chintzy sofa, with Duncan at the other.

He did not hesitate. "So you found out," he began. "Frankly, I wasn't surprised."

"No?"

"No, I'd dreaded it. I suppose I suspected it all along, but I didn't really want to face up to the fact that my own son could have done something like that."

She was still. "Your son?"

"Yes, Patrick. As I assume you've discovered."

"Why do you think it was him?" she asked gently.

He laughed. "Because it's obvious. The house was locked last night. This morning the painting was back in its original position, as if nothing had happened. There are four or five copies of the keys — mine, my wife's, my daughter's, my son's, and a spare set we keep in a drawer."

Isabel asked him where his wife was. He replied that she was in Paris and would be away for the next two weeks. He had spoken to her on the telephone, though — to give her the good news. "Needless to say, she's delighted."

"But I still don't see —"

He interrupted. "I assumed that you spoke to him after you discovered the truth."

Isabel shook her head. "No, I didn't."

"Then he must have realised that you knew."

She was not sure what to say. "Do you think so?"

"Yes."

He looked up at the painting. "He's gone on and on about redistribution — he's harped on about it for years. But I never thought he'd take his animosity to me and my concerns to such an extent." He shook his head ruefully. "Never. I would never have dreamed it."

"Are you sure it's him?" said Isabel gently.

He looked at her in surprise. "What do you mean? Who else could it be?"

"You have two children," said Isabel.

He laughed. "Alex? No, that's out of the question."

Isabel looked down at her hands. I could tell him, she thought. I could list the factors that pointed to his daughter: her financial need, her attachment to the painting, her deliberate involvement of Isabel through Martha.

Duncan now rose to his feet and took the few steps that brought him close to the painting. He gazed at it, his back to Isabel.

"Do you know something?" he said, without turning round. "When I asked Martha to contact you, I never imagined that you would be able to sort the whole thing out. I hardly dared hope. I expected that you would be a comfort to me in the whole business — as I told you — but I had no idea that you'd bring the matter to a successful conclusion."

Isabel sat where she was. "When you asked Martha?"

He seemed surprised by her question. "Yes. I got in touch with her. I didn't want to speak to you out of the blue. I suppose I'm afraid of rejection." He looked at her and gave a curious, self-deprecatory shrug. "Who isn't? We're all a bit weak, I fear."

"I don't think it was your son," said Isabel.

Duncan appeared to weigh this — but not for long. "You don't have to protect him, you know. I'm not going to do anything about it, as I told you. After all, he's still my son."

Isabel stared at him. "Do you love him?"

"Of course I do. In spite of everything. I'll get over this."

She was astonished. "So this will make no difference to your relationship with him?"

Duncan sighed. "Probably not. We are very far apart, you see, in many respects. And I don't think this was directed against me. The painting was going to come

284

back — he was merely going for the insurance company. He hates people like that — fair game, in his view."

"What if I told you," said Isabel, "that it was definitely not your son? What if I said that it was somebody else altogether?"

He sat down again. She had his full attention. "Why? What do you mean?"

She closed her eyes briefly, trying to order her thoughts. "It was somebody else, but I cannot reveal who. I'm sorry. But I assure you that I am one hundred per cent sure that it was not Patrick."

Duncan looked confused. "Then who . . .?"

"I can't reveal that," Isabel repeated. She had made her decision. It had all fallen into place and she knew what she had to do. "You yourself said that the important thing is that the painting is back."

He corrected her. "You said that."

"No, you did."

He looked doubtful. And Isabel thought: did I say it, or did he? And if we can't remember who said what, then how could anybody be sure about who spoke to Martha? But one thing was clear: it was right not to tell him that his daughter was behind the theft. If she was, which Isabel thought was probable. Or perhaps not . . . "I think I should get back to Edinburgh," she said.

"I owe you a great deal," said Duncan. "I'm very grateful to you."

She had been about to stand up, but at this, she remained where she was. "Then I'm going to ask something of you."

He was guarded. "Yes?"

"I'd like you to make some gesture towards your son," she said. "You said that you loved him. Well, he doesn't think so."

He began to protest, but she cut him short.

"Yes, I mean it. He thinks that you disapprove of him."

"He disapproves of me," blurted out Duncan.

"Disapproval can sometimes be an act of self-defence," Isabel pointed out. "And in this sort of situation it's not necessarily a good idea for people to blame each other for starting things. You have to short-circuit all that. You have to forget about it. Tell him that you value him. Tell him that you are happy with what he is. Don't deny it. He's not going to change his nature, you know. Tell him that that's all right. Say it. Embrace him. Put your arms around him and say that you're proud of him and you love him."

He stared at her.

"Or lose him," she said.

She rose to her feet, glanced one final time at the Poussin, and began to leave the room.

She was back in Edinburgh well before lunchtime. Jamie had been practising that morning — he had a demanding concert coming up in which he was playing Mozart's bassoon concerto, and he was working his way through that, ironing out difficulties, making sure that his playing was as polished as possible. Now he was ready for lunch, which he suggested they have in the garden as it was a warm day — one of the warmest

286

of the year so far — and they could eat on a picnic rug on the shady part of the lawn. Isabel agreed, and prepared a plate of sandwiches and a jug of the slightly tart lime cordial that she had made a few days previously.

Sitting on the rug, she told Jamie about her trip to Munrowe House and about the conversation she had had with Duncan. "So who was it?" he asked.

Isabel picked at a sandwich. "Ham," she said. "You should have the ham ones and I'll have tomato. Who was it?"

He took the ham sandwich from her. "Yes. Who was it?"

She extracted a tomato sandwich from the small stack on the serving plate. "Who was it? Sometimes it's difficult to say. You think you know the answer, then you don't."

"But you must have some feeling about it," pressed Jamie.

"The daughter," said Isabel. "I may be wrong, but I think it was her. The last thing I wanted to do was to tell Duncan that. He is very fond of her and I'm not sure that it would be helpful for him to know that she's dishonest. Frankly, I think it could even be the end of him — that knowledge."

Jamie understood. "So you kept that from him?"

Isabel nodded. "I did. I think I had to." She paused for a moment. "But it could have been somebody else. I'm not sure. It could even have been Duncan — I doubt it, he was so obviously delighted about having the painting back that I more or less dismissed the idea, but it's theoretically possible. Just."

Jamie was silent. He had started on the ham sandwich and was making quick work of it. Within a minute, it had disappeared, and he reached for another one.

Once their lunch was over, they lay down on the rug. Isabel, feeling relaxed and relieved that the Poussin was back in its home, reflected on the fact that the best solutions in life are sometimes the vaguest and least clear-cut. That was true, no matter how much we strove for certainty, for the cut and dried, for the harsh truth that admitted of no nuances, no qualifications. I am glad that I do not live in a world that requires such certainty of me, she thought. I am glad.

"Look at those clouds," said Jamie, gazing up at the sky. "Look at them."

"Yes," said Isabel. "They're very beautiful, aren't they? Clouds are very beautiful and yet so often we fail to appreciate them properly. We should do that. We should look at them and think about how lucky we are to have them."

She turned to Jamie, lying beside her. He was still on his back, his hands tucked behind his head, making a rough-and-ready human pillow. Had she been able to write haiku, she thought, she would write one to him now. *You beside me / The grass beneath / I think . . .* and so on. But she could not, and what she wanted to say to him now was all jumbled up inside her. She could kiss him perhaps; that might express her feelings every bit as eloquently as if she were to speak at length.

288

But she felt a piece of tomato on her teeth and she did not want to kiss him until that had dislodged itself, or been dislodged.

"Look at the shape of the clouds," she said. "What do you see in those beautiful clouds, Jamie?"

She thought he might find a shape of the clouds that they could treat as an omen, a portent perhaps, but he did not. Instead, he waited for a few moments, waited until a bee that had been crawling on a nearby flower went on to something else.

"I see you," he said.

THE MINOR ADJUSTMENT BEAUTY SALON

Alexander McCall Smith

With Mma Makutsi busy with motherhood, cobras and a senior aunt, Mma Ramotswe must grapple alone with two puzzling cases. First she is approached by Mma Sheba, the executor of a deceased farmer's estate, who has a feeling that the young man who has stepped forward may be falsely impersonating the farmer's nephew in order to claim his inheritance. Then the proprietor of the Minor Adjustment Beauty Salon comes to Mma Ramotswe for advice. The opening of her new salon has been shadowed by misfortune. Not only has she received a bad omen in the mail, but rumours are swirling that the salon is using dangerous products that burn people's skin. Could someone be trying to put the salon out of business?

THE HANDSOME MAN'S DE LUXE CAFE

Alexander McCall Smith

Even the arrival of her baby can't hold Mma Makutsi back from success in the workplace, and so no sooner than she becomes a full partner in the No. 1 Ladies' Detective Agency — in spite of Mma Ramotswe's belated claims that she is only "an assistant full partner" — she also launches a new enterprise of her own: the Handsome Man's De Luxe Cafe. Grace Makutsi is a lady with a business plan, but who could predict temperamental chefs, drunken waiters and more? Luckily, help is at hand, from the only person in Gaborone more gently determined than Mma Makutsi . . . Mma Ramotswe, of course.

DREAM ANGUS

Alexander McCall Smith

Divine Angus might grant you sight of your true love in a dream; you might even fall in love with him — but he'll never love you back. He's too busy making mischief, until he is trapped by his own romantic games and falls for an unattainable woman, doomed to seek her forever.

In 20th century Scotland, Angus's troubled alter ego searches for his true family; a psychotherapist who helps people understand their dreams, his life seems to parallel that of his mythic namesake.

Mesmerically weaving together the tales of the Celtic god and the Scottish scientist, Alexander McCall Smith unites dream and reality, leaving us to wonder: what is life, but the pursuit of our dreams?

SIDNEY CHAMBERS AND THE FORGIVENESS OF SINS

James Runcie

Six new stories about the full-time priest and part-time detective, set in 1960s Cambridge. On a snowy Thursday morning in Lent 1964, a stranger seeks sanctuary in Grantchester's church, convinced he has murdered his wife . . . Sidney attends a shooting weekend in the country with his wife Hildegard, where they find their hostess has a sinister burn on her neck . . . A firm of removal men "accidentally" drop a Steinway piano on a musician's head outside a Cambridge college . . . Sidney's friend Amanda receives threatening pen letters when at last she appears to be approaching matrimony . . . During a cricket match, a group of schoolboys blow up their school's science block . . . And on a family holiday in Florence, Sidney is accused of the theft of a priceless painting.

TOP SECRET TWENTY-ONE

Janet Evanovich

The dead ends are turning into dead bodies. Stephanie Plum is getting desperate. She's running out of leads in the search for Jimmy Poletti, who was caught selling more than cars out of his New Jersey dealership. Even Joe Morelli, the city's hottest cop, is struggling to find the criminal wheeler and dealer. Stephanie's No. 1 temptation, Ranger, is also struggling. There's a killer in town with a personal vendetta against him. If Ranger wants to survive, he'll need Stephanie's help — and to reveal a piece of his mysterious past. Death threats, highly trained assassins and highly *untrained* assassins are all in a day's work for bounty hunter Stephanie Plum!

EXTRAORDINARY PEOPLE

Peter May

Paris.

An old mystery.

As midnight strikes, a man desperately seeking sanctuary flees into a church. The next day, his sudden disappearance will make him famous throughout France.

A new science.

Forensic expert Enzo Macleod takes a wager to solve the seven most notorious French murders using modern technology — and a total disregard for the justice system.

A fresh trail.

Deep in the catacombs below the city, he unearths dark clues deliberately set — and as he draws closer to the killer, discovers that he is to be the next victim.

Hedy's W

ABOUT THE AUTHOR

Jenny Lecoat was born in Jersey, just fifteen years after the Nazi Occupation of the Channel Islands. Following a Drama degree at Birmingham University she moved to London and pursued various careers as a stand-up comic, presenter and magazine contributor, before becoming a full-time television writer in 1994. She worked on a wide range of series including sitcoms, children's programmes and dramas, until a growing interest in factual and biographical stories inspired her to revisit her island roots. Her feature film *Another Mother's Son*, telling the story of her family's resistance activities during the war years, was released in 2017. *Hedy's War* is her first novel.

She is married to television writer Gary Lawson and now lives in Hove, East Sussex.

Hedy's War

Jenny Lecoat

First published in Great Britain in 2020 by Polygon,
an imprint of Birlinn Ltd

Birlinn Ltd
West Newington House
10 Newington Road
Edinburgh
EH9 1QS

www.polygonbooks.co.uk

1

ISBN 978 1 84697 531 8
eBook ISBN 978 1 78885 278 4

Bri British Library Cataloguing in Publication
A catal logue record for this book is available st
from the British Library.

Typeset by 1type.com

  s Ltd, Elcograf S.p.A

Preface

This novel is based on true events. In 1940, young Hedwig Bercu, a Jewish girl who had recently escaped the Anschluss, found herself trapped on the tiny island of Jersey when Nazi Germany invaded the Channel Islands. The extraordinary story of Hedy's struggle for survival, including the role played by a serving officer of the occupying forces, was first documented almost sixty years later, and is the foundation for this fictionalised account. Some names have been changed.

For more background information, please see Acknowledgements.

For those courageous Channel Islanders
whose acts of kindness, resolution
and resistance under Occupation
saved the lives of others.

And for Gary.

Jersey, Channel Islands
Summer 1940

The sun's heat had begun to mellow, and the gulls were cruising for their final catch of the day when the siren sounded. Its wail climbed and fell, calling out over the jumbled slate roofs and church spires of the town, and across the patchwork of potato fields beyond. In St Aubin's bay, where the waves lapped and fizzed on the sand, its warning finally reached Hedy's ears as she lay dozing by the sea wall, and woke her with a jolt.

Rising in slow motion, she scanned the sky. Now she could also hear a faint, tinny whine in the east. She tried to steady her breathing. Perhaps it was another false alarm? These warnings had become a daily event these past two weeks, each time the reconnaissance planes merely circling, then disappearing back out to sea with cameras crammed full of blurry images of main roads and harbour walls. But this time something was different. The engine sound contained a note of brutish intent, and now several tiny black dots were emerging in the distant blue. The whine became a hum, and the hum a strident drone. Then she knew. This was no reconnaissance mission. This was the start.

For days now, the islanders had watched the black smoke rise and mushroom on the French coast, felt the vibration of the distant blasts pulse through their bellies and rattle their bones. Women had spent hours counting and re-counting the tinned foods in their larders, while the men squashed into banks to withdraw the family savings. Children had yelled their complaints as gas masks were forced over their heads. By then, all hope had vanished. There was no one here to deter the aggressors, nothing between them and their shimmering prize but flat blue water and an empty sky. And now the planes were on their way. Hedy could see them clearly now, still some distance away, but from the outline she guessed they were Stukas. Dive bombers.

She spun around, looking for shelter. The nearest beachside café was almost a mile away. Stopping only to grab her wicker bag, she sprinted for the stone steps leading to the walkway above, and took them in three bounds. At the top she scoured the promenade; a hundred metres towards First Tower was a small seafront shelter. It contained nothing but a single wooden bench on each of its four exposed sides, but it would have to do. Hedy hurtled towards it, grazing her shin as she mistimed the leap onto the low plinth, and threw herself against the bench. A moment later she was joined by a panic-stricken young mother, probably not much older than herself, gripping a small white-faced boy by the wrist. By now the planes were over St Helier harbour, one arcing across the bay towards them, the noise of the engine so deafening that it drowned out the boy's screams as the woman pushed him to the ground. The violent rat-a-tat of machine gunfire stung Hedy's ears as several bullets found the sea wall and zinged off in random directions. A second later, a distant explosion shook the shelter so hard Hedy thought the roof might collapse.

'Was that a bomb?' The woman's face was ashen beneath her tan.

'Yes. Near the harbour, I think.'

The woman gave her a brief, confused look. It was the accent, Hedy knew – even in a moment like this it still set her apart, marked her out as an alien. But the woman's attention quickly turned back to her child.

'Oh my God,' she muttered, 'what have we done? My husband said we should have evacuated when we had the chance.' Her eyes fixed on the sky. 'Do you think we should have gone?'

Hedy said nothing, but followed her companion's gaze upwards. She thought about her employers, the Mitchells, staggering onto that filthy, inadequate cargo boat with their screaming child, and nothing but a change of underwear and a few provisions stuffed into a brown packing case. At this moment, with the aroma of burning aviation fuel in her nostrils, she would have given anything to be with them. Her knuckles turned yellow on the slatted bench. Corkscrews of charcoal smoke drifted across the bay, and she could hear the little boy beside her sobbing. Hedy swallowed hard and focused on the questions bouncing around her brain like a pinball. How long now before the Germans landed? Would they round people up, stand them in front of walls to be shot? If they came for her, then . . . ? There was no point finishing that thought. Anton, the only person on this island she could call a friend, would be powerless to help her. The shelter vibrated again, and she felt its fragility.

Hedy remained crouched silently, listening to the planes loop and dive and the crack of explosions a mile away, until at last the sound of the engines began to fade into the distance. An ageing gentleman with dishevelled white hair stumbled towards them, and stopped to peer into the shelter.

'The planes have gone,' he called. 'Try to get home as quickly as you can. It can't be long before they get here.' Hedy's eyes fixed on his jacket, which was covered in dust and uneven patches of blood. 'Don't worry, it's not mine,' the man assured her. 'Old fellow walking near the harbour took a bullet in the leg – we had to get him to the hospital.'

'Are there many hurt? Or . . . ?' Hedy glanced towards the little boy, not wanting to finish the question.

'Some, yes.' The man's voice faltered a little, and Hedy felt a surge of anguish. She pressed her fist to her lips and swallowed

3

again before he continued: 'They bombed a line of potato trucks waiting to unload at the harbour. I mean, for God's sake, what's the point of that?' He shook his head and gestured towards his destination. 'Hurry now.'

The man hastened away. Hedy hauled her shaking body to its feet, wished the woman good luck and set off along the promenade towards the town, wondering how on earth she would get back to the Mitchells' – assuming the house was still there. She tried to hurry, but her skinny legs felt weak. She imagined Hemingway cowering beneath the sofa in the empty living room, his grey feline fur stiff with terror. Already she was half regretting disobeying Mr Mitchell's instruction to have him put down. The animal's trusting eyes had melted her heart at the door of the vet's surgery. Now she wasn't even sure if she'd be able to feed herself, never mind a cat.

By the time she reached the outskirts of St Helier town she could hear the bells of the ambulances and the random shouts of desperate men trying to work as a team. Smoke rose in perfect columns from boats and buildings in the windless summer evening; cars lay abandoned on the roads at odd angles. There were a few people about: some searching for the missing, some wandering aimlessly, and one old couple on a bench, sobbing. Hedy walked on, forcing herself to put one foot in front of the other, deliberately edging her mind towards reality. The seas around the island were probably already full of U-boats. Soon she would once again be surrounded by those grey-green uniforms and hear the barking of orders. She pictured the bang on the door, Wehrmacht hands grabbing at her elbow, the house abandoned with dirty dishes still on the table. Anything was possible now. She recalled only too well the way the Germans had behaved in Vienna.

Especially towards Jews.

She pressed on, pushing her body weight forward, willing herself home. She needed to reach Hemingway and give him a hug.

'I have these. But might they get us into trouble?'

Anton stood in the doorway of his bedroom holding out a pair of once white, now grey, ribbed cotton underpants. Even from her seat by the window Hedy could see they had not been washed. She felt the tiniest smile creep around her lips at the word 'trouble'; Anton could be so cautious sometimes, just as he could be absurdly optimistic at others. His face, like her own when she accidentally caught herself in the mirror, was pale with anxiety and exhaustion. Anton lived alone and Hedy suspected that he, too, had sat up for the last four nights, staring sleeplessly over deserted streets, counting down the curfewed hours with fearful expectation.

'Too late to worry about that,' Hedy replied. 'And they said a white flag. They didn't specify what it should be made of. Look, everyone's doing it.' They poked their heads out of the first-floor window into the sunshine. Below was a neat town street, lined with apartments built over shops and businesses, with doors that opened directly onto the pavement. Outside each window hung some kind of household fabric – an apron, a baby's nappy, an ancient undergarment. Defiance in the face of defeat. Anton nodded his agreement and Hedy, taking care to use only the tips of her fingers, took the underpants and tied them to the broom handle, then eased it out of the window, resting the brush end on a chair and weighting it down with a towel. As they did so, the sound of the vehicle engines swelled in their ears. 'Here they come now,' Hedy murmured.

The first car appeared at the end of the high street, clearly visible from their viewpoint – a smart open-topped Bentley filled with senior officers in full uniform. The second was a gleaming Daimler with several more. Behind them followed a dozen or so less impressive Fords and Morrises containing lower-ranked soldiers and a couple of motorcycles with sidecars at the rear – all stolen, Hedy supposed, from the garages of local residents, as the arriving military could hardly have had time to transport such vehicles from France. Even from up here, the delight on the Germans' faces was clearly visible. Presumably after months in the cold muddy fields of Europe, the creamy white beaches and tree-lined lanes of this picturesque island had come as a happy surprise to them, just as they once had to Hedy.

'Look at them.' Anton's voice was thick with anger. 'You'd think they'd conquered the whole of England, not a few British islands off St Malo.'

'For them it's the first step,' Hedy muttered.

'We're not expected to salute them, are we?'

Hedy peered into the windows opposite. Behind every one stood morose local residents, staring with impotent hatred at their new masters. There had been no more bombs since Friday night, and the damage around the harbour and Weighbridge was already partly repaired, but everyone knew that today marked the true beginning of subjugation. Watching their captors arrive, the people willed their fury into the invaders' hearts, their sullenness their only defence.

Hedy shook her head. 'They won't make us salute. They'll want to convince us how civilised they are – show the world how they intend to run Britain. What was it they said?' She picked up the leaflet from Anton's little table, and brushed away the dried granules of mud from the flower bed where it had landed. 'Here it is: "the liberty of peaceful inhabitants is solemnly guaranteed".' She snorted. 'We'll see how long that lasts.'

Anton squeezed her shoulder for reassurance. She felt the warmth of his hand, her first physical contact with anyone since saying goodbye to the Mitchells' little girl, and had to chew the inside of her lip to keep the tears at bay. They stood like that for several moments, until the line of cars finally disappeared and the windows above the pavement began to close. There would be more soldiers, of course, in the coming days – many more – but the islanders had had their first glimpse of the enemy, enough for one day. Anton returned to his usual easy chair by the fireplace, carefully positioned to hide the torn linoleum beneath. It was a small, scrappy apartment, but it had a cosiness far more comforting than her ex-employers' sprawling, deserted house, and the smell from the bakery beneath made it homely. It was a place where she had always felt safe.

'There's no point thinking the worst,' Anton said, reading her thoughts.

'All right for you.' She slumped down on the only other chair and tucked one leg underneath her, as always. Her fingers fiddled constantly with the ribbon on her dress. 'I'm so stupid! Why didn't I go to America when I had the chance?'

'You know why.'

'I could have found the money somehow! I shouldn't have given up so easily.'

Anton lent forward in his chair. 'Look, there are so few Jews left on the island – a dozen maybe? – it's probably not worth the Krauts seeking them out.' He must have seen the cynicism in her eyes, for he went on: 'I really don't think it will be as bad as it was in Vienna.'

Hedy tossed her hair. 'No? Even if you're right, even if they don't target my people, do you realise how vulnerable we'll be now? We're foreigners here, foreigners who speak German! We'll be caught in the crossfire.'

'The Jersey people won't turn on us that way, they know exactly why we're here.'

'Anton, they dragged you off to that internment camp barely six weeks ago, just for being an enemy alien!'

'Only until they checked things out, then I was back home again. That's what I mean – people here are pretty reasonable.'

'You Catholics!' Her voice sounded high and jagged. 'You think the world is full of saints! You think the locals won't

7

remember that the Austrians threw flowers and cheered when the Germans crossed our border?'

Anton pushed his mop of thick dark hair from his eyes and sat back in his chair. Despite her affection for him, it was one of Hedy's constant disappointments that Anton avoided arguments. It was partly a dislike of confrontation, partly a genuine desire not to cause unhappiness. Perhaps that was why she had never felt any romantic attraction towards him, despite all they had in common. How much more protected she might feel now, if things had been different between them.

Anton shifted in his chair, manoeuvring to change the subject. 'I must try to get some sleep tonight,' he said eventually. 'The bakery will re-open tomorrow. Mr Reis reckons we'll be mobbed with people panic-buying, but I'm not so sure. I think most people will try to carry on as if it's a normal day.'

Hedy gave a bitter laugh. 'Oh yes, of course. Like you say, the shops will open, order of the Commandant. And we'll all go about our business like nothing's happened. That's what people do, isn't it? We'll hang up our blackout blinds and move our clocks forward an hour to fit German time. And we'll tell ourselves it'll all be fine.' Her breath was coming in short gasps.

Anton moved towards her. 'Hedy, don't.'

'Everyone will walk around town, pretending we're not terrified of being arrested. And me, I'll sit around waiting to be packed off God knows where on the next boat. But you're right – apart from that, it'll be just like any normal day.' The last words left her as a scream as she sank to her knees, the sobs jerking her body. 'I can't take this, Anton, not again. Please, don't let them take me away.'

Anton held her gently in his arms, muttering words of comfort, then passed her his handkerchief. Hedy cried into it for a full ten minutes while Anton made hot tea, and sat Hedy down in his own chair to drink it. Then he put Rachmaninov on the gramophone, and they both sat in a companionable stillness, listening to the soaring melodies until the sun began to dip. Hedy watched the sky above the rooftops turn from pale gold to pink, her thoughts in freefall. She thought about her parents back in Vienna, whose precious letters would no longer reach her. She thought about Roda, with her silver laugh and wild hair; how brave her sister had been, stuffing that envelope of schilling notes down her knickers as they pushed their old Steyr motor car into thick, concealing undergrowth, two kilometres from the Swiss border. She wondered if Roda ever made it to Palestine. Then Hedy closed her eyes and dozed for a while. When she woke, Anton provided more tea and some stale macaroons he'd taken from the shop. He gave her a leftover tinned sardine to take back for Hemingway. Finally, as the sky grew royal blue, it was time for her to go.

'I'll get my jacket and walk you back,' Anton said. 'You shouldn't be out on the streets alone.'

Hedy blew her nose and ran her fingers through her hair to push it back into shape. Tonight was a threshold, a time for putting things in order, for packing and storing away. Tomorrow she would buy a bolt for the front door. A large black steel one that would slide into its socket with a solid click. Metal was what she needed now.

Outside the window, the strongest, brightest stars were beginning to push through the darkness. As she stared at them she thought of the protestors on the streets of Vienna, down on their hands and knees scrubbing pro-independence slogans from the pavements. The Krauts had laughed and pretended that the kicked-over pails and crushed fingers were an accident, and the chalk and paint eventually washed away. But the words and colours of the messages were burned into her memory for ever, and the resolve never left those protestors' eyes.

Anton returned with his jacket. Hedy handed him back his handkerchief.

'Keep it.'

Hedy shook her head. 'No thanks. I won't be needing it any more.'

★

The morning of 16 September, a day ringed in thick black ink on Hedy's calendar, dawned bright and clear, though a stiff breeze persisted from the direction of the harbour. The elements had been unpredictable in recent days; a fierce storm had blown in from the Atlantic straight into the Gulf of St Malo, bringing sharp showers and a wind that whipped around the corners of the town's streets, blowing women's hats from their heads and catching the new swastika flag that now hung outside the town hall. Such squalls were unusual for the island's mild climate, not when the leaves were still green on the trees and the evenings were still so light. Yet Hedy had heard no one complain about it; perhaps because there were no longer any tourists to drive away, or perhaps because it seemed a fitting reflection of the island's new mass depression. Last night, when she had wandered by the sea wall of St Aubin's bay watching German NCOs rolling out miles of barbed wire along the beach, it seemed to her that even the waves were receding quicker than before, as if they no longer wished to stay in this infected place.

Hedy pulled her cardigan a little tighter over her dress as she made her way towards the town's main shopping street, wondering why the purposeful rhythm of her heeled peep-toe sandals echoed so loudly as she hurried along the pavement – so much so that passers-by turned to stare at her, seemingly affronted by the sound. Click-clacking into King Street, it slowly dawned on her that the volume was due to the disappearance of motorised traffic. Apart from occasional German vehicles, the streets of St Helier were once more a maze of pedestrian streets, where every sharp noise bounced and ricocheted around the walls in a mimic of bygone times. She made a mental note not to wear heels in public again. She had not spent the last weeks as a ghost in her own community, slipping into the streets occasionally to buy food or take some air, only to draw attention to herself now.

Still, she was grateful to have found a new apartment in the centre of town, within easy reach of the shops and the covered market on Beresford Street. It was a big step down from the Mitchells' family home, but with that property now under legal stewardship, a chilly bedsit at the top of a town house was some kind of home, and better than getting stuck out in the country parishes. Already the shops had sold out of bicycles, and Hedy had spotted a few ageing nags harnessed to tatty old Edwardian carts, piled up with produce from St Mary and St Martin, bringing steaming piles of horse dung back to the modern tarmac roads. Pretty soon, Hedy mused, the streets of Jersey would sound and smell like the streets of her childhood.

She checked her watch; it was a little after nine fifteen, giving her just enough time to buy new stockings before her appointment. This morning she'd chased Hemingway around the apartment with a newspaper after he'd laddered her last pair, shouting at him that she wished she'd left him behind. Bare legs would simply not do – and certainly not today, when it was vital that she look and feel her very best. She hurried on towards De Gruchy's department store, passing several local housewives all wearing the same expression – a wary, hunted look of fearful expectation. Each of them quickened their pace as they passed groups of bantering German soldiers – scared to be so close to the enemy, afraid to run in case it should be misinterpreted. And there were scores, perhaps hundreds, of soldiers in the town now, browsing the shop windows and loafing in the parks. How the Reich could spare so many boats to transport them all, Hedy could only wonder. Crossing the road to avoid a boisterous group of off-duty privates sharing cigarettes and slapping each other's shoulders, she reached the store, pushed open the heavy glass door and made her way through the various elegant counters to the hosiery department.

'Excuse me?' Hedy tried to neutralise her accent as much as possible without sounding like a parody. 'I would like to buy some stockings.'

The assistant, a woman in her forties with hair in a top-knot bun, inclined her head as she prepared her customer's bad news. 'I'm sorry, madam, we're completely sold out.'

Hedy glanced down at the display drawers under the counter's polished glass top, and saw that they were almost empty. 'You have nothing in the back, perhaps?' She beamed a rictus smile, afraid this obvious approach might backfire, but the woman shook her head.

'Sorry, I can't help you.' She leaned forward conspiratorially, her sickly floral perfume rising uninvited up Hedy's nostrils, and hissed: 'It's *them*. They come in here all friendly, but look! Gone through the whole place like ruddy locusts – sending it all back to their families, see, 'cause they've had nothing in their shops for months. Winter coats, kitchen stuff, fabric, you name it. You tried to buy cheese this week? Can't get it for love nor money.'

Hedy matched her low volume. 'Can you not refuse to serve them?'

'This Jerry officer came in, said if we do, our managers will be thrown in prison. But where's the new stock going to come from, that's what I want to know? You see them down the harbour this week, sending all our Jersey Royals to France? What are we supposed to eat? Tell you what . . .' The woman's face brightened as an idea occurred to her, and her voice lowered even further. 'You can have the stockings I'm wearing right now if you can get us a couple of pork chops by tonight? It's the old man's birthday and I've got nothing for him but a bit of leftover tripe.'

Hedy stared at her, considering. The thought of putting on a strange woman's dirty stockings was unpleasant, but more dispiriting was the realisation that even if she wanted to, she was in no position to strike that kind of deal. Only this morning she'd noticed that the butcher at the end of her road had stuck up a sign reading 'Regular Customers Only'. Special deals were doubtless available to friends and the favoured in this insular little place, but Hedy had no such traction. She saw her future stretching ahead, an endless queue in which she was always at the back, getting what no one else wanted or nothing at all.

'Thank you. I appreciate the thought but I'll try elsewhere.'

The assistant shrugged to indicate that Hedy was wasting her time. And so it proved to be. Voisins store, the haberdashers at the top end of town, even the funny little shop behind the market where the old ladies went for crossover pinafores and flannelette nightdresses all gave her the same story. By ten minutes to ten Hedy found herself defeated, heading towards her appointment with still naked legs, and her mother's disapproving voice ringing in her head, telling her that nice girls never went out like that.

As soon as she turned into the Royal Square, still bearing the giant white cross of surrender painted on its pink granite paving, she saw the crowd. A chaotic queue of men, snaking around the block into Church Street, huddled together in twos and threes, all shuffling their feet and muttering furtive expletives to each other as they waited to enter the makeshift records office set up in the library. It was, Hedy realised, the registration line for local men between eighteen and fifty-five – a manifestation of the Nazis' desire to list, classify and number, and a preparation for future identifications. From now on, the seeking out, hauling up and dispensation of Jersey people would be as easy as taking a memo from a pigeonhole. What was the English expression? Like shooting fish in a barrel. The wind blew again, and she shuddered.

From somewhere in the centre of the crowd came shouts of anger. Hedy craned her neck to witness a young man in a flat cap gesticulating at two German privates, shouting that they had no right to treat law-abiding citizens this way. She watched the soldiers lead the man away, her heart thumping in her chest, and closed her eyes momentarily. Then she straightened her dress, swung away from the crowd and set off again without looking back. At the far end of the square she turned into Hill Street and, holding her head high, walked briskly into the Aliens Office.

★

Lieutenant Kurt Neumann dropped his duffel bag onto the waxed floor of his new quarters, and headed straight for the French windows at the end of the sunny room. He could already feel a grin spreading across his face, like a kid at his first funfair. What a view! If only he had a camera. The garden was gorgeous. Puffy white blooms of alamy roses and exotic seaside shrubs surrounded a neat lawn. At the end was an ornate iron gate, and beyond that – the sea. Or, to use the proper English word from his new dictionary, the *seaside*. This was not the ocean that Kurt was used to, that scary, churning plain that threatened to swallow ships and suck down soldiers. This was a sweep of sparkling sapphire, licking at a beach of ash-blonde sand and bubbly black seaweed. It beckoned you into it, dared you to rip off your boots and run barefoot along its soft, welcoming shore. If he didn't have a deployment briefing in ten minutes, Kurt would have done exactly that, right now. He shook his head in wonder and gratitude at getting a posting here.

The Unterfeldwebel who'd collected them from the harbour a little after dawn had suggested a guided tour of the island before dropping each officer at his allocated billet. In the back of the gleaming Morris Eight convertible, Kurt's immediate neighbour, a Lieutenant Fischer who proudly mentioned three times that he was from Munich, spread a map over his knees and bombarded their driver with questions about geographical positions and plans for fortified defences. But Kurt, apart from the odd nod of fake interest, simply sat back in the leather seat and looked around, happy to let the information wash over him. There was plenty of time for work later. Right now he wanted to absorb every detail.

The island, it seemed, was basically a rectangle. They drove first along St Aubin's bay on the south side, past the quaint granite harbour with its bobbing fishing boats, and over the hill to St Brelade where lush green vegetation tumbled down to a white sandy bay. The road took them up the west side with its vast beach and rolling dunes, then ten kilometres along the north coast, with its majestic cliffs and picture-postcard bays of blue-green water. On the east side, the terracotta moonscape of a barren rocky shore revealed itself as the tide slid out, and the glorious, centuries-old Mont Orgueil Castle rose skywards. At each bend in the winding roads, in every dip and under every arch of thick emerald foliage, Kurt felt a rush of excitement. But by now Fischer and the other officers were checking their watches, muttering about finding their billets and reporting in. Kurt nodded in agreement, while thinking how he'd like to return here with his old chum Helmut after the war; apparently there were plans afoot to turn all the Channel Islands into a high-class resort for the military when all this was over. They could stay at one of those big hotels on the Esplanade, hit the bars, meet some girls. They'd have a ball.

His billet turned out to be a pretty semi-detached house on the east side, in an area named Pontac Common. The interior smelled of polish and lavender, and had been decorated tastefully in muted floral patterns by its previous Jersey owners. Standing in the garden and looking out towards the sea, Kurt wondered where they were living now. The late summer sun warmed his face despite the chill wind, and bees buzzed among the flowers. Fischer, who was marked on the list as Kurt's new room-mate, appeared through the French windows behind him, smiling in approval at the view.

'Some place, isn't it?'

'Beautiful,' Kurt replied.

'Needs a lot of pulling into line, though. The whole garrison, I mean.'

'Really?' Kurt noticed that he was wearing an Infantry Assault badge and a bronze Close Combat clasp.

'Public relations directive from Berlin.' Fischer sniffed and stubbed out the end of a small cigar on the lawn. 'There was a lot of co-operation with the local government in the first weeks – personally I think that sends out a bad message.' Kurt nodded, wondering what that meant. 'Apparently they've not even rounded up the Judenschweine yet.'

Kurt dragged deeply on his cigarette, sensing that the fun part of the day was coming to a close. 'Do they intend to?'

'They're being registered this week. Then we'll see.' Fischer took in a huge lungful of sea air. 'Yes. I reckon we can really do something with this place.'

★

Hedy watched as Clifford Orange, Chief Aliens Officer of Jersey, arranged himself behind his desk, running his hands over the surface as if savouring its solidity. He was a middle-aged man with skin that bloomed and flaked around his cheeks; his hair was thinning but he sported a small moustache and eyebrows so heavy they looked like they might crawl away of their own accord. From the ceiling hung a chandelier, far too large for the room; the sun poured through the window and splashed off the gleaming floor. Beyond the pane, Hedy could see the trees in the town churchyard. She sat down on the upholstered chair in front of Orange's desk and folded her hands in her lap on top of her handbag, hoping it might convey conformity and obedience. She offered a small smile but Orange was already lost in the file laid out before him.

'So, Miss Bercu. Let me refresh my memory. You are twenty-one years old, you arrived in Jersey on the fifteenth of November 1938, and you currently reside at 28 New Street, correct?'

'That's correct, the top flat.'

He glanced up at her with a curious look. Hedy suspected it was her command of English that intrigued him. She wondered if he'd expected her to bark like a dog.

'When you arrived here you were in possession of a recent British visa in the name of Hedwig Bercu-Goldenberg, a foreigner's passport issued in Vienna the previous September, and a registration card recording your status as a Romanian national, issued in Vienna in May 1937 in the name of Hedwig Goldenberg.' He put down the document and looked her in the eye. 'Can you explain the variation in your nomenclature?'

'I think I have already explained: Bercu was my stepfather's name, and Goldenberg was my mother's.'

'Your stepfather?'

'I don't know who my real father was. After I was born my mother married a Romanian, and I took his name.'

Hedy swallowed at the end of the sentence and became painfully aware of a film of sweat on her upper lip. She had rehearsed this story a dozen times with Anton in her apartment, but saying it out loud in a formal environment felt different.

Orange removed his fountain pen from its holder and with great precision made a note on the document. 'So, Goldenberg being a Jewish name, you are in fact Jewish?'

'No.'

Orange placed the cap back on his pen and laid it to one side, ensuring that it sat in perfect parallel with the blotter. 'You're not Jewish?'

'I was raised a Protestant. My stepfather is Jewish and my mother adopted his religion when they married, but I have no Jewish blood.' Hedy attempted the smile again but this time it wouldn't come. Every word of the lie grew like cotton wool in her mouth. Orange's eyes darted over her and she realised he was staring at her hair, which she had pinned up especially for today's interview. She knew its tawny blonde colour, a gift from her grandmother's side of the family, would be her greatest alibi today, particularly to someone like Orange who had probably only seen pictures of Jews in books. But now he seemed to be assessing its authenticity. Perhaps he had been told that all Jewish women wear wigs.

'You're telling me that your mother, whose name is Goldenberg, was in fact Protestant?'

'Yes.' Her hands were now gripping her bag as if it might fly out of her lap at any moment.

Orange rose from his seat and walked over to the window, gazing across at the Norman church tower in what he clearly hoped suggested a pose of judicious concentration.

'You see, Miss Bercu, I am in a most difficult position. I trust you understand the relationship between the Jersey authorities and the new German Field Command?'

'Not entirely.'

Orange smoothed his moustache with his thumb and forefinger. 'It is one, I fear, of immense delicacy. Jersey civil administration continues as before, but we must now accommodate and execute the orders of our new masters. And the Germans have requested that all Jews living within the Channel Islands must be registered separately from the remainder of the populace.' He turned back to face her. 'So you see I would be failing in my duty should I fail to register any Jewish persons with German Field Command.'

Hedy tried to clear her throat surreptitiously before answering. 'But I am not Jewish.'

He sighed just loud enough to let her hear it. 'If you'll forgive me, I find your explanation unconvincing in the light of the documented evidence. If you were somehow able to prove your heritage—'

'Why is it I who must provide proof? If you don't believe me, is it not up to you, or the Germans, to provide proof that I *am*

Jewish?' She stopped and bit her lip, remembering Anton's advice to placate, not provoke. In her lap, her nails dug into her palms.

Orange was glaring at her now, and returned to his seat as if to wrap things up. 'On the contrary,' he replied. 'The Field Commandant's instructions state quite clearly that where any doubt exists, one should take the precautionary measure of classifying that person as Jewish.'

Hedy took a deep breath. She sensed she had only seconds left. 'Mr Orange . . .' She was careful to pronounce the 'g' softly in the French style, not hard like the English fruit. 'I have seen in Vienna how the Germans treat the Jews. If you register me as a Jew, I will be watched constantly. I may be imprisoned, perhaps worse. You will be placing me in grave danger.'

Orange frowned at her, a father disappointed in his errant child. 'No active measures have been taken against Jewish citizens.'

'That doesn't mean they are not planned.'

'If you are so fearful of the Germans why did you not evacuate in June?'

'I would have done, if England had accepted my current visa status.' She dabbed at her top lip with the back of her hand. 'If you submit the information I have told you today, the Germans will accept your word. There is no reason why anyone should question my race status for the rest of this war.' She raised her eyes to meet his, a final appeal. Orange looked from her face to her file and back again, before closing the file.

'I'm sorry, Miss Bercu, but given the information I have, it would be remiss of me not to classify you as Jewish by Romanian parentage within the current regulations. If I were to bypass the rules, and the Germans were to discover at some later date that I had done so, I could risk not just my own position but the whole relationship of co-operation between the Jersey Government and our occupiers, on which this island's security depends. I'm sure you understand.' She continued to stare at him and, suddenly uncomfortable, Orange began to chatter on with false cheerfulness while shuffling his papers. 'You really have nothing to worry about, you know. Whatever irregularities may have occurred in your home country, registration is simply a formality here, part of the German zeal for good administration. Those of us in government have found most of them perfectly reasonable and courteous. We simply have to play by their rules for the foreseeable future.' She knew he was waiting for her to stand, but Hedy remained where she was, as if refusing to move from this chair might somehow alter the course of her destiny. 'Anyway, I think that's all for today.'

It was over. Hedy stood with difficulty, trying to recalibrate her new position. Her fate had now been sealed, her life transformed by the stroke of a pen. She glanced about her, noticing other things in the office – the brass banker's lamp set at a perfect forty-five degree angle, the shelves of perfectly aligned alphabetical files on Jersey law. And in the furthest, dimmest corner, a globe on a stand, bearing a fine coating of dust, unturned in many months. She had never stood a chance.

Orange held out his hand for her to shake. 'Good day, Miss Bercu.'

Hedy stared at his hand without extending her own, then looked him straight in the eye.

'*Fick dich selbst.*'

And she turned on her heel and left.

1941

S t Ouen's bay on the west coast was the wildest, most dramatic side of the island. Five miles of pristine sand, curved into a perfect arc, provided an open graveyard for the foam-topped rollers that glided up the gulf from the Atlantic, rising and swelling before crashing onto the sand with the force of advancing tanks, blasting white spray into the air. The bay was broken only by rocky outcrops at each end, and La Rocco Tower half a mile out, a stubborn little edifice from the days of Napoleon still holding its own against the bay's strong currents. Hedy loved that little tower. This was her favourite place to walk, even though the bitter wind blew straight through the disintegrating fabric of her old woollen coat. And for want of proper glue, the sole of her left lace-up shoe, by now her only remaining pair, was trying to separate itself from the leather.

Spring had refused to appear this year. The sun that should by now be warming the soil, coaxing the flowers and tomatoes into premature season and injecting its unique, nutty flavour into the island's potatoes, glowed pale and watery. Hedy made her way along the path between the sharp blades of seagrass, feeling the penetrating sand grate between her toes. Behind the open spread of the beach, undulating sand dunes seeped into the gentle slopes of nearby farmland. If any Allied counter-attack should come, it would surely be here. Little wonder that this bay was now the focus of Hitler's obsession with steel and concrete, shoring up his beloved Atlantic wall against a force he was certain was on its way. Feeling the vibration of distant trucks, Hedy turned to see a column of grey and khaki trundle its way up the Five Mile Road, weighed down with cargoes of metal and cement. Mines were being planted all along the shore, and new defences were springing up from La Pulente in the south to Grosnez in the north, hulking grey towers with shadowy armament slits, squat concrete bunkers and gun emplacements. St Ouen's would never look the same again.

The bus back to town was due in twenty minutes. Hedy considered a final stroll down to Le Braye slip, but decided against it; there was only one service today, and if she mistimed her return she knew she would not have the energy to run to catch it, nor to walk the six kilometres back to town. In recent months she had learned the role of fats in the human diet, and what happened when they were removed. Shivering, she stuffed her hands in her pockets, shuffled to the bus stop, grateful for the stone bench beside it, and slumped down, waiting for her breathing to return to normal. That was when she spotted the copy of yesterday's *Evening Post* lying on the grass behind the seat.

Hedy looked around in surprise, half expecting someone to appear and claim it. Newspaper could be used for kindling, stopping draughts or cleaning windows – discarding an entire edition was unthinkable, and the paper's owner must have been furious to discover its loss. Thrilled with her treasure, Hedy flicked through the eight dual-language pages, filled with orders and propaganda disguised as news. Later she could have fun scouring the columns for translation errors, the ones deliberately left in by the Jersey editors to let their readership know exactly which articles had been dictated. And she would read the exchange and mart columns too, even though Hedy had long ago exchanged any possession of any value she could afford to part with.

As she sat reading, her eyes caught the headline on page three: 'THIRD ORDER relating to measures against Jews.' The same proclamation had been printed the previous week. Hedy had no wish to read it again and tried to turn the page, but found herself drawn in by ghoulish fascination.

... shall be prohibited from carrying on the following economic activities:
(a)   wholesale and retail trade;
(b)   hotel and catering industry;
(c)   insurance;
(d)   navigation;
(e)   dispatch and storage;
(f)   travel agencies, organisation of tours;
(g)   guides;
(h)   transport undertakings of all descriptions, including the hire of motor and other vehicles;
(i)   banking and money exchange;
...

The list ran on to the bottom of the page, but Hedy folded the pages back together and stuffed the whole paper into her coat's inside pocket. Depressing as it was, in the end this latest order made no difference to her. No one would employ a Jew anyway, for fear of upsetting the Germans. Even her last job as a school cleaner was deemed too risky by the headmaster, who packed her off with a week's wages and some excuse about unsatisfactory toilets. For three months now she had lived on nothing but her meagre savings and the charity of Anton, who saved every burnt crust in the bakery and often slipped her a few pennies to buy rations. But this morning as she wrapped up for her walk, she had noticed how the clothes hung loose on her body, and her skin, once creamy and lustrous, had become dry and sallow. This, she sometimes thought, was how it would end. The Germans weren't going to shoot her after all. They were just going to starve her to death.

The bus arrived, packed, and Hedy, having counted out the fare in small change, wriggled through and found a seat at the very back. Here she could take in the scenery without getting drawn into conversation. Too often she had seen people recoil at her accent, taking her for a German secretary or even a spy. Invisibility and silence were a simpler option these days. The bus pulled away up the hill and Hedy craned her neck to see La Rocco Tower disappear in the rear window, the water swirling and sucking at the rocks beneath.

At least tonight she had something to look forward to. Anton had offered to pay for her to go to West's cinema to see *The Wizard of Oz*, and although she had seen it six times since the picture house got stuck with it last year, it was a welcome change from another evening alone in her apartment. In the early days the cinema had sold mugs of cocoa in the interval, though nothing so lavish was available now. Hedy's stomach growled and her mouth watered at the memory, and for the rest of the journey she forced herself to count trucks of soldiers on the road ahead. Thinking about food achieved nothing but misery.

She alighted the bus at the Weighbridge and made her way to the cinema where the queue was already winding out of the building and down the street. It was always Jersey folk here, the Germans preferring films in their own language at the Forum picture house, though the field police sent down the occasional spy to keep an eye on events. Hedy searched the queue for Anton, and for a moment thought she had arrived before him. And then she saw. In the centre of the queue, his tousled hair combed back into an impression of slickness, Anton was squashed tightly against a woman, a little older than himself, with a pale oval face and light blue eyes. Her black hair, worn in a homemade copy of a Greer Garson crop, made her look younger than her thirty-odd years, and a little vulnerable. She and Anton stood arm in arm, and Anton was laughing at something she'd said – a gurgling giggle Hedy hadn't heard in quite a while. Hedy felt a rush of curiosity. She had often seen Anton stare blushingly at pretty girls in parks and cafés, but he had never had the courage to ask anyone out before. Hedy edged towards them and waited.

Anton beamed and breathed in deeply as he always did before speaking in English. 'Hedy, this is Dorothea. We met last week when she came to the bakery.'

Dorothea ignored Hedy's outstretched hand and rushed at her cheek, her lips already pursed for a kiss. 'Anton's told me so much about you,' she gushed. 'I know what good friends you are. I do hope we can be friends too.'

The woman's fingernails, Hedy noticed, were bitten down to the quick, and her movements as fluttery as a baby bird. But the most startling thing was the strength of her Jersey accent, a twanging inflection Hedy had learned to recognise. Hedy glanced at Anton, surprised by his choice of a local girl. She smiled at Dorothea. 'I like your haircut.'

Dorothea flushed with obvious pleasure. 'Thanks, my mother does it. It's easier to manage like this when you can't buy shampoo.' Hedy's hand went automatically to her own lank, papery locks. 'You're from Vienna too?'

'I am, from Romania originally.'

'And you're a Jew?'

Hedy took half a step back. Her eyes, bright with accusation, moved directly to Anton, but to her annoyance Anton's gaze never left Dorothea. Hedy peered ostentatiously around the queue, indicating that this wasn't a conversation for a public place. Eventually she answered quietly. 'I am registered as a Jew, yes.'

Dorothea, oblivious to Hedy's discomfort, shook her head with sympathy. 'I think it's awful the way they're treating you. I don't know why Hitler hates Jews so much. How are you supposed to manage if you're not allowed to work?' Hedy felt suddenly aware of her frayed coat and gaping shoe. But then an idea lit up Dorothea's face. 'I tell you what I saw the other day – an advert for translators.'

'Translators?' Hedy stared at her, confused.

'That new transport compound the Germans are building at Millbrook? Apparently they want people who can speak English and German to work in the offices. You should apply. Your English is wonderful!' she added with a broad smile.

Hedy's mouth opened and shut, at a loss how to reply. She turned to Anton for a reaction but her friend, finally aware of the brewing storm, had developed a fascination with his own feet. A painful silence expanded in the space between them, until Hedy cleared her throat and spoke deliberately slowly. 'You are suggesting that I, a Jewish girl, apply for a job in a German office?'

'They're probably desperate,' Dorothea replied, as if dispensing a compliment. 'Not many local people speak German – well, it's such a hard language, isn't it? The advert said the pay was good too.'

At that moment a boy in a maroon uniform far too big for him pushed open the doors to the cinema, and Anton stepped forward.

'You said you needed the Ladies', Dory? Go ahead and I'll get the tickets.'

Dorothea gave him a loud kiss on the cheek and hurried off. Anton checked she was out of earshot before turning to Hedy, looking like a child awaiting the cane. 'Please don't judge her, Hedy,' he muttered in German. 'She's got a heart of gold. She's just not very worldly.'

'Anton, what are you playing at?' Hedy's voice came out as a hiss. 'Telling my business to a total stranger?'

'It just came out – we've shared a lot of things this week. Don't worry, she's completely trustworthy.'

'You hardly know her! In any case, she's an islander – she'll get labelled a Jerrybag going out with you.'

Anton refused to meet her gaze. 'She knows I'm not German.'

'Let's not have that discussion again! Good God, Anton, did you hear what she said to me? Does she even know what this war is about? She's a *shoyte*!' Hedy shifted to try to force herself into Anton's eyeline but he continued to glance about him, intent on everything but her.

'Lots of people are having to work for the Germans now, whether they want to or not. In your position it might be worth considering.'

'*My position?*' Hedy glared at him. 'My position is, those bastards drove us from our homeland and view me as no better than an animal! And you're saying I should help them with their administration?'

'I'm saying you need money.' Anton's voice was quiet but steady. 'Hedy, you're my friend. I worry about you. I want to help you but every week it gets harder. What Dorothea is suggesting might be a practical solution . . .' He reached out for her arm.

She brushed his hand away. 'So this is how we behave now? We just accept what's happened – make friends with the Krauts?' She threw her arms in the air, exasperated. 'I can't believe you're taking her side. Or that you're even interested in a woman like that. You know what?' She tugged her coat a little tighter around her. 'I'm going home. I don't want to see the stupid *Wizard of Oz* anyway.' And turning so that Anton would not see the hurt in her eyes, she stomped off. When she finally found the courage to glance back, the queue had disappeared into the cinema.

★

The concrete steps of the house were badly cracked, and the communal door beneath the once ornate portico was so swollen from rain and lack of paint that it barely closed. Hedy slunk into the building and began the long climb up the wide, unlit staircase to her apartment. She heard the creak of dry, ancient wood as she stepped slowly onto each step, and felt as if the sound were coming from within her. Resentment mixed with acid in her empty stomach and ripped at the lining. How would she fill her evening now? The BBC news at nine o'clock, with more depressing reports of Allied defeats in North Africa? Climb into bed with Hemingway and a library book, pull the heavy curtain that separated her 'bedroom' area, and close out the world for a few hours? Her spirits sank at the thought. She knew she'd been hasty walking off like that. That idiotic, petulant temper from her father's side. But it was too late now.

On the first floor she heard the predictable scrape of Mrs Le Couteur's door as it opened an inch, saw one droopy eye peering out from the darkness. In her first weeks here Hedy used to call out a greeting to her neighbour to reassure her, hoping that it might allay the old widow's suspicions and perhaps build a little trust between them. But Hedy had never received more than a grunt in reply, and after she found the pensioner in the downstairs hallway, holding Hedy's mail up to the light to assess the contents, Hedy had given up. Now she ignored the old bat as she passed by, and heard the door click shut again as she continued her steady ascent to the top floor.

The apartment was gloomy, with only the last grey fingers of dusk throwing a little light onto the linoleum. It was bitterly cold. Hemingway padded across to greet her, and Hedy picked him up and held him close, glad of his warm silkiness on her face. But quickly realising there was no food about her body, the ungrateful beast wriggled out of her arms and returned to his basket in front of the fireplace. He sniffed at the empty grate, throwing her hopeful looks.

'Some chance,' Hedy muttered, pulling down the blackout blind. Then, with a slow, reluctant stretch, she took one of the precious candles from the box under the sink. They had cost most of her remaining savings on the black market, and she'd meticulously nicked the wax of each one with a knife, limiting her nightly usage. No Hanukkah ceremony this year. Taking a match from the box on the windowsill, she struck it carefully so that it would light first time without splitting. The wick flared and she placed her hands around its small gold flame.

Now the chill of the room began to bite, bringing with it a crowd of righteous justifications for her stormy departure. She had a right, did she not, to feel upset at Anton's carelessness? Betraying his only friend, in the face of such *meshugas* – from a woman he'd only just met! *Might be worth considering?* This, from the man who complained when he was forced to serve German soldiers in the bakery? If there was one thing she'd always admired about Anton it was his moral compass. Had he just tossed it aside for the sake of a pretty face?

On the tiny stove was a milk saucepan containing the last inch of the cabbage and swede soup she had cooked the day before. The smell of it hung in the air like sour washing. For a moment she debated leaving it for breakfast, but hunger, as always, beat common sense, and soon she was scooping it greedily into her mouth, swallowing faster than was good for her. She sucked hard on the tin spoon to get the last drops, licked the inside of the saucepan until she could taste nothing but metal, and slumped down onto the wooden chair at the little table, staring into the flickering flame. Then, even as she told herself it was a bad idea, she pulled open the shallow drawer tucked beneath the table and slid her hand in, feeling around till she found the small bundle of papers. Drawing the candle closer, she unfurled the thin sheets and sifted through to the last letter, dated April 1940 – exactly a year ago.

'Our darling daughter,' it began in her mother's spidery hand. Several vacuous and suspiciously cheery sentences about the lovely weather and the helpful neighbours followed. And finally, the darkly coded final paragraph: 'But there is talk of us going on a holiday.' Hedy stared back at the flame. Not once in all their years of marriage had her parents ever discussed going on holiday. She closed her eyes and conjured up her mother, warming her hands by the old kitchen range. She thought of Roda – ebony-haired, giggling Roda, posed as she always was in Hedy's mind in a broad sun hat and holding a long pole, tilling the soil on some Palestinian kibbutz. After a while Hedy smoothed down the sheet of paper and returned it to its bundle and its drawer, this time locking it with its small metal key. Reading these letters never brought comfort, any more than recipe books killed hunger pangs. Not for a month would she read those again.

She sat back in her seat but the image of Roda persisted. Roda who had flirted with the German guards when they were questioned that night near the Swiss border, laughing coquettishly over her shoulder to avoid showing her papers, winking at some grinning Nazi to get across the border. Hedy had brimmed over with admiration for her that night. Roda would do whatever she had to in order to survive. She was too bright, too plucky to do anything else.

Hedy, you're my friend. I worry about you.

Very slowly, as if to pull a trick on herself, Hedy eased the copy of the *Evening Post* from her pocket. She opened it on the table and flicked through the pages, this time ignoring the Jewish order and speeding through to the classifieds at the back. It was there, on page seven, a box advertisement.

WANTED: translators fluent in both English and German for office work at NSKK Transportgruppe West, Staffel Vt. Excellent rates. Applications in writing by 15th May.

She read it again, then a third time. The room was perfectly silent, and the only light came from the candle flame and its yellow reflection in Hemingway's staring, questioning eyes. The rent was due on Friday. Once paid, she would have nothing left to buy her rations. A burning pain crept across her chest as she tore around the edges of the advertisement and placed the little rectangle of paper on the table. The room was still cold, but she realised she was sweating.

★

'Private? This one's ready.'

The NCO approached with a clipboard and jotted down the registration plate of the Opel Blitz truck. He then offered the document for signature, and tore off the copy. 'Shall I bring the next one through, Lieutenant?'

'No, I'm going to break for lunch. Give me half an hour.' Wiping his greasy hands on a piece of rag, Kurt Neumann stretched his aching back, slicked his hair back into place and headed for the officers' mess. Rabbit stew on the menu today. Proper stew, with mashed potatoes! This time last year he was living on tins of Fleischkonserve (remembering it still made him belch a little) and that awful rye bread that broke your teeth. His tummy rumbled in happy anticipation.

Crossing the compound, Kurt coughed to clear the dust from his throat. The fine, pale powder of Lager Hühnlein got into everything – clothes, eyes, even socks. That was what you got for throwing up such a vast, sprawling complex in a few short weeks. The scale of the place was impressive, with rows of prefabricated administration huts, material storage units and fortified pathways for heavy vehicles to run in and out all day. From here, according to Field Command, 'the greatest construction of fortifications the world had ever seen' would be planned and implemented.

Privately, Kurt found the whole concept a bit daft. After all, if Churchill wanted to take back these islands by force, wouldn't he have done it by now? Why pour so much money and energy into ruining beautiful scenery? But Kurt knew better than to voice such thoughts to fellow officers – and certainly not around fanatics like Fischer at his billet, or the employees at this place. The Organisation Todt, or 'OT' as the military engineering section was known, was dominated by a real bunch of reprobates – very different from the professional, disciplined guys he'd served with in France. At mealtimes they sat in tight groups, chain smoking and laughing too hard at jokes he found cruel. On one occasion he'd seen a local lad, a kid with a funny walk who was employed to clean out the latrines, kicked in the groin by an OT officer for some apparent disrespect. Kurt had felt sickened by the incident, but hadn't reported it. He told himself there was no point, as no action would be taken. As Helmut had cautioned him all through their schooldays, better to keep your head down when there was nothing to gain. And apart from the OT thugs, he enjoyed his work here. Supervising the work of the mechanics, ticking off inspection lists, signing off the imported trucks – these were all jobs he could do in his sleep. A little fiddling with the Buick engines, a little paperwork – hardly the front line. He could almost be back at engineering college.

There was a queue at the mess hut, so he decided to have a smoke and wait it out. Leaning against the wall of a storage hut, he tapped a Gauloise, his new favourite brand, from a pack in his pocket, and was about to light it when what he saw made him stop, the flame of his lighter still flickering in the breeze. A pale, skinny girl with tawny blonde hair was standing between two of the admin blocks, looking around her in some confusion. Her hair was neatly pinned up, but despite the warmth of the day she wore a shabby wool coat and shoes that looked as if they'd seen better days. She looked anxious, and she clearly needed a good meal, but what struck him most were her eyes. They were the large, frightened eyes of a woodland creature, yet there was a hint of defiance there too. He was about to ask if she needed assistance when she spoke first.

'Excuse me, I'm looking for OT Feldwebel Schulz in Block Seven?'

Kurt smiled, surprised. 'You're German?'

She shook her head. 'From Austria. I'm here for' – she hesitated, as if the words hurt her mouth – 'for the translator's job.'

He couldn't stop staring at those eyes. They were the colour of the sea in Rozel bay. 'Block Seven is the next hut on the left. Here, let me show you.'

'No, thank you.' Her voice contained the chill of compulsory courtesy. 'I can find my own way.' Kurt watched her walk across the uneven terrain, her figure swaying as she moved, not taking his eyes off her for a second until she turned the corner and disappeared.

An hour later, his belly now full of rabbit stew, Kurt was passing the entrance to Block Seven with a stack of signed dockets, when he saw the girl again. This time she was leaving the hut, and as she did so she shook hands with a pudgy little man with wire-rimmed glasses whom Kurt assumed to be Schulz. It was an odd, perfunctory handshake, as if neither of them wanted to partake in it, and both wanted it over as soon as possible. Kurt watched the girl as she walked down the path towards the barbed-wire boundary and the exit gate, then he called Schulz over.

'OT Feldwebel?' The man nodded. Kurt towered over him. 'That young woman – she was here for the translator's job, yes?'

'Yes, Lieutenant.'

'Are you taking her on?'

Schulz squirmed a little. 'No choice I'm afraid, sir. She's fluent in both languages. We've had so few applicants.'

'I don't understand. Is there a problem?'

Schulz blinked very quickly as if someone had kicked sand in his face, and scratched the end of his nose. 'Not at all, sir. I'm sure she will prove entirely acceptable.' Kurt sensed that Schulz was holding something back, but couldn't be bothered to pursue it. His attention was still half on the girl's disappearing figure, so he smiled vaguely and indicated Schulz could go. Then, still holding the dockets in his hand, he felt a surge of curiosity that pressed him forward. At least, that's what he told himself afterwards.

Checking that no one was watching, he crept down the path after the girl, taking care to keep his distance. Reaching the gate, she turned left down the narrow country lane beyond. Throwing the guards a quick salute, Kurt strolled out of the compound after her. Still keeping well back – after all, if she turned to question him what would he say? – he followed the girl to the next bend. There, what he saw made him step back and press himself into the steep grass verge for fear of intruding on this private moment.

The girl was leaning on a rusty iron gate leading to a neighbouring farm, her forearms resting on its top bar. He couldn't see her expression, but the droop of her slender shoulders suggested intense sadness, even despair. She raised one pale, slight hand to her face and wiped her cheeks. With the other hand she pulled out the pins at the back of her neck until her hair fell in soft curls, then she threw back her head to loosen it further, carefully bunched the pins together and placed them in the pocket of her coat. Kurt watched, transfixed, scarcely breathing, afraid she might turn and see him, while at the same time wishing that she would. But the girl didn't turn around; she continued to stand perfectly still, leaning on the gate and staring out across the field before her, as if taking in the scents and perfumes of the surrounding countryside. The breeze caught her hair and the edges of her coat, redrawing her silhouette, and Kurt fancied that she had closed her eyes. Then, as a flight of swallows moved across the sky above her, she leaned forward over the gate and vomited hard into the field below.

★

Town was busier than usual, perhaps due to the morning rumours of French cheeses on sale in the covered market. Hedy stood on the corner, watching housewives hurry past with half-empty shopping bags, and cyclists with rubber tubing for tyres swerving to avoid potholes. She looked about her, trying to make up her mind. Anton's apartment was a short walk to her right, but if she turned left towards New Street she would be home in eight minutes. She had a strong urge to race back to her apartment, feel the comfort of Hemingway's purring on her belly. But she knew this chill between her and Anton had stretched on for too long, and it was time to end it. Today, especially, she craved Anton's easy company and optimistic reassurance. She turned to the right and felt her footsteps quicken as she neared the shop. Without knocking, she pushed open the side door to the flat and started up the stairs. But what she heard next froze her in her tracks.

'In through the nose, out through the mouth . . . slowly now.' The voice – male, filled with authority – drifted towards her on the stale air that smelled of must and flour. Hedy's stomach tightened as she continued on tiptoe, trying to identify the speaker. It certainly wasn't Anton, nor was it his boss Mr Reis. She tried not to make a sound, hesitating as she reached the top.

'Anton?' The apartment door was ajar, and she pressed on it until it swung wide enough for her to see inside. Sitting upright in the centre of the room on a wooden chair was Dorothea, her eyes closed in concentration, her breaths quick and shallow, her brunette crop sticking to her forehead. She was holding her hands together in front of her as if in prayer, and her chest jumped with a persistent cough. On her right, his hand resting reassuringly on her shoulder, was Anton, and on her left stood a short middle-aged gentleman with grey flecks around the temples and round horn-rimmed spectacles. The man turned to nod at Hedy before turning back to his charge. Hedy looked from one to the other in confusion, till she spotted the large leather bag, partly open, and the stethoscope peeping out from beneath the gentleman's flannel jacket.

Anton's eyes flicked towards her. 'Dory had an asthma attack.'

A shameful burst of irritation flared immediately. What was this woman doing here, if she was ill? And why was she relying on Anton, when she surely had family of her own? But taking in her clay-coloured skin and the beads of sweat around the forehead, Hedy pushed her other feelings down. An empty stomach, Albert Einstein once advised, was not a good political adviser.

'Fortunately,' Anton was saying, 'Doctor Maine was willing to come here from the hospital.'

'Are you all right?' Hedy asked. Dorothea opened her eyes for a moment and acknowledged Hedy's question with a desultory waggle of her fingers. 'What caused this?'

'She was upset.' Anton gave a little shake of his head, warning Hedy not to pursue it further. Hedy tentatively placed her bag down on the table, unsure if she should stay, while the doctor continued to listen to Dorothea's lungs through his stethoscope. Finally he straightened up.

'You must try to avoid situations that make you anxious, Miss Le Brocq. Prevention is better than cure, yes?' His voice, which had the Jersey lilt to it, was honeyed and kind, though cracked with tiredness. The bags under his eyes reminded Hedy of her uncle Otto, and when he turned to include her in his smile she found herself smiling back. 'Stocks of epinephrine are low, like everything else,' he continued. 'We may not be able to get it at all in a couple of months. There are a few home treatments that can help – mustard oil, ginger – but I doubt you'll find those in the shops these days. Try to get her to the hospital if it happens again. House calls are becoming limited to absolute emergencies.'

'I thought doctors were allowed private cars?' Anton asked.

'Yes, but our fuel allocation is less than two gallons a week. That can mean difficult choices sometimes.' He scribbled out a bill in a chaotic hand and gave it to Anton, who looked at it with surprise. The doctor waved his hand. 'What can money buy you now? A loaf from your delightful Austrian bakery will more than cover it. Good day to you all.' And with that he collected his bag and slipped quietly from the room, leaving a faint smell of cigarette smoke. To her surprise, Hedy found herself a little saddened by his exit.

Anton went to the sink in the corner to get Dorothea a glass of water. Hedy followed him, speaking softly in German. 'So what happened?'

Anton kept his eyes on the running tap, but answered in German too. 'Her stepfather found out about me and threw her out of the house. Dory's going to live with her grandmother for a while until things calm down.' He caught her eye for a split second. 'Please don't say I told you so.'

'Fine, I won't say it.'

Anton shut off the tap and turned towards her. 'I'm sorry, but I like her. And she likes me. What should I do? Dump her to please everyone else?'

Hedy reached out to touch his arm. 'You've only known her a few weeks. Is it really worth this much trouble?'

'It's only trouble if you choose to see it that way. Her family will come around eventually. Like Dory says, if it makes us happy, it must be right.'

'And what if the Germans force you into the army?'

'I'm classed as a food producer, so that won't happen. Unless the war drags on.' He shrugged to indicate there was nothing more to say, then took the water to Dorothea and held the glass to her mouth. Dorothea sipped it slowly, keeping her hand on his. Hedy stayed by the sink, watching the two of them, listening to Dorothea's shallow, grainy breaths. The window was open, and the grubby lace curtain blew up a little in the breeze. Somewhere outside, a mother shouted at a crying child.

Anton broke the moment, speaking deliberately in English. 'How come you're in your best dress?'

Hedy hesitated, reluctant to share her big news now. But Anton would find out soon enough anyway. 'I got that translator's job at Lager Hühnlein.' She watched their astonished faces for a moment before adding, 'You were right – they were desperate.'

Anton smiled for the first time. 'But that's wonderful. Dory, did you hear that?'

Dorothea nodded and took her deepest breath yet to reply. 'That's great news, Hedy. I knew it would work out for you.' She smiled with real warmth, and at that moment Hedy realised that, probably thanks to Anton's diplomacy, Dorothea had no idea of the upset she'd caused that first night.

'If I had any other choice . . .' Hedy stopped. Such rationales, even from her own lips, sounded hollow and pathetic.

'Some acorn coffee?' Anton gesticulated towards his little stove.

Hedy shook her head. 'Another time maybe – you've got enough on your hands.' The remark prickled with resentment, and she saw the hurt in his eyes, instantly wished she could take it back.

'Well, I'm really pleased for you, Hedy. Come to the bakery soon and tell me all about it.'

The child outside the window was wailing now, and the room seemed stifling. Hedy felt a sudden need for fresh air. She forced herself to smile. 'All right, I will. Bye.'

On her way down the stairs, she heard him call after her: 'You've done the right thing, you know.'

But Hedy pretended not to hear.

★

The clock on the back wall read four: the predictable aching hour, when the strain of sitting hunched over her ancient Adler typewriter since early morning produced a shot of hot pain behind her left shoulder blade, and the pressure required to hammer down the stiff keys burned her tendons.

Hedy sat back on her rickety wooden chair and took a moment to stretch her back and massage her throbbing wrists. She wondered if the other girls in the office suffered the same way. Those big blowsy Bavarians, imported from the Fatherland to type and file all week, and screw their soldier boyfriends all weekend. If they shared her pain, they never showed it. Hedy gazed up at the narrow window of the hut, the shafts of sunlight taunting her with their promise of a glorious afternoon beyond. The room was airless, its fluorescent lights flickering pointlessly even on a bright day like this, and from her neighbour Derek, a sallow, nervous youth who was one of the only other non-Germans in her block, emanated a perpetual smell of mould. Hedy suspected it was because, like her, he had nowhere to dry wet laundry. She suspected she probably smelled the same. If so, she didn't care. Let them smell her. Aware of the sweeping gaze of Fräulein Vogt, the block supervisor, she took another list of German building company bids and stuffed a translation form into the Adler's roller.

Today was Saturday, the end of her first month in the office, and it was pay day. She hoped that collecting the small brown envelope might lift her crushed sprits. The job itself was undemanding – translation of correspondence, payrolls, allocations – and the wages were decent. But the misery of it weighed heavier than even she had expected. The long hours, the dust, the stuffiness, the exhausting one-hour walk twice a day on so little food – all that was bad enough. But a conscience, it transpired, could not be assuaged or scrubbed clean. Each morning she watched as the trucks, filled with dead-eyed mercenaries, rumbled off to their construction sites to reinforce anti-tank walls and build new airport runways, knowing that she was now a part of it. Survival, it seemed, was an expensive business for the soul.

Schulz, whose eyebrows had almost shot out of his head when he'd first seen the red 'J' on her identity card, had allocated her a desk in the furthest, dimmest corner of the hut, clearly anxious that her racial status might cause a riot. But it soon became clear that senior OT staff were keeping Hedy's classification to themselves. For that at least, Hedy was grateful. Those vapid Aryan typists, who stared right through her as if she were made of paper, would doubtless be far less passive in the shadowy pathways between the work huts, should they discover the truth. She accepted her corner seat without complaint, kept her head down and got through her work with speed and minimal speech – though here, at least, her accent acted as a cover, rather than a liability. She ate alone in the canteen, made no eye contact. Other than her supervisor, and occasionally Derek when he ran out of something, she drew no attention from anyone. Were it not for the perfectly formed dollop of saliva that, with vengeful secrecy, she spat onto the floor of the latrines on every visit, she might not have been there at all.

The only exception was the German lieutenant she had met on the day of her interview. They had passed each other on the footpaths several times, and each time he greeted her with a broad smile and some small courtesy in German. She replied with a mumbled hello, knowing that a word interpreted as inappropriate or disrespectful could mean dismissal. But there was an unexpected warmth in those eyes, almost a mischievous twinkle, that she liked. And secretly, when she had gone through an entire week without one meaningful conversation, she quite looked forward to these fleeting moments of normality. Strange what tricks loneliness could play on the mind.

Just as she pulled her finished sheet from the roller, Vogt, a pinched woman with exceptionally long, yellowing fingernails, approached Hedy's desk. On it she placed her wage packet, followed by a list of names and addresses and a bundle of petrol coupons. 'Allocation lists,' she squawked in her strangled, parrot-like voice. 'To be done this afternoon. Coupons are for immediate dispatch. When you have completed each list, place the recipient's form and the appropriate number of coupons in the sealed brown envelope.'

'Does each recipient get the same number of coupons each week?'

'No. If fuel stocks are low, they may receive fewer.'

'And is that information provided on the form?'

'No explanation is required. The difference will be compensated to them the next week, or when stocks recover.'

Hedy nodded and began to fill in the forms as requested, but her mind scattered with a dangerous thought. If recipients had no idea how many coupons to expect each week, then she could, in theory, allocate any number she chose, and pocket the rest. Her heart began to hammer in her chest. Petrol coupons were worth a fortune and could be exchanged for anything. Every week she saw black market meat, eggs and sugar sneaked across market stalls, at prices even her new wages wouldn't meet. This could be her key to that magic kingdom. But what if the forms were checked before dispatch? Grey, irregular shapes appeared on her paperwork, and she realised her palms were sweating.

She tried to focus, think clearly. Getting caught was unthinkable. Theft of German property had sent plenty of islanders to jail – as a Jew, it would mean deportation. But still her mind danced and dived, picturing not just the prize, but the satisfaction. Scoring a point. Getting one over. She breathed in and out slowly and deeply, while observing the other employees from beneath her brows.

Over the next hour she watched each worker take their paper-work to the front desk and place the coupons in the collection boxes. Each time, the copies of the documents were stamped by an administrator and piled high on Vogt's desk like a layer cake, but at no point did anyone bother to check them. Hedy calculated that so long as the correct amount of coupon bundles were counted in the stock room, no one would be any the wiser. And even if some delivery driver complained about a reduced allowance, there was no way anyone could trace the variation back to her.

At ten minutes to six she still hadn't made up her mind. By now she was fighting to control her trembling fingers. Then, as the large hand on the clock eased almost to the twelve, she saw Vogt turn away to deal with a pile of signatures. Hedy picked up a form for an Irish construction company with an allowance of thirty coupons, and rolled it into the Adler. With rivulets of sweat tickling her armpits, she typed the number twenty-five in the box, at the same time slipping five coupons into the inside pocket of her coat which hung on the back of her chair. No one, she was certain, had seen her. As the end-of-shift bell shrieked on the wall, she stood up, delivered her remaining forms and envelopes to Vogt's desk, and walked out of the hut at a regular pace.

The evening was golden, with the sun still high in the sky and a gentle breeze on the air. She barely needed her coat, but she didn't dare remove it now; anyway, overdressing on this semi-starved island was commonplace these days and no one gave her a second look. The dust particles stuck in her eyes and throat, and her heart was pounding, but she looked straight ahead and continued walking. She told herself this was destiny. The ease of this opportunity was surely the hand of fate, as if the universe was forcing her to take this chance to even the score. She moved with the flow of workers down the slope towards the south gate, her booty nestled securely next to her heart. Bodies jostled and pushed past her in their eagerness to get home. She manoeuvred her way through them, making sure she kept her footing firm on the path. She was almost at the gate. She was almost free. Then she felt the hand on her shoulder.

Turning, she saw his face close to hers. For a second all she saw was the uniform and thought she might pass out.

'Hedy, isn't it? Kurt Neumann, remember? We met the day you were hired.' He must have seen the colour drain from her face because he added quickly, 'Don't worry. This isn't about work – I'm not even part of the OT. I wanted to ask you a favour.'

She stared at him, half expecting the coupons to come to life, burst through her coat and hurl themselves into his face. She breathed in slowly, trying to get a grip of herself. 'Yes?'

'I know you're one of our translators. I have this article from the *American Journal of Science*, about the future of the motor car, and I was wondering if you might translate it for me?' Hedy opened her mouth but no sound came out. 'I do speak English, but I know yours is far better than mine! I'd be happy to pay you, or I could thank you by buying you a drink sometime. Maybe dinner?' He smiled, and it was an authentic smile – warm, full of optimism and ideas. It made the crow's feet around his eyes crease up. His teeth were white and even. Hedy sensed that the acid swirling in her stomach was rising up.

'Dinner?'

'Look, I understand,' he assured her. 'If you don't want to be seen in public with a German officer. But we do have access to our own stores. I could bring food to your home. Do you like cheese?'

'Cheese?' She cursed herself. This kind of panicked reaction was exactly how she would be caught.

'Or whatever you like. No funny business, I promise. I was in the Deutsche Jungenschaft, you know. Perfect manners.' He gave a little laugh, inviting her to join in. Hedy wrenched her facial muscles into a laughing position. 'So what do you say?'

'Sure.' She felt the space around her shift and blur. Her only conscious thought was that this man clearly did not know that she was Jewish. Every particle of her body was screaming at her to get away. In her peripheral vision, she was scouting the exits.

'Great. Well, I'll put the article on your desk and you let me know what night is good for you, all right? See you.'

Another brilliant smile and he was gone. Hedy turned and continued down the path out of the compound. Her legs seemed to swing weightlessly beneath her, and the lane swam unseen in front of her eyes. She hardly exhaled until she reached the main road, and for the remainder of her journey home she had to stop several times to catch her breath at the roadside. Not until she was back in her apartment was she able to take stock of what had happened. As the reality sank in, she began to laugh, a frightening cackle of hysteria that sent Hemingway scurrying under the bed, and forced her to sit down at the table. For several minutes she wondered if she would ever stop.

With a shaking hand, she pulled the coupons from her inside pocket and stared at them. She had got away with it. And aside from her own fear, there was no reason why she shouldn't get away with it again. Perhaps every week. She felt a flush of pride. She had swindled her overlords, scored a victory. No longer a collaborator, she was now a resistance fighter. Hiding in plain sight within the snake pit, trickling poison into their nest, throwing a V-sign to the entire German nation.

There was just one problem. She appeared to have invited a German officer to her home for dinner.

Anton's apartment was as clean and neat as Hedy had ever seen it. Every surface had been scrubbed with hot water and there was even an egg cup of daisies and buttercups on the table. Two places were set with chipped plates and old tin cutlery, and a pot of cabbage and swede stew bubbled away on the single electric ring. Hedy stirred the pot with a bent metal spoon, wishing that Anton owned a wooden one. If she'd known there wasn't one in either of the drawers of his little dresser, she would have brought her own from home, and saved the ends of her fingers from blisters. She turned the heat down just as Anton burst through the door of the apartment, his hands stuffed into his jacket pockets and an uneasy look in his eyes. Hedy wiped her hands on a ragged tea towel.

'Forget something?'

'I need something to read while I'm sitting down there.' He took a Stefan Zweig novel from the half dozen books on the shelf and shifted it from palm to palm. 'How long do you think the Kraut will stay?'

'Couple of hours at the most. Thank you again for offering to do this. I really didn't want him coming to my place.'

'Are you sure you want to go through with it?' Anton's face was taut with concern.

'If I bail out now he could get angry, say that I led him on. And I don't want to give him any reason to get suspicious.'

'But what if he, you know . . .'

'If anything happens I'll stamp on the floor, or scream. But it won't. He's not like that.' The words left her mouth easily; she realised that she meant it, and wondered why.

'So long as he doesn't find out you're Jewish. What if he wants to see you again?'

'He won't. I plan to bore him to death. You know I can do it.' They exchanged a small smile across the room, but Anton still looked unsettled.

'And you're certain he has no idea about the coupons?' Hedy shook her head with confidence. 'I still think you're crazy. Stealing right under their noses . . .'

'It's only trouble if you choose to see it that way.' She left a deliberate beat, waiting for Anton to get the reference. 'How is Dorothea? Still at her grandmother's?'

Anton pursed his lips a little, but let it go. 'Yes, for the moment.'

'No more asthma attacks?'

'No, thank God. What will you do with the coupons? Sell them?'

Hedy couldn't help a little grin of triumph. 'I thought about it. But I've decided to give them to Doctor Maine.'

The gawping expression on Anton's face was just as she'd imagined it. '*Give* them?'

'Then it becomes an act of pure resistance, not just petty theft or selfishness. It's an atonement, for taking wages from the Krauts. My own personal *mitzvah*.'

Anton shook his head. 'Maybe our faiths aren't so far apart after all.' He waved his novel. 'I'll be just downstairs.'

Hedy listened to Anton's clumping footsteps heading down to the bakery. She straightened the table settings, pulled the two paper sheets of the translated article from her bag, and laid them out. Turning off the electric ring, she smoothed her skirt and fiddled with the buttons of her blouse. A violent churning in her stomach caused her to burp ferociously.

At six, she went to the window from which she and Anton had waved their makeshift white flag almost a year ago, and peered out. Neumann, holding a canvas bag, was making his way up the road. He saw her face and smiled. Hedy gestured to him to come up, and a few seconds later he was standing at Anton's door, a sheepish grin on his face. Hedy did her best to smile back, though the sight of a man in full German uniform in Anton's familiar little apartment was overwhelming. She stood aside to avoid any physical contact as she ushered him inside. He hovered near the door politely, as if wary of looking too much at home; his dark blond hair was slicked back with some kind of oil, his eyes bright with childlike excitement. After bidding each other good evening, they stood awkwardly in silence.

Eventually Neumann gestured to the sheets of paper on the table. 'Is this my translation?' Hedy nodded. 'Thank you, I will read it when I get home tonight. You have excellent handwriting.'

'May I see what you brought?'

Neumann was already lifting his bag onto the table and unbuckling the flap. From it he pulled two small plucked chickens, a Camembert cheese, a large white loaf, a packet of real French coffee, a bar of plain chocolate and two bottles of Bordeaux. Hedy gazed at the display, feeling the drool rise in her mouth.

'This is for you of course – not to be shared with me,' Kurt assured her.

'Thank you, Lieutenant,' Hedy replied. She had made a promise to herself to be polite at all times.

'Call me Kurt, please.'

Hedy scooped up the provisions, leaving only the wine and bread on the table, and stuffed it all into one of Anton's cupboards, shutting the door as if to pretend none of it existed. She gestured to him to sit, and dished the meagre vegetables into mismatched bowls. Kurt opened the wine and poured a little into chipped cups, they both mumbled a toast to the end of the war, and Hedy cut the bread with a knife. Then they sat eating in silence. Hedy mopped up every morsel of the stew with the delicious bread crusts. She had forgotten what real bread could taste like. Once or twice she glanced up at him and caught him watching her eat, but she was too hungry to find it disturbing.

Eventually Kurt made a polite enquiry about her early life in Austria; Hedy answered in the fewest words possible, pretending that her move to Jersey had been due to a job opportunity. And how did she like working at Lager Hühnlein? Hedy replied that she liked it well enough, although the dust was sometimes irksome. A half-hour dragged by, stumbling and uncomfortable, the conversation bumping awkwardly along, like a plane that couldn't take off. Hedy sipped her wine at a snail's pace. It was months since she'd drunk alcohol and a loosened tongue was the last thing she needed now. When Kurt spoke of his passion for American cars, Hedy drew him out on the subject, calculating correctly that the topic would occupy a good few minutes. But eventually he drained his second wine, and placed the cup down with intention.

'Hedy, I don't wish to be rude, but I would prefer not to spend this evening discussing the Ford motor company.'

She rose to her feet and began clearing the table. 'So what would you prefer to talk about?'

The German shifted on his wooden chair, trying to assume a pose of relaxation. 'I'd just like us to get to know each other.'

She lowered the crockery into the sink, keeping her back to him. 'There's nothing special about me. There are plenty of German girls at the compound who would prove far more interesting, I'm sure.' She bit her lip as soon as she'd said it, knowing he wouldn't miss the dig. She was right.

'You know, not all Germans, even in the military, are the master-race enthusiasts Hitler would like you to believe.'

'Really?' She rubbed at the dirty bowls with her fingers so she didn't have to look at him. 'I thought that was one of the main reasons for your country going to war. Do you not consider yourself superior to Slavs? Or Jews?' She glanced up into the shard of broken mirror that Anton kept above the kitchen sink for shaving, and saw that her cheeks were flushed. She must have drunk too much wine after all; this was a suicidal path.

'Can I tell you something in confidence?' Kurt replied. Hedy said nothing, which he seemed to take as consent. 'Between you and me, I believe Hitler attacks those groups to elevate his own position – they're nothing but scapegoats. Personally I've never had a problem with any Russian or Jewish person.' She heard him give a small sigh. 'Look, would you sit down for a minute? It's hard talking to someone's back.' Hedy dried her hands and sat back down on the edge of her chair. 'Thank you.' He leaned so close to her that she could see those tiny crow's feet around his eyes. His breath smelled of the soft red wine. 'You know, Hedy, I'm not a military man. When I was a little boy, all I ever wanted to be was an engineer. I did my apprenticeship in a shipyard, and then one day, my company was told we had to make tank engines instead of trawlers, and we all had to wear this.' He indicated his gabardine wool tunic, unbuttoned at the top. 'Next thing I know, we're at war and I'm servicing Panzers. Men my age had no choice.'

'So you just . . . accepted it?'

'It was that or prison. Sometimes when a force is that strong, it's pointless, arrogant even, to think you can fight it. Like King Canute, the king who drowned because he believed he could stop the waves just by the power of his own command? You know that story?'

She sniffed. 'Everyone knows that story. And that version is wrong anyway. Canute didn't drown, and he wasn't trying to stop the tide.'

'He wasn't?'

'Canute was a good king. He was trying to prove to his egotistical nobility that no man can challenge the power of God, even a monarch. It was a gesture of humility.' She fought the urge to move back to the sink. She felt too exposed here, too close to him.

Kurt was laughing. He had a beautiful laugh. 'Well, I guess I learned something today.' He smiled, inviting one in return;

she refused it. 'All I'm saying is, I didn't choose to do this, or to be here. I really didn't have any option.'

'So in your view you share no responsibility for what your country is doing, or the pain you are causing?' The words seemed to tumble out of her mouth.

'What I'm trying to say is—'

'What about the people I saw in Vienna, being put on trucks and driven away?'

He reached across the table, and for a second she thought he was reaching for her, but his hand went towards the wine bottle, which he emptied into his cup. 'I agree with you that's wrong.' He took a long swig. 'Moving people around like cattle, it's cruel and unnecessary. But they'll be put on good farmland, among their own kind.'

'Farmland? You think they're moving the . . . those people to *farms*?' The wine was mixing with her fury; the fountain was now unstoppable, her earlier promises of caution and courtesy forgotten. 'Most of them have never been heard of again! You're telling me they weren't taken to some forest and shot?'

'A lot of those stories are propaganda.' There was irritation in his voice now. 'You think the Allies aren't capable of that? What did you hear about us before we came here? I bet you were told we'd rape the women and eat babies alive! Of course there are stupid, ignorant people on my side, as there are on yours. But that doesn't mean we're all the same.'

Hedy rose to her feet, and to her alarm, he did too. He was a good head taller, and she realised that one blow could knock her unconscious. She heard a door bang somewhere below and wondered if Anton was preparing to sprint up the stairs. Yet still her mouth ran on. 'Why should I believe that? You wear the uniform of a Nazi, you accept the pay of the Nazis, you carry out the orders of the Nazis. What else are you but a Nazi?'

He stared at her with an expression she couldn't fathom. It wasn't the anger or contempt she'd expected, it looked more like disappointment. He raised his arm, and for a second Hedy thought the blow was coming, but he just picked up his canvas bag from the table and threw it over his shoulder.

'And you?' he barked. 'You are an Austrian; we are technically countrymen. You work for the same people as me, you take their wages. You invite me here to get your hands on my food, but you continue to treat me like an enemy. And you know . . . ?' He pulled his cap down tightly on his head. 'If you lump an entire race together, and believe every person is the same – then you're no better than Hitler.'

Hedy stared at him. Her hands were trembling but she managed to keep her voice steady. 'I think you'd better go.'

'All right.' He moved towards the door then turned back. 'You know, despite everything, I would like us to be friends.'

'Thank you for the food.' She tried to hold her chin high, determined not to show weakness.

Kurt looked despondent, but merely shrugged. 'Thank you for the translation, and for dinner.' And then he was gone. Hedy stood for a moment, her hand on the table for support, as Anton rushed in, his face full of anxiety, and put a tentative arm around her.

'It's all right. He's gone.'

'I shouted at him.' Her whole body was shaking now.

'Don't worry. He won't report it. How would it make him look, complaining that he'd been upset by a young girl? He won't say anything.'

Hedy nodded but the trembling continued. It went on long after Anton opened the second bottle of wine, poured her a large cupful and insisted she drink it while she reported the night's events to him. She was still unsteady and a little nauseous when, having thanked Anton for everything, she scurried home, the precious groceries wrapped in newspaper under her old coat, and gratefully pulled the bolt across the door of her apartment. Lighting the stub of a candle, she breathed deeply and tried to talk herself down. Maybe she was simply shocked by her own rashness, speaking to a German officer that way? Or it could be a reaction to the unaccustomed alcohol. She drank cold water from her kitchen tap. Perhaps she was a little ashamed. Behaving that way to a man who, after all, had been kind to her and treated her like a human being.

It was at three in the morning, when the dream woke her, that she knew the lie was starting to crack. A dream of such sexual charge that it drew sweat from every part of her and tossed her blankets from the bed. Kurt's hands on her body, his lips on her mouth, her hips arcing up to meet him.

In the shadowy darkness of her apartment, Hemingway arched his spine and hissed at her.

★

'I hear they're finally confiscating the Judenschweine wireless sets.' Fischer shoved the gear stick into third with ludicrous force, causing a grinding in complaint. Kurt winced at the sound. 'Can't believe it's taken them this long. I mean, if anyone's going to transmit information to the British mainland it's those devious little kikes, right? Should have been a priority.'

Kurt gave a vague nod, but kept his eyes fixed on the world outside. The day was warm with a cloudless sky. Fishing boats bobbed in the harbour, and on the far side of the quay the outline of Elizabeth Castle sprawled in the bay. The best policy for these morning journeys, he'd discovered, was to focus on the landscape. At first Kurt had found Fischer's daily diatribes amusing – in fact Kurt had rather enjoyed lobbing in new statistics and arguments, watching his colleague's face grow pink and sweaty. But now the guy just got on his nerves. And Fischer drove the staff car as if he were breaking a wild stallion, speeding up to stop signs and slamming on the brakes at the last minute. Kurt mentally ran through the other guys in his billet, wondering if anyone else could give him a ride to work. He'd ask around tonight.

This morning was even worse than usual, because in the back-seat was the odious Geheime Feldpolizei operative, Erich Wildgrube. At least, secret police was what everyone assumed him to be: the man studiously avoided direct questions. He was forever hanging around the barracks and social clubs, pumping out a stream of questions disguised as casual curiosity. His piggy eyes swivelled constantly, and he always wore a leather trench coat, felt Alpine hat and a musky cologne that turned Kurt's stomach. Kurt could never figure out why someone whose entire job depended on anonymity deliberately drew so much attention to himself. Kurt didn't trust Wildgrube further than he could piss.

Fischer was pointing to a large white V-sign that had been painted on a granite wall. 'And there's another thing. Have you seen how many of those have appeared around town? God knows where they're getting the paint.' He shook his head in bewilderment at the islanders' persistence.

Wildgrube leaned forward, his whiney, girlish voice cutting through the sound of the engine. 'It's pure insubordination. Needs to be clamped down hard, or the rot spreads. Don't you think, Neumann?' A whiff of cologne brought Kurt's breakfast part way up his gullet.

'Sure,' Kurt replied. 'Nothing spreads like rot.'

There was no reply, and Kurt wondered if he'd overplayed his hand. But they were now approaching Millbrook, his drop-off point, and with relief Kurt hopped out, giving the roof a double bang to imply cheeriness, and jogged into the compound. With luck, there'd be a nice long list of jobs for him today. A full schedule meant no time to think about Fischer, Wildgrube or even – well, no point going back to that one now.

In fact, it turned out to be a swine of a day. His entire morning was taken up with some misaligned pistons on the crankshaft of a Horch 108 that caused him to miss lunch, and he spent the afternoon chasing a bundle of dockets his junior mechanic had put in the wrong pigeonhole. By the time six

o'clock came, Kurt was hot and grubby, and decided that tonight he would try out the new officers' club in town. He usually avoided those places – the sight of the young French whores depressed him. But there was always a decent stock of the local apple brandy and enough friendly faces to take his mind off things. He was just about to shout to his NCO engineer for a lift home when he saw her.

She was leaving Block Seven, wearing the same clothes she always wore – those tatty lace-up shoes and, for some strange reason, a heavy winter coat that was falling to pieces. She walked with an even, deliberate step, and her hair rippled gold in the breeze. Kurt slowed, wondering whether to hold back and let her pass through the exit gate first. They hadn't spoken since that awful night, even though he'd seen her at a distance several times and pictured their next encounter more often than he'd like to admit. He'd thought about apologising, but what was the point? He'd not really done anything wrong. And if she hated all Germans as much as she claimed, it was a loser from the start. Best to put it down to experience and move on – plenty more fish in the sea. Except that none of the others seemed to interest him. And he had fallen asleep every night with Hedy's green eyes imprinted on his memory.

Kurt pushed back his shoulders. No more of this schoolboy creeping around, he would clear the air once and for all. He walked purposefully in her direction. Hedy turned, as if sensing his approach, and then something extraordinary happened. To Kurt's astonishment, she smiled at him. It was the first full, true smile he'd had from her, and the effect on his heart rate was a shock. He responded with a grin of his own, hoping his partial erection wouldn't be obvious in his uniform trousers. Pushing through the crowd of employees towards her, Kurt felt a surge of optimism, possibilities flooding in, lifting him. As he drew breath to speak, a harsh German voice shouted from behind him, 'What is this? To whom do these belong?'

Kurt turned. Behind him stood OT Feldwebel Schulz, who, in his right hand, held a bundle of ten petrol coupons, now covered in mud and footprints. His nervous, blinking eyes scanned the crowd, evidently expecting a reply. Kurt looked around too, then his gaze landed on Hedy. The colour had drained from her face and her hand was sliding into her coat towards her inside pocket. She fumbled around inside but her hand emerged, empty. At that moment, their eyes locked, and Kurt understood everything. Then, as if hearing another person's voice somewhere in the distance, he heard his own.

'Yes, they belong to me. Thank you, I must have dropped them.'

From that second, everyone seemed to move a little more slowly, and when Kurt recalled it later, it seemed as if the events were lit by bright floodlights, like a film set. Hedy stared at him in pure disbelief. Kurt forced his eyes away from hers as Schulz marched towards him.

'Why were these in your possession, Lieutenant? Do you have an allocation?' The evening sun was catching Schulz's glasses, giving him the appearance of a blind robot.

Kurt thought fast. 'Actually, no. I got them from one of the drivers in exchange for tobacco.'

'Which driver, sir?' Schulz shifted to his other foot, embarrassed by the inappropriateness of the situation.

'I don't know – there's scores of those guys. They all look the same to me. Is this a problem?'

'Yes, Lieutenant, indeed it is.' Schulz's cheeks were flushed red. 'This represents an illegal transaction of Reich property! Officers are meant to set an example.' His voice dropped an octave. 'I'm sorry, sir, but I will have to report this.'

Kurt felt a trickle of sweat run down his back. 'Come on, Henrik, seriously? It's just a few coupons – everyone does it.'

'Perhaps so, sir, but you have admitted it.' Schulz hung his head, clearly not relishing his duty. 'I must talk to my superior.

Please be in my office in thirty minutes.' And he stomped off, stuffing the evidence into his top pocket.

The onlookers began to disperse, murmuring quietly among themselves. Kurt forced himself to wait several seconds before glancing back to Hedy. Her face still registered incredulity but there was something else there now, a nameless emotion that turned Kurt's insides to caramel. She looked as if she were about to say something, but Kurt warned her off with the tiniest shake of his head and a wink. He spun on his foot and walked back towards his cubbyhole office. He looked back only once, and was glad to see that Hedy had already gone.

The military police arrived within an hour. A little after eight, Kurt was escorted to a Black Maria where one of the two MPs opened the door for him and offered him a cigarette for the journey. Kurt blew perfect smoke rings through the rear bars of the van as he watched Lager Hühnlein disappear behind them. What he still couldn't figure out was why, at that moment, he felt more at peace than he had in months.

★

'Two weeks?'

'That's what all the typists are saying. Apparently they want to make an example of him.'

Anton pulled a face. 'Mr Reis's neighbour was in the Jersey section last month for black market trading. I hear that jail's pretty grim.'

'Better than being sent to France, I suppose. I would take him some food, but —'

'No!' Anton put his hand towards her, the index finger raised. 'You stay away, or you'll make them suspicious. And I think you ought to look for another job.'

Hedy sat back on her haunches, watching Anton wiggle his homemade fishing line deep under the rock. It was an ingenious contraption: a coat hook tied to a length of old hosepipe, partially braced with a length of broken broom handle. Ormers, even small lobsters, could be prised from these gloomy depths if you were lucky.

'You know as well I do, I wouldn't get another job.'

'But you need to protect yourself. What if Neumann finds it too tough in there, and decides to tell them the truth?'

Hedy blinked in the glare of the white sky, and peered across the lunar wilderness of rocks and shining pools towards La Roque beach. They were a long way out, and the people on the distant shore were no more than coloured dots. One of them was Dorothea, waiting by the sea wall for their return.

'If he was going to rat on me he would have done it by now.' Hedy hoped her tone sounded pragmatic.

'Maybe, but what kind of reward will he want when he comes out? He obviously likes you, and now he has information on you. He could take advantage.' Anton's probing was becoming more frantic, as if he could taste the seafood meal lurking just out of reach. Still nothing moved in the pool except minuscule, transparent fish, no longer than a fingernail, shooting through the water in a thousand directions, and a few shore crabs, smaller than silver sixpences, scuttling over the sandy floor to the shelter of the next stone. Such tiny creatures, Hedy thought, with no defence system; their only hope was concealment. She stood to stretch her legs.

'So what should I do? If I leave now, that would look more suspicious. And my address is on record – if he wants to blackmail me, I can't stop him.' She wiped the film of sweat from her top lip and fiddled with the strip of torn curtain fabric she had wrapped around her hair for a scarf. The day was hot, and every nerve in her body felt too near the surface of her skin. 'How long do we have before the tide turns?'

'Twenty minutes, if that. Then we have to head straight back.' Anton checked the watch in his pocket. 'Dorothea says it comes in really fast down here. This island has one of the biggest tides in Europe, about twelve metres – it's really powerful.'

Hedy nodded. 'All right, then let's at least try to get some limpets. No point going home empty-handed.'

She headed for a patch of jagged rocks, on the far side of the gulley, and crouched down out of the sun. Taking her improvised chisel – a piece of slate stolen from a building site in town – she chipped at the dull yellow pyramids on the shadowy underside of the rock, until a few fell into her basket. Anton chose a different clump of rocks to work on, and for a while there was no sound but scraping and the breath of their exertions. Above them rose the silhouette of the ancient Seymour Tower, a memorial to other wars and older struggles. Hedy glanced at her friend a few times, but his eyes stayed on his work. Soon their fingers were numb and their knuckles bleeding from the barnacled rock. They had twenty-seven limpets between them, barely enough for a snack.

Anton gave a weary sigh. 'Let's call it a day. Don't want to take any chances.' They began their slow journey back towards the shore, slipping and staggering on the wet rocks, grasping at each other to steady themselves.

As the silence lengthened, Hedy reached for a safe topic. 'So what were the main headlines on the BBC last night?'

'Germans are closing in on Leningrad. If the Russians can't stop them and Roosevelt doesn't step in soon, this might all be over by Christmas.' He stopped, drew a tiny pouch of tobacco from his pocket and rolled the slimmest cigarette he could. 'Does this mean you handed your wireless in?'

Hedy nodded. 'If I didn't surrender it, they'd only search my apartment. No point taking stupid chances.'

'And I trust all this has brought an end to your petrol coupon business too?'

'I'm not a fool, Anton.' Then she added: 'Although if I'd known the seam on my pocket had come loose, none of this would have happened.'

'What about Doctor Maine?'

'I feel bad for him. But there are plenty of black marketeers he can go to.'

The rocks flattened out as they moved towards the shore, and now they were crunching on drying seaweed. Hedy looked up and made out the slim figure of Dorothea sitting on an old blanket by the sea wall, her legs tucked neatly to the side beneath her homemade skirt, waving at them. Hedy let slip a sigh she intended to be inaudible, but Anton's frown told her that it wasn't. He rolled the limpets around the basket in his hand before turning to look at her.

'There's a freshwater tap over by the slipway – I'm going to go and rinse these off. I'll be a few minutes. You go and keep Dorothea company.' Hedy met his eyes and saw determination. 'Go on. I won't be long.'

It was a stand-off, and Hedy knew it. Feeling like a schoolgirl, she shuffled through the dry sand of the upper shore. Dorothea shifted herself along the blanket and patted the space next to her feet. 'How did you get on?'

'Not so good. Twenty-seven limpets.'

Dorothea laughed. 'Don't worry. I can put them in a potato pie; they'll still give some flavour. Ah, look, you grazed your hand!' She took a small lacy handkerchief from her bag and dabbed at Hedy's knuckles before Hedy had a chance to decline. 'It's a messy business, low-water fishing. But worth it, if you come away with some supper. Hey, look what I got today.' She pulled a small black tube from her bag and twisted it to reveal a stub of pink lipstick. 'It belonged to my grandmother; she said I could keep it. Would you like to use it?'

Hedy craned her neck for Anton, who was still messing about by the slipway. 'No, thanks.'

'Sure? It's Coty. A good one. And I bet it's your colour.'

'Honestly.' Hedy bent down to brush her bare legs with her fingers. The coarse grains were clinging to her damp feet and shins, making her skin itch. She yearned to follow Anton to the water tap to rinse it off, but understood that abandoning her post was not an option. She was about to ask a polite question about Dorothea's family when Dorothea casually remarked, 'Anton tells me they put your lieutenant in prison?'

Hedy stared at her, dumbstruck. In the corner of her vision, she could see Anton making his way back towards them. She wanted to slap him.

'Anton told you?'

'Of course. I think it's so romantic,' Dorothea trilled. 'It's like a movie – going to prison to save the woman you love.'

Hedy's skin felt as if it was crawling with insects. Her voice came out tight and loud. 'It's nothing like that! Why would you say that? He felt sorry for me, that's all.'

Dorothea's face became childlike. 'Hedy, I'm sorry if I've offended you. But . . . it's a big gesture to make out of pity. Are you sure that's all it was?'

'I don't know why he did it! Perhaps he felt bad for upsetting me the night we ate together. But really, you think I would have a romance with a Nazi officer?' The words seemed to hang and twist in the air, and she could feel the blood pumping to her cheeks.

At that moment Anton's shadow loomed over them. The basket of wet limpets hung loose in his fingers, dripping onto the sand. 'What's this?'

Hedy stood up, glaring at him with all the outrage she could muster. 'Dorothea seems to think there is some kind of love affair going on between me and Lieutenant Neumann. Where on earth would she get such an idea?'

Anton pushed sand with his foot. 'I'm sure no one is suggesting any such thing. How about we all go back to town and find somewhere to get a cold drink?'

'No, I'm sorry, I'm not feeling so good. I need to go home.' It was true. She needed to find some shade. She needed to get this sand off her, clean herself, cool down, calm down.

Dorothea held out the basket of limpets. 'At least take your share.'

Hedy pushed it back. 'I can't eat them anyway. They're not kosher.'

'I think some things shouldn't matter in wartime.' Dorothea's voice was oddly calm, and when Hedy looked up she saw that the woman was staring at her with a disconcerting intensity. 'Hedy, you know you can trust me, don't you?'

'I'm not sure who I can trust any more.'

She turned and walked briskly across the beach to the slipway, scrambling onto it with difficulty. At the tap she ran cold water over her legs and only then, struggling to get her shoes onto her damp feet, did she look back. Anton was sitting with his knees pulled up, rubbing his eyes and head in the slow rhythm of exhaustion. But Dorothea was still looking at Hedy, the blue of her eyes glinting in the afternoon sun.

★

The thin column of light angling in through the high barred window lit up Wildgrube's oiled hair like a brightly jewelled cap. Together with his earnest expression, he looked like a commedia dell'arte character, and Kurt had to suppress a smirk. Wildgrube stood with his feet neatly together, as if on parade, looking down at him.

'Of all the people I might suspect of something like this, Kurt, it would never have been you.'

Kurt drew deep on the cigarette Wildgrube had given him, and watched the smoke drift through the sunbeam. The wooden bench under his backside was slightly damp and full of splinters, and he still hadn't got used to the smell of shit and piss in this place. But he was damned if he was going to give this idiot the satisfaction. He shrugged, as if he didn't understand what the fuss was about. He'd got rather good at that shrug over the last few days.

'To be honest, Erich . . .' He watched Wildgrube flinch a little at the use of his Christian name. Two can play at that game, Kurt thought. 'I knew it was against the rules, but I never saw it as a serious issue. I mean, half the guys I know have some kind of deal going on the side. I hear the head of the secret police has quite a little business going with one of the local butchers.'

Wildgrube's lips pressed together to hold in a remark, and Kurt detected the smallest twitch in his left eye.

'You are misinformed. my friend,' Wildgrube replied. 'Black marketeering takes valuable supplies out of circulation, causes hardship and risks insurgence among the civilian population. It is viewed very dimly.' He turned and did a strange little walk up and down the narrow cell while he composed his next sentence. Kurt took another long drag on his cigarette. 'I am still shocked that you, a respected officer, would so casually flout these rules, knowing the damage it would do to your reputation. You are fortunate that the Russian campaign is progressing so rapidly, otherwise you might find yourself leaving this jail and being put on a plane to the Eastern Front.'

Kurt sucked the last dregs of his cigarette and stubbed it out on the floor of the cell, grinding it into the cold black stone. He felt a weight lift. A fortnight in this hellhole he could cope with, even losing his leave was a price worth paying. But the possibility of a transfer east had kept him awake every night since this began. In those long, dark hours he'd found himself questioning his motives and coming up with no real answers. Sure, saving a pretty girl from prison was a noble thing to do, but if it meant dying on the Pripet Marshes? And for what? He'd only been given one tiny indication that she felt anything for him at all – in that single split second in the compound when she'd looked at him with thankfulness and . . . Affection? Bemusement? Pity, that he was prepared to behave like such a sap? Yet he'd carried that treasure of a moment in his head ever since, and promised himself that no matter what punishment was handed down, he would not betray her. Whether that made him Don Quixote or the biggest fool in the Wehrmacht he still wasn't sure. He only knew that he wanted to see her again, as soon as possible.

Kurt hauled himself up from the bench, pleased that Wildgrube was so much shorter than him, and gave the policeman a friendly pat on the arm. 'You're absolutely right, Erich. And believe me, this is the only lesson I'll need. I assure you I'll be a good boy from now on.'

Wildgrube's eyes narrowed a little. 'It is not a question of being a "good boy".' It is about maintaining the right attitude towards our great Reich and our beloved Führer.'

'Of course.'

They stood like that for what felt a long time, neither wanting to break first. Eventually Wildgrube gave a loud sniff and banged on the door for the guard to release him. As he turned to bid Kurt farewell, Kurt saw the trace of a smile around his thin mouth.

'When they let you out, come and find me. We'll have a drink together – put all this behind us, yes?'

'Sounds good.'

Kurt watched the door slam shut and heard the footsteps disappear down the corridor, until the only sound remaining was the groaning of a sick prisoner in a neighbouring cell. He sat on his bench and leaned back, watching the sunbeam catch new bumps and cracks in the wall as it crept upwards, and his thoughts turned to King Canute.

★

The leaves on the trees in Parade Gardens were turning yellow and brown, and bulbous, rain-filled clouds scuttled across the sky. It was almost September. As Hedy made her way past the Don Memorial, several bored off-duty German soldiers lolled on the granite plinth or leaned on the replica cannons, smoking

French cigarettes and chatting. There was a louche, tainted quality about them. One of them gave a low whistle as she passed, and she turned her head away in disgust.

The café was on York Street, close to the General Hospital. It was a dim, inconspicuous little place with a faded awning above the window and a brown interior made darker by heavy lace curtains. A perfect venue for her meeting. The door pinged as she pushed it open. She was relieved to find the place empty, except for the bored-looking waitress and one old lady in a window seat, eking out a cup of bramble tea and staring blankly at passers-by. Hedy tucked herself behind a table at the rear, ordered a cup of carrot coffee and settled down to wait.

Five minutes later, the bell rang again and Hedy looked up. He was standing in the doorway, wearing a long brown raincoat and an old Homburg, his eyes darting around to seek her out, while taking care not to make direct contact. He shuffled to the table next to hers and sat down, pretending to study the menu. Hedy sipped her drink and kept her gaze on the window. She heard him order a glass of milk from the waitress, his voice noticeably strained and weary, then heard the rustle of his newspaper. Hedy waited until the waitress had gone into the back larder to get the milk jug, pulled a small package from her bag, stretched across and deftly placed it on his table. She sat back, cup in hand.

With equal nimbleness, Doctor Maine took the slim bundle and slipped it into his coat pocket. Only then did they allow themselves the smallest exchange of smiles, an acknowledgement of a transaction well done. But in that fleeting moment, Hedy saw that the shadows beneath his eyes were darker than ever, and the hair around his temples greyer than before. And she knew that she'd been right not to tell him about the events at Lager Hühnlein, just as she'd been right not to tell Anton that she had no intention of giving up her theft of petrol coupons. Everyone was under enough strain, already living with too much fear and uncertainty, without the anxiety of knowing other people's secrets. Occupation was making enigmas of them all.

Hedy drained what was left in her cup, left the correct money on the table and slipped quietly back onto the street. She felt pleased with herself, admiring of her own courage and fortitude, and tried to connect with the feeling, to record it in her memory. Because she knew that this might be the last time she could feel such an undiluted emotion. From now on, if today turned out as she planned, every future achievement would be weighed against *shanda* and found wanting.

The previous night she had lain awake in her bed, so afraid of the darkness and her own thoughts that she let the remains of a precious candle burn right down to its end. The flame had flickered in the draughty room, throwing shadows and shapes onto the curtain, but she'd barely seen them. Instead, she saw her mother bent over, weeping and inconsolable, and her father in the raging temper of his life. She saw Roda, staring with incomprehension at a sister she no longer knew, and Anton with his head in his hands, just as he had looked that day at the beach. But what she saw most was Kurt, and that tiny wink that had communicated so much. The picture was already fraying with repetition, but it sent a pulse of longing through her. She ached to touch herself, but guilt kept her hands above the blanket in the cool damp air. She closed her eyes and turned over, burying her face in the pillow. But there she found nothing but German soldiers marching down Grabenstrasse and SS guards kicking at the curled-up bundle of an elderly Jewish neighbour as he lay dying on the street. Each time, the image was dispersed by Kurt's smiling face pushing its way to the fore. And as her battered wind-up alarm clock showed three o'clock, she let her resolve slip away, and her hand slipped down beneath the blankets to silence her body's throbbing demands.

By the time Hedy reached Newgate Street, her heart was thumping. She turned into the narrow, deserted road, aware of her own footsteps on the cobbles. Halfway down, a dimpled metal door was set into the imposing granite wall; a large metal ring served as a knocker, and beneath it was a small sliding hatch. Hedy edged past the door and stood waiting on the opposite side of the street, in the shadow of the prison walls. Spots of water began to polka dot the cobbles, and as the rain grew heavier it seeped into her hair and shoulders, but still she waited, silent and motionless.

Finally, the door opened. Kurt, wearing his uniform tunic and cap, and carrying a paper parcel of his belongings, stepped out into the street. She watched him lift his eyes to the sky and breathe deeply, then he turned and saw her. For a moment she feared what she saw was anger. But the smile came again. Relieved, she returned it. She raised her finger to her lips, then walked towards him.

'Twenty metres behind,' she whispered, 'no closer.'

Kurt nodded.

Hedy began walking back to the main road. Now and then she glanced over her shoulder or made some excuse to turn, and saw that he was still following. They walked, so intimate in their distance, up to the Parade and through the slender streets of town cottages and business premises, until they reached New Street and Hedy's front door. Hedy climbed the steps and slipped inside, pausing only a second to see the distant figure of Kurt at the end of the road, measuring his steps to control his speed. Leaving the door ajar, she climbed the two staircases to her apartment, thankful that Mrs Le Couteur's door remained firmly closed. Her key turned in the lock just as she heard the tread of Kurt's footstep at the bottom, and she hurried inside. Standing quite still in the centre of the tiny room, she breathed heavily, steam rising off her coat, streaks of wet hair stuck to her forehead. The room reeked of last night's boiled vegetables – hers or a neighbour's, she couldn't be sure. She heard him coming up the stairs. Hemingway, sensing danger, ran under the bed and stayed there. Then Kurt was standing in the doorway, looking directly at her, trying to get the measure of the situation. He pulled the door behind him and took off his cap.

For a moment, neither of them moved. Hedy had no sense of his thoughts. He took a step towards her, then another, and reached out his arms. Hedy felt herself melt into him. His lips, which tasted faintly of stale tobacco, were on hers, and he was kissing her with a tender ferocity that sent desire shooting through her body, his hands pushing through her hair and feeling for the back of her neck, squeezing her arms and shoulders, reaching down towards her breasts. Hedy reached out one last time for her conscience, but rules and certainty were already gone, and longing dragged her towards a pit of pleasure. By the time her dress was on the floor she couldn't have told you her own name.

4

The open truck was crammed with soldiers – perhaps twenty-five, thirty. As it sped by, churning up dust and fallen leaves, and blurring the uniforms into a smear of greenish grey, Hedy pressed herself against the hedgerow, taking care to keep her face buried in her scarf. The truck rumbled on towards the bend in the lane, but before it turned she caught the face of one young private, pale and vacant, staring out towards the headland. Hardly more than a schoolboy, his eyes were glazed, his lips pressed together as if to hold back some imminent torrent. From beneath the brim of her old felt hat, Hedy watched his features smudge, then disappear, before she slipped down the footpath that led to the sea.

In tiny Belcroute bay the waves slapped rhythmically at the water's edge. The tide was still coming in; soon the glassy rock pools would disappear in gushes of silvery water, absorbed back into the ocean. Hedy clambered over the slimy rocks, leaving her hands free to break any slip, steering well clear of the flat areas of the beach where mines might be laid. She looked for the line of discarded seaweed on the shingle, and was relieved to see the ragged marker lay a good two metres beyond the low sea wall. Soon the spring tides would swell the flow, trapping any careless visitor and forcing them to scrabble up to the steep woodland above. But today she would be safe.

Edging around the corner where the foliage still grew thick, she threw a quick glance over her shoulder to make sure no one was following. Then, reaching the familiar gap between the rocks she had come to view as her own, she crouched down and snuggled into the gap, making sure to keep her back tight against the slab so that no one walking on the pathway above could peer over and see her. The breeze was stiff, but the sun still held a little warmth, and its position told her it was around midday. She pulled off her hat and made herself comfortable, knowing she wouldn't have long to wait.

So far, November had been a harsh month. The bread ration had been cut again. There were rumours circulating about further restrictions to the gas supply. And the arrival of more German troops from France, hundred after hundred swarming off boats in St Helier harbour, had caused a collective wave of despair through the community. What were all these soldiers for? What would they do here? It could only mean more orders and new harassments. Still, sitting here with the sun's rays on her eyelids, and no sound except the lapping water, there was no denying an old, familiar sensation rising in her chest. It was happiness. She'd almost forgotten it. Resting her head back, she smiled as the feeling flowed down her arms and pooled in her fingertips. She breathed it in, letting her thoughts drift.

Then, as always, came the payback. The sinking chill of fear and guilt.

It had been like this right from the first day – that rainy afternoon in her apartment, with the thin light bleeding through the skylight onto their naked bodies, the two of them still and exhausted on the counterpane. They had stayed for hours squashed together on her tiny bed, sharing confessions of their first stirrings of attraction and waiting for darkness to fall so that he could slip away unseen. That was when it began in earnest. This psychotic pendulum of joy and self-hatred punching it out in her solar plexus – random fits of laughter as she walked to work, and frantic crying in the early hours. It was exhausting – but not the worst part. The worst was the one constant emotion that never truly went away, but bubbled under the surface all day and night. The terror.

Several times she was seconds away from blurting out the truth. Two tiny words, she often told herself, and it would be over.

Two words: 'I'm Jewish.' It wouldn't have been so dangerous, right at the start. She could have dismissed his anger with a shrug – did he really not know? Was it her fault that he, an officer, didn't know the employee background of his own compound? And if he'd raged and yelled, stomped about her apartment in indignant haste to find his clothes, she'd have gambled that he could never tell anyone, for fear of retaliation. It would have been simple.

But she didn't tell him. Not that day, nor the next time, nor any of the wild, furtive encounters they had shared since. As her affection for him grew, so did the fear of his disapproval. After a while she became crazy enough to think she might never need to tell him. She dreamed up a universe in which the issue would simply never come up. Until one day, months or years in the future – this part she left deliberately vague – he would turn to her over a meal in a pavement café, smile, sip a glass of wine and say, 'By the way, you never mentioned . . .' But alone in her bed, Hedy knew it was already too late.

A low whistle from the other side of the rocks snapped her eyes open. A few seconds later, Kurt's loping figure appeared around the outcrop. She watched him climb towards her, his long limbs moving with grace and confidence, until he dropped down close to her and steadied himself. She waited for those crinkly eyes to find her, holding out her arms towards him. Then he was on top of her, embracing her, kissing her long and hard, murmuring that she looked beautiful and how he'd missed her in their days apart. As they squeezed together between the rocks, he opened his canvas bag to reveal half a loaf, some tiny French apples and a few tomatoes. She snuggled into the space beneath his left arm, and for a while they ate their lunch in silence.

Finally Kurt wiped his mouth with the back of his hand. 'You hear about Sidi Rezegh?' Hedy shook her head. 'Afrika Korps crushed the British 7th Armoured Division. If we take Malta, it could all be over in a few months.' Hedy stared down at the last hemisphere of tomato in her palm, letting him pick up on her silence, and felt his twitch of regret. 'I'm sorry. But that's what we both want, right? For this to be over?'

'What about the Eastern Front?'

'Still gridlocked. The snow must have arrived by now. God knows what it must be like for those poor bastards. I just hope Helmut's not out there.' He caught her questioning look. 'My best mate since we were kids, he's like a brother. He's in the Panzers now.' He peered at her, his head on one side. 'Hedy, why don't you have a wireless? All the other locals have one.'

Hedy threw the piece of tomato into her mouth and chewed longer than was necessary, trying to remember the correct lie. 'I told you, mine broke. You can't buy them any more.'

'Maybe I could get hold of one, use my contacts? Then I could listen to the BBC news with you. More accurate than the rubbish we have to listen to.'

She touched his knee. 'Thanks, but I don't want you spending that kind of money. I can get the news from you, or Anton.'

'Ah, the famous Anton. Are you ever going to let me meet him?' Hedy threw him the wry look that bagged up a dozen previous conversations, but Kurt merely shrugged. 'If he's that good a friend, he'll understand, surely? And isn't he in the same position, dating that local girl?'

'You'll meet him one of these days. You ever hear from Helmut?' Her tactic was blatant and she knew he'd spotted it, but he let it slide.

'One letter in the summer, most of it censored. Don't even know where he is. I worry about him.' He threw his apple core into the rocks and turned to face her. 'When can I come to your apartment again? I mean, this is great, but' – he slipped his hand down to her breast, his thumb gently circling her nipple – 'I miss you.'

Hedy felt her sex ache in response, but she could also hear distant voices further along the headland path. She pushed his hand up towards her neck.

'I miss you too, but it's too risky here.'

That smile again. She could smell the apple on his breath, the oil he used on his hair, and she fought the urge to place his hand back where it had been.

Kurt pushed himself up on one elbow. 'I really don't think you need to be so cautious. At least two of the officers in my house are seeing island women. And it's not like you're a Jersey girl anyway.'

'That's the point. The locals are already suspicious of me, with my nationality and my accent. I could be labelled a spy, kicked out of my apartment. I have to be doubly careful.' Sensing his disappointment, she continued quickly. 'Mrs Le Couteur's cough sounds better, though. If she's well enough to go to her sister's on Friday, you can come over then.'

He nodded. 'I'll make sure I see my friend at the supply store and get' – to Hedy's delight he blushed slightly – 'what we need. Oh, and I almost forgot – a present for you.' He reached into his pocket and pulled out a bar of Stollwerck chocolate.

Hedy gasped at the sight of the smart blue wrapper with its familiar curly brand script, holding it like a baby bird in the palm of her hand. 'How did you know this used to be my favourite? You want to share it now?'

'No, it's for you. I can get more next week. Save it till you really need it.' He turned his face towards the sun. 'I love this spot. How long before the spring tides?'

'About ten days.'

'And then this beach will be cut off completely?'

'Water will come right up to the wall – perhaps over the top with a storm tide.' She sensed the question in his eyes. 'That's when the wind and tide rise together, and force the sea levels up. I saw one here a couple of years ago. It was frightening.'

He took his hand in hers and closed his fingers around it. 'We'll have to find another meeting place. Be too easy to get trapped here.'

Hedy merely nodded, put her head on his shoulder and let the low autumn sun melt her thoughts away.

'Swedes, swedes, beautiful swedes,
We sing the praises of dear old swedes,
Oh yes, they're just all right,
They fill you up till you're blown up tight,
Swedes, swedes, succulent swedes,
They're all a fellow needs,
We all adore 'em, give us some more of 'em,
Beautiful, beautiful swedes.'

The five singers, chaotically costumed in various remnants from the Green Room Club's pre-war wardrobe chest, conducted the crowd with lusty enthusiasm. Chains of clasped hands formed along each row of seats, a forest of swaying arms silhouetted against the stage, while eager faces turned to each other, chuckling at the silliness of it all.

Hedy, holding tight to Anton on her right and a white-haired old lady on her left, sang as loudly as she could, giggling between breaths. This had been a great idea after all. She'd hesitated last night about accepting Anton's spare ticket, mainly because she'd been hoping that Kurt might be free this afternoon. But after she found Kurt's note in the pocket of her coat, saying that he'd been called to some local authorities meeting, she'd decided that a trip to the theatre might be a nice distraction. Now she wondered why she'd not been before. The pretty Victorian Opera House, with its gold trim and laurel mouldings, reminded her of her local theatre in Vienna, where her father had taken her to matinees as a child. That smell of polished wood and dusty old velvet, the mood of expectation . . . And so what if she recognised the lead actor from the stall in the fish market, or that the stage was lit by three car headlights fixed in the orchestra pit and powered from car batteries in the wings? What did it matter that the curtain had to rise at four, so that people from the country parishes could get home in time for curfew? Here, there was colour and song and escape, and for once the bubbling dread was firmly caged.

She leaned across to shout in Anton's ear, 'Isn't this wonderful?'

Anton smiled, but Hedy saw that there was nothing behind it. He looked distant, remote. Now that she thought about it, Anton had been in a strange mood since they'd met earlier that afternoon. The volume of her singing dropped a little, and she began slipping her friend sly little looks. Leaning back to glance at Dorothea on Anton's far side, she scanned for signs of argument or sulking. But Dorothea was grinning at the stage with wide, unblinking eyes, singing her heart out along with the rest. If there was trouble in paradise, Dorothea was clearly not aware of it.

The thick red curtains swung across to announce the interval, and with a clatter of lifting seats the audience began to file out to the bars and lavatories. Hedy leaned across her two companions. 'Shall we get something to drink?'

Anton wrinkled his nose. 'They won't have any real tea or coffee.'

'No, but I saw a sign on the way in that they have the best parsnip coffee in town! Come on, my treat?'

Dorothea glanced between the two of them with bush-baby eyes. 'You mean both of us?'

Hedy felt a flutter of embarrassment. She'd been trying for weeks now to be more friendly towards Dorothea. The romance had showed no sign of fading, and knowing she needed to make an effort for Anton's sake, she'd showered Dorothea with enquiries about her health, her grandmother, even her machinist job at the Summerland factory. But the woman's obsession with old movie magazines and endless chatter about hairstyles made for poor conversation, and her persistent girlish snickering, at things that really weren't that funny, set Hedy's nerves on edge. Until now she'd been confident that she'd kept her irritation hidden, but Dorothea's remark revealed that Hedy's tight, impatient smiles had concealed nothing. Now she'd have to repair the damage.

'Of course both of you! Come on, or we won't have time to get served.'

The three of them shuffled out of the auditorium and down the stairs to the tiny theatre bar, where they joined the long line of ragged locals queuing for whatever paltry fare was on offer. Everyone was so used to queuing these days, it hardly raised a comment any more. Hedy opened her bag to find her purse, but Anton placed his hand over it.

'Don't be silly. I don't really expect you to pay.'

Hedy bridled. 'Why not? I'm earning now. And after all the times you've paid for me—'

'It's all right – put your purse away.' His voice had an edge to it.

'Anton, what's wrong? You've been grumpy since we got here.' She looked to Dorothea for agreement, but Dorothea ignored her. Hedy had noticed that Dorothea, like Anton, was wary of any form of conflict.

'I'm fine, I'm just tired.'

'Ah, poor old Anton.' Hedy leaned into his ear and began to sing an old lullaby in a melodic whisper: '*Schlaf, Kindlein, schlaf! Der Vater hüt't die Schaf, die Mutter schütttelt's Baüme lein . . .*'

Anton yanked himself away. His scowl was so fierce Hedy took a step backwards. 'Hedy, for goodness' sake! You want to get us beaten up?' He wiped his ear with his fingers as if to remove the melody. 'You think *I'm* in a strange mood, what's wrong with *you* lately? You've been acting like you were drunk or something, these last few weeks.'

'I was only teasing you, that's all!'

'No, it's more than that. Something is going on with you.'

Hedy felt the blood rise to her cheeks. She hoped he would put it down to the stuffiness of the bar, which suddenly felt overwhelming. 'I'm just trying to stay cheerful! Wouldn't hurt you to try it. Everyone's tired, everyone's hungry, but what's the use in complaining? Dorothea, don't you think so?'

But Dorothea was staring at her as if she'd just worked out the last clue in the crossword. 'I know what it is! It's that lieutenant, isn't it? Have you seen him again?'

The air grew hotter. Hedy prayed her voice was still working. '*What?*'

'That's it, isn't it? What was his name – Kurt?'

She knew her only option was to attack, though her cheeks were aflame now.

'For goodness' sake, Dorothea, not this again!'

'I'm right, aren't I? You've seen him.'

At that moment, Hedy hated her. Treating it like some schoolgirl joke behind the bicycle sheds! How could the woman not grasp the severity of this? An elderly couple carrying chipped teacups bumped into the three of them as they pushed their way back through the crowd. The old man muttered an apology, but Hedy barely acknowledged him. She took a deep steadying breath. 'I told you, I met him that once when he came out of prison, to thank him. That's all.'

'You've not seen him since?' Anton asked.

'Why would I?'

'Because you really like him? Same as he likes you?' Dorothea's face was full of eagerness and concern, with no hint of judgement. Hedy almost envied her naivety.

'I don't know what goes on in that head of yours, Dorothea, but you really don't know me at all. And can you please not say things like this in a public place? Go back to your seats – I'll queue for the drinks.'

But Anton was still pawing for an argument. 'You two sit down – I'll get them.'

'Anton, for the last time, I said I'll pay.' Hedy reached for her purse again.

'And I said put your money away!' He pushed at the bag, which slipped from Hedy's arm, falling to the floor with a thud and sprawling the contents across the pink carpet. Each of them looked down to see the intimate story laid out beneath them. Hedy's leather purse, a Christmas gift to her from the Mitchells before the war; a lace handkerchief bought from the local market in happier times; and a half-eaten bar of Stollwerck chocolate, still in its bright blue wrapper.

For a moment none of them spoke. They simply stared down at the chocolate as though it were a hand grenade. The queue for the counter moved forward; two women in battered straw hats behind them, realising that Anton's trio had no intention of following, shrugged and manoeuvred in front of them.

Hedy lifted her eyes to meet Anton's and saw the anger.

'And I suppose' – his voice had steel within it – 'I suppose you bought this down the market?'

Involuntarily, Hedy put a hand to her cheek, leaving Dorothea to scrabble on the ground for the spilled items. 'I got it from a secretary at work.' The phrase swung in the air like frozen washing, stiff and wrongly shaped.

'I don't believe you.' Anton had never before said those words to her. 'You told me you never speak to anyone there. And yes, your face is crimson.'

Hedy felt the wall start to crumble. She didn't have the strength for this, not with him. It came out as a whisper. 'Anton, I'm sorry. I should have told you. But . . .'

Dorothea was instantly at her side, placing the bag back on her arm, putting one hand around Hedy's shoulder while the other stroked her hair. 'Hedy, don't apologise! No one can help who they fall in love with. And it's no different from me and Anton.'

Hedy kept her eyes fixed on Anton, whose face was setting with controlled fury. His voice stayed low. 'It's totally different. Have you told him?'

'Told him?'

'Don't play games. Have you?'

'I . . . no.'

Anton shook his head. At the counter, the straw-hatted women were telling the girl serving them about the best recipe for carrot jam. The clink of teaspoons being placed into cups was suddenly deafening.

'All that talk at the start . . . how you hated them, how scared you were! I did everything I could to protect you. And now this!' Hedy gazed down at the carpet. The patch in front of her was reduced to a bald, stringy trellis of fibres, scuffed apart by thousands of footsteps over the decades. 'Do you want to be imprisoned, maybe deported? Is that what you want?'

Dorothea's hand was still in her hair. Hedy wanted to smack it away but dared not draw any more attention.

'Don't be cruel to her, Anton. It's not her fault,' whispered Dorothea.

But Anton was buttoning his jacket and retying the scarf around his neck. 'Actually, it is. Are you coming with me or staying here?'

Dorothea cast a pained look at Hedy, but Hedy nodded at her to go. With a final squeeze of Hedy's arm, Dorothea followed Anton out of the bar. Hedy heard their feet on the staircase, her eyes still determinedly on the carpet, then at a slow, measured pace she made her own way out of the theatre by another exit. With luck, she would just manage to get home before the tears began.

★

Low sunbeams streamed in through the vast arched window at the end of the council chamber, bouncing off the polished table and lighting up the medals pinned on the German's chest. The reflection was so dazzling that Kurt, directly opposite, was forced to sit back in his seat to avoid being blinded. Why a mere administrator like Doctor Wilhelm Casper, who looked as if he had spent the entire Great War in a variety of offices and wouldn't know one end of a rifle from the other, should have such an impressive array of decorations, Kurt could only speculate. He glanced at the twenty or so other faces around the table to see if anyone else shared his scepticism, but the other German faces all displayed taut little smiles, while the Jersey heads were slumped despondently over their paperwork. The only other person Kurt recognised was a baby-faced lance corporal called Manfred, who he had recently met on a reconnaissance trip to one of the new north coast bunkers. A fellow Dresdner SC fan, Kurt had found Manfred friendly and curious out in the field. But here, under the gaze of the great and the good, Manfred kept his head down over his notebook, barely acknowledging Kurt's presence.

Kurt cast a wistful look at the bare boughs of the birch tree outside the window as they bounced in the wind against the evening sky, and suppressed a sigh. He didn't even know why he'd been summoned to this stupid meeting. The subject he was here to advise on – the adaptation of the local airport to accommodate new Luftwaffe fighters – was listed on the agenda as 'Other Business Time Permitting', and as it was now nearing six, it was obvious that his presence was a total waste of time. He could have been with Hedy today. Saturday was usually a good day to avoid her neighbours, with many of them out queuing at the market or visiting family. They could be tucked up in that tiny bed together right now. He felt a surge of resentment as his mind drifted to the mossy scent of her hair, the softness of her fingers, that supple, responsive body.

It was more than that now, though. Of course he'd had girlfriends back home – a couple he'd been quite keen on at the time – but what he'd felt in recent weeks, this new depth of emotion, genuinely shocked him. He found himself thinking about her all the time, wanting to share any interesting moment of the day, longing to hear her voice. It was affecting his attitude to his colleagues too. In the kitchen of his billet, he would often hear the other officers laughing as they swapped stories about some girl they had flirted with, or fucked in the back of the clubhouse. They would slap each other's knees in boyish congratulation over some brunette who had given them head in the back of a car for a kilo of fish, one crowing that he'd had both mother and daughter in return for 200 French cigarettes. Kurt had never felt comfortable around this kind of talk, but now he found it positively distasteful. More than that, it baffled him. What satisfaction lay there? What challenge, what discovery? Sure, at the start it was lust that had driven him towards Hedy. But now . . . now it was that internal darkness that kept him coming back for more. The mix of anger and sadness in her eyes that masked a mystery so complex it frightened him. How could a woman give her body to him with such abandon yet simultaneously hide so much? Like a fisherman at the end of the day who has caught only tiddlers, but knows that great, fat fish still swim beneath the surface, Kurt couldn't drag himself away.

'Some additional fuel restrictions,' Doctor Casper was droning through his interpreter, a slight, bespectacled young man who could have passed for Casper's own son. 'From next week gas will only be available between seven a.m. and two thirty p.m., and between five thirty and nine p.m. And Field Command wishes to procure the contents of the island's current wood stores. We will, of course, be happy to negotiate a settlement on an amicable basis.'

A new voice piped up: 'That firewood is needed by the local population for heating and cooking. What if we do not wish to negotiate?'

Kurt turned his attention back to the table to see who had spoken. A tired Jerseyman with thinning grey hair and wire-rimmed spectacles, who Kurt understood to be the local councillor for labour issues, was glaring at Casper with ill-disguised contempt.

Casper merely shrugged. 'Then, Mr Le Quesne, we will take it anyway. Field Command must place the needs of the island garrison before the needs of . . . *Einheimische*.' Casper wiped his dry lips with his fingers as if the word 'locals' had caused an unpleasant taste. 'We also require that the contents of your glasshouses be placed at the disposal of the military.'

Kurt looked down at the papers before him, careful to keep his expression neutral. Inwardly, he flinched. Every day for months now he'd listened to his colleague Fischer bleat on about the idiocy of the local Superior Council members – these dumb provincials, with their stubborn refusal to accept the natural, common-sense orders of their masters, and their rustic small-mindedness that prevented them from helping themselves. Even Kurt himself, watching Hedy eke out her meagre vegetables for the week, had privately wondered if these shortages had more to do with the failings of local agricultural policy than Field Command's interference. Yet here was the new governor stealing food from the locals and not even bothering to lie about it.

'Oh, I think we fully understand the status of the "locals", Doctor Casper,' Le Quesne chipped back, undimmed. 'Your imprisonment of my messenger boy, whose stammer prevented him from apologising when he brushed against a German officer on the street, made that crystal clear. As has your latest measure – ordering us to seize the proceeds of all Jewish businesses.'

Kurt looked to Casper, wondering if this would result in a sharp rebuke or something worse, when another Jersey voice rang out from the far end of the table. It came from a flaky-skinned fellow sporting a moustache and heavy eyebrows.

'I don't believe, Mr Le Quesne,' the newcomer chimed in nasal tones, 'that deliberate antagonism will serve anyone here. Last year, you yourself were one of the strongest advocates of the Jersey Superior Council retaining civil authority, that we might act as a bridge of communication, so to speak, between our German visitors and the local population. On that basis, implementation of Doctor Casper's wishes is both our duty and obligation.' The speaker turned to Casper and offered him a simpering smile that turned Kurt's stomach.

'I am grateful,' Casper replied with a nod, 'to Chief Aliens Officer Mr Clifford Orange for his pragmatic and courteous response. And as time is running on, I believe, on that basis we should conclude.'

Casper snapped his folder together, as did his uniformed minions, and rose to his feet. Kurt, grateful for the release, but with his anger still churning, followed the line of obedient uniforms out of the chamber and towards the grand marble stairs of the council building. As they made their way down the steps, he found himself next to Manfred.

Kurt greeted him with a pat on the shoulder. 'Hey, Manfred, what did you make of that?' He was careful to keep his voice under the level of communal chatter.

Manfred looked up at him, apparently taken aback to be addressed by a senior officer. 'Sir? You mean the meeting?'

'Did you know that we were requisitioning food from the locals to feed the garrison?'

Manfred nodded. Kurt spotted a tic in the boy's eye. 'Not surprising, I guess, sir. Our being here has pretty much doubled the population. Only so much they can bring over from France.'

'Doesn't really fit with the promise we made, though, does it? About guaranteeing their liberty.' Manfred gave no reply, but threw Kurt a tortured look.

'You don't have a view on this?'

'No, sir.'

'I thought you wanted to make Obergefreiter next year?' Kurt pressed him. 'If you want to climb the ladder, you have to express an opinion occasionally.'

'Yes sir, but . . .'

Sensing his discomfort, Kurt waited for the rest of the contingent to move on before taking Manfred to one side. In the pink reflected glow of the giant swastika flag that hung in the entrance, Kurt took his remaining tobacco from his breast pocket and offered Manfred a roll-up, which the youth happily accepted.

Kurt waited for him to take a deep drag. 'But what?

It was Manfred's turn to lower his voice. 'Lieutenant, you're a good guy, sir. I – I admire you, you know? But if people know I've had this kind of conversation with you—'

Kurt raised an eyebrow. 'Because of that petrol coupon business?'

'Lieutenant Fischer, he says we need to be careful who we mix with. And that guy with the hat . . .'

'Erich Wildgrube?'

'Yes, him. He drops in at all the barracks, talks about watching out for the bad apples.'

'So much for paying for your mistake and moving on.'

'See, sir, my family depends on my wages.' Manfred took another deep drag on the precious tobacco, holding it down before he spoke. 'Making Obergefreiter is important. They need me to do well, you understand? If it was down to me . . .'

'Don't apologise. You run along. And, Manfred? Don't worry – this conversation never happened, okay?'

Kurt slapped the lad on the shoulder and pushed him towards the door, giving it a moment before he followed. He'd suspected as much, but the confirmation hurt. Fucking Fischer, fucking Wildgrube. Fucking pointless rules and mindless fucking loyalties. He stepped out into the chilly darkness and set off towards the coast road, deciding that the long walk back to Pontac Common would do him good. But his mind continued to bounce from one ugly image to the next. German soldiers loading up barrows from the greenhouses of local farmers. Wildgrube's ugly, pasty face with those furtive little eyes. But mainly Kurt kept thinking of King Canute, sitting stubbornly on his throne, gasping for air between the crashing waves as the tide moved unceasingly towards him.

★

The paraffin lamps around the shop gave off an eerie blue glow, throwing strange, looming shadows on the tiled walls. From the darkness of the street, the empty display window revealed the story within, like watching a movie on a screen. At the rear, Anton, in his white apron and pillbox baker's cap, moved effortlessly around the room, sweeping the floor and wiping down surfaces in a series of methodical arcs, while at the front counter the ebullient Mr Reis, visibly slimmer these days, was patiently explaining to the last customer of the day that he had nothing left to sell her at any price. Even from her viewpoint on the bench across the street, Hedy could see the woman's desperation as she waved a pair of children's shoes in front of him, pleading for a bartering deal on the burnt rejects she hoped lay under the counter. But the old man continued to pacify her, smiling apologetically and patting her hand, until eventually she nodded and let herself out through the shop door, shuffling down the road with her shopping bag swinging empty at her side.

The freezing seat penetrated the thin fabric of her coat as Hedy shifted her sitting position. She watched Mr Reis close the door behind the customer and pull the bolts across – three of them now, due to the recent night-time raids on food premises – and turn the sign to 'Closed'. Ten more minutes, and Anton would be upstairs in his apartment. She decided to give it fifteen before she followed him up there; give him time to shake off the bakery dust and feel a little more conversational. Assuming, of course, that he let her in at all.

Her breath came in unsteady little pants as she climbed the stairs. The door to the flat was ajar and she could hear Anton padding around, no doubt trying to figure out what kind of evening meal was possible. As she neared his apartment door, his voice from within took her by surprise.

'Come in, Hedy. I know it's you.'

Hedy slunk in, leaving the door open, staying close to the wall. 'How did you know?'

'You were sitting on that bench for half an hour. I'm not blind!'

'Can we talk?'

'Yes, but Dory will be here in ten minutes.'

Hedy tiptoed across the floor and took her old seat by the window, one leg tucked under her body as always. It was months since she'd been here. How long ago it seemed, cooking that meal for Kurt in this very room.

'You must be freezing. I'm afraid I've nothing much to offer you,' Anton continued. 'But I can warm some water for you? Maybe with a spoonful of sugar beet syrup?'

Hedy nodded her gratitude, and Anton busied himself in the kitchen area.

'How'd you make the syrup?'

'Skin a turnip and boil it for hours.' Anton banged the tap above the sink with the flat of his hand to get it to work properly. 'But you didn't come to talk about that, did you?'

Hedy clenched her fists and stared at the back of her hands as she spoke. 'I want to apologise. I understand why you're angry. I'm angry with myself. Me and Kurt . . . it was the last thing I wanted to happen, but . . .'

Anton continued to fiddle with pots and matches. 'Is it serious?'

'Nothing's been said, exactly, but . . . I really care about him. And I think he feels the same.'

'Well, that's something, I suppose.' He looked at her properly for the first time. 'Sorry I lost my temper. But you're like a sister to me. And the fact that you lied for so long—'

'I was ashamed. And I also wanted to protect you. The less people know, the less trouble they can get into – sometimes it's safer to lie.' She rubbed her forehead with the palm of her hand. 'And I seem to be getting rather good at it.'

'What do you mean? Anything else I ought to know?'

A short silence. To hell with it, she thought. 'I'm still stealing coupons for Doctor Maine.'

His face was a picture. '*What?*'

'Actually, I never stopped. I still meet him every week to deliver them. Kurt doesn't know. No one does.'

Another silence endured, longer than the first. Then, to her relief he broke it with a grin of disbelief. 'For God's sake, Hedy. Do you have a death wish or something?'

'Apparently.' A manic giggle escaped from her nose; she attempted to sniff it back up. 'Papa always said I never made things easy for myself. But I don't think even he could have imagined this.' Another giggle leaked out. 'Stealing from my enemy during the day, and sleeping with him at night. I know . . . I must be out of my mind.'

The chuckle fizzed between them for a moment, faded. Anton put down the matches. 'You have to tell Kurt – I mean, about your race classification. He will find out eventually.'

'I'm seeing him tomorrow. I'm going to tell him then.'

'And you're prepared for him to end it? Because he'll have to, if he wants to protect himself.'

'I know.' She got up, crossed over to Anton and gave him a hug. 'Thank you. I'm so sorry, Anton. Sometimes I don't know what I'd do without you.' But as she spoke the words, she felt a stiffness, a retreat. 'What did I say?'

'I haven't been entirely honest with you, either.'

The water in the tiny saucepan began to boil but neither of them moved.

Hedy's first thought was that Dorothea was pregnant. 'Tell me?'

'I've been drafted.'

Hedy's stomach seemed to drop into a lower space. 'You mean . . .'

'Letter arrived that day we went to the Opera House. I've not even told Dory yet. I'll be signed up in a few weeks, assigned

86

local duties. After that, who knows? Way things are going, it could be the Eastern Front.'

She felt light-headed. Her hand instinctively reached out to grasp the counter top and steady herself. 'But you're a food producer. You're classed as an essential worker.'

'Obviously they've decided they need soldiers more.'

Hedy felt her throat closing. She blinked hard but the tears leaked out anyway. 'But it's not fair! You're not German!'

'We're both technically German citizens now.'

'But you . . . you might . . .'

'Might not come back? Of course. But if I refuse, they'll shoot me anyway.'

'Who would shoot you? What's happened?'

Hedy and Anton both whipped around to see Dorothea standing in the doorway, her eyes wide with fear; her grandmother's coat swamped her tiny frame, making her look even more vulnerable. Anton moved quickly towards her and enveloped her in his arms.

'I've had my orders to join the Wehrmacht. I'm so sorry, Dory.'

Dorothea let out a howl of despair, burying her face in his chest. 'No! No, I need you here! What if you get hurt or killed? I can't bear it!'

Hedy hung back, embarrassed to be a witness to such an intimate moment, yet sensing that to leave now would be as bad. She could hear Dorothea's breaths becoming shorter and wheezier, and tried to recall what Maine's advice had been in the event of another attack. Her eyes darted to Anton's store cupboard, wondering if it contained any mustard. But what happened next pushed any such thoughts from her head.

'I know, and I want to make sure you'll be protected, whatever the future holds,' Anton was saying. 'That's why today I got this.' He reached into his trouser pocket and pulled out a small box. As he opened it, Hedy could just make out the glint of something shiny. 'It's not new, of course – it belonged to Mr

Reis's aunt. But it's small, so I think it might fit you. The stone is an opal, I think.' Taking Dorothea's hand, he stared into her stunned, tear-stained face. 'Dorothea, will you marry me?'

Dorothea clapped both hands to her mouth to muffle another cry, this one mixed with joy. 'Oh, Anton! Of course I will!' She flung her arms around his skinny body, clinging so hard his spine made a faint cracking sound. They both turned towards Hedy.

'You hear that, Hedy? She said yes! We're getting married!'

Hedy looked from one to the other as they hugged, kissed each other long on the lips, then hugged again. Her throat was still full of rocks from Anton's first news; events were now turning to quicksand beneath her feet. She saw Dorothea's beaming, tear-streaked face and felt a surge of pity and loss, though who it was for, she couldn't say. Eventually she gained enough control to croak out the compulsory sentences: 'Congratulations, I'm so happy for you both. Everything will work out, I know it.'

She'd been mistaken, she thought, as she gathered up her coat and bag, wished them luck and hurried down the narrow stairs towards the street. She wasn't getting any better at lying at all.

★

Pulling her scarf tighter around her neck, Hedy perched on one of the granite bollards placed along the quay for boat anchorage, and knocked her feet together to get the blood flowing. The icy gusts from the ocean beyond rippled the black water around the fishing boats. The locals called this little marina, tucked away at the back of the main port, the French Harbour. This had been her idea for a meeting place this evening – quiet but not secluded, private enough for the conversation she planned, but public enough to summon help if things should turn ugly. The road here from the town was lined with harbour warehouses, hulking great slabs with ribbed doors that roared like engines as they were rolled up and down. Behind her rose the vast, impenetrable walls of Fort Regent, raised by Royal Engineers over a century before. This was a charmless, transient place where no one ever lingered, but simply did what whatever job needed to be done and moved on. Appropriate, then, for her task today: deliver her message and walk off into the darkness.

All day long, typing reports in that soulless crate of an office, she had played out this moment in her mind, feeling the dread rise. Yet what, exactly, was she dreading? Perhaps he would fly into a rage, but in all these weeks she'd never seen anything to suggest that was likely. Kurt could, in theory, report her to the authorities; miscegenation was unquestionably a sackable offence, and who knew what he might be driven to in desperation. But the fear that nudged persistently, like a rubber band twanging on her wrist, was the anticipation of her own future: months, maybe years, trapped in this island prison, without Kurt for comfort. The secret meetings, the softness of his hand on hers, his kindly questions about her day – they were all that had made the last months bearable. But she had promised Anton, and she knew herself that to stretch this out any further was suicidal. It had to be tonight.

Suddenly she heard a strange sound some distance away – a collective shuffling and heavy breathing, like a herd of small animals. It was getting closer. Anxious, she stood and peered down the road that led back to the Weighbridge and main harbour. In the fragments of remaining light she could just make out an approaching group of people. It wasn't a troop of German soldiers, whose rapping boots could be heard for miles, but there were guards at the fore, wearing the uniform of the Organisation Todt. Then, as they came closer, she saw it. Lumbering towards her was a stinking cloud of broken humanity. Skeletal, shaven-headed men, some old beyond their years, some no more than boys, shuffling along in a frightened pack, their eyes on the ground to avoid those of their guards, who grinned as they swung their rubber truncheons for any imagined offence. Despite the cold, the prisoners were dressed in nothing but rags, their feet bound only in cloth. Several had visible injuries, many others the obvious stains of shit and vomit. As one sharp breeze brought the smell of them into Hedy's nostrils, the bile rose in her throat until she retched. She wanted to turn away, in horror or respect, but could not.

The guards drove their victims on at a quick pace; as they passed by, not one raised his face to look at her; they simply stumbled on, saving every gram of energy for the march ahead. Hedy was so shocked that she hardly noticed Kurt approaching from the opposite direction.

'Did you see that?'

Kurt nodded. 'Slave labourers, for the defence construction. Third boatful this week. It's hideous.'

'But did you *see* them? They're half dead already! How can anyone treat human beings that way?' She searched for Kurt's eyes in the gloom, and realised his focus was miles away. Anger erupted inside her. 'This is what your people are doing in the name of your superior race! Can you still tell me you don't feel responsible? Do you still think this is nothing to do with you?'

'It's about all of us!' His voice was cracked and sour, a tone she'd never heard before. 'You think this stupid fucking war doesn't touch everyone? All our lives will be ruined by this, all of us!'

Hedy stared, stunned, cancelling a dozen questions in her head. She reached out and touched his arm. It was all it took. Kurt sank back onto the granite bollard, made a small choking sound and began to weep. She stood silent for a moment, then slowly put her arms around him and cradled his head on her chest. His sobs shook his body while he tried to get control of himself. When at last he spoke it came in forced, intermittent bursts. 'Had a letter from Helmut's mother. His unit was attacked by Russian planes. Some of them made it, but—'

'But?'

'Helmut's tank took a direct hit.'

Hedy pulled his head closer to her. 'Oh, Kurt, no! Are they certain?'

He nodded. 'They identified him by his dog tag.' The sobbing began in earnest again. 'The last time I saw him, he told me to take care of myself. He told me!'

Hedy said nothing, but continued to hold him, stroking that soft, dark blond hair. She thought again of her parents, perhaps still sitting around that kitchen stove, more likely rounded up onto some truck and driven God knows where. She felt his grief blend with her own, and twist painfully in her chest.

'It's all right, Kurt, it's all right. I'm here. I'm here.'

They stayed there on the frozen quay for what seemed like hours, until Kurt pulled away and stood up straight, brushing the tears from his face.

'I'm sorry. I feel a little better now.'

Hedy nodded. 'We all need to cry sometimes.'

'So what was it you wanted to tell me?'

'Me?'

'You said in your note that you needed to talk to me about something important. It sounded serious.'

She looked out across the glistening black water, the shadowy shapes of the boats. How she'd love to climb into one now and sail away into the void, swallowed up by the darkness. Her voice was tiny. 'Yes . . .'

'Well, let me say something first. It's something I've wanted to get out in the open before, for a long time, but I wasn't sure you . . .' She held her breath, half anticipating a question. Did he already know? Perhaps someone at work had said something. His hands reached for her face. 'Anyway, tonight I have to say it. Hedy, I love you. I have done since the start. I'm still not sure if you feel the same, but I know this is it for me. I always want us to be together. So it's up to you now.' She pressed herself even closer to him, letting herself melt into his body. The buttons of his uniform dug through her coat into her flesh. Her face ached with the contortions of emotion, and she could feel her heart hammering. 'So, now it's your turn. What did you want to say?'

Hedy screwed up her eyes. For the first time in years, she wished for a true faith. A faith like her mother's, one that brought the gift of guidance. Yet she already knew what she had to do. Even now, it was not too late. She just had to push her emotions aside, drag common sense back in. Find the kind of strength the rabbis used to talk about, the kind her sister Roda could summon at will. She pulled back to look at him and placed her frozen hand on his face.

'I wanted to tell you . . . that I love you too.'

He grinned, and kissed her with passion and tenderness. Afterwards, she tried to recall her feelings at that moment – shame, relief, anger? But all she could remember was the pleasure of that kiss.

5

The atmosphere on the street was tangible, Kurt thought, as he strode along St Saviours Road in the pink glow of the afternoon sun. In two weeks it would be Christmas. A novel kind of holiday this year, one without turkeys, trees, nuts or even presents for most of the kids. It would be little better in Germany, he was sure, but that brought no comfort here. If you stretched out your hand into the cold, still air, you could rub the bitterness between your thumb and forefinger and feel its grit. The 'ghosts' whom other officers often spoke of – the glass-eyed, unseeing locals who had for months ignored every German on the street as if they were invisible – now stared directly at Kurt as he walked by. Some exuded pure hatred, some just the gloating anticipation that the end was near. It was now 'only a matter of time' they muttered to themselves or to each other on street corners, just loud enough for passing soldiers to hear. The game had changed; the tide had turned. The Yanks were in.

Poor fools, Kurt thought. Yes, Pearl Harbor had swung the compass around. But with the Americans focused on the Pacific Theatre, it couldn't possibly have much effect in Europe for at least a year, probably more. All this meant was a longer, greater, more destructive war, with no guarantee of victory on either side. And for what? The questioning voices that had whispered to Kurt for months were now shouting so loudly they were waking him in the early hours, leaving him staring at the ceiling while Fischer snored peacefully in the bed beside him. What the hell were they all doing here? Parading around this island in their ridiculous uniforms, torturing Slav prisoners, tormenting the locals with cold and hunger. Just yesterday the senior OT officer had lectured the compound staff on the importance of pride in their great nationalist work. The schedule was vital, he told them, for the security and success of the Fatherland. The same day, Kurt had received Helmut's last letter, dated two weeks before his death. Inside he felt something taking shape, an icy crystal of disgust. He thought of Hedy, the only light in his life, and felt grateful that he'd kept his promise to keep their relationship private. At first he'd thought her obsession with secrecy tiresome, creeping around and inventing stories to satisfy his colleagues' questions. But now, with the locals' attitude shifting, he saw the sense in it.

A twisting murmuration of starlings filled the bright winter sky, and he smiled at the thought of the evening to come. Hedy's nosy downstairs neighbour was away at her sister's, and he was off duty till tomorrow morning. As he passed a forlorn little group of children, singing 'Away In A Manger' outside an unrelenting house, he felt a rush of Christmas cheer and goodwill, and flipped two coins into their cloth cap. Turning into New Street, he began the final stretch towards Hedy's building; he imagined her standing by her tiny stove, stirring a pot, and quickened his pace in excitement.

So lost was he in his thoughts that when he first heard the voice he didn't realise it was aimed at him. Only when the shout of 'Leutnant!' became 'Leutnant Neumann!' did Kurt turn to see the figure on the other side of the street. Wildgrube raised his silly Alpine hat in a greeting as he hurried across the road. Kurt tried his best to smile but suspected the result was unconvincing.

'Good evening, Lieutenant.' Wildgrube's voice sounded even more whiney and high-pitched than usual. 'And where, may I ask, are you headed this fine afternoon?'

Kurt stared at him, trying to remain expressionless. Was this a coincidence, or was the guy actually following him? If so, for how long? Kurt's immediate concern, though, was that he was no more than ten metres from Hedy's front door.

'Actually, I was just taking a stroll.' It sounded fake and Kurt knew it.

Wildgrube's smile was stretched to breaking point but his eyes were empty. 'Really? Around here?' He looked about him with theatrical puzzlement. 'Hardly the most scenic choice!'

'I thought I might head up to Vallée des Vaux – it's about fifteen minutes that way. Still green up there this time of year. Have you been?'

The policeman corrected the angle of his hat as he replaced it on his head. 'I confess I have not. I did not know that you were such a keen walker?'

Kurt kept his expression friendly, doing a dozen lightning calculations in his head. If Wildgrube had followed him all the way from his billet, he must be receiving information on Kurt's movements. Had he received a tip-off of some kind, and if so, from whom? Fischer was the most likely candidate; he had hardly spoken to Kurt for weeks following Kurt's prison sentence, and he and Wildgrube were definitely chummy. But Kurt was always discreet around Fischer, and it was doubtful the Nazi had anything specific to report. Kurt's guess was that this was a simple fishing expedition.

He smoothed back his hair to indicate composure. 'Keeps me out of trouble.' He hoped Wildgrube would appreciate the self-deprecating reference, but the spy's expression didn't change. If Kurt was going to throw him permanently off the scent, he was going to have to come up with something good. 'All right, Erich, you've got me. I'm not planning to walk up Vallée des Vaux . . .' He tried to look suitably embarrassed. 'I heard there was a new "officers' club", over on Rouge Boullion. One of the guys in my house went last week, came back with some stories! I thought I might stop by.'

At this, Wildgrube smiled properly, with intent. The effect was rather chilling. 'Ah! You are looking for some female company, perhaps? The kind whose company is, let's say, reliable in its outcome?'

'Exactly.' Kurt forced out a laugh. 'Like I said, you got me.'

Wildgrube joined in his laughter. 'You don't have to be embarrassed about such natural needs, Lieutenant! Tell you what – I wouldn't mind checking out the place myself. Would you mind signing me in?'

Frustration rose in Kurt's gullet and threatened to choke him. The trap had snapped shut – any lie he told now would be too obvious, and he had no doubt Wildgrube would follow him anyway. Now he would be stuck with this reptile for the rest of the night, while Hedy waited alone up there, confused and disappointed. He longed to glance up at her window to throw her some explanatory look. But he kept his eyes firmly fixed on Wildgrube's face and, accepting his fate, pulled the plug.

'Sure, if you like.'

'Great. After we both get laid I will buy you a nice Scotch whisky. How about that? It will be a chance for us to get to know each other better.'

Kurt's brain continued to whir as they set off up the road. Perhaps there was an advantage to this nightmare. If Wildgrube still had Kurt marked as a potential troublemaker, this was Kurt's chance to allay suspicions, maybe even soften him up for information in the future. He planned the evening out in his mind – he'd been through enough of these nights back home to know how it would go. Wildgrube would knock back a couple of whiskies then make a big deal of picking the 'best' woman in the place. Meanwhile, Kurt would cover his tracks with the youngest, most vulnerable kid he could find, and pay her for a half-hour conversation about her family, tipping her enough to buy any lies he required later. He and Wildgrube would drink the rest of the night away, while Kurt threw in a few remarks about his previous 'foolishness' for good measure. That way, the night would at least be an investment. It was the thought of not being able to let Hedy know that hurt the most.

Only when they were a good twenty metres past Hedy's door did Kurt make the excuse of retying his boot lace in order to sneak a glance up at her window. He had barely a second to take it in, but swore he saw her at the edge of the attic pane, peeping down into the street. Not daring to make even the smallest sign, he took a deep breath before rejoining Wildgrube for the short walk to the officers' club and the miserable young whores who waited for them.

★

'Maybe a little tighter around the waist? I'm so skinny now – well, who isn't these days! I don't want it to hang off me or I'll look like I'm wearing an old sack!'

Dorothea giggled and pulled the dress tighter on her body, indicating to Hedy where the fabric should sit.

Hedy, squinting with concentration, pulled the darts a little further out and pushed the pins into place. 'Like that?'

Dorothea stepped down from the chair and stood back, craning her neck to try to view the dress from different angles. Hedy took the tiny vanity mirror from her dressing table and held it up for her, wishing that her landlord provided a full-length mirror as part of the furnishings.

'That's much better. I love the texture of this dimity, don't you? I mean, it would have been lovely to have something new . . .'

Hedy obediently rubbed the fabric between her fingers. 'Yes, but no one expects new clothes these days, even for a wedding. Anton's borrowing a suit from Mr Reis's son, isn't he?'

'I know.' Dorothea sighed. 'It's just . . . you know how you always planned your wedding, dreamed about what you would wear, right from when you were a little girl?' Hedy raised her brows as if in agreement, even though it was a topic she'd never given a moment's thought. 'I even used to walk my dolly down the hallway to "Here Comes The Bride", with an old lace curtain draped over her head! Still, this is a lovely dress. And I think with that little white hat . . .' She twirled herself around Hedy's apartment, her head flicking back for approval.

Hedy opted for a stock response. 'You'll look lovely. Anton will be proud of you. But you should probably take it off now – it's like an icebox in here. And you don't want to get it dirty before the big day.'

Dorothea unzipped herself at the side and wriggled out of the dress, trying to avoid the pins, babbling as she did so. 'Still can't believe I spotted that hat in the exchange adverts. I mean, what are the chances of the perfect hat popping up just this week? Well worth a bar of soap and an old bedsheet! Now all I need is gloves to match, but that's probably over-optimistic.'

Hedy sneaked a glance at Dorothea's pale, bony body beneath her slip, wondering how much of it Anton had seen and what he would think of it. She wondered if that was how she looked to Kurt; perhaps it was fortunate not having a proper mirror after all. 'And listen, Hedy, I wanted to say thank you for doing this. I loved making things before we had to trade the Singer, but I've never been much good at hand-sewing. My grandmother would have helped if she could, of course, but her eyesight is so poor now. Then I thought of you, and when Anton told me you'd volunteered, I was just . . . well, it means a lot to me.'

Hedy, avoiding Dorothea's eyes, knelt on the floor and placed the pins back in their old tobacco tin one at a time. She knew what her mother would call her at this moment – a *Farshtinkiner*, a louse. Only three days earlier, Hedy had visited Anton at the bakery. She'd gone on the excuse of returning a borrowed book, but in truth intended to talk to him about this marriage, perhaps even persuade him not to go through with it. She'd even manoeuvred him into the privacy of the bakery's backyard, away from prying ears. If she could just make him see that he had only proposed through guilt, through a fear of leaving Dorothea without a widow's pension . . . Surely he would understand this was no basis for a marriage?

Of course, the conversation had never got that far. No sooner had Anton closed the outer door, he had badgered her about Kurt, demanding to know what had happened – had she told him the truth? How had he reacted, were they still together? Hedy rushed headlong into a passionate defence of her procrastination: if Anton had only seen Kurt that night! The man was broken, and it would have been inhuman to pile on so much grief in one day. And she'd honestly intended to tell him at their next meeting, if only Kurt had not been followed by that dreadful secret police officer. But she would tell him the truth the next day, she swore, or at least the day after. And as her mouth sprayed its pitiful nonsense, she watched Anton nod wearily, his hair and lashes covered in fine grey flour, too stooped and exhausted by his impending conscription to argue. She knew he saw right through her. Overwhelmed by her own hypocrisy and spineless-ness, Hedy had hurried from the bakery without bringing up the wedding at all, guiltily agreeing over her shoulder to help in any way she could. She'd slouched home, comparing the open, straightforward girl she'd been at school with the selfish, scheming reflection that now jumped out at her from dark shop windows. This infected boil of lies and self-delusion swelled a little more each day, contaminating people who were supposed to love each other, poisoning her own soul. She cursed this stupid, pointless war.

She looked up at Dorothea and forced a smile. 'You're welcome. I just hope I do a good enough job.'

'I know you will. And you must come round for supper at the new house. Did I tell you about the place Anton's found for us on West Park Avenue?'

'You did.'

'The rent's a bit steep, but it's got the prettiest fireplace in the front room and a sweet little yard at the back.'

'And brass knobs on all the doors,' Hedy chipped in, hoping she'd take the hint.

Oblivious, Dorothea slipped her shoes back on and wriggled into her old woollen dress. 'I can't wait to be Mrs Anton Weber! Now, here's your invitation.' She pulled a homemade card from her bag, cut from some old packaging and painted in what looked like whitewash.

Hedy read the text, handwritten in pen and ink: *Dorothea Le Brocq and Anton Weber request the pleasure of Hedy and Kurt at the States of Jersey Register Office, followed by a reception at 7 West Park Avenue.*

'I know how sensitive you are about your relationship,' Dorothea added, 'but it would be wonderful if you wanted to bring him.'

Hedy shook her head. 'I'm sorry, it's just not possible. Kurt and I can't be seen together in public.'

Dorothea reached out for her hand. Her fingers were like ice. 'But you've been courting for months now, and we've still not met him! What if he just came to the reception at our place? No one there would judge you.'

Hedy re-read the card. 'I thought you wanted the reception at the Pierson pub?'

Dorothea kept her eyes and fingers on the buttons of her dress, even though it seemed to Hedy that she had already finished buttoning it. 'We were, but it seemed a waste of money for just five or six of us.'

'Five or six? But what about your family, friends?'

'Well, Nana will come to the ceremony, of course!' The false brightness splintered in her voice. 'But she won't have the stamina for the reception too. And Mr Reis has to run the shop. So it's just you and Kurt, Doctor Maine if he's free – and I'm hoping my schoolfriend Sandy will come, if her dad agrees.'

'But your parents?' Hedy felt a wave of pity.

'We're honestly happy with a small do. It'll save us trying to scrape together food for lots of people.'

Hedy watched Dorothea fold up her wedding dress with ritualistic care, stroking the fabric as if it were a kitten, placing it in a neat bundle on Hedy's table. She continued to touch it, as if the garment held some magic power she didn't quite understand, yet believed in utterly. Once more, Hedy wondered what she was really thinking. The woman seemed almost ethereal at times, a spirit from another world. But when she spoke again her voice was stronger. 'We just want our best friends there, that's all that matters!' She patted the bundle down and managed a big, generous grin. 'So, you see, there's no reason why Kurt shouldn't come.'

Hedy decided the safest course was to let the subject drop. 'Thank you. I'll think about it.'

Dorothea pulled on her coat, arranged her hat and headed for the door. 'Thanks again for this, Hedy. If there's ever anything I can do for you in return . . .'

Hedy hesitated. She had, in actual fact, been brewing an idea for several weeks, but was still unsure if she wanted to ask such a huge favour of this ditsy girl. Deciding that this was not the right time, she was about to say no, when Dorothea, evidently detecting something in her body language, stopped with her hand still on the door latch. Hedy found herself pinned by those intense eyes glinting from the other side of the room.

'What is it? Tell me?' said Dorothea.

'It's nothing. At least, it can wait till after the wedding.' Hemingway rubbed himself against her leg, as if prompting Hedy to ask the question.

'Please, Hedy. Anything?'

'Well, it's just that . . . I've heard nothing from my parents in twenty months, nor they from me. They can't even receive mail in Vienna, being Jewish.'

Dorothea shook her head. 'It's so unfair.'

'But I have an old schoolfriend, Elke, who I think still lives there. If I use a false name and I'm careful what I say, I think

I can slip a letter into the franking pile at work. But what I need is a safe return address . . .'

'So how can I help?'

Hedy suppressed a sigh, and reminded herself that Dorothea was doing her best to be helpful. 'I was wondering if I could write care of your new house?'

Dorothea blossomed. 'Oh, of course! Use our address by all means.'

Hedy nodded. 'Thank you. It's a . . . what is the English phrase? A long shot. But it's all I have.' It was Hedy's turn to pat the wedding dress. 'I'd better be getting on with this.'

Dorothea waved goodbye with her fingertips, the way a child waves to its mother, as she let herself out the door, and Hedy heard the fading sound of her feet skipping down the stairs and the humming of the wedding march in her high, frail voice. Hedy picked the dress up from the table to plan her work, wondering, with an unsettled feeling, how long that voice would be a significant sound in her life.

★

The day was cold and monochrome, but the wind had dropped and the bulbous flint-coloured clouds were still clinging to their rain. Hedy stepped as lightly as she could across the Royal Square, walking carefully so as not to disturb the ancient glue on the sole of her shoe, and enjoying the sensation of wearing stockings for the first time in months. She had been saving them for weeks, for just such a special occasion. Of course Kurt must have bought them on the black market, and they must have cost him an absurd amount of money, which made her feel both guilty and delighted. She wore the same old crepe dress and the same old cardigan she wore for every event other than work, but the slippery thrill she felt when her legs brushed together did give a sense of occasion to the day.

She was unsure which door led to the registrar's office, but as she turned the corner by the town church, the crowd on the steps led her straight to it. Hedy watched as a family party gathered on the steps. The bride was a local lass of no more than seventeen, with an empire line dress that Hedy was pretty sure was designed to hide the middle trimester of pregnancy. Holding her hand, wearing a suit he'd probably had since school and an expression of pure misery, was a spotty youth, hemmed in between a surly, stocky man Hedy took for the bride's father and his slit-mouthed wife in a tight floral dress. A shotgun wedding if ever Hedy had seen one – yet the steps were crowded with siblings, aunts and cousins, kissing the bride and clucking around, glad of the excuse to break their grim, daily routine with a family celebration.

Hedy squeezed past them and into the building, following the signs until she found the waiting area. She found herself in a vapid charmless space, despite its gleaming oak floor, and only a stone's throw away from the Aliens Office where she'd been interviewed by Orange, over a year ago. It had the same smell of wood and musty papers, and oozed municipality, bringing to mind shuffling queues for permits and bored secretaries smashing down on staplers. Two wedding parties sprawled over the plain benches against the wall, laughing and chatting excitedly. On the third bench sat Anton and Doctor Maine, silent and expressionless.

Hedy stood in the doorway for a moment, taking in the two of them. Doctor Maine was in his Sunday best, but she could plainly see the scruffy old shoes beneath his flannel trousers. He looked abandoned, somehow, almost derelict, his skin dry and sallow. She had never found out how old he actually was. Younger than his face suggested, she was sure of that. But they had agreed early on to keep conversations, and especially personal details, to a minimum: it was unwise to be seen chatting together too regularly, and safer to remain in ignorance in case either of them should ever be caught. All Hedy knew from their snippets of conversation was that his wife was effectively an invalid, and that he had very little in his life beyond his work. On several occasions, when Kurt brought Hedy little treats of tobacco or fresh rabbit meat from the German stores, she had passed on what she could to the doctor, knowing that he had no access to such luxuries. He never asked questions, just smiled with gratitude and tucked the contraband away in his medical bag before hobbling away up the road. She had never heard him complain about anything. Abandoning caution just this once, she leaned across to kiss his cheek.

'How are you, Doctor Maine?'

'I'm well, my dear. And please, call me Oliver.'

Hedy sat down between them, pulling her coat down over her knees to hide the two moth holes in her dress, and turned to Anton. His suit was oversized, but it was a quality cut in dark charcoal grey, and with the sprig of wild cyclamen in his buttonhole, and his roguish hair beaten down with the last of Mr Reis's Brylcreem, he looked genuinely handsome. Hedy gave him her broadest grin.

'You look very smart.' She brushed his shoulders, feeling the subtle padding of his jacket beneath her fingers.

'Thanks. Is Dory here yet?'

'Don't worry, she's on her way! Remember she's bringing her grandmother. I imagine she can't walk very fast.' She trawled her mind for a safe topic of conversation. 'Is Dorothea's friend coming? Sandy, is it?'

'Apparently not. Will Kurt be joining us later?'

She opted to keep it simple: 'I'm afraid he couldn't get the time off.'

Anton shrugged. 'More sherry for us, then.'

They sat waiting in silence. In the unusual warmth of the crowded room Hedy's eyelids began to droop, and her mind drifted to the last wedding she'd been to, around five years earlier. Her cousin, draped in white lace over satin, swirling through the local hall; the melodies of the *klezmer* band; the thunder of three score pairs of feet on the dance floor. Otto had told his favourite joke about the tailor while his wife pretended to scold him, and her parents had danced together as if they were teenagers. Hedy opened her eyes, found herself staring at the lattice windows and the naked branches of the trees in the churchyard, and stifled a sigh.

Moments later, Dorothea arrived, resplendent in her fitted dress and hat. She was accompanied by her grandmother, a bird of a woman with gnarled arthritic hands, but with the same look of wilful determination that Hedy recognised well. Dorothea's eyes glistened with excitement behind the birdcage net that hung across her face, painstakingly arranged to look like a casual draping. She hugged her husband-to-be, then took Hedy's hands in hers and squeezed hard.

'It means everything that you're here today,' she whispered.

A small, neat official approached them with a clipboard. 'Le Brocq-Weber party?' His voice was clear and travelled easily, and he pronounced Anton's surname with an excessive German accent. Hedy glanced around, and saw every pair of eyes across the waiting room slowly turn towards the three of them. Adults pulled children closer, older locals made a clucking sound with their tongues, and heads bowed together, muttering at a volume too low to hear, but Hedy knew what the content was. And without any doubt at all, it contained the word 'Jerrybag'. She glanced at Dorothea to see if she had noticed, but the bride-to-be was fiddling with the buttons on her gloves and grinning at everyone in her party.

'Shall we go in?'

The five of them pressed into the little ceremony room, fitted with nothing but a few chairs, a plain blue rug and heavy oak desk. Before the Occupation there would no doubt have been beautiful arrangements of flowers set around the room, and perhaps a musician in the corner playing harp or guitar. Both

Dorothea's grandmother and Doctor Maine hurried towards the seats at the very front, as if to give the impression of an enthusiastic throng. Almost before everyone was settled, the registrar began reading from his book, and Anton and Dorothea were muttering the few essential phrases as instructed. Anton slipped onto her finger a slim gold band – a sacrifice that Hedy knew had cost him his last warm sweater ('I'll be in uniform in a few weeks anyway' he'd pointed out with a shrug). And then it was over. Anton and Dorothea kissed each other self-consciously, and her grandmother applauded the happy couple, though it was barely audible in her soft cotton gloves. The five of them traipsed out of the room and into the street, where the old lady threw some homemade confetti made from the ripped pages of Dorothea's movie magazines, and everyone laughed for no reason, and stood looking at each other on the chilly grey pavement.

'Well,' Anton volunteered eventually, 'I suppose that's that. Shall we go?'

★

Kurt's feet ached; they filled his boots like throbbing weights as he dragged them up the pathway towards the door of his billet. He could feel each toe, swollen and stinking, in the thick wool of his socks – socks that hadn't been washed in at least four days. All he wanted in the world at that moment was a bowl of warm water and a chair. He wasn't even bothered about lunch, or the fact that he'd forgotten to go to the officers' supply store for more tobacco. Nothing mattered now except to get his damn feet into the open air and give them a good soak.

For three days solid now he'd been working seventeen-hour days, arriving at the compound at first light and returning to Pontac Common long after the evening meal had been cleared away. Yet still new orders continued to clog up his pigeonhole.

In recent weeks the stream of foreign workers had become a flood, causing construction activity around the coast to rocket, and, exponentially, the orders for trucks to more than double. Trucks for material transportation, trucks for moving men from one site to another, trucks for tools and cooking utensils and food supplies – the last of which Kurt suspected was for the OT guards, rather than the poor devils slaving under them. More manpower at the compound had been promised, but had not yet arrived, and last night, sick with exhaustion, Kurt had announced that he would be taking Saturday afternoon and evening off, and if Field Command had anything to say about it they could take it up with him on Monday morning. Now he had one overriding hope – that either the kitchen or his own shared room would be peacefully empty, and that he could spend the next few hours on his backside, feeling water swirl around his toes and reading a trashy novel.

As he pushed the door of the little house, he knew instantly that his first wish was not to be granted. Loud voices and the smell of French cigarettes poured from the kitchen, where three officers were engaged in a highly competitive game of auction rummy. As he headed for the stairs Kurt shook his head, musing at the odd, pointless ways young soldiers found to fritter away their free time. But of course, he considered, he was hardly planning to use the afternoon any more productively. Remembering where he should have been, he felt a niggle of annoyance. He adored Hedy, no question. But dear Lord, she could be an irritating little tyke at times.

It had been a fractious, difficult evening at her apartment last week, resulting in the closest they had come to a row since their first date. Kurt had spotted the homemade wedding invitation propped up on Hedy's dressing table, and questioned her deliberate avoidance of the whole topic. Surely, he argued, this was the ideal day to meet everyone? Wouldn't it be rude to refuse? Hedy, who was frying up some chicken livers he'd brought her on the little electric ring, and had been in a splendid mood till that moment, immediately went on the defensive. They'd had this discussion a hundred times! Secrecy was paramount, as Kurt knew, so why was he even contemplating the idea? It was such an overreaction that Kurt became instantly irritated, and got hold of the argument like a puppy with a slipper.

'I understand you wouldn't want me at the ceremony,' he protested, scattering cutlery on the table with unnecessary force. 'But if the reception literally consists of the happy couple, you and your doctor friend, in a private house, I really don't see the problem.'

'Someone might see you coming in.'

'Someone might see me coming here! You know I'm always careful. And Anton will be a Wehrmacht soldier himself in a few weeks' time.'

'Exactly. They've got enough problems with Dorothea's family boycotting the whole day, without us adding to it.'

'Surely that would make them even keener to see a friendly face! Are you ashamed of me or something?'

'Of course not.' She sounded genuine, but he noticed she kept her attention on the chicken livers.

'Then what's this really about?'

But he never did get a satisfactory answer, and later he'd found the invitation torn up in her rubbish bin. Lying awake later that night, listening to Hedy's soft snores beside him, Kurt decided that it was some kind of psychological block she had developed. She'd over-thought this meeting with her friends, building it up in her mind until it became an unassailable mountain. As soon as the wedding was over, Kurt decided to confront it. After all, some day in the not-too-distant future, it would be him and Hedy toasting their future together. They'd never actually discussed it, but given their mutual feelings it seemed inevitable. What kind of wedding would they have, if she couldn't come to terms with the fact that he'd been forcibly conscripted into this damn army?

The thin afternoon light seeped through the landing window as he plodded up the stairs towards his room, his lumpen feet feeling like sacks of coal on the treads. In his mind, he struck bargains with some imagined deity, promising all kinds of generous behaviour in the week ahead, if he could just get a few hours to himself. But as he pushed the door open, the first thing he saw was Fischer sitting at the little writing desk, files and papers piled in front of him. Kurt did little to hide his frustration, and by the look on Fischer's face the disappointment was mutual. Pulling off his boots with a sigh of relief, Kurt hurled himself onto his bed without speaking for several minutes, wondering whether he had the energy to fill the china bowl on the washstand, but eventually he felt compelled to be polite.

'Are they making you take the office home with you now?'

'Idiots in there don't even know how to calculate a percentage,' Fischer snapped back. Kurt suppressed a smirk. Fischer had been transferred from agriculture to one of the internal security departments a fortnight earlier, a change Kurt assumed would suit him perfectly, but the man had been in a filthy mood ever since.

'Percentages of what?'

'Payments from Jew undertakings, as laid out in the fifth order. Ninety per cent of proceeds to the Jersey Department of Finance and Economics, ten per cent to the General Commissioner for the Jewish Question. I mean, how hard is that?'

Kurt hauled himself to his feet and shuffled over to the washstand. Yes, there was water in the jug – it was cold, but the thought of going downstairs to heat it up was too gruelling. He poured some into the bowl and shuffled back to his bed.

'There can't be many cases to check, though, surely? I mean, there's only a handful of Jews on the island?'

'Quite enough,' Fischer spat from the side of his mouth, 'to cause problems. All have to be accounted for, own business or not.

Little rats get everywhere. You know they've even got one of them working for us?'

Kurt pulled off his socks, noting with some glee Fischer's wrinkling nose as the pungent smell reached his nostrils, and plunged his feet into the water. Immediately he wished he'd made the journey downstairs for hot – this was not the sensation he wanted at all. 'Who's that, then?' He was barely listening. Since his conversation with Manfred a few weeks back, Kurt had decided to let Fischer's regular rants go in one ear and out the other.

'Some Jew bitch in your compound, working as a translator. Bercu?' He flipped a sheaf of paper. 'Yes, Hedwig Bercu. Good job the other employees don't know what she is, there'd be a riot. I mean what kind of message does that send, putting one of them on our own pay roll?'

Kurt sat very still. The sensation of the icy water around his feet seemed to be spreading, as if the cold was moving up through his legs and into his chest. 'Did you say Hedwig Bercu?'

Fischer nodded. 'Why? You know her?'

Kurt felt his head shaking, though he didn't recall trying to move it. 'No . . . Heard the name perhaps.' Fischer's eyes were on his face, curious, searching. 'Are you sure she's a Jew?'

'It's on her identity card, signed off at the local Aliens Office!' Fischer sniffed with irritation and turned back to his papers, though Kurt sensed he was still being watched. 'Too bloody soft, this administration. I'd have had the lot of them on a boat the first week . . .' His voice became fainter, turned into white noise.

Very slowly Kurt removed one foot, then the other, from the bowl of water. Two foot-shaped dark patches formed on the rug next to his bed. His feet were no longer painful, but his heart was banging in his chest and he felt a little queasy. After what he hoped was an acceptable pause, he stood up.

'I'll leave you in peace. Got something I need to do.'

★

It was a sweet little house, Hedy thought, as the four of them trooped up West Park Avenue, self-conscious in their best clothes, chattering gaily to keep embarrassment at bay. Not a fancy property, but a good location, and you could see the blue of St Aubin's bay from the end of the road. It formed part of a terrace, a well-kept row of Victorian villas on the western edge of town, with bays at the front and attractive arched windows on the upper floors, highlighted with decorative stones in contrasting colours. Anton had done well to find a place like this, and on a private's wages; no wonder Dorothea was so excited about it.

Anton opened the door with a flourish, and made a big comedic fuss about lifting Dorothea over the threshold, even though he could probably have lifted her tiny frame one-handed.

Giggling like a child, Dorothea beckoned Hedy and Doctor Maine inside from the hallway. 'Come in, come in. My grandmother gave us a bottle of sherry that's almost three-quarters full! Anton, we can get to use those new glasses Hedy gave us!'

Hedy winced, thinking of the two uninspiring glasses she had found in the exchange adverts in the *Post*, which were certainly not designed for sherry. But she and the doctor trooped in behind them, both making the requisite oohs and aahs as they entered the small formal sitting room at the front of the house. Hedy's first impression was that it was remarkably tidy, but she quickly realised that it was, in fact, just very empty. There was nothing on the walls but a patterned paper from the turn of the century; the only seats were two simple wooden chairs and a green baize foldaway table designed for playing cards. Doctor Maine offered one seat to Dorothea, and Hedy insisted the doctor take the other, making herself as comfortable as she could on the bare floorboards and trying to look as if this was the most natural position in the world, while praying that the rough wood beneath her legs wouldn't ladder her precious new nylons.

Anton came in carrying the bottle of sherry, the new glasses and two chipped teacups Hedy recognised from his old apartment, and proceeded to pour everyone a drink. Dorothea apologised for the cold and promised that it would warm up once they got a fire going. The little group leaned in to clink their vessels together.

'To the happy couple,' Doctor Maine volunteered. 'May your life together be long and joyful.' Hedy took a sip and threw Dorothea a nervous look, hoping that the irony of the toast, indeed the entire day, wouldn't tip her into tears. But the bride was grinning from ear to ear, her head perpetually tipping against Anton's jacket and her fingers constantly wiggling to touch some part of him. She was thoroughly relishing every second of the occasion.

'I just wish we could have taken some photographs,' she burbled, 'but we plan to go to Scott's and have some taken in the next few days. I mean, you must have a reminder of the happiest day of your life, mustn't you?'

'And guess what?' Anton volunteered. 'Mr Reis's family saved some of their ration for us. We've got some delicious Pont-l'Evêque cheese with enough bread to make toast. And Dory's grandmother has made us a delicious caraway seed cake. So we can celebrate in style.'

'I'll get some plates from the kitchen,' said Dorothea, draining her sherry glass.

'No, let me,' Hedy chipped in, eager to get her rapidly chilling body off the freezing floor, and even more eager to eat. 'A bride on her wedding day should do nothing but sit and look beautiful! I'm sure I can find everything.' She pulled herself up and started towards the kitchen.

That was when it came. A loud rat-a-tat-tat on the front door. Not the cautious, friendly knock of a curious neighbour, but the determined, righteous hammering of one who expects to be admitted. For a second, everyone froze. Dorothea's smile vanished, replaced by a look of bewilderment. Hedy looked anxiously towards Anton, knowing that he, too, suspected one of Dorothea's family might show up to cause trouble. Handing his teacup of sherry to his bride, he marched quickly into the hallway with the stance of someone expecting a fight, while the three of them sat very still, listening. The visitor spoke before Anton could get a word out, and as he did so, Hedy's stomach lurched.

'I'm sorry to interrupt your party, but I must speak to Hedy at once.' Seeing the colour drain from her face, Doctor Maine and Dorothea both gaped at Hedy, while they all waited for the next sentence. 'I am Kurt Neumann. Could you get her for me, please?'

Hedy stumbled into the hallway. Kurt, in uniform, was standing on the doorstep. For some reason he seemed taller than usual. Hedy's voice came out as a croak. 'I thought you had to work today?'

'May we speak in private?'

His formality terrified her. But somewhere inside she already knew the reason, and from the look of him, Anton did too.

Anton gestured to the end of the hallway. 'Please, be my guest.'

Hedy walked down the hall into the unfamiliar kitchen, hearing Kurt's footsteps directly behind her but not daring to turn and look at his face. They found themselves in a dull, chilly little room with black-and-green checked linoleum, and a gas water heater over a deep ceramic sink. The gas supply was currently on, and Hedy could hear the sputtering of the tiny flame inside the white metal cylinder. Strange, she thought, the rooms in which your life changes for ever are never the places you would imagine. She positioned herself by a small leaf table covered with a chenille tablecloth, and forced herself to face him, though she kept her eyeline firmly on his knees.

'What is it?' The question was insulting and she knew it.

'Fischer says your registration card classifies you as Jewish. Is it true? Are you?'

Even now – and she marvelled at her own idiocy – part of her was still preparing to continue the lie. She thought about the story she had used at the Aliens Office about her surname being inherited and having no Jewish blood, and almost began to tell it again. But when she opened her mouth, nothing came out. In that second she realised she was exhausted by the pretence, sick of the imagined scenarios. Whatever was about to happen, it was better that it was now.

'Yes.' Her body began to tremble. She tried to calm herself by picking at the tassels of the tablecloth, twisting them between her fingers. Still she couldn't bring herself to look at his face, but the bewilderment in his voice told her everything.

'I told you that very first evening that I didn't believe in any of that master-race nonsense.' He paused, selecting and rejecting various sentences. 'Since I've been here, witnessed what's happened, that feeling has only grown stronger. And you knew that.' Another pause. 'So after all we've been through together the last few months, all that we've said . . .' He fell silent. The sputtering of the gas flame filled the painfully empty space. 'I've only got one question: why? Why didn't you tell me?'

Hedy had assembled three of the tassels, and began to plait them. She remembered how she used to plait Roda's hair in her bedroom, finishing it off with a silken bow.

'I wanted to. But I left it too long. I didn't know how you'd react.'

He gave a snort of disbelief. 'For heaven's sake, Hedy! I spent two weeks in that stinking jail for you! But apparently'– his arms rose in exasperation then dropped back to his sides, lifeless – 'apparently that meant nothing.'

'Of course it did . . . does . . . it means everything. I'd have been arrested if it wasn't for you.'

'Yet you still thought I was capable of turning against you?'

Hedy began another plait, then returned to the first. She could feel the fabric start to fray in her fingers. Soon that section would be completely bald.

'I know it's hard to understand, but you don't know what it's like to be picked out, hated by everyone.'

'Try walking down King Street in full Wehrmacht uniform—'

'It's not the same! When the Anschluss came, I saw people turn on us. People who'd been friends for years, who we thought we trusted. Hiding becomes an instinct. I hated lying to you, but . . .' With a supreme effort, she lifted her eyes. The hurt she saw was shocking. 'I'm sorry. I was just . . . scared.'

'But this wasn't just about you. You've put me in danger too, without my knowledge, or consent.'

'I know.'

For a long moment he said nothing. Then his features softened and he took a step towards her, stretching out his hand to touch her fingers with the ends of his own. She let go of the tassels as she felt the softness of his skin.

'Hedy, I would never do anything to hurt you.'

She bit her lip, a chastised child sent into a corner. Her logic of the last few months was disintegrating, and suddenly seemed ridiculous. This war had driven out every gram of trust she once had. 'You mean it?'

'I swear.'

The ball of anxiety in her stomach began to unravel and she felt a swell of optimism. 'I know that now.' She reached out her other hand, but as she did so, he released her and pulled his arm backwards. Instantly, something shifted in the space between them. The room grew colder, tiny icicles seemed to form within her bones.

'Yes, I think you do. But it's too late.'

The icicles broke into every organ. It was hard to catch her breath. 'Why?'

'If you can hide something so important for so long, treat me like the enemy, compromise my safety . . .' He shrugged, drained. 'Without trust, there's no point going on.'

Hedy could hear her teeth grinding in her head. Her jaw felt stiff. 'I said I'm sorry . . . and I mean it.'

Kurt shook his head. 'I know . . . and I believe you. But it makes no difference.'

It was too much. Every nerve in her now felt raw and exposed. A wall rose up, high and protective. 'That's an excuse. You just don't want to risk being with me, now that you know. You're scared you'll be charged with Rassenschande, lose your commission and be packed off to the Russian Front.'

His face changed at that moment. She could feel the fury.

'You know damn well that's not true. I'd have willingly taken that chance.' He turned and walked back towards the kitchen door. 'You know that first night, when you were angry with me? Called me a coward for getting swept along by the Nazi machine? I've thought a lot about that. I'd actually decided you were right. But now . . . now I think you're the coward. Goodbye, Hedy.'

She heard his footsteps in the hallway, his mumbled apology to Anton and Dorothea for spoiling their day, and the sound of the front door slamming shut. Just at that moment, the gentle popping of the gas light in the cylinder fizzled out.

The last thing she recalled was Anton's concerned voice asking if she was all right, the soft swish of her body sliding down the wall onto her haunches, and the gasping of her lungs as she dropped her head onto her arms and sobbed.

6

1942

There was sleet in the air. Fine feathery specks whirled in corkscrews, then vanished into dark spots as they landed on the pavement. Every person shuffling along the street, bundled against the wind in threadbare old coats hunted down from cobwebbed attics, kept their chins on their chests and elbows tucked close to their bodies, occasionally releasing a hand to brush away the frozen flecks. How sad, Hedy thought, that something so fragile and beautiful could cause such pain; her fingers, gripped around the straps of her battered handbag, were now a cruel, livid purple, and stinging as if her skin had been torn away.

She hesitated at the junction, considering a detour via Rimington's, the fruiterer at the top of King Street – a rumour had gone around her building last night that some early rhubarb had been spotted in the town. But a diversion that way would mean coming back past the Aliens Office, and after last month's encounter Hedy decided she would prefer to miss out altogether than clap eyes on that hated place. She walked on, trying to push the memory of that meeting from her mind, but anger brought it bouncing back. The officiousness of the assistant registrar, and his imperviousness to her obvious distress as she'd showed him the brief official note she'd been handed by Feldwebel Schulz the day before.

You are instructed that all registered Jews are requested to attend an interview with German Field Command at College House.

Jews must present themselves at the address below at the earliest opportunity.

No reason, no explanation. Hedy had rushed down to the bureau in the faint hope that they might offer some kind of strategy or information. But the registrar had merely scratched his head, shrugged and said that if the Germans wished to see her, she'd be advised to comply. Hedy had thanked him in a tone bordering on sarcasm and walked out, already resolute that she would do no such thing. She tamped her anxiety down, telling herself that given the mere handful of Jews involved, the implementation of the order might be postponed, perhaps eventually overlooked. But hope and optimism were scarce commodities right now. Since Anton's wedding, each day had become a tunnel of sludge to be trudged through, each waking dawn another plunge into numbness. Most mornings, the sheer effort of climbing out of bed seemed insurmountable.

It was three months now, thirteen whole weeks, since she'd spoken with Kurt. She'd seen his gangly figure once or twice across the compound, talking with mechanics or carrying boxes of parts from one hut to another, but she'd never got close enough to see his face, or hear his voice. He was probably staying out of her way, keeping close to the motor block and eating only in the officers' mess. She told herself it was for the best, the right thing for both of them in the end, but her body argued violently every night, and she'd wake from dreams with her arms wrapped around a damp pillow. She had been lonely, desperately so, in that first year of Occupation, but this – this was a whole new realm of misery. Now she understood what they meant by a broken heart.

She had tried, in the first days, to shift the blame. Kurt, Clifford Orange, Hitler, anyone but herself. But curled up in a bawling heap on the floor of her apartment, the truth had oozed out of every pitiful argument and drowned such nonsense. Kurt was right. When it came to the tough decisions, she was the coward.

She had had a thousand opportunities to tell him in those early days, but found a thousand and one reasons to avoid it. She had let down not just him, but her family, her entire faith. And now she was paying the price. She spent her days at her typewriter, producing meaningless reports, avoiding eye contact with everyone around her, and her evenings alone, reading whatever books were left on the sparse shelves of the library, and watching the windows of her neighbours turn black one by one until the town sat in darkness. Once or twice she caught herself wondering if it mattered what happened to her any more; if they wished to imprison or shoot her, let them do it. But thoughts of her distant, scattered family kept her going. And today, at least, she had a clear and meaningful purpose. She wrapped her scarf a little tighter and turned down towards the harbour and the distant crowds.

The boat was packed. Every metre of rail, every tiny patch of deck contained four or five soldiers squashed together, beans in a tin, leaning, loafing or waving to others on the quay. Others continued to stream up the gangplank, an endless caterpillar of hunched, reluctant men. The quayside, too, swarmed with people: Wehrmacht officers rubbed shoulders with local bobbies, Jersey dockers with secret police. Up above, pale faces leapt out from the mud-green uniforms, most of them smoking or staring out to sea. A few were visibly distressed, clearly in no doubt where they were headed now. Despite the best attempts of the Nazi propaganda machine, facts had filtered through even to the lowliest troops, through coded letters, snippets of BBC news, whispers of military personnel from France. The stories had torn through the troops like a flash fire – the disaster of the Battle of Moscow, entire divisions wiped out by the Red Army and the blizzards. Now these young men knew they were being ripped from the cushiest post in Western Europe to be dumped into a frozen hell. Some young Germans were said to have committed suicide on receiving their new orders.

Hedy spotted Dorothea first, not far from the gangplank,

and fought her way through. Dorothea was dressed in an elegant black coat of her grandmother's which, although it had seen better days, suited the drama of the occasion, and a navy scarf tied over her cropped hair made her skin look even whiter than usual. She was standing in front of Anton, her eyes bloodshot and teary, staring at him as if trying to burn every detail of him into her memory. Anton himself stood tall and square-shouldered in his uniform, exclaiming some proud defiance to the world. It was the first time Hedy had seen him in full Wehrmacht attire, and it made her shudder.

Anton noticed her and pressed his lips together in an attempt at a smile. 'You made it. I'm glad.'

'Of course. So . . . this is it.' The banality of her remark embarrassed her, but her mind felt fogged, devoid of anything useful. 'Do you know how long the crossing is?'

Anton shrugged. 'No idea.'

Hedy could see that Dorothea was shaking. Her breath was thick and wheezy; Hedy wondered what they would do if she had an asthma attack right here in the open. 'How are you bearing up, Dorothea?'

Dorothea tried to smile, but her lips trembled, preparing for a cloudburst.

Anton kissed her on the cheek and squeezed her arm. 'Darling, would you just give us a moment? I promise it won't take long.'

Dorothea nodded meekly and drifted away towards the harbour wall, using the opportunity to squash a lace hankie into her eyes. Hedy stood silent, waiting, already knowing what Anton was going to say.

'Hedy, I need you to promise you'll look after her.' He was reaching for her hand, grabbing at it, crushing it in both his own. 'Her grandmother is so frail, she may not last the year, and there's no sign of Dory's parents relenting on this marriage. She's stronger than she seems, but there's only so much she can take.'

Hedy opened and closed her mouth, searching for the right

words. 'I'll try, Anton, really. But I'm not sure that I—'

'I'm not asking you to love her like I do, I'm just asking you to look out for her. You're not far away, you could drop in on your way home from work, just check on her, you know?' His grip on her hand increased, and she felt sure she heard a bone crack. 'She'll look out for you too, of course. You're both on your own now.' He bit his lip so hard that it turned white. 'If there was anything I could do to change this . . .'

Hedy closed her eyes. It was too much, this sadness. How was anyone supposed to bear this weight, this endless avalanche of misery? She felt the desperation of Anton's grasp, and knew there was only one answer she could give. 'Of course I'll take care of Dorothea, Anton. I promise.'

Her words seemed to soothe him, and with a final squeeze he released her hand. 'Nothing from Kurt, I suppose?'

'There won't be. It's over.' Saying the words aloud opened dangerous gates, and she swallowed hard. This was no time to fall apart, she owed Anton that, and she wouldn't want to give the Germans the satisfaction. She raised her chin. 'Don't worry, we'll be all right. You take care of yourself.'

Anton beckoned to Dorothea who flew back to his side and buried her face in his shoulder. Just then a raucous shout came from down the quay: '*Letzter Aufruf! Alle an Bord! Schnell!*' There was a forceful thrust of people towards the gangway, and for a moment the three of them were carried along with it. Hedy grasped Anton's arm and kissed his cheek, then Dorothea pressed her lips to his, her arms so tight around his neck Hedy feared she would damage him. Then Anton was lost inside the mud-green caterpillar, the great flow of despair rippling up to the decks above, and Hedy and Dorothea were left standing on the quayside, waving at a peach-coloured dot they knew to be Anton's face, their own features twisted into parodies of smiles. They remained there, shivering on the cobbles, as ropes were unwound and heavy chains thrown, watching as the vessel slowly manoeuvred out of its mooring towards the harbour mouth and the open sea, and for once Dorothea said nothing.

When at last there was nothing to watch, they turned to each other. Hedy reached out and placed a hand on Dorothea's arm, knowing that this was her first call of duty. 'Would you like to go and find somewhere warm for a cup of something?'

Dorothea dabbed her eyes with her sodden hankie. 'Thank you, Hedy, that's sweet of you. But no, I just want to go home.' She turned, then spun back, digging deep into her pocket. 'I'm sorry, I almost forgot. This came for you yesterday.' She pressed an envelope into Hedy's hand, then went on her way, walking slowly up the quayside, her black coat billowing in the wind, looking for all the world like the tragic heroine in the final scene of a romantic movie.

★

Holding the note out of sight, below the level of her desk, Hedy read it again. It was a small cream-coloured sheet, smaller than a regular letter, already crumpled from constant folding. In the top corner a round, circular rubber stamp read 'Le Comité international de la Croix-Rouge, Genève'. And there, at the bottom, were the permissible twenty-five words that had imprinted themselves on Hedy's mind for ever.

> Hope all well. Your mother and father departed January, holiday. Return date uncertain. Sent love. No news Roda or others. Moving, no further letters. Elke.

Hedy sat back in her chair, let her eyes drift around the office. Luck was on her side this morning; Supervisor Vogt was busy at her desk with some administrative catastrophe, real or imagined. And the clatter of typewriters – that exasperating din and the overture to so many persistent headaches – today became a comforting noise that helped to shut out the rest of the world. With quiet, deft movements, Hedy refolded the letter, returned it to her handbag on the back of her chair, and held a materials quality translation in front of her face, frowning, to give the impression that she was dealing with something of great complexity and importance.

It had been such a chance, writing to Elke. It was years since they'd seen each other – Hedy wasn't even sure that the family were still at the same address – and it carried a huge risk that her old school chum might betray her or her parents. They had been close once, but who knew what transformations people had undergone since the start of this insanity? Elke might have been in the Bund Deutscher Mädel by now. But somehow, Hedy's letter had reached her, and Elke had found the courage and means to reply.

Holiday. Her mother must, at some point, have used that word with Elke to describe deportation, and Elke had repeated it, knowing Hedy would understand. Now, each time she closed her eyes, she saw an open truck, crowds of Jews being pushed aboard, the butts of Karabiner rifles poking the soft flesh of their backs. She saw her parents, exhausted and terrified, huddled together on someone else's packing case, hugging what possessions they could carry in their arms. And then the long, petrifying journey to . . . at that point, her mind shut down. There was only so much horror any mind could absorb, she supposed, and she was currently at her limit.

The clock indicated it was almost lunchtime. She'd had no breakfast, but in her current state she couldn't think about eating. From the moment she'd opened her eyes that morning, knowing what she had to do, acid had forced its way into her gullet, generating waves of sickness. But weeks had passed since Dorothea had handed her the envelope on the dockside, and over many sleepless nights she had exhausted every other option. Seeing Vogt still bent over her desk, Hedy placed her bag over her arm and slipped silently from the room as if making an early dash for the canteen, ignoring the irritated looks of the Bavarians who were still key-smashing at their desks.

Out in the fresh spring sunshine, she hurried down the dusty, uneven paths towards the officers' mess. Fifty metres before the entrance was a small patch of scrubby grass, which gave a clear view down towards the mechanical yards. Pretending to fiddle with her shoelace, she waited there for several moments, half praying that she hadn't already missed him, half wishing that he wouldn't show up at all. Then she saw him. That unmistakable outline, that walk – and there, there was the bubbling laugh she knew so well. Not as deep and throaty as she'd heard in the past – this one was a little on the tight side as he responded politely to some colleague's joke – but the memory of it made her smile. At that moment he saw her, and she watched his entire body react, a tiny backward rearing such as a horse might make with a bad rider. She stood still, staring, hoping that he would understand from her expression alone. And sure enough, a second later Kurt made excuses to the men he was with, and began to walk towards her.

At first, the proximity of him almost wiped her mission from her mind. If anything, he looked taller, more handsome; he had lost a little weight, but that faint scent of sweat and engine oil punched her into the past, and those eyes pinned her to the spot. He said nothing, but stood before her expectantly. It was impossible to guess what he was thinking.

'I have a favour to ask you.' The words finally tripped out, and she kept her eyes fixed on his, anticipating a refusal. But what came back was a friendly nod, an encouragement to continue; he must have known this was important for her to approach him so brazenly. 'I received this.' She took the Red Cross letter from her bag and handed it to him, taking care not to let their hands touch. The paths were now thronged with people on their way to lunch, and Hedy glanced anxiously about as Kurt read it, wondering if she should have picked a more private place. But most people seemed to be fixed on getting to the canteen, eager to get to their one reliable meal of the day, and passed the two of them without interest.

Kurt handed the letter back to her. 'You think they've been taken away to some ghetto or prison?'

'I don't think there's any doubt. They might already have been shot.'

'I'm sorry, Hedy, really I am.' The kindness in his voice pricked her defences and she had to drive her nails into her palm to focus her mind. 'But what do you want me to do?'

'I just want to know . . .' Her voice was shaky; she could hear the cracks in it. 'I just want to know where they were taken, what's happened to them.'

'But how can I help?'

'I thought perhaps you might have some contacts out east, maybe someone in Berlin who could check the records . . .' Now that her thoughts were words, they suddenly sounded ridiculous. It was obvious that Kurt wouldn't know any more than she did. Afraid he would think this was all an excuse to strike up a conversation or perhaps something more, she added: 'I know it's unlikely, but I'm desperate. And I have no one else.' She saw it then – that old look of affection, the look that had once calmed her fears and made the whole world seem bearable. To her shame, she felt a tear pop out and roll towards her mouth. To add to the agony, he reached out his hand and, with his index finger, brushed it gently away.

'I can't guarantee anything, and it may take a while. But I'll do my best. I promise.' The affection faded then, replaced with something between sadness and disappointment.

Hedy wiped away another tear and tried to stand up straight. 'Thank you. I'm still in Block Seven. You can find me there any day.'

She turned and walked quickly back to her block, unable to bear the idea of sitting in that canteen surrounded by people. She would work through her lunch hour, hammering out those reports until six o'clock, fingers thumping the keys, head filled with nothing but quantities of cement and addresses of delivery companies. She wouldn't make eye contact with Vogt, or her neighbour Derek, or give any of them the opportunity to notice her. After that she would hurry home, rush through her meagre meal and climb into bed at the earliest opportunity. There, she would bury her face in the pillow so that no one in the surrounding apartments would hear her. And then she would weep and howl like a wounded animal into the early hours of the morning.

★

'But why? Why are you making us do this?'

Dorothea's voice rang out over the clatter and hubbub of the room. Her eyes were wide with innocent confusion. Hedy glanced nervously at the German private behind the makeshift table, as he grabbed Dorothea's Bush wireless set and pushed it along the surface towards the rising bank of radio sets at the end. For a moment Hedy feared the soldier might retaliate, but she quickly realised that the look on his face wasn't aggression but incomprehension. The man didn't speak English.

'Dorothea, just walk away,' Hedy muttered, at the same time checking out the number of other armed Germans in the room and the position of the exits. 'He doesn't understand you. And I want to get out of here.'

In fact, Hedy hadn't wanted to come to the parish hall at all. It was a nest of German soldiers, festooned with swastikas, and being amongst it made her skin crawl. But when the announcement of the radio confiscation had been made in the evening paper the previous week, Dorothea had come straight round to see her, begging Hedy to help her deliver the bulky device with its heavy wooden surround. Remembering her promise to Anton, Hedy had no choice but to agree.

She looked around. The room was packed with furious, murmuring Jersey folk, slamming their beloved family wirelesses on the table top, snatching their paper receipts from the Germans' hands with flushed, bitter faces. The idea that they would be returned at the end of the war was so pitiful a lie, it was almost funny – everyone knew that these highly desirable items would be packed onto a boat headed for the Continent by this afternoon, and that all of them would be gracing the drawing rooms of Nazi Party officers by the start of next week. Meanwhile, the locals would now be completely shut off from the real war, dependent solely on the risible misinformation of the German-controlled press. Hedy, already without a wireless for over a year, had grown used to the pressing silence of the long evenings without music or human voices. But her regular visits to Dorothea's to listen to the BBC were a vital link to the world, even if she did have to spend much of the time pointing out the locations on Dorothea's ancient atlas. This new level of isolation frightened her as much as anyone.

Eager to get back to the anonymity of the street, Hedy pulled at Dorothea's arm. But Dorothea was still facing the soldier out. 'I think you understand enough,' Dorothea was saying. 'I would just like to know what good you think this will do.'

Hedy stared at her charge, baffled. The woman had never so much as contradicted Anton in public (or, Hedy suspected, in private) yet here she was, fearlessly accosting an enemy soldier. Hedy looked around to see a second German, heavily-built and with a rifle slung low across his chest, craning his neck to watch the exchange from the far side of the room. One signal from the first, Hedy knew, and they would both be arrested. Arriving here this morning, they had already seen one local man dragged off following a scuffle in the queue that flowed out onto the pavement.

This time Hedy's grip was more forceful. 'I mean it, we need to leave now.'

Her heart leapt as she felt a hand upon her back, pushing her away from the table and towards the exit. Dorothea, she realised, was being similarly propelled. There was a good deal of strength behind the pressure, so much so that she was halfway across the floor before she managed to turn and see the cause. To her relief, it was a weary-looking, grey-haired gentleman with thinning hair and wire-rimmed spectacles, wearing a fixed but beatific smile.

'I can answer your questions, ladies, but I suggest you don't pursue the matter here.' His voice was as tired as his appearance suggested, but Hedy recognised the inflections of a Jersey accent, similar to Doctor Maine's. He continued to drive them forwards until they were all standing on the pavement, squinting in the bright sunshine after the gloom of the parish hall.

There, he turned to them and offered his hand. 'Deputy Ned Le Quesne, pleased to meet you.' Hedy and Dorothea both returned the gesture. The name meant nothing to Hedy but Dorothea was peering at him with curiosity.

'From the States?' Dorothea asked.

'States Labour Department, for my sins.' He smiled but Hedy sensed there was some truth to the apology. 'I'm sorry if I appear unchivalrous, but I didn't want you to get into trouble. I'm afraid Jerry have been quite forceful about this latest nonsense; there have already been a number of arrests.'

'I just want to know why. Why are they taking our radios away?' Dorothea pressed him.

Le Quesne glanced over his shoulder and encouraged them a little further down the road. 'Simple revenge, I fear. The tide of the war has turned in recent weeks. So they hope to punish us and, at the same time, keep the truth from us to destroy morale. But we shan't let that happen, shall we?'

Hedy glanced back at the parish hall, where two youths were arguing with a German private, drawing attention from other soldiers. A woman in her sixties, emerging onto the pavement, was weeping on her husband's shoulder.

'We certainly won't!' Dorothea was shaking the old man's hand. 'And I say my prayers for our troops every night.' Hedy drew a breath at the disingenuous irony of this remark, but the Deputy was already bidding them good day and heading back towards the parish hall.

Dorothea turned to her. 'Thank you so much for your help, Hedy. I couldn't have carried that here on my own. Would you like to come over this evening? I've got enough potatoes to make vegetable rissoles, if you have a couple of carrots you can share?'

Hedy hesitated. The BBC news and the discussions that followed it were the only thing that had made recent visits to West Park Avenue bearable, as they kept Dorothea off the subject of movie stars or, worse, how much she missed Anton. The thought of an evening with nothing but conversation between them was a grim prospect. But her promise to her old friend kept tapping her on the shoulder.

'Thank you – maybe just for an hour.' She protected her eyes with her hand as she looked upwards into the blue, feeling the warmth of the sun burning her skin. 'It's hard, the first night without your radio. I remember.'

'Oh, we can still listen to the news.' Dorothea's tone was bright.

'I don't understand?'

'I handed in my wireless, just as they asked. I just didn't hand in the one in the attic.' She beamed as she tripped lightly along the road in the direction of the park, leaving Hedy watching her, astonished.

★

'Same again?' Kurt, with a broad smile, raised two fingers towards the skinny, bored waitress. 'This brandy is excellent. I might see if I can get myself a bottle at the stores.'

Wildgrube knocked back the dregs of his own glass – his fourth large one tonight by Kurt's reckoning – and licked his lips in agreement. Even in the muted light of the club, Kurt could see that his face was starting to flush, the puce-coloured streaks echoing the heavily applied rouge of the club hookers. Already his gestures were becoming expansive, and his watery eyes danced around, taking in the latest batch of Normandy whores, enthralled by his own sense of wellbeing. Kurt suspected that he didn't receive many social invitations.

'Now, my father' – Wildgrube took a drag on his cigarette and continued as if Kurt hadn't spoken – 'worked in a factory. No interest in his appearance. Used to clip my ear when I spent my money on quality shirts and decent shoes, called me a little fairy.' He threw his head back and laughed uproariously. Kurt mirrored the laugh precisely, at the same time using the moment to empty most of his own brandy into the aspidistra on the ledge behind his shoulder. 'But look at me now! Just these cuffs alone . . .' He displayed the crisp white cuffs of his shirt as if modelling them for sale. 'Always pressed to perfection. I tell you, the housekeeper at our billet – ugly as a bulldog, but my God can she iron a shirt! And her stews are pretty good too!' He patted his belly and laughed again.

Kurt pretended to take a sip from his nearly empty glass, thinking that the woman probably pissed heartily into every dish she served him. He glanced at the clock – seven thirty. It was the fourth time he had brought Wildgrube to the club in three weeks, and experience told him that by eight he should be able to push him in any direction he wanted. The tricky part was catching him in the golden moments between professional discretion and passing out.

Kurt's first invitation to join him on a 'boys' nights out' – a phrase Kurt had picked deliberately, knowing that it would appeal to the spy's ego – had been met with scepticism. Wildgrube possessed the bullied child's instinct for knowing when anyone was looking down on him, and Kurt had to work hard to convince him that the whole thing wasn't some practical joke. But Kurt knew that, whatever reservations or suspicions Wildgrube might have about him, they would eventually drown under the weight of curiosity and desperation for approval. On the first three occasions Kurt had played it safe, keeping the conversation to German architecture and what cup size created the best female figure, while also dropping in meaningless titbits about himself and the others in his billet. But Kurt was beginning to assess Wildgrube's powerlessness and indiscretion around booze. How the man had risen through the ranks with such an obvious flaw was baffling, but then, Kurt thought, on that basis how would you explain Göring? In any case, Kurt sensed that tonight, if he could get the levels of enjoyment just right, he could move in for the kill. And Wildgrube appeared to be having a whale of a time.

'This is wonderful. I love this place.'

Kurt nodded. 'Good to get away from the hoi polloi, spend time with your own kind. Not that I'm in your strata, Erich. Access all areas, cosy chats with all the big boys – am I right?'

Wildgrube shrugged, lapping it up. 'I know a lot of people. Not just here.'

Kurt twirled his glass in his fingers. 'You mean, in Berlin?'

'Oh yes. Got friends there who've done very well for themselves. Inner circle, you know?' Then his manicured hand brushed away the topic like an imaginary fly. 'How often do you come here on an average week?'

Kurt thought quickly, aware that his answer could well be checked later for accuracy. 'Not too often. Don't want to make a pig of myself!'

Wildgrube laughed hard and slapped his thigh. 'You see that one?' He pointed to a young blonde of around seventeen, wearing a tight flimsy dress and tossing her hair in an obvious bid for sales. Kurt wondered if her mother knew where she was and what she was doing. 'That's the one I'm having later. Fantastic little arse, don't you think?' He leaned towards Kurt, conspiratorial. 'Though I have heard that some of the new ones are not that clean. Might just tit-fuck her to be safe – don't want to catch a dose of something.'

The waitress put down two new glasses with a wide, artificial smile. Kurt raised his towards Wildgrube's for a toast, and heard the glass almost crack as Wildgrube went in too hard.

Kurt decided it was time to change tack. 'So tell me, Erich, how's it going in your department?' He let the term hang in the air, vague enough to be interpreted as ignorance. 'Who's giving you trouble at the moment?'

Wildgrube blew dismissive air through his thin lips. 'Ah, you know. The usual suspects. Black marketeers. Dumb Einheimische who think they're Rosa Luxemburg. You know, some of the labourers we brought over have escaped from their compounds? Turns out some of the locals are actually hiding them in their homes!' He knocked back half the brandy in a single gulp. 'Serve them right if they get raped or robbed, stupid fuckers.'

'And how are things back home? Is it true the Führer's planning a new offensive against the Soviets?'

Wildgrube tapped the side of his nose to indicate that Kurt had overstepped the mark. Kurt, realising his mistake, held up one palm and turned his head away, as if deferring to a greater power. But the next moment Wildgrube was pulling back to the forbidden path, prudence swirling in the bottom of his glass. 'Big man's doing great work there. Of course, the best stuff is hush-hush.'

'I'll drink to that.' Kurt held up his glass again, and once more Wildgrube drained his own in one. Kurt leant in and glanced ostentatiously around him, deliberately whipping up a sense of drama. 'But come on, give me a clue at least? Something to do with the Jews, am I right?'

Wildgrube wagged his finger, with a look a parent might give a naughty child they're about to forgive. 'You're a bugger, Neumann! Of course it's the damn Jews. Finally found a solution. Bloody clever too. But' – all the fingers went up now, suggesting a barrier that could not be crossed – 'I can say no more. Tell me . . .' He beckoned Kurt in further. 'These pretty little bitches. Which one is yours?'

Kurt grinned, pretending to be entranced by the game, and cast a slow, thoughtful gaze around the room. The decor in the club was gaudy, a collection of gold-plated light fittings and red velvet armchairs that probably looked ghastly in daylight. Everywhere he looked drunken officers and grim-faced, malnourished women sprawled. In the far corner, Fischer was sitting with some of his hardline cronies, playing some kind of drinking game with a pack of cards. Dear God, Kurt thought, why was he even putting himself through this, for a woman he'd sworn never to see again? Images of Hedy floated through his mind. That soft mouth and those sea-green eyes; her startled expression when he entered a room; the smile that sank softly into a pillow. The last months without her had been the most unhappy he could remember. A dozen times he'd walked from his billet all the way to New Street and stood outside her building, waiting for a glimpse of pale skin or tawny hair at the window. Once he had even got as far as the door. Each time, a prickling resistance – pride, perhaps a sense of betrayal – held him back. But the thought of being with any other woman left him limp and dispirited.

Wildgrube was waiting for his answer, his tongue lolling at the side of his mouth like a raw clam. At random, Kurt picked out a tall, willowy brunette draped across the end of the bar. 'That one.'

Wildgrube laughed again. He would laugh at anything now. 'Ah, you like them tall and dark? For me, has to be a blonde. Nice Aryan girl.' He picked up Kurt's brandy, mistaking it for his own, and finished that too. 'Soon that'll be all that's left, you'll see! They'll get all the scum in the end. Every one of them.'

Kurt sensed the door was opening, and warned himself not to push too hard for fear it might slam again. At the same time, he knew he didn't have too long – Wildgrube was so drunk now that he could barely make segues between his own sentences. 'Let's hope so, eh? Won't be easy, mind.'

Wildgrube scoffed. 'Shooting fish in a barrel. They don't know, see. No idea where they're headed, what they're walking into.' His speech was slurring now. 'SS chum showed me some photos last time I was home. Genius – way they pack them in, nice and easy.'

Kurt kept his body perfectly still. 'Pack them in?'

Wildgrube gave a smile that Kurt would remember for years afterwards. 'That's the beauty of it.' He cocked his head to Kurt, telling him to come a little closer. 'Keep this to yourself, now – this is just between us, understand?'

★

Hedy was fast asleep when the banging started. Her first response was rage. So many nights recently she had lain awake until the dawn chorus began around four, dragging herself to work in a state of exhaustion. Tonight was the one night she had actually managed to drop off at a reasonable hour, and now some idiot . . . For a few seconds she thought it was coming from one of the other apartments. Then she realised it was coming all the way from the communal street door. Someone was demanding entry, and someone – probably Mrs Le Couteur – was opening it. Hedy spun around to the clock: almost three. Now she was upright in bed, her ears pricked like a wild animal. Pictures of German soldiers with arrest warrants swam in her mind. Grabbing a woollen cardigan from the chair, she jumped out of bed and ran to the apartment door, pressing her ear against it. That was when she heard the footsteps on the stairs and the familiar voice: 'Hedy? Hedy, please, I know you're in there.'

With her heart almost jumping out of her chest, Hedy pulled back the bolts and threw open the door. Outside, the hallway felt shockingly black and draughty. Kurt stood swaying on the landing, his hair sticking up at strange angles, a wild expression on his face. As soon as he saw her he threw himself into her arms, knocking her backwards several steps. Cautiously she placed her arms around him and somehow manhandled him across the threshold.

'Kurt, what's happened? What are you doing here?' His face was buried in her neck now, and it sounded as if he was crying. Hedy disentangled herself and managed to get a firm grip on his arm. She pulled him into the apartment and steered him towards the chair by the table, where he slumped as if he hadn't sat down for a week. She could smell the alcohol on him, strong and sour. She raised the blackout to relieve the intensity of the darkness, then sat down next to him.

'Tell me what's happened.'

He looked up at her, the moonlight from the window lighting one side of his features. She could see that he was crazy with booze-heightened emotion, but as he stared at her he seemed to sober up, and with one gentle hand pushed the hair back from her face the way he had when they were lovers.

'Hedy, I am so sorry.'

'For what?' Her mind was spinning with awful possibilities.

'I didn't believe you, didn't believe any of it. Thought it was just stories. I didn't think people could really behave that way.'

'Like what? What are you talking about?'

'I honestly thought . . . they said it was farmland. Just relocation. I didn't know. I swear to you I didn't know.'

And then it began to tumble out – the facts that Wildgrube had confided, and the connections Kurt had put together for himself. The secret plans, the liquidation of the ghettos, the burning of synagogues with Jews locked inside, the round-ups, the 'special' cattle trucks, the purpose-built extermination camps. The separation of men and women at the gates, the classification of prisoners, the removal of belongings, the overalls, the forced labour, the trickery of the fake showers, the chambers piled up with bodies.

Hedy sat in silence beside him as the phrases kept coming, sometimes choking him, sometimes spewing out in a bilious stream. The words landed on her like burning tacks, blistering her skin. Crematoria . . . chimneys . . . gas. As the words became pictures, and the pictures a reality, she began to lean away from him. She wanted to hit him in the mouth to shut him up, to stop this knowledge from reaching her brain, to punish him for being one of them. And at the same time she wanted to hold him, and tell him that he couldn't have known – who could ever know something so inhuman, so incomprehensible? As Kurt ranted on, she felt herself growing smaller, shrinking down like Alice in Wonderland. By the time he got to her parents, confessing that if they had been transported they were probably already dead, she was a speck of humanity on the vast expanse of the earth, tiny and inconsequential.

Slowly, in small sputtering fits, he reached the end of his story and fell into a deep, brooding silence. Hedy rose slowly, staggered across to the sink and vomited for several minutes, clinging to the porcelain, feeling the wet streaks on her face, but too numb to move. Eventually she hauled herself up, rinsed out her mouth and dragged herself to the bed. Kurt moved slowly to join her, and they sat, wordless, staring at nothing but the shafts of moonlight arcing their way across Hedy's pillows. Then, as Hedy remembered it, she must have fallen asleep for a few moments, because when she stirred, the moonbeams had been replaced by a dim leaden light in the distant sky, returning outlines of furniture in the bedroom and hints of colour to their skin. Somewhere outside, the first birds began to call to each other.

Kurt put his hand on her knee. 'Tomorrow I'm going to walk into College House with my Walther P38 and take out the Field Commander.'

'Don't be stupid.'

'I mean it. I have to do something. You were right: I've been a part of this, I'm responsible. I have to find some way to atone for what we've done.'

'You'd be dead before he hit the floor.'

Kurt shook his head. 'Doesn't matter what happens to me.'

'It would do no good. Berlin would just send someone else.'

'Then I'll go to Berlin, take out the lot of them. I have to do something, Hedy, I have to make this better. And somehow I have to win your forgiveness.'

Hedy felt a surge of tenderness. She took his face in her hands. 'Kurt, listen. That stuff I said months ago – I was just angry. You're not responsible for what they're doing. You said yourself, you had no choice, no more than Anton. And you have to stop talking like this. No suicidal mutiny on this little island is going to save a single Jew.'

'But I have to do something . . .' His voice was growing weaker, like a child.

'You already did, Kurt, don't you see? You saved me! But for you, I'd have been sent to one of those camps!' She gripped him harder, her fingers pressing the blood from his face. 'That's not war, that's not hatred – it's goodness, it's love! That's who you are!'

He placed his hands on her shoulders, and a calm seemed to descend on him. 'Then let's fight them – both of us! I don't know how exactly, but we can try, can't we? If we've got each other, then we've both got a chance. Maybe we can get out of this alive, together. Please, Hedy?'

She looked at him, knowing that he meant it, and in her gut she felt something lift. It was hope, and possibility. She breathed in deeply, and whispered, 'I've never stopped stealing petrol coupons.'

He stared for a moment, as if she'd spoken in another language, full of incomprehension. Then he started to laugh. 'You never stopped stealing coupons? You never stopped?' She could feel the tension seeping from his body, until he became helpless with laughter and fell onto his back, pulling her on top of him. 'Oh, Hedy, I'm so proud of you! I love you so much!'

He pulled her body towards him then, and kissed her with an intensity that melted her, that stirred a sense of life within all this destruction, and soon their two bodies merged, rolling back and forth across the mattress as the dawn pushed through the tiny attic window.

7

It was a spring tide. The ocean had been dragged so far out of Belcroute bay that the shingle gave way to gleaming, rarely exposed sand at the water's edge. Blurred, shadowy outlines of rocks could now be seen beneath the calm turquoise water. Like sharks, Hedy thought, lying in wait beneath the surface. The morning was hot and clear, but she shivered anyway. As if reading her mind, Kurt extended his arm and pulled her into his body a little tighter. With a sigh, she leaned into him and rested her head on his shoulder.

It was the kind of day that summer tourists would have embraced just a few years ago. Then, there would have been women in swimsuits lounging on the magnolia sands around the corner in St Brelade's bay, and children splashing each other in the shallows. There would have been ice creams and blankets, and the air would have been pierced by excited shouts. Now, it was hard to find any sliver of coast free from mines and barbed wire. And these days, Hedy found it hard to look at such fortifications.

Since the night of Kurt's revelations, she found many sights painful. High stone walls, bars on windows, the small train that ran along the front of St Aubin's bay to transport building materials. Children crying, people coughing. The hiss of a gas heater. Everything she saw and touched projected her into the horror. She saw the tiny square of sky through the vent in the boxcars used to transport them. She reeled back as the doors opened and the limp bodies were disgorged, smelled the shit on the floors and heard the clank of the oven door as the bolts sealed her inside. And she would think of her mama and papa, the same people who had cuddled and sung to her, washed her hands at the kitchen tap while she stood on a stool, and she couldn't put the two halves together. How was it possible that this had happened to them? To anyone?

She had faked an illness for a week to stay home from work, knowing she couldn't trust herself around the Germans. Kurt had waited for Doctor Maine outside the hospital and acquired a sick note for Hedy to give to the compound authorities, as well as a prescription for a small bottle of brandy. For six days she had lain on her bed, watching the sun appear and disappear in the skylight above, wondering if she, too, would die, not much caring either way. But on the sixth day she felt hungry, ate a little vegetable soup, and poured a bowl of water to wash herself all over, grateful for the sensation of the sponge against her skin. If she was the only one of her family left, she considered, she carried a responsibility now. She needed to stand up straight again, get a grip on herself. She forced herself to do some dishes, buy her rations – and even, the next week, return to work. And as the days grew longer and warmer, honeying her skin and melting the frozen tundra beneath it, she began to perceive a future again. Because now she was no longer on her own. She and Kurt were finally, properly together.

Over a long, intense evening, crouched in this very spot among the rocks and huddled against the wind, they had formulated the basis of their new relationship, consisting of three heartfelt promises. First, that both of them would carry on with their lives as if nothing had happened – although in reality they would do every little thing they could to wreck the system while they waited for their deliverance. Second, they would repeat nothing to anyone of what they had learned; a leak of such sensitive information could too easily be traced back to Kurt's conversation with Wildgrube, and the consequences could snow-ball quickly. Plus, with letters from Anton so few and infrequent, there was no point in upsetting Dorothea any further.

Their last undertaking proved a little more complicated. Kurt insisted that Hedy needed to move – too many neighbours in the New Street building would be aware of Kurt's nocturnal visit, making future contact there risky. Hedy, sick of the stairs and Mrs Le Couteur's (now quite blatant) snooping, willingly agreed. But a trawl through the rentals column in the *Post* revealed no affordable apartments within walking distance of Hedy's work; every town property was now filled with soldiers or local farming families kicked off their land in the early months of Occupation. For several days Hedy had scoured the library notice board and the scant offerings of the rental agency, but found nothing.

Once again, it was Doctor Maine who came to the rescue. Without even enquiring why Hedy needed such help, the doctor pushed a note through her letterbox, informing her that a patient of his on Pierson Road had died, and that the woman's son was giving notice on her apartment that week. Hedy was there within an hour. It was a small, dingy basement, close to Anton and Dorothea's house, with a distinct smell of mould; the only view was people's feet as they passed on the road outside, and the no-pets rule meant leaving Hemingway behind. But it was cheap and convenient, furnished with a double bed, and the spivvy-looking landlord seemed happy to take her money without references. Hedy thrust the first fortnight's rent into his hand before he had time to reconsider. The next day she fed Hemingway his last meal, stroked his little grey head, pinned a note to his collar, and left him outside the door of the new lady tenant who was always stroking him in the hallway. Then she took her old wicker bag stuffed only with a few garments, a toothbrush and her parents' beloved letters, and moved into her new life.

Now she and Kurt met as often as schedules and security allowed. They used hidden locations such as Belcroute or, on occasion, Hedy's new apartment, Kurt slipping in with his own key after dark and sneaking away early before he was missed at his billet. Neither of them ever joked about the excitement of the subterfuge. Both knew it was far too serious for that.

Hedy shuffled a little closer to him as they squashed together on the pebbles between the jagged boulders, and squeezed his hand. 'Did you manage to find out any more about getting a crystal radio set?'

Kurt nodded. 'That radio and gramophone shop near Anton's old flat? Apparently the owner makes them for people in the back room. But there's a waiting list, and I suspect he only helps people he knows.'

Hedy pushed her bare toes into the tiny warm stones at her feet. 'Guess I'll have to carry on relying on Dorothea.'

'I'm so sick of the nonsense the RRG puts out.' Kurt picked up a pebble and threw it down the beach where it bounced on the shingle. 'They're still reporting the Pacific like Midway never happened. And as for what's going on in the east . . .' An image of Anton squatting in some dugout flashed in Hedy's brain. She quickly pushed it away. 'It's madness – everyone knows it's all lies. Even Colonel Knackfuss has a radio in his office for listening to the BBC.' He picked up another pebble, but Hedy, mindful of the footpaths above them, gently took it from him. 'The Yanks are hammering our cities. At this rate there'll be nothing left by the end.' He turned to her with an ironic smile. 'I'm starting to think Sydney might be a good place for us, afterwards. Can't get much further away than that!'

Hedy forced a smile in return. As wonderful as it was to be with Kurt again, talk of a future beyond the war still frightened her. He dropped a lot of such references into the conversation, mentioning the style of house he'd like to live in, or a boy's name he particularly liked. No doubt Kurt thought it showed confidence and commitment; he was certain that in a postwar world, mixed marriages would be lawful, perhaps even encouraged. Hedy kept her own thoughts private: that laws don't change people's minds, and that the hatred between Jews and Germans would likely last for generations. Nor did she mention that this new world terrified her, that she dreaded an Austria where her family no longer existed and the neighbourhoods of her childhood had been razed. To Hedy, the coming years seemed so fraught with danger and complexity that she blocked the idea out. Surviving each day, each week, was as much as she could manage right now.

She shivered again and changed the subject. 'Remember that peg-leg fisherman Oliver Maine told me about?'

'The one who sells black market fish?'

'I found his mooring the other day, near some steps at the English harbour. Bought a mackerel before the German inspectors arrived to take his catch.'

'A whole mackerel? Lucky you!'

'Oliver says the guy's building a boat in secret, somewhere out at Fauvic. When the time's right, he plans to use it to escape.'

Kurt wrinkled his nose. 'Have to be some boat to reach England from here. If he heads for the French coast, he'll be shot before he's landed.'

'Still, it shows you people are fighting back. And the mackerel was delicious – I'll go back again next week.'

Kurt pushed the hair from her face. 'Take care. This new Jewish curfew . . .'

Hedy dismissed the comment with a wave of her hand, even though the same anxiety had kept her awake on many nights. 'I keep an eye on the time. Anyway, I'm an insurgent now, aren't I?'

Kurt laughed. 'I nearly forgot.' He rummaged in his pocket, drew out a bundle of paper Reichmarks and pressed them into her hand. 'There you go. Resistance wages.'

Hedy pulled a face. 'I don't like taking money from you.'

'I told you, this is for both of us – for emergencies. Are you keeping it somewhere safe?'

'Behind that loose skirting board by the bed.'

'First rule of revolution: always have a stash of money you can access quickly.' He grinned, and Hedy saluted to join in the game. Perhaps Kurt was right – perhaps a little self-delusion was no bad thing for the spirit. She tucked the money away in her bag, and when she turned back Kurt was still watching her.

'Look at you! You are so gorgeous. Can I come over this evening?'

'If the coast is clear. Come the long way round, through the park – make sure you're not followed.'

He nodded, placing his other arm around her. 'I'm always careful. Now give me a kiss.'

She didn't need to be asked twice.

The café was tiny, with a dark interior, chipped paint and grubby curtains. The air was filled with the scent of charred vegetables, the only food that had been cooked here for many months, and the tablecloths had long ago been scrapped for lack of any detergent to wash them in. Pictures of happier times, poorly painted (by the proprietor, Hedy suspected) hung on the walls under thick layers of dust. As usual, it was empty, the owners presumably keeping the place running as a reason to get out of bed in the morning, rather than to provide a meaningful service. But it was a useful private space, away from prying eyes. Hedy took a corner seat, asked for any kind of hot drink they could provide – they all tasted the same anyway, no matter what you called them – and waited for the doctor to arrive.

Fifteen minutes later, her drink cooled and stewed in its cup, the shop door pinged and Maine shuffled in, lifting his heavy doctor's bag over the backs of the chairs as he pushed his way through the tables. He glanced around to choose an appropriate seat, but Hedy caught his eye and gestured for him to sit at her table, as the elderly woman at the counter –

probably the owner's mother – had such poor eyesight she barely knew who she was serving. He slumped onto the seat opposite, placed his bag on the floor and smiled. 'Good day, my dear, and how are you?'

'Mustn't grumble.' She had recently learned the phrase from listening to local women in the covered market, and now liked to drop it into conversation whenever she got the chance. Checking that the old lady's attention was elsewhere, she slid the envelope of petrol coupons across the table. 'And yourself?'

'A little tired, but aren't we all? How is your friend?'

A code had evolved between them over the months: 'your friend' meant Dorothea, 'your other friend' meant Anton, and 'your additional friend' referred to Kurt. They also referred to the petrol coupons, on the rare occasion they needed to, as postcards.

Hedy pulled a face to indicate she was giving only part of the story. 'I saw her yesterday. I think the stress of her situation is affecting her.' She patted her chest to clarify her point, and the doctor nodded. In fact, Hedy had stayed at Dorothea's house for an hour after the end of the news bulletin the previous night, alarmed by her enduring cough and the disturbing bluish shade of her lips. In recent weeks Dorothea's health had noticeably declined, worsened by a poor diet and her anxiety about Anton. She often said herself that she dreaded another winter under Occupation. Yet she often seemed more focused on her movie scrapbooks than the details of the BBC reports, and Hedy often had to repeat the salient points to her after the broadcast. In truth, Hedy was finding the role of guardian increasingly testing; it certainly involved a lot more than popping round every few days to make sure she had food in the cupboard.

Maine reached into his bag, drawing out a tiny jar of pale flakes. 'Grated ginger,' he muttered, pushing the jar across the table towards her. 'From a patient of mine. It's far from fresh, but she can sprinkle a little on her evening meal. Or add it to a chest rub, if she can find any oils.' He gave a wry smile. 'Six years' medical training, and I'm reduced to dispensing folk treatments like some old peasant woman.'

Hedy reached across for the jar, letting her fingers cover his for a moment. She remembered how, at their first meeting, he had reminded her of her uncle Otto. Otto was likely dead now, caught up in the same haul as her parents, and this man was probably the only person left of that generation who she trusted. She wished she could just climb into his lap and have him sing her a lullaby.

'Thank you. I don't know what we would do without you.'

Maine smiled with a rare vulnerability, revealing the gratitude of a man who received few compliments. He was on the edge of a reply when the room was filled with a violent rushing noise, and the café door flew open. Their hands sprung instantly apart, and each of them pinned themselves back in their seats. All eyes were on this sudden, alarming intruder.

'You got any water there? Give us a glass, would you? I've a terrible thirst.'

The man was tall and well built, his thick-set features pulled into a scowl, his rusty hair unkempt. His voice was deep and powerful, and Hedy knew at once that he had an accent, though she did not know then that it was Irish. The man stomped up to the counter, where the old lady quietly poured him a glass of water and watched him down it in one go, as if huge men burst into the place every day demanding drinks.

The envelope of coupons, Hedy realised, was still sitting on the table. She glanced up at the doctor, indicating that he should put it out of sight, when she realised that Maine was turning in his seat, trying to keep his face out of the newcomer's eyeline. Hedy felt a rising panic; something frightening was happening, but she wasn't sure what. At that moment the man at the counter looked towards their table and peered at Maine's face, seeking out the features.

'The doctor, is it?' Hedy's stomach somersaulted. 'Fintan Quinn – you patched up my mate down the hospital two weeks back, after that fall, remember?'

Maine smiled at Quinn. Hedy wondered if it looked as unconvincing to its recipient as it did to her. She pulled the envelope back to her side of the table and dropped it into her lap, out of sight.

'Indeed. Is he recovering well?'

'Ah, sure. He's back on the job, good as new now.'

Quinn helped himself to another glass of water while Hedy's mind galloped on. If that was the extent of their relationship, there was no need to panic. All the man had seen was a doctor he barely knew, sitting in a café with a young woman. She breathed deeply, scoffing at herself – some resistance fighter she was, panicking at every passing remark. But what the man said next almost stopped her heart.

'And you – you work up at Lager Hühnlein, don't you?'

Hedy turned to Quinn and nodded, calculating that an obvious lie could backfire. Now she could see his face full on, it did look vaguely familiar. Yes, she had seen him driving trucks of cement and girders in and out of the compound, his arm casually draped from the window, that blank, ruddy face perusing the site. He stood out from the other mercenaries because of that rumbling voice and wild ginger hair. Hedy gave him a cool, courteous smile, hoping to hit the sweet spot between encouragement and hostility.

'That's right.'

'Thought I recognised you. Never forget a face.'

The man downed the second glass then turned and headed for the door, giving them both a small American-style salute with two fingers as he passed. Then he was out the door as rapidly as he'd entered.

Hedy and Maine stared at each other for several moments, communicating only through nervous glances. As soon as the old lady disappeared into the back, Hedy pressed the coupon envelope into Maine's hands. She leaned forward to whisper across the table. 'You think he saw anything?'

Maine shook his head. 'What could he see? It's just an envelope.'

Hedy sat back and nodded, breathing out for what felt like the first time in several minutes. 'It's just that we've been linked together, by someone who can identify both of us . . .'

Maine leaned in, his turn now to cover her hand. 'My dear Hedy, from what I saw of those gentlemen at the hospital, I don't believe they'd even be interested. All any of them cared about was how quickly the chap could get back to work, so that they didn't miss a day's pay.'

'But if he were to find out about . . . *me*.' She was careful to observe their unwritten rule, never to say the word 'Jewish' in public. 'You know they deported those women from Guernsey a few weeks ago?' She bit her lip, wishing she could tell him all she knew of their probable fate.

He patted her fingers. 'You have cause to be careful, and I know you always are. But you have enough real worries, without inventing new ones.'

Hedy nodded, forcing a smile, vowing that the next time she saw the peg-leg fisherman she would buy an extra mackerel for the doctor and his wife. 'You're right. This bloody war, it's making me so edgy. But perhaps a different venue next week?'

'That would be sensible, I think. You want to leave first? I'm not on call till four.'

Hedy paid the woman for her drink and slipped out into the cobbled street, trying to shake off the sense of anxiety that had planted itself in her stomach. It was a warm afternoon, and as she reached the park the sun on her skin felt like treacle. She tossed her hair a little and instructed herself to relax, to live a little in the moment. After all, she had done good work today. The coupons would enable Maine to reach dozens of sick people in the parishes. She was expanding her contacts to acquire food supplies – and tomorrow night she would see Kurt again. There was still much to feel thankful for, she reminded herself, as she slipped silently through the backstreets of St Helier, passing the swastika flags and soldiers without a second glance.

★

Kurt shifted uncomfortably on the wooden bench, eyeing the other officers nearby. All were smoking or engaged in stilted, distracted conversations. It was a high-ranking affair, to be sure – no one under the rank of lieutenant, and a generous sprinkling of captains. It was clear that none of them knew why they had been summoned today, and equally clear that this was something big. The sun, strikingly warm for September, poured through the casement windows of College House, turning the grey stone corridor into a slow-bake oven; several of the older officers had already turned an unhealthy shade of puce. Much longer stuck here, Kurt thought, and Berlin might have to replace the entire Field Command.

He looked around the grand interior with its ancient flagstones and crafted wood trim, the perfect example of the British Victorian boarding school it had been before the war, and tried to imagine snotty-faced boys tumbling through these hallways. Where were those kids now? Probably stuffed in some prefabricated wooden hut, compulsory German grammars perched on their knees. This place must have seemed a daunting enough environment to a young lad; now, inhabited by the uniformed pen pushers of the Field Command, it reminded Kurt of a hive, and the buzzing, claustrophobic cells around a queen bee.

On the far side of the room he spotted Fischer, deep in some private conversation with an administrator. Fischer had been chummy with Kurt lately, apologising for the mess in his half of their shared room, and offering Kurt a substantial amount of the cigarettes his brother had sent from Germany. But there was a coldness beneath the camaraderie, and Kurt was aware that conversations at the billet often ended abruptly when he entered a room. Kurt knew Fischer's game but continued to ignore it. If Wildgrube and his gorillas chose to spy on him from time to time, he'd just have to make sure he gave them nothing to see; he was scrupulous now about looking over his shoulder. And the way things were going on the Continent, they could all be out of here within six months.

A uniformed lackey emerged from a wooden double door and waved them forward. Kurt followed the crowd into the large meeting room, finding a space to stand at the back with a decent view of the senior commanders around the table. The windows here were even larger, the stuffy heat even more unbearable. Whatever this news was, Kurt thought, let it be delivered quickly.

Colonel Knackfuss himself was seated at the centre of the table. Kurt stared at the man's stiff decorative collar, biting into his craggy neck, and the tiny scabs at the side of his head where some barber had shaved the stubble growth with excessive speed. The officers arranged themselves around the room as the colonel's deep-set eyes remained fixed on the paperwork before him, evidently glad of the extra time to prepare his statement. Then silence fell, and Knackfuss's rasping tones rang out.

'I summoned you here today because the Swiss Government has recently asked the German High Command to consider an exchange of prisoners of war. As you may be aware, several thousand German citizens are currently interned in Persia by order of the British.' A lightning exchange of confused looks pinged around the room. What did this have to do with the administration of the Channel Islands? 'One year ago,' Knackfuss continued, 'when the internment first came to light, an order was issued that, in retaliation, Feldkommandantur 515 should immediately deport all British residents not born within the

Channel Islands, at a ratio of ten to one for those held in Persia.' The silence deepened as minds began to turn over, unravelling the significance. Kurt sensed that a number of people in the room had actually stopped breathing. 'This order was never enacted. In January of this year I made known my objections to 319 Infantry: it is my view that the British-born islanders serve as a shield to attacking Allied forces, and that such a deportation would create additional defensive problems, including potential resistance. However . . .' Knackfuss shuffled the papers before him, as if it might somehow alter what was typed upon them. 'However, the new applications of the Swiss have brought this situation to the attention of the Führer, who is displeased that previous orders were ignored. Berlin now insists that the deportations be carried out as directed: that is, all British subjects without permanent residence, and all British men between the ages of sixteen and seventy born on the British mainland, along with their families, be sent forthwith to internment camps in Germany.'

Knackfuss lowered his papers and scanned the room, giving his officers permission to react. A low rumble of muttering rolled through the room. Several heads had dropped in anticipation of what the next weeks would involve, others maintained expressions of cautious neutrality. Fischer, Kurt noticed, was one of those glaring at Knackfuss, clearly incensed that one so senior should question the Führer's orders. The heat of the room fizzed in Kurt's bones and made him nauseous. He tried to think of mountain streams and glasses brimming with ice cubes.

'We calculate that the number of islanders affected,' Knackfuss went on, 'amounts to approximately two thousand, around one in twenty of the population. The announcement will be made in the *Evening Post* on the fifteenth, that is, in five days' time, with the first deportations taking place the following day.' The muttering grew louder. Kurt heard distinct phrases such as 'twenty-four hours?' and 'got to be kidding!' bubbling up in pockets around him. Knackfuss, aware of the disturbance, raised his own volume against it. 'This will present significant challenges, but gives us the advantage of surprise. The less time people are given to organise their personal affairs, the less opportunity they will have for opposition.'

He gazed around the room – making mental notes, Kurt suspected, of the less forgiving faces and to whom they belonged. Fischer had now arranged his own visage into a model of impartiality; Kurt made a feeble attempt to copy it, but when he caught his reflection in the window, he just looked mildly deranged. 'There may well be resistance,' Knackfuss continued, 'but this order comes from the Führer himself with the highest priority, and no exceptions can be made. I need not tell you that this remains highly classified information until it is publicly released, and that no mention of this will be made outside this room, other than to those within Field Command involved in the practical arrangements. That is all. *Heil Hitler.*'

A forest of hands rose in salute, and then Knackfuss was gone, whisked away to some private office deep within the building. The explosion of conversation went off like a bazooka. Kurt muttered something to his neighbour about making a telephone call, and slid silently from the room, down the grand corridor and out through the nearest exit. As he trotted down Mont Millais towards the town, the queasiness persisted. He looked at each local he passed – ordinary men and women going about their daily business, heading home on lunch breaks, shopping or pushing prams. How many of them would have their lives turned inside out within a few days? How many kids and elderly people would not survive the journey? How many more would perish in internment camps? But Kurt knew full well the real reason for his churning stomach. This order meant that all pretence of reasonable behaviour from his administration was now finished. If Berlin was prepared to treat British subjects with this degree of contempt, a new sweep of foreign nationals and Jews would likely follow. He would have to see Hedy tonight and warn her. They would need to stash more money behind the skirting, and he would suggest she keep a bag packed at all times.

The sun was burning the skin on his face, cooking his body through the thick wool of his tunic. It was already far too hot for September. But the distant high clouds were static, and the stillness in the air promised an even hotter night to come.

★

It was a noise Hedy had never heard before in these streets. A cacophony of singing, wailing and roars of defiance, individual voices occasionally cutting through the hubbub and rising to the surface. Somewhere to her right was a rousing chorus of the song she had heard sung in public houses in the months before the Occupation, 'There'll Always Be An England'. To her left came the anguished high-pitched cries of a woman and her children. On Commercial Street a group of men had gathered in an ominous, illegal group of ten or twelve, yelling and gesticulating to the world at large. Pushing her way past them and the milling crowds blocking the thoroughfare, Hedy grabbed hold of Dorothea's hand for security as they pressed on towards the harbour.

As the narrow street gave onto the open expanse of the Weighbridge, the sight stopped both of them dead. Hundreds of people in small groups, standing or collapsed on their haunches, all of them bundled in layers of clothes far too hot for the day's searing heat. Each clutched a battered packing case, or a roll of blankets tied up with string. Grim-faced men herded their families; their wilting, red-faced wives dispensed fragments of scorched swede to their hungry young, while older children bounced screaming toddlers to no avail. Wherever she looked Hedy could see people hugging each other. Many were weeping. Families, neighbours, work colleagues – people who had all considered themselves locals until the previous night, when a sharp rap on the door and a sheaf of papers had brutally delivered a different interpretation. Women who had escaped the order ran to friends and in-laws who had not, pressing into their hands whatever treasures had been found at the back of the store cupboard – a tin of tunny fish, a couple of undersized apples. Men sweating in their winter coats thrashed out hurried deals with pals and neighbours over the upkeep of properties, custody of businesses, care or disposal of family pets. The scene formed a grey, raucous mural of despair.

Hedy turned to Dorothea to see her hand clasped to her mouth. 'I didn't believe it till now. How can they do this?' Dorothea looked around, searching. 'I have to find her.'

Hedy followed her gaze over the sea of heads. 'I'm not sure you'll be able to find anyone in this crowd.'

'I have to try.'

They tiptoed through the chaos, stepping over legs, children and belongings, peering into assembled groups. The sun was now reaching its height, and Hedy yearned for shade.

Suddenly Dorothea gave a shout. 'That's her! Over there!' She pointed to a small group sitting in a semi-circle on the ground near the bottom end of Commercial Buildings. 'Sandy? Sandy, it's me!' Hedy found herself dragged along by Dorothea's fierce grip, bumping into people and stumbling over luggage, until they reached the family group. One of them was a woman of Dorothea's age, with striking dark hair and olive eyes, a winter coat tucked under her bottom as a cushion. Next to her, a man Hedy assumed to be her father, sporting ruddy cheeks and a booming voice, was engaged in an intense conversation with another gentleman. As they drew near, Hedy realised that the second man was the deputy they had met on the day of the wireless collection.

'But why have the Jersey States allowed this to happen?' the father was shouting. 'We've lived in the island for thirty years, Le Quesne, do we have no rights?

The deputy's eyelids were heavy, as if the simple challenge of wakefulness was too much for his ageing body. 'We have done everything in our power. We refused to serve the notices, but the Germans dragged parish officials from their homes and ordered them on pain of imprisonment.'

'You're supposed to protect us. It's a damned disgrace.'

Le Quesne trudged off, only to be accosted by another furious deportee.

Dorothea threw her arms around her friend. 'Sandy! I had to come to say goodbye. Do you have any idea where they're sending you?'

'All we know is that it's some camp in Germany,' the woman replied. The phrase turned Hedy's stomach. 'They only told us last night.' She looked composed, but Hedy could sense the turmoil underneath.

Dorothea took a small jar of sugar from her bag and pressed it into Sandy's hand. 'I've been saving this for something important, I want you to have it.'

Sandy smiled with gratitude, but her father immediately stepped forward. 'We don't need anything from your sort, thank you.'

'Daddy, please!' Sandy jumped in, but the old man pushed himself in between her and Dorothea.

'You're married to one of them – you're on their side. You stay away from my daughter. Go on, clear off.'

Seeing the hurt on Dorothea's face, Hedy took hold of her elbow to draw her away. But to her surprise Dorothea drew herself up. 'I may love a man in the German army but I know whose side I'm on, thank you very much.' She reached out and squeezed Sandy's hand. 'Take care of yourself, my love.'

She turned on her heel and walked away. Hedy hurried after her, knowing she could lose her in a moment. 'That was brave.'

Dorothea shrugged. 'It's not the first time. Won't be the last.' Then she stopped, her head on one side. 'Listen – there are people down there singing the national anthem.' It was true.

'God Save The King' was now plainly audible from a large group over by the quay. 'Let's go and join them.'

'I don't think that's a good idea. The Jerries are jumpy today, they could start shooting.'

But Dorothea shook her head. 'Let them. These are my people, I'll not let them be packed off to God knows where without letting them know how I feel about it.' She marched off in the direction of the quay.

Hedy hesitated, half wanting to go home, half feeling that she should support Dorothea. Duty finally forced her on, but as she traipsed along behind Dorothea's purposeful figure, she felt a twinge of admiration. The island community had already spat this woman out as trash, yet here she was defending them. Anton had been right, Hedy reflected, about her good heart.

The two of them picked their way through the crowd until they reached the quayside and the improvised choir of locals, self-consciously attaching themselves to the edge of the throng. As a scrappy version of 'Keep The Home Fires Burning' started up, Dorothea joined in, tentative at first, then belting it out with gusto. She sang as if it were the last song of her life, her usual wheezing temporarily vanished. Hedy, looking around for soldiers and spies, timidly mimed along. The song ended and was immediately replaced with 'We'll Meet Again'. Then another, noisier version of the national anthem, and a somewhat chaotic rendition of 'Run, Rabbit, Run'. Minutes turned into hours, and as the Germans continued to stare vacantly above the heads of the rebels, Hedy, finally familiar with the words and tunes, let her voice ring out and reverberate in her chest in a way she had forgotten it could. Now and then she and Dorothea would turn, in the middle of a phrase, and grin at each other.

The sun slowly arced around to the west, and as it did so the mass of people and the baked paving stones beneath their feet intensified the heat of the day, shimmering off the quayside in distorted waves. By the time the first boat began to board, the

Germans' rifles were primed and aimed at the crowd, ready to stop any last-minute rebellion. The singers' voices, hoarse as they were, grew louder and more defiant. And at that moment Hedy was struck by a single, powerful certainty. Kurt's suspicions were right: everything that had happened in the last two years had simply been a rehearsal. The real Occupation was only now beginning – a new, bitter wind was blowing in. Soon, perhaps sooner than anyone imagined, everything was going to change. At that moment and with great clarity, Hedy understood that she was no more than a cork bobbing on the surface of the harbour, waiting to see where the current would take her.

She took a deep breath and bellowed out the final chorus of 'Pack Up Your Troubles', and her voice travelled out across the water and into the void.

8

1943

The clock on the wall showed 5.55. Hedy tore the last sheet from her typewriter and placed it on the pile of finished reports. She scanned the room, noting the position of every staff member, calculating their precise stage of departure; she knew all their habits well enough by now. Bruna, the tall girl from Munich who always brushed her hair for two minutes before leaving, presumably to impress her endless succession of boyfriends. Rosamund, Miss Vogt's pinch-lipped favourite, who always lingered by the supervisor's desk in the hope of soliciting a compliment on her day's work. Smelly Derek with his stench of mould, who fussed over his station each night before putting on his jacket, obsessed with leaving everything perfectly tidy. It was vital that Hedy chose exactly the right moment to transfer the petrol coupons from her desk to her coat, just when everyone was distracted. Pretending to look for something in her bag, she waited for her moment. Then, as Derek bent over to tuck the dust cover under his machine, Hedy moved, deftly slipping the coupons into her inside pocket. Another sweep of the room told her that, as usual, no one had noticed. Projecting an air of calm indifference, she took her bag from the back of her chair, collected her coat, and strolled out into the dusty exterior of the compound.

Walking towards the exit gate she kept her eyes ahead of her, as always. It was rare for her to catch a glimpse of Kurt at this time of day – normally he was over in the warehouses, doing the last stocktake of the day – but they had long ago agreed that they should never be seen speaking to each other at work. On the occasions when they did pass each other on the pathways, both of them would look the other way or, in Kurt's case, manufacture a conversation with a colleague as a sleight of hand. Hedy had never trusted anyone at Lager Hühnlein, but now she viewed everyone as a potential enemy. People could be seen whispering in quiet corners of the canteen, in the shadows of filing cabinets or outside toilet cubicles – rumours about spies and collaborators, about imminent Allied raids and possible German reprisals. It was impossible to separate cynical German employees, who genuinely wouldn't have cared if you stole an entire desk from under their noses, from secret police operatives snooping for information. Even harder to tell the difference between resistance-minded locals and those who would sell their own grandmothers for a cash reward. The only safe option was to keep your mouth shut at all times and, if asked anything, profess complete ignorance.

Last year's fears of a new, more repressive phase had proved all too correct. Paranoia was now the default mood of the German authorities. Rations had been cut for several months as 'punishment' for the sinking of German ships, and a number of local people, including a recalcitrant canon, had been sent to punishment camps for listening to the BBC news. Worst of all had been the announcement made one cold, wet day in the early spring that, in retaliation for an abortive British commando raid on the sister island of Sark, a further two hundred islanders were to be deported. Neither Hedy nor Kurt needed to be told that this latest seizure would be certain to include the few remaining Jews.

Frantic, they discussed options. The Jersey authorities, Hedy asserted, would be useless; she adamantly refused Kurt's suggestion to interfere on her behalf, arguing that it would be sure to arouse suspicion and put them both in greater danger. Finally, in desperation, Hedy approached Feldwebel Schulz, who sulkily agreed that in the light of her work at the compound and the difficulty of replacing German-speaking employees, he would request an exception be made in her case. It seemed a meagre hope. For three weeks she had lived in dread, her nights tormented with fitful sleep, her days broken by stomach cramps and diarrhoea. Several times Kurt delivered news of another Jewish arrest or disappearance (clearly some had gone into hiding with friends, a dangerous solution in Hedy's view), always reassuring her that the longer she escaped attention, the more optimistic they could be. Other individuals, he pointed out, were being deliberately overlooked if Field Command deemed it expedient to do so. But his pallor, and the way his fingers trembled as he lifted a cup to his lips, gave his real feelings away.

No formal decision was ever announced. But by the fourth week, with arrests petering out, they began to suspect that this particular storm had passed. Perhaps Schulz's request had been accepted, or maybe Hedy's refusal to attend the College House interview the previous year had caused her name to drop off a list. Whatever the reason, it seemed that, for now, life could return to whatever currently passed for normality. Till the next time.

By the summer, she and Kurt felt sufficiently confident to return to their tiny acts of sabotage. Shut away in the privacy of Hedy's flat, they would entertain each other with their stories: of how Hedy had deliberately placed over seventy audit sheets in the wrong files, a mistake impossible to trace back but which took two hours for the administrators of Block Three to correct. Or how Kurt had turned a blind eye to the faulty wiring connections of a young mechanic in his charge, causing the truck to break down on its first girder delivery of the morning. They never fooled themselves that such actions made any real difference, but the laughter they shared in repeating them had a caustic edge to it, and stoked their yearning for revenge.

On nights like that, their lovemaking often had a cold, urgent undercurrent, as if sex was the one channel where their rage could be safely expressed. At other times the boyish gentleness of Kurt's touch brought Hedy to tears. She felt shame for ever doubting him. Never had she known anyone so kind, so utterly himself. She loved his attempts to supplement her weekly supplies with whatever he could bargain for at the military stores, the way he gleefully passed on any news of in-fighting or incompetence in the local administration. Best of all were the times he was able to create an excuse at his billet and stay the whole night. Then they would have long whispered conversations into the early hours, reflecting on how Hitler had risen to power and how Europe might prevent such collective madness ever recurring. Because, as summer turned to autumn, bringing with it the fall of Italy, they became ever more optimistic that the Allies would win. All they had to do, Kurt reminded her, was survive, and see the end. Worn down by his certainty, and recognising how many bullets had already been dodged, Hedy had recently begun to believe that some kind of future might be possible.

The sky was darkening as she set off down her usual route, following the lane towards the main road, then along St Aubin's road towards First Tower. Her new second-hand coat, a successful barter made by Kurt for some French candy, was a vast improvement on her old one, which had worn away to threads and buttons, but constant undernourishment meant she always felt the cold. Her mouth watered at the thought of the small piece of fish she had purchased at huge expense from her friendly fisherman the previous day. She'd also managed to save a swede and a few potatoes from the previous week, and Kurt had given her a small candle he'd stolen from his billet. Tonight she would eat like a queen.

She was just passing the arched gate of the old Sun Works tea-packing factory when a hand on her shoulder caused her to cry out. Spinning round, her first reaction was relief that she saw no uniform. Then, as she caught a proper view of the man's face beneath his cap in the half-light, relief was quickly replaced by fear. She recognised him even before he began to speak, the strength of the accent jerking Hedy straight back to the café where she and Doctor Maine had sat over a year ago.

'I know about your little sideline. Do us a deal and I'll say nothing about it.'

Hedy swallowed, her mind racing. Quinn, that was the fellow's name. Was he talking about the coupons? How could he possibly know? Was he bluffing? She tried to arrange her face in a way that suggested innocence and confusion. 'I don't know what you mean.'

The Irishman now had a tight grip on her arm. Hedy glanced about but there was no one else on the street. He had chosen his moment carefully, and at that second she realised he had probably followed her all the way from work.

'You know. Those petrol coupons, the ones you've been filching away.'

Hedy's heart sank. Had Quinn spoken to someone in her office? Had someone there seen her after all? Did he know there were coupons in her pocket right now? She decided it was worth one last throw of the dice. 'I don't understand.'

The grip of his hand tightened, his fingers now biting through her coat and hurting her skinny arm. 'I think you do. You get them for your doctor friend.'

Hedy felt the blood drain from her head. 'Nonsense.'

He squeezed her harder and Hedy whimpered. 'I'm not stupid. My girlfriend knows there's coupons going missing from your office.' Bruna, Hedy thought. Bruna, that Bavarian bitch, whose romantic interests were clearly now stretching beyond the German NCOs to include OT employees. 'Then I remembered – you and the doc together that time. I knew there was something going on. Guilt written all over you.'

'You're crazy.' It sounded like a lie.

Quinn smirked. 'Don't worry. I'm saying nothing. All I want is a cut. Couple of coupons a week and your secret's safe.'

Hedy stood as still as she could, hoping that a lack of resistance would calm him, quickly trying to calculate the best way out. She could give him two of the coupons right now and get away from him, which was what her body was begging her to do. But she reminded herself he was a mercenary. The man had no loyalties, and any fool could see where this kind of blackmail would lead. Two coupons today, ten next week, a hundred the week after. Either she would be caught by Vogt, or she'd fail to deliver and Quinn would betray her anyway. Her only chance was to close this down now.

'I'm sorry, but you've made a mistake.' She looked him straight in the eye, rebellious. 'I'm just a translator. I don't steal. I've nothing to give you.'

Quinn stared at her with impotent impatience. Clearly he had not envisaged this reaction and was at a loss where to take it now. Hedy could hear the blood pumping in her ears, and fought to keep her thinking clear. If she was right, Bruna's accusation was likely based on suspicion rather than certainty. And it had often occurred to Hedy that other people within the office were probably stealing too. If Quinn took Hedy's word now, perhaps he would walk away and try his luck elsewhere. For a moment she thought she sensed a retreat. Then fury blasted from him. 'You've got some nerve for a Kraut bitch, you know that? Well, they're all going to know about you now, and you'll be sorry. You'll see how sorry.'

Hedy felt his clutch release, then he was gone as quickly as he'd arrived, bounding up the road towards First Tower in a loping run. Hedy leaned back against the painted wooden gates of the factory, unable to stand unsupported. Rivulets of sweat ran down her chest between her breasts, though she was cold and shaking. All thoughts of home and dinner had now evaporated. There was only one coherent thought in her mind. It was all over.

★

She sewed the final stitch, cut the cotton with her teeth and held the coat up in the dim light of the apartment to examine it. It was good workmanship – her mother would have been proud. Provided you didn't feel or press the hem, no one would ever guess there were items concealed there: her toothbrush (impossible to replace now, and the thought of not brushing her teeth, even with the crushed cuttlefish 'toothpaste' of recent months, repelled her); the bundle of notes from behind the skirting board, finally stepping up to its rightful role; her mother's precious letters. She shook the coat a little – as she hoped, nothing moved or called attention to itself. She considered taking the small bag of essentials she kept packed, at Kurt's insistence, under her bed. But she quickly realised that the risk of walking through town with such an item, inviting searches and questions, was too great. In any case, she needed to remain as small and unobtrusive as possible.

She remembered herself and Roda preparing to escape across the Swiss border all those years ago, and tried to recall everything her sister had said. 'Money for bribes' – that had been her mantra. Anything else could be acquired later. It was funny really, Hedy mused; everyone in the family always thought of Hedy as the sensible, hard-headed one and Roda the romantic one who would fuss over girlish possessions and crack under pressure. But it was Roda who organised, chivvied and made all the harsh decisions, even volunteering to drive them through the mountains on those treacherous roads. Now it was Hedy's turn to show what she was made of.

The knock on the door paralysed her. Could Quinn have raised the alarm in the few hours since his threat? She searched for the small tear in the curtain fabric that allowed her to peek out without being seen, and pressed her eye to it. Dorothea. She leaned back against the bedstead, wondering whether to answer, weighing up the pros and cons of speaking to Dorothea today. Then she moved quickly to the door.

'I just wanted to tell you,' Dorothea began chattering before she was across the threshold, 'an old friend of Anton's told me today that there's been a shipment of French cheese. Of course the Jerries have taken most of it, but there'll be a little on sale in the market tomorrow if you get there first thing.' She beamed at Hedy, so proud of her news, so childishly hopeful of gratitude.

'Thank you. But I won't be able to get to the market tomorrow.'

'If I take your ration card, maybe I can get some for you?'

Hedy looked at those innocent, pale eyes. She knew she was about to break her promise to Anton, and felt a tug of remorse, but it was too late. The decision was made.

'Dorothea, I'm sorry, but I have to go away for a while.'

'Go away? What do you mean?'

'Something's happened. They're going to find out I've been stealing petrol coupons.'

Dorothea's mouth fell open. 'You're still doing that?'

Hedy nodded. 'And I can't take the chance. If I stay here, I'll be arrested and deported.'

'You want to come over to my house?'

To her own surprise, Hedy gave a little snort of laughter. 'I need to go a little further than that.'

Dorothea slumped into the only chair, her face even whiter than usual. 'Is Kurt going to help you?'

Hedy hesitated, considering a lie. But she already knew she was going to need Dorothea's help. 'Kurt doesn't know. I haven't told him.'

Dorothea's eyes grew wider with each second. '*Doesn't know?* Hedy, you can't just vanish!' She shook her head in disbelief. 'Kurt loves you. And you love him. Don't you?'

'Which is exactly why I have to do it this way.' Hedy moved around the room, tidying the books, pulling the bed covers straight, trying to keep her hands occupied. 'Kurt has a record for coupon theft already. Once they know about this, they could easily connect us. God knows what they'd do to him.'

To her embarrassment, she could see Dorothea was starting to cry.

'No, this is all wrong. Where will you go?'

'I have a plan. But I can't tell you. It's better no one knows – in case they question you.'

'You're not going to try and get off the island?' Dorothea's breath was becoming wheezy.

Hedy made a scoffing sound and turned her face away. 'That would be foolish and dangerous.'

'You can't do this alone!'

'It's all taken care of.'

'Doctor Maine? Is he helping you?'

'No!' Hedy was shocked at the volume of her own voice. 'He's to know nothing about this. That way, if they question him, they can't prove he was involved in any of it.' She wiped her cold sweating brow with the back of her hand. 'It will only be for a while, till things settle down.'

At this point Dorothea broke down completely and buried her face in her hands. Hedy watched her cry, too distracted to reach out, too scared to shed any tears herself. Then she crouched down beside her to get Dorothea's full attention. 'I need you to do something for me.' Hedy took the sheet of paper she had spent so long writing out on her last precious sheet of writing paper, folded several times for want of an envelope. 'Please give this to Kurt. I don't want to leave it in the apartment in case someone else finds it first.'

Dorothea took the note and pressed it to her rasping chest. 'Of course. But, Hedy, are you sure? Whatever you have planned, it sounds dangerous.'

'Doing nothing will be worse.' Hedy pulled on her coat and buttoned it up to the neck. 'I'm really sorry.'

'For what?' Dorothea looked genuinely confused.

'For dragging you into this. For leaving you on your own.'

'Oh, Hedy, don't worry about me.' Her voice had a new steeliness. 'Just take care of yourself, for God's sake.'

Hedy put her hands in her pockets to pull the coat more tightly around herself, feeling the weight of its new additions in the hem. Her voice wobbled a little as she forced out her reply: 'Of course. Don't worry, it's all going to be fine.'

★

He was just emerging from his tiny office when he saw them. A group of six or seven female employees – typists, he assumed – were gathered on the pathway from the canteen, talking with great animation. Their heads were bobbing together as if discussing something very important, but the way they kept glancing over their shoulders to check who was listening suggested that it was also rather shameful. Some gossip about a boyfriend, Kurt supposed. Perhaps a pregnancy? He knew, through an overheard conversation at his billet, that Fischer had just been through a similar panic with his married girlfriend, and had felt a twinge of smugness that he and Hedy were always so careful. Eager to show how uninterested he was, Kurt stepped off the path and gave the women a wide berth. But just as he passed them, a German phrase jumped out at him.

'At least you weren't in her block! Who knows what I might have caught!'

Kurt tried to dismiss it, but something told him that he needed to hear more. Deliberately dropping a couple of the files he was carrying, he bent down and began to shuffle them back together. He didn't have to wait long.

'What's the management playing at anyway, employing Jews? I hope they find the bitch and shoot her.'

Slowly Kurt rose and sauntered towards them. Unsure how else to approach it, he decided to pull rank.

'Ladies, you're blocking the path. What's so important that you have to stand around here gossiping?'

The tallest of the group, with blonde hair worn in a single

plait, stepped forward. 'Sorry, Lieutenant, but we've just found out that there was a Jew working in Block Seven. Apparently she's been stealing petrol coupons.'

Kurt gave a little cough to cover his involuntary gasp. 'Really? And where is she now?'

'No one knows, sir. She hasn't been in for two days. It's not right, though, sir.'

'It's scandalous,' chipped in a pug-nosed brunette. 'People have been sitting next to her all this time and never knew. I think we should have been told.'

Kurt looked at them, their angry, contorted faces scowling in unison, then turned and marched quickly in the direction of Block Seven. His heart was beating so fast he felt sick. Could it be true? How had she been caught? And how come he hadn't heard about it? Arriving at the hut, he opened the door and scanned the room, but saw only a handful of secretaries working through their lunch hour. Hedy's coat was not on the rack.

Without waiting to give notice to anyone, he dumped the files on a colleague, pulled on his tunic and ran from the compound, jogging the two miles to her apartment, arriving soaked and gasping at her door. Shouting Hedy's name, he wiggled his key frantically in the slot until he managed to get inside. The apartment was deserted. The bed was neatly made, a few garments still hung in the cupboard, and for a few terrible moments Kurt was certain that she had already been arrested. But then he took some deep breaths and began to look around. Her toothbrush was missing, the drawer where she kept her parents' letters was empty. With trembling hands he got on all fours and pulled the loose skirting away from the wall – the Reichmarks, too, were gone. He gasped with relief – clearly this was a planned escape. But where the hell had she gone?

Only when he reached Dorothea's house, and was greeted with her anxious, pallid face and Hedy's note, moistened by Dorothea's sweating hand, did the panic begin to return.

'I'm sorry, Kurt,' Dorothea muttered. 'I tried to make her tell me, but she thinks it's safer for us not to know.' She stood before him, arms crossed over her chest against the chill, looking up at him, wide-eyed. He placed his hand on the foot of the hall banister for support and read the note again. He had already read it three times, but could not accept that it told him nothing.

My darling Kurt,
They know about the coupons. I have to disappear. I wanted nothing more than to see this out with you, but I won't risk your life along with mine. I don't want to be a coward this time. Perhaps, if the fates are willing, we will find each other again when this is all over. I love you more than anything. Take care of yourself.
Hedy.

Kurt sank down onto the stairs, rubbing his eyes and pushing strands of hair back from his face. He had to work out all the possibilities, eliminate them one at a time, but all he could think about were those eyes – that brooding darkness behind the green, the very quality that had drawn him to her. Always secrets, thoughts that were never expressed, even to him. It was obvious now that this was something she must have plotted months ago, a premeditated plan for just this kind of eventuality. He cursed himself for not seeing it earlier, for not forcing her to open up. At least the fact that she had taken her few treasured possessions probably ruled out suicide.

He turned back to Dorothea. 'She said Maine is not helping her?'

'She was very clear that she didn't want to involve him. Said this way he would be safe.'

'But she has no one else here, no one!' He thought for a minute. 'What about Anton's old boss?'

'Mr Reis? I don't think she's seen him for months. Anyway, I heard he was in the hospital.'

'But who else would she trust enough to shelter her?'

'Kurt, I think she may try to escape the island altogether.'

His stomach lurched. 'She wouldn't be that crazy, would she?'

'When I asked her, she agreed it was stupid and dangerous. But I noticed that she blushed a little, and she wouldn't look at me.'

Kurt hauled himself to his feet and began to pace. 'She could get herself shot just for being on the beach! And what would she do? Stow away on some boat? She knows there's no sea traffic to England.'

Dorothea nodded. 'The only place she could reach is the French coast. And what good would that do?'

A small electric charge fired in his head. 'The French coast?'

'Yes?'

Kurt's heart began to hammer again. 'I think I might know where she's gone. But I need to hurry.'

Dorothea asked no further questions but merely nodded. 'I still have Anton's old bicycle hidden in the larder . . .'

★

Hedy woke with a jump, astonished that she had been asleep. She tried to stretch out her legs but they had grown numb with stillness and cold; she could no longer feel her toes at all. The smell of wet wood and paint was in her nostrils. Pulling her coat tighter around her, she peered into the darkness, trying to identify the unfamiliar shapes: the tools hanging on nails, the ropes on hooks. Rising above her, filling three-quarters of the space with its bulk and forcing her into one small corner, was the hull of a wooden boat. Through the ventilation window near the roof, the crescent moon shone a perfect rhombus of silver light onto the rough splintered wall; she pressed her ear against it, and heard the distant waves creeping their way up the beach in sucks and splashes. She guessed it must be four or five in the morning – only another hour or two to wait.

Crunching, uneven footsteps on the shingle forced her upright, breathless. A moment later the door shuddered open, and she recognised the stocky silhouette with heavy whiskers around the chin, and the soft, gruff voice.

'*Ça va?*'

'*Bien.*'

She watched the fisherman's dark figure limp into the hut and move around the hull, checking each section with his fingertips. Jean-Paul's limited English and Hedy's meagre smattering of French restricted conversations to single words and gestures. They knew virtually nothing of each other, and Hedy felt far from ready to trust him; when she had produced her precious bundle of Reichmarks for payment, he'd snatched at it with an eagerness that alarmed her. But certainty was a luxury she could no longer afford. All that she had managed to glean, in her months of buying Jean-Paul's mackerel at the harbourside, was that his wife had died a year or so earlier, and that for some reason he held the Germans responsible for her death. The look of disgust on his face and the voluminous, aggressive spitting that accompanied the recounting of his tale told Hedy all she needed to know: the fisherman hated the Jerries and felt he had little left to lose.

She wondered now if she had ever, truly, expected the plan to get this far. The notion of using this mythical, illegal boat for her own ends had popped into her mind the moment she'd heard about it, but at the time it was only a fantasy. Then, during those long, tortured weeks waiting to know if she would escape deportation, it had mutated into something possible, an emergency option should everything fall apart. Yet even then, in saner moments Hedy assumed the old man would laugh at her – tell her that the boat was not seaworthy, or that this 'escape plan' was just a joke, a good story for the harbour taverns once the war was over.

Two nights ago, he had stared cynically at her when she showed up at his mooring at dusk, attempting to explain her objective with random French words and bad mime. He probably thought she was working for the enemy, because he merely grunted, hobbling about the deck of his fishing vessel on his wooden leg and gesturing for her to push off. Only when she wrote down the sum she intended to pay did he seem to take the idea seriously. Half an hour later, after painful, repetitive communications and a great deal of staring out to sea, Jean-Paul, as she now knew him, spat thoughtfully onto the deck of his fishing boat and offered his hand to shake.

The first stages of the escape were clear in her mind, thanks to the old man's scribblings on scraps of newspaper. She would hide in the boathouse, tucked away down a lane on scrubland at Fauvic beach – an area known to be light on patrols and surveillance. Just before dawn, when the tide was high enough to launch, Jean-Paul would guide his vessel carefully around the rocks, then row them out to a safe distance before starting the outboard engine. Fourteen miles to the east – storms, riptides and patrols permitting – they would reach a quiet cove south of Portbail on the French coast just as darkness fell in the late afternoon. But here the plan grew vague and, if Hedy thought about it too much, quite insane. It was likely she would have to swim to shore, in darkness and freezing water, a task she knew might be beyond her. Then she would have to hide out in barns and outhouses around the German-occupied village for several days until she could find someone to help her. After that, her only idea was somehow to make contact with the French Resistance, who would help to get her over the border to Switzerland.

But crouched in the dark corner of the boathouse, it all seemed frighteningly remote, and Hedy tried not to look that far ahead. Instead, she told herself for the hundredth time that here, on this tiny occupied rock, discovery and death were a certainty, and at least this way she stood a chance. Her stomach rumbled, and she sighed, wondering when she might eat again. Kurt's smiling face came to mind and drew an embryonic sob to her throat, but she pushed the image away. She had done the right thing, the only loving thing she could. Now the decision was made, the money spent, there was nothing to do but sit here and wait for the rising tide.

★

Kurt could feel the muscles in his thighs begin to ache as he pushed the pedals harder. He'd convinced himself in recent months that he'd remained fairly fit even on his restricted diet, but this journey was telling otherwise. The rusty state of this ancient bicycle and the improvised tyres made from an old garden hose were certainly no help. His lungs burned, begging for more oxygen, as he pumped his way up the St Clements road. By his calculation of the tides, he had half an hour – assuming he was even going to the right place. But as soon as he'd remembered Hedy's story of the fisherman and his secret boat, he knew it was his best and only chance. The sky in front of him was just starting to turn cyan blue above the rooftops as he cycled east. She would be out to sea long before the sun brought its full strength. Stopping was not an option.

As he cycled, adrenaline inflated his anger. Why, why would she do this, when she could have come straight to him? An attempt like this was suicide – surely she had to see that? But even in his fury, he recognised her calculations and understood. Her stubborn, stupid independence made him want to scoop her up.

He pressed on up La Rue de Fauvic, passing tiny granite cottages. Beyond them he could just make out the open fields. Ahead lay a dark expanse that he prayed was the sea. He must be close now. Arriving at a T-junction, he peered through the emergent half-light to see, on the far side, a track running on ahead. It had to lead down to the beach – he could feel the wind and smell the salt in his nostrils. Looking in every direction to make sure he hadn't been spotted, he summoned the last of his energy to pedal across the tarmac road and onto the rough earth track, horribly aware of the sound of the wheels in the thick silence. As the track came to an end and the sea rose up to meet him, he dismounted and threw the bike to one side. He ran the last few yards and peered over the sea wall, then, spotting a break indicating a set of steps, hurried down them.

He scanned the beach to his left and right. The tide was high; waves were breaking rhythmically on the shore, hiding every rock and boulder beneath. His heart began to calm and the blood roar in his ears eased. But it had all been for nothing. The whole area was completely deserted. If Hedy ever was here, he was too late. And wherever she and her fisherman were now, there was nothing he could do to save them. A pain spread in his chest as he pictured the remainder of the war without her. He saw her bloated body washed up on the beach, or lying in woods with a bullet in her back. He stood staring at the horizon for several moments, rooted in misery.

A sound further down the shore drew his eyes to the south. In the semi-gloom he peered in its direction until he made out a shape – a bulky grey form that seemed to be moving at the water's edge. He staggered towards it, his brain finally making sense of it; now he could see the open wooden boat, with what looked like a small engine at the stern. He stumbled on, tripping over rocks, slipping on seaweed. Yes, there were two figures, pushing it into the water – both short, slight. And one of them . . .

'Hedy!'

His voice echoed across the beach. Both figures froze. He could see her clearly now, the shape of her shoulders and the way her body was leaning. The person with her, an old man, jumped back from the boat and raised his hands as if expecting to be shot. Kurt continued to lurch towards them till he was no more than five metres away, then stopped. Hedy was staring at him, white and shaking with fear and cold. As a child, Kurt had once entered the shed in Helmut's garden to find Helmut's father on a chair, about to put a noose around his neck; the expression on Hedy's face now was identical. For a moment no one moved, unsure where this would go.

'Kurt, I'm sorry.' She was clinging to the edge of the boat, either to support the boat or herself, Kurt wasn't sure. The boat was bouncing furiously in the surf, rolling with each incoming surge. 'I have to do this alone.'

'No.' Kurt spoke in English and deliberately kept his voice low and steady – the worst outcome now would be some kind of fracas. It seemed that the fisherman wasn't armed, but Kurt had no idea what the guy was capable of, and in this state of mind he wasn't sure about Hedy either. 'Hedy, this won't work. There are patrols out there. You won't get out of island waters.' He gesticulated at the little vessel; it looked pretty professional for something built in a shed with no proper materials, but a glance told him all he needed to know. 'Even if this reached France, you'd never make it past the beach.'

'I have to try. If I stay I'll be sent to a camp.' Her voice was choked with terror.

'Hedy, listen, please. I know you're afraid. But we can find an answer.' He remained quite still, keeping his focus on the two of them. If they decided to jump into the boat and start rowing, Kurt knew he probably wouldn't have the strength to pull it back. The fisherman, realising Kurt was unarmed, had now dropped his hands and was hanging firmly onto the other side of the hull. He was looking from Kurt to Hedy, waiting to see what the next move would be. In the incipient pale gold of the horizon, Kurt could now see the man's face – he seemed to be chewing slowly on some unseen root or tobacco, and beneath the leathered skin and whiskers his expression indicated he might be willing to put up a fight, if only to save his profit.

Kurt turned his attention back to Hedy, who had begun to buckle from the centre, as if someone had taken out an air stopper.

Her voice dropped to a whisper. 'It's the only way.'

'No. There's another, better way. Hedy, I'll keep you safe, I promise. But please, if you do one thing for me in your life, do not get in that boat.'

Hedy looked from him to the fisherman. She turned her head to look out across the bay, gazing at the navy-blue line of the horizon against the rapidly lightening sky. At that moment, to Kurt's relief, he could see reality descend, the recognition of the futility of it all. As her hopes drained away, she let go of the boat and swayed for a few seconds, then toppled backwards into the shallow water, arms flailing, head struggling to get above the surface. Kurt ran to her, hauling her sodden body from the water and held her, both of them trembling. Hedy was now weeping openly, while the fisherman stood silently by, staring at them with a blank expression, his jaw still moving as he chewed away, the boat beneath his hands bobbing up and down on the morning waves.

★

Hedy peeped through the hole in the curtain. It was almost dark, and the wind was picking up – she could hear it blowing through the high trees on Westmount.

'Make sure to weigh everything down properly,' Kurt reminded her. 'And be careful that no one sees you coming back. Is everything packed?'

Hedy peered into the wicker bag containing the clothes and personal effects that would travel with her. Everything she owned was in that bag, except for her coat that lay across her bedstead, still damp around the cuffs and hem. She hadn't had the heart to open it up and see what remained of her parents' letters, but suspected they were now papier-mâché. She would slit the hem open to retrieve her toothbrush later.

'Yes, that's everything. It's almost time. What will you do?'

'I'm going to go through the apartment, make sure there's nothing here that leaves any clues. What about the key?'

'Push it through the letterbox when you leave,' Hedy instructed. 'We won't be coming back.' She covered her mouth to stop a nervous belch. Acid swirled painfully in her empty stomach, but it wasn't food she craved, it was a cigarette. At that moment she would have traded anything for a quality smoke. But neither she nor Kurt had any tobacco left, and anyway, in her current state it would probably make her sick. She slipped on her coat, shivering as the damp sections touched her skin, then picked up the small pile of clothes they had chosen carefully together: a cotton shirt, a scraggy V-necked pullover, a tweed skirt and a battered pair of ladies shoes Kurt had bought at great expense from a black marketeer. She shoved the clothes down the front of the coat and buttoned it up, holding the items in place with one hand. 'I'll be as quick as I can.'

'Be very, very careful.'

She slipped out of the apartment, and began her journey down Pierson Road, one hand pressed to her chest to keep her little stash safe. The street, unsurprisingly so close to curfew, was deserted. She had to move quickly, silently; remembering the young deer that used to wander in the forests around Vienna, she tried to imitate their delicate footsteps. What luck, she thought bitterly, that she was now the same weight she had been at thirteen. Breathing hard, she hurried across the Esplanade and towards the seafront, her head constantly turning, her eyes darting to every flicker of light or perceived movement. Thank heaven there was barely any moon tonight, and a fair cover of cloud.

She reached the seafront, stepping delicately across the small railway track the Germans had laid last year to transport their building materials, and made her way to the steps leading down to the beach. After a last check for patrols, she began her descent. The stone risers were too high for comfort, and she had to take extra care not to slip – a tumble and a broken ankle now would put an end to everything. Finally she reached the beach. A few metres down the shore on either side were fences of barbed wire and signs declaring mines, but there was enough space around her for the plan to work. With her breath coming in thick, nervous pants, she pulled the clothes out of the coat and laid them on the sand. It seemed criminal to throw such items away, and for a moment she wondered about keeping the pullover. But she reminded herself that she had to make this look realistic. This was a piece of theatre, and as such needed some level of sacrifice. Folding them into a neat pile, she took the carefully worded note from her pocket and placed it on top. Searching around for the largest stone she could find, she picked it up and placed it on the note. Then she stood back to assess her work, knowing that she had only one chance to get this right.

Out in the bay the sweeper light of a sea patrol swung across the black water. She thought about Jean-Paul, counting his money in the dark corner of some tavern. Her last sight of him had been his stooped, hardy body hauling the boat back to its secret boathouse, perhaps unwilling to attempt the journey alone, or perhaps just deciding to postpone his adventure for another day. She hoped one day he'd make it, but understood that she would probably never know. He was part of the world she was leaving behind.

She had resisted Kurt's idea for several hours. Not because she thought staging her suicide an implausible idea – many islanders had been driven to it in the last couple of years, and she had more reason than most. It was more that in a small, heavily guarded community, permanent concealment seemed impossible. And could she even survive such a life? Whatever hardships she had faced up till now would seem like nothing. How long would it last? A year, two? Five, six, seven? The numbers spun in her head, meaningless, terrifying. But she had no other option. Kurt was right: if actual disappearance was out of the question, an illusion of it was the next best thing.

Taking a last look at the picture story she had created, she tiptoed back up the steps to the seafront and across the main road.

She hurried past what had once been the People's Park, now the headquarters of the Organisation Todt, walking as quickly as her legs could carry her, looking around her all the time. At the same time, she couldn't help but enjoy that fresh air and savour the scent of the ocean and the evergreens. She took in the glory of the stars, the majesty of the cumulus clouds scudding across the sky, and tried to imprint it on her mind. It would be a long time before she saw all this again.

She reached the narrow entrance to the alleyway that ran behind the terraced backyards of West Park Avenue and, with one final confirmation that no one was watching, scuttled down the passage until she reached the gate of number seven. Lifting the wooden latch, she let herself into the yard, crossed quickly to the back door and tapped four times as arranged. It opened immediately and Hedy stepped inside, shivering with cold and fear. Kurt was already standing in the kitchen, his features tight with anticipation. Dorothea hugged her briefly, then, without a word, closed the door and pulled across the heavy black bolt.

9

Kurt stood in the hallway of his billet, listening hard. Fortunately – or unfortunately, depending how one looked at it – this was a creaky old house, and every footstep on the upper floors could be heard downstairs. Other officers were moving around, padding across their rooms, crossing to the bathroom, closing doors. This was a useful time of day, he figured, when those on night shift had already left, and the rest of his colleagues were taking advantage of this break to wash, write letters home or snooze on their beds. In about fifteen minutes Fischer and the rest would pile downstairs for their evening meal, prepared by housekeeper Mrs Mezec, a local woman who came in daily to collect laundry and cook for the officers. Evidently she was a cousin of the original residents who had evacuated in 1940, and considered this a way to keep an eye on the place. She only spoke if absolutely necessary, and pocketed her wages each Friday with a sullen nod. Most of the officers ignored her or made tasteless jokes about how grateful she'd be for their attentions. Kurt often sniffed his dinner before eating it, knowing full well what revenge he would take in her shoes.

Strolling into the kitchen with what Kurt hoped looked like casual interest in tonight's menu, he found Mrs Mezec stirring a pot on the stove, and smiled at her. She acknowledged him without anything resembling a greeting. Kurt adjusted the chairs around the kitchen table, as if preparing for a dinner party, then sat down.

'What is dinner tonight, Mrs Mezec?'

'Pork stew.'

Kurt nodded with enthusiasm, wondering which poor local farmer had had their valuable porcine asset grabbed by soldiers and loaded onto a pick-up. Still, this meant there were likely to be further cuts of meat in the larder. Hedy had refused pork in the early days, but any such cultural taboos had long been discarded.

'Sounds delicious. Oh, by the way, the window in the bathroom is jamming again. Would you mind taking a look at it, please?'

She turned to him with a look that could sour milk. 'I'm not a handyman.'

Kurt beamed at her. 'Of course not, but you have a . . . what is the English word . . . a knack.'

Mrs Mezec laid down the wooden spoon in her hand and, without trying to hide the roll of her eyes, shuffled out of the kitchen to see to it. Kurt leapt up and opened the larder door, taking care to place a finger on the ball catch to prevent it making a pinging sound. It was dim inside, but as he suspected, a decent-sized leg of pork lay on the back shelf, covered by a sheet of muslin. All Kurt needed was a sharp knife to hack a slice off the front. He was about to take one from the drawer when he heard footsteps on the stairs. Damn it – he would have to sneak down in the early hours to compete his mission. He moved quickly to the sink and pretended to be washing his hands.

'Evening, Neumann.' Fischer was dressed smartly and smelled of scented soap. Where the hell he had got hold of something like that, Kurt could only guess. There were rumours that Fischer had now moved on from his pregnant married lover, and was now screwing the widow of some local aristocrat. 'Waiting for dinner?'

'I am. I'm starving.' Kurt kept his tone light and playful. 'Good day?'

Fischer grunted and threw the local paper onto the table. 'Bloody waste of time. Had to attend the burial of those Allied seamen washed up on the beach. Bigwigs decided to send a guard of honour and a firing party, show "respect". I ask you, what's the point?' Indeed, Kurt thought, considering how we treat them while they're alive. But he kept his jovial expression pasted in place. Fischer gestured to the paper. 'Think there's a photograph in there somewhere.' Kurt obediently took the paper and leafed through it while Fischer droned on. 'What sickens me is that the Allies are placing sea mines all round the islands, trying to stop our supplies coming across from France, but top brass still insist we doff our caps when we manage to blow them out the water.'

Kurt mumbled a passive agreement, but was no longer listening. There, in the middle of the paper, was a photograph of Hedy. It was a professional shot in a formal pose, and from her normal weight and creamy complexion he knew it must be an old one, presumably taken before the war. Perhaps she had had some portraits done as a gift to send to her family in Austria. Her hair, thick and lustrous, was swept back from her face; those eyes he knew so well were looking up towards something or someone to the right of the camera; and there was both a trace of a smile and a sense of sadness in her expression. But what drew Kurt's gaze was the text above it in German, and the same lines in English below:

NOTICE

The German authorities are looking for Miss Hedwig Bercu (see photograph), typist, of no nationality, 24 years of age, formerly residing at West Park, 1 Canon Tower. She has been missing from her residence since November 4th, 1943, and has evaded the German authorities. Any person who knows the whereabouts of Miss Bercu is requested to get in touch with the Feldkommandantur 515, who will treat any information with the strictest confidence. Anyone concealing Miss Bercu or aiding her in any other manner makes himself liable to punishment.

It was signed by the Field Commander, with today's date.

Kurt read and re-read the notice. Of course, he'd been expecting this. It was ten days since Hedy had effectively vanished from the outside world, and despite her efforts, it wouldn't have taken the secret police long to trace her address once they decided to find her. What was worrying, though, was that the notice mentioned nothing about a suicide. Had they not found the clothes and the note? Did they not believe it? Or was not mentioning it here some kind of trap? He glanced towards Fischer, wondering if the Nazi had deliberately led Kurt to the paper, knowing he would see the photograph. Perhaps this was all an elaborate ruse to gauge his reaction. Kurt's mind was still grabbing at possibilities when he realised Fischer was still talking to him.

'Don't you think?'

'Hmm?'

'I'm saying, next time we should just chuck the bodies in a hole and be done with it. Either that or burn them for fuel. Damn freezing in this house!' Fischer laughed at his own joke.

Kurt thought about the crematoria at the camps and imagined punching Fischer across the kitchen. Instead, he folded up the paper and smiled. 'Yes, it is. You know, an engineer friend of mine got hold of a load of logs last week. I'll pop over there, see if he'll sell us a couple.' He held up the newspaper, opting for a double bluff. 'Mind if I borrow this? There's a picture in here of that missing Jew – this guy lives near the compound, maybe he's seen something.'

Fischer, giving nothing away, merely nodded. Kurt walked into the hall, took his greatcoat from the peg, and slipped quietly out into the night. If he jogged some of the way he could be at West Park Avenue in thirty minutes.

★

'Okay, I am going to knock now.' Hedy laid her ten cards on the table.

Dorothea leaned over to look at them, and her face creased a little with embarrassment. 'You need at least three for a run, Hedy.'

'I have three – Queen, King, Ace?'

'But Ace is low in this game, remember?' Dorothea sat back in her chair with the kind of bright smile you'd give a child. 'Never mind, let's deal again. You've almost got it.'

'Do you mind if we stop?' Hedy heard the tightness in her own voice. 'I'm a little tired.'

It was a feeble excuse, but the thought of sitting at this table any longer, playing yet another round of this pointless game, set off a rising panic that was becoming all too familiar in recent days. As usual, it was accompanied by sweating, breathlessness and a barely controlled desire to run out into the street. It was all she could do to stay in her chair. Dorothea collected the cards and tucked them back into their pack.

'You're right, we've been playing for hours. Shall I see what we've got in the larder for dinner?'

Hedy stared at her new housemate, mystified by her stoicism. As if they might open the larder door and find shelves groaning with cold chicken and homemade tarts, and it were merely a matter of deciding what accompaniments to serve. Her unrelenting cheeriness, the determined avoidance of any alarming thought or memory, baffled Hedy; once or twice she'd actually wondered if Dorothea was quite right in the head. Just the other night, Dorothea had pulled the wireless from the cupboard under the stairs, and they had crouched in the doorway listening to the BBC news at the lowest possible volume, poised to thrust it back into its hiding place at a second's notice should anyone knock on the door. The news was depressing, the main headline being the Allied defeat in the Dodecanese. Yet at the end of the broadcast, Dorothea packed the wireless away and returned immediately to her movie scrapbooks, humming a jolly American big-band tune to herself, as if none of it had really touched her. The melody sawed at Hedy's nerves like cheese wire as she tried to occupy herself looking up the island of Leros in Dorothea's old atlas.

Hedy also noticed that Dorothea had begun to duck any mention of Anton, although Hedy had seen her kiss his photograph on her way up to bed. Hedy was only allowed to mention his name in the context of the past, and even then only happy memories were acceptable. Any talk of local trouble was closed down too, whether it was last week's night-bombing raids that almost shattered the windows, or public notices about the salt shortage. Conversely Dorothea would drag her adored movie stars into any conversation, as she did the imagined lives of the knitted dolls she kept on her bedroom windowsill. She introduced them to Hedy one by one, explaining the stories behind their names, and gazing into their expressionless woollen eyes as if she could read their thoughts. Sometimes Hedy looked at this overgrown, delusional kid and had to remind herself that this was the same woman who had bellowed patriotic songs into the faces of hostile Germans at the quayside.

She realised that Dorothea was waiting for an answer to her question.

'Of course,' Hedy replied, 'let's take a look.'

When Kurt had first suggested Dorothea's house as a hideout, Hedy had dismissed the idea. For one, she was certain Dorothea would never agree to such a dangerous arrangement on a permanent basis. And she would go crazy, she pointed out, finding Dorothea's company difficult enough over a couple of hours.

But Kurt had put up irrefutable arguments. Practically no one on this island could link the two of them, as they'd only been seen in public together a handful of times. Neither of them had any friends who might drop round or ask awkward questions, and with Anton away there was plenty of space. In any case, what alternatives did they have?

Dorothea said yes. She hadn't hesitated for a second, even when Kurt had spelled out the risks to her quite openly. On the night of Hedy's arrival, she seemed excited by the idea of a houseguest, flitting from room to room finding spare blankets for the old single mattress she and Kurt had hauled into the attic space through the tiny hatch. Beneath the eaves she had pushed back old packing cases and ancient, mouldering rugs to create a bed area, and placed up there a precious candle in a holder and a few books to read. Hedy could move freely around the house during the day, so long as she stayed away from the windows. Should anyone unexpected come to the door, a carefully placed dresser beneath the attic hatch and a short hook-on ladder would enable Hedy to climb into her hiding space and have the cover back within half a minute.

Hedy concentrated all her efforts into trying to feel grateful, but the reality of her new imprisonment was already taking its toll. Her new sleeping arrangements, despite her host's best efforts, were a particular torture. The pitch black when she blew out the candle was a nightmare; every settling sound of the house manifested as the scurry of a mouse or rat, and locating a precious match to allay her fear was nigh impossible. Hedy had taken to sleeping in her clothes as the space was so cold, and calls of nature either risked a catastrophe with a bucket or simply had to be ignored till daylight. She had started napping in the front room during the day to compensate for her sleepless nights, but was jolted awake by every footstep or raised voice on the street outside. For the first time, Hedy was starting to feel more anxious about the condition of her mind than of her body. A sense of obligation and gratitude kept such thoughts buried, and in any case she didn't want Dorothea fussing over her any more than she already did. But knowing that the one thing that would calm her would be a stroll in the fresh air, knowing that even this simple pleasure was now out of bounds, made her want to curl up into a ball and scream.

There was also the unsolvable issue of food. As Hedy's ration card could no longer be used, they were now forced to survive on a single ration, plus whatever extras Kurt could provide on the days he made it to the house. The two women were now as dependent on him as Kurt was reliant on their sense and security. Sometimes, in her fitful afternoon naps, Hedy dreamed of a three-stick tripod, bound with twine and trembling on a wasteland, whipped by a wind that threatened to send it flying into pieces. Then she would wake with a shout, and when Dorothea asked if she was all right, would pretend it was a childhood dream of monsters. She never knew if Dorothea believed her, but no further questions ever came.

The coded knock at the back door alerted them both. Checking at the kitchen window, Dorothea nodded that it was Kurt and hurriedly let him in. Hedy ran to him and hugged him, fighting disappointment when she saw he was carrying nothing more substantial than an evening paper.

'I'm sorry,' Kurt said, reading her thoughts. 'Fischer came down at the crucial moment. But I'll try and get down to the kitchen later tonight. I thought you should see this.'

He showed her the notice in the newspaper. Hedy read it several times and stared at the picture. It had been taken in 1939, and the physical changes in four years shocked her; she wondered if Kurt was thinking the same thing. She folded the paper and handed it back.

'We knew this was coming. Maybe they haven't found the clothes and the note yet. It's not like people are using the beaches.'

'Maybe.'

'Can you stay a while?'

Kurt shook his head, despondent. 'I'm meant to be out getting logs, I need to get back.' He stroked her face with his fingers. 'Do you have enough food tonight?'

Hedy made a titanic effort to smile. 'We'll manage. Don't worry.'

Kurt kissed her lightly on the lips then slipped out into the darkness of the alleyway and was gone again. Hedy felt a strong urge to weep, but choked it down. Dorothea's fingers fluttered on the back of Hedy's neck in an attempt to comfort her before propelling her towards the larder.

She opened the door. 'Right, then – what do we have here? How about a nice mashed swede with a boiled potato?'

'But there's barely enough for one.'

Dorothea laughed pointlessly. 'You boil the water and I'll cut the swede up, all right?' While Hedy ran freezing water into a pan, Dorothea took the vegetable and began to slice it on a wooden board, her hands pushing the knife expertly through the flesh, softly humming to herself a melody that Hedy vaguely recognised. She turned to Hedy. 'You know that one?'

Hedy forced herself to answer. 'It's from a movie, I think?'

'*Top Hat* – Fred Astaire and Ginger Rogers. It won the best song of 1935. Did you see the film?'

'I don't remember.'

The phrases from the newspaper notice were running through Hedy's mind. *Missing from her residence . . . evaded the German authorities . . . concealing Miss Bercu . . . liable to punishment . . .* Dorothea's knife kept disappearing into the swede, the slices falling one after the other, helpless against the gleaming metal. Over and over the blade sawed its way through the pale flesh. Hedy felt bile rise in her throat and realised that even tonight's meagre meal may be beyond her.

'Did you know,' Dorothea was saying, 'that Ginger Rogers had to fight the director to wear that dress? You know, the beautiful one with all the feathers? But she won, and it looks amazing, the most beautiful gown in any movie. When we've had dinner, I'll show you a picture. And I'll show you some of the other gowns of hers. She's got such style, don't you think? Would you like that?'

Hedy heard her own voice from the end of a long tunnel, as she forced out the smallest smile and replied, 'Yes. Yes, that would be fun.'

★

Kurt stood still on the pathway, his eyes skyward. All over the compound, workers had stopped to do the same, transfixed. The plane, clearly visible in the blue winter sky, climbed then dived, displaying its RAF roundel to the world. Anti-aircraft guns could be heard firing at it from every direction, and when smoke began to pour from its rear end, there was a gasp as everyone thought it had been hit. Kurt held his breath, waiting for the plane to tumble towards them, taking out houses and civilians in its path. But the plane turned to climb again, and the letter 'V' began to form in smoke in the sky.

The muttering around the compound grew to a full-throated hum as questions were thrown, one to another. Was it the beginning of a daylight raid, or just a warning of worse to come? Then, when the plane shut down its smoke and sped away northwards towards the English coast, most agreed it was probably a Christmas message of support for the islanders from Mr Churchill. Good for him, Kurt thought to himself, though an airdrop of food parcels would have brought these people a lot more joy.

He turned to head back to the metal lean-to where the latest collection of pick-ups were awaiting repairs. That was when he saw him. He would know that hat anywhere, perched idiotically to one side, bobbing through the crowd. And when those piggy eyes found Kurt and crinkled in a fake smile, Kurt knew immediately that this was not a social visit. Deciding that it was safer to begin on the front foot, Kurt approached him with his hand held out.

'Erich, how are you? It's been a while.'

Wildgrube's clammy hand slithered out to shake his own. 'It certainly has. A long while.'

Instantly, Kurt realised his mistake. Following that hideous night in the officers' club, Kurt had felt far too angry to face the man again in a social situation. Frankly, he didn't trust himself not to have one too many drinks and say something stupid, maybe even start a fight. He'd effectively dumped Wildgrube as a drinking partner, always coming up with excuses whenever Wildgrube suggested another 'boys' night' or boozing session. Apart from a birthday party Wildgrube had thrown for himself, to which Kurt had reluctantly shown up for half an hour, their recent encounters had been limited to official engagements, or bumping into each other in town. It was obvious now that Wildgrube felt slighted, and would take his revenge.

Kurt could have kicked himself for not seeing this one coming. He offered his warmest smile. 'So what can I do for you?'

Wildgrube pulled a small booklet from his inside pocket, flicking through it till he came to the right page. Kurt could see that it was a book of portrait photographs – people of interest to the secret police. He shoved it under Kurt's nose. 'This girl. You know her?'

Kurt didn't need to look, but made a show of peering at it. It was the photograph of Hedy that had appeared in the local paper. His blood began to pump, but his mind spoke to him softly – how he behaved in the next minute could change the entire course of his life.

'I saw that photograph in the *Post* a couple of weeks back. She's gone missing, hasn't she?' He looked back to Wildgrube, and saw that the man's eyes had never left his own.

'She has. Does she look familiar to you?'

Kurt thought fast, trying to calculate how much Wildgrube already knew, feeling the man's hot, sour breath on his face.

'A little.' He groped in his memory for what he had previously admitted, trying to recall the content of numerous conversations. 'Is this the Jew who was given a job here?' Wildgrube gave the tiniest nod. 'She doesn't look Jewish, actually. Maybe that's how the mistake occurred – someone forgot to check her papers.'

'But you remember her?'

'From around the compound.'

'Nothing else?'

'Afraid not.'

Wildgrube took back the booklet and tucked it into his pocket. Kurt knew from the twitch at the corner of the policeman's mouth that he had an ace to play, and was enjoying the anticipation of pulling it out. What a tragic little bastard, Kurt thought, getting his kicks in life from cat-and-mouse games like this.

Wildgrube made the most of his moment, dragging it out until the last possible second. 'Unfortunately, Lieutenant, that does not fit with what other people have told me. OT Feldwebel Schulz recalls quite clearly that when she came here for her job interview two years ago, you showed quite an interest in her. He remembers that you followed her down to the gate as she left.'

Jesus, Kurt thought, how did these people remember such details? Did they have nothing better to think about?

'Well, if Schulz remembers that, I probably did. To be fair, she's pretty cute . . . If you didn't know,' he added quickly.

'And other people here recall that you have been seen talking to each other on several occasions.'

Kurt stalled. They had been so careful in recent months. And of course Wildgrube could be lying. But there were other times, before he knew the whole picture, before he became conscious of security . . .

'I might have spoken to her once or twice. But to be honest, Erich' – Kurt tried to grin, uncertain he could pull off – 'I talk to a lot of girls. I mean, I don't take notes!' He chuckled, but Wildgrube's expression did not change.

'Are you aware that this woman was stealing petrol coupons for some considerable time?'

Kurt blew air between his lips with some force. 'So it's true. I heard the secretaries gossiping about it. You caught her?'

'We have sufficient grounds for her arrest.'

'And that's why she went missing?' Kurt girded himself, waiting.

'No doubt. Now this vermin is loose, unaccounted for. And her interest in petrol coupons does, I'm afraid, create a strong connection to you.'

Kurt breathed in. Attack was his only option now. 'Damn it, Erich, will you never let this go? I made one mistake, years ago, and served my time for it. Half the employees are pilfering something! Am I to be linked to everyone you catch for the rest of my time here?'

Wildgrube stared at him, emotionless. 'So you know nothing about this woman or where she might be?'

'Why on earth would I?' He threw up his hands in exasperation. 'But the size of this island, I wouldn't have thought she'd be hard to find.'

'That's the interesting thing.' Wildgrube readjusted his Alpine hat to an even more ridiculous angle. 'We found a pile of clothes on the beach, with a suicide note written in her own hand – we checked it against examples in the office.'

'Well, there you go. That answers your question, doesn't it?'

'It would, it would. Except for one thing. You are aware of the tidal system around these islands?' Kurt gave a neutral shrug, even though he knew exactly where this was going. 'It is one of the largest tidal ranges in the world. As we have seen from the bombing of ships in the vicinity, the bodies invariably end up on the island shores. Just last week a storm tide threw up all sorts of debris. Yet, no body has been reported. Not one sighting, after a month.'

'Maybe she weighted herself down, or the body hit a mine.'

'Perhaps. Or perhaps the whole "suicide" is a ruse and she is still somewhere on the island. If so, we will find her, and both she, and anyone assisting her, will be dealt with appropriately.' Wildgrube brushed imaginary fluff from his coat and lifted his hat. 'Good to talk to you again, Kurt. Thank you for your help in this matter. We shall speak again, I'm sure.' And, with a ludicrous little bow, he puttered off into the crowd. Kurt watched the hat dip and weave away. One word spun round and round his brain like a mantra. *Scheisse . . . scheisse . . . scheisse.*

*

It was Christmas Eve. The distant sound of carollers could be heard across the park, and doors up and down the street banged throughout the day as housewives scurried into town and back, sniffing out every shop rumoured to have festive treats in store. Most returned empty-handed. The small patches of sky visible at the top of the windows were already the colour of slate, sucking the colour out of the chimneys and rooftops; somewhere, beyond the clouds, the sun was preparing to set.

Hedy sat with her chin on her knees, hugging her shins for warmth, and wriggled to get comfortable. No fat reserves, she'd recently discovered, meant that sitting for long periods, even with a cushion, was a painful experience. But what else could she do? She had spent the afternoon wandering aimlessly from room to empty room, searching for the balance between warming up and burning calories, but last night even climbing the stairs to the attic had left her panting and dizzy. Her weakness frightened her. What if there was an emergency that meant she needed to run? What if she got really sick? Approaching Dr Maine for any kind of treatment would mean drawing him into this conspiracy. So far, no further arrests had been reported in connection with her case, implying that either Quinn had kept Maine's name out of it, or that the Germans had chosen not to pursue a useful individual based on hearsay. Dorothea told Hedy she thought she'd seen Maine leaving the hospital two weeks before, though it was dark and she couldn't be certain. Hedy had desperately hoped that she was right.

She looked at the calendar on the wall – a homemade affair made from movie magazine cuttings, the dates marked out in stubby pencil. Images of Christmases in Vienna floated across her mind – the lights in the squares, the creaking, laden stalls of produce in the market. Though the family had never celebrated it at home, she'd always loved the atmosphere on the streets, soaking up the excitement of Christian friends and neighbours. One year, Roda had been given a huge box of yellow and pink bonbons by an admirer. She wondered what Roda was doing today – if she were still alive.

She had been living in Dorothea's house for a little over six weeks now. For every seven days, they had between them two ounces of margarine, seven ounces of flour, three of sugar, four ounces of meat, plus four and a half pounds of bread. Tea was a flavour barely remembered. Salt was now impossible to obtain unless you could get access to seawater. Each Friday, Dorothea burst eagerly through the door, beaming all over her pallid little face, and laid the week's fare on the kitchen table. For a few moments they rejoiced as they devoured an acceptable lunch – perhaps a slice of tongue to go with a crust of tasteless Occupation bread, or a scrap of imported mutton that could be stewed into an edible form with some potatoes. Then they would force themselves to stash the rest of the goods in the larder, and eke out their supplies for the days to come. Kurt still brought whatever he could, but knowing that he was under surveillance, his visits were currently reduced to once or twice a week, often empty-handed. Last Sunday he stayed no more than ten minutes, giving Hedy only the briefest hug and kiss on the forehead; sometimes she wondered if that particular deprivation wasn't the most painful of all.

Hours drifted by. It was now completely dark outside, and cold in the house. Hedy didn't dare to light a fire; there was so little wood left, and in any case it would have been reckless to display any signs of life while Dorothea was absent. She compromised by lighting the paraffin lamp. From next door came the sound of festive merriment – numerous voices raised in excitement. Hedy tried to remember what it was like to have raucous, carefree fun like that.

When the hands of the clock reached eight, she felt her anxiety rise. Dorothea never stayed out this late in the evening, even when she visited her ailing grandmother. She had left at lunchtime, muttering something about visiting a cousin in St

Martin's. It had struck Hedy as odd at the time – Dorothea had never mentioned this cousin before, and it was out of character for her to be so evasive about her movements. Hedy guessed that she was up to something, but was sensible enough, or cowardly enough, not to ask.

Eight thirty. Hedy began to wonder what she'd do if Dorothea didn't come back. There was no telephone, and anyway, who would she ring? There was no means of finding anything out; she couldn't even go out and buy a newspaper. She would be dependent on Kurt's next visit, not just for information but for her next meal. As the minutes ticked by, her anxiety grew, and it took every shred of self-discipline not to pull back the curtains and peer out in to the dark, deserted street.

Suddenly she heard the clip-clop of a horse's hooves and the grind of heavy cart wheels. Horses rarely came down this street, and never at this time. Hedy rose from her seat and, taking the paraffin lamp with her, moved to the doorway between the sitting room and hallway, breathing heavily. From outside came bizarre sounds – scraping, banging and the grunts of people straining to move heavy objects. And then, another noise – a high-pitched screech that sounded like . . . No, Hedy told herself, she was imagining it. It couldn't possibly be . . . ?

The front door flew open and the noise crashed into the house like a double-decker bus. Squealing, gasping and clattering. Hedy gaped, astonished, as Dorothea slammed the front door behind her and pressed herself against it, a mixture of panic and triumph on her face. At the same time Hedy let out a shriek as something at knee-height brushed quickly past her legs. Her eyes followed the squealing sound that accompanied the shape, and there it was, careering down the hallway towards the kitchen – a young pig. She stared at Dorothea, too shocked to speak.

Dorothea's voice was shrill with excitement. 'Quickly! Trap it in the kitchen!' Breathless, she pushed Hedy towards the kitchen door. 'I was going to bring it round the back, but I was afraid it might escape up the alleyway. We have to kill it before the neighbours hear.'

Hedy looked from Dorothea to the pig, which was now careering around the kitchen in panicky circles, looking for a way out.

'Are you *insane*? Neither of us knows how to butcher a pig.' She pressed herself against the wall, half expecting the animal to attack her. A familiar sentence from her childhood was running through her head: 'And the pig, because it has a cloven hoof that is completely split, but will not regurgitate its cud; it is unclean for you. You shall not eat of their flesh, and you shall not touch their carcasses; they are unclean for you.' She had long abandoned kosher rules – pork being one of the only meats occasionally available on the island – but killing it herself? That was an entirely different matter.

But Dorothea had a glint in her eye Hedy had never seen before. 'We can do it, between us. We can use this.' Dorothea began rummaging through an old wooden crate in the hallway, which she used for storing old newspapers, as Hedy looked anxiously towards the animal, now head-butting the walls in its desperation to escape. From the bottom of the pile of papers, Dorothea produced a slim, flat item that, in the dimness, Hedy could barely make out. Only when Dorothea undid the catch and pulled it from its sheath did Hedy realise she was holding a knife, about twenty centimetres long with a clean, gleaming blade. 'Anton left it with me when he went away, in case I should ever need it. It's sharp enough.' She held it out to Hedy like a prize.

Hedy put her hand on the wall to steady herself, scarcely believing this was happening. She was aghast at this stranger before her, a crazed, fearless lunatic who stashed forbidden weapons and murdered wild animals in her own kitchen. 'No, Dorothea, I can't! I can't even touch it. Really!'

Dorothea placed her hand on Hedy's arm, gentle but firm. 'I can't do this alone. You have to help me.' Hedy's head continued to shake, but Dorothea's grip grew tighter. 'I mean it. If just one neighbour gets wind of this, they could call the Germans down here.' She listened for a moment, hearing the revelries next door. 'They're having a party – perfect. Come on!'

She walked purposefully into the kitchen, stuffing the blade down the front of her brassiere. The pig became even more agitated. Its trotters were clattering on the kitchen floor like a satanic tap dance. Hedy could see the hairs on its leathery skin, make out the pink moistness of its snout. She wanted to scream, but Dorothea's voice was calm. 'Keep that door closed, or it'll get loose in the house. Get the old tin bath, the one that's meant for the firewood – that should be big enough.'

Too frightened to disobey, Hedy manoeuvred herself towards the larder, making sure not to turn her back on the animal. She groped in the dark for the container on the larder floor and grabbed the end of it, hauling it noisily from the cupboard and skidding it across the kitchen floor with her foot.

'Good. Now we just have to catch the bugger!' Dorothea hissed. Hedy held the lamp a little higher. 'Just keep thinking about the pork steaks we'll have! Right . . . I'm going to try and trap it in this corner. Copy me, keep moving forwards.' Dorothea opened her arms and made some low whooping noises to encourage the pig backwards into the far corner. Placing the lamp on the side – the last thing they needed now was to be plunged into total darkness – Hedy extended her arms and moved forward too, creating a pincer movement between the two of them. The squealing grew louder, and Hedy longed to close her eyes and shut it all out, but her eyes remained fixed on their terrified prey. As she got close, Dorothea dropped to her knees and grabbed the pig by its middle, forcing its backside into the corner.

'Grab its front legs, Hedy, quickly!' Her tone was so urgent that Hedy did as she was told, thrashing with her arms to find the animal's legs, turning her face to the side in terror of being bitten, until she managed to grab one and then the other. Dorothea somehow managed to turn herself around until she had got a proper grip of its back end and lifted the animal by its rear legs. 'Get it into the bath, on its back! Try to hold it still while I cut its throat.'

Hedy heard her own voice, shrill, half screaming: 'I can't, I can't!'

'You can! It's only a wee one, it's not that strong. Now lift!'

With huge effort they managed to swing the struggling beast up and into the tin bath. Hedy fought to hold a pair of legs in each hand as the animal twisted and writhed. Suddenly there was a squirting noise and the smell of shit was in her nostrils. Hedy retched violently, knowing that actual vomit was not far behind.

'Quickly!' Dorothea was screaming herself now. Party or no party, the neighbours were going to hear something soon if they didn't finish this fast. Just then, Hedy saw Dorothea pull the sheath knife from her brassiere and slice it forcefully across the pig's throat. The squealing stopped instantly, but the thrashing grew worse.

'Again, again!' Hedy cried. 'It's not dead!'

Dorothea pulled the knife free where it had got stuck in the flesh and slashed again. Immediately the flailing stopped, and the animal lay limp in the bath, half submerged in its blood and shit. Hedy rushed to the kitchen sink and vomited green bile and water, having nothing else in her stomach. By the time she turned back, Dorothea had hauled the animal up by the neck and slit its belly from top to bottom, spilling guts and organs into the disgusting soup beneath. Her hands and wrists were covered in blood and gore. When most of the blood had drained she let the carcass slip down, and looked towards Hedy with a look of overwhelming relief. Only then, hearing the wheezing in her breath and seeing the tears in Dorothea's eyes, did Hedy understand the superhuman effort it had taken her to accomplish this. Hedy moved towards her and squeezed her arm. 'Well done. That was extraordinary.'

Dorothea shut her eyes and shook her head. 'Come on. We need to get this thing cleaned up – I'll bury the entrails in the park. Then . . .' She smiled. 'Then we can make our Christmas dinner!'

★

Hedy moved the mouthful of pig's liver across her tongue, savouring it, letting the flavour transport her. She had already consumed one of the kidneys and a portion of its heart, but had saved the tastiest part till last. A little juice ran from the corner of her mouth and she saved it with her finger, pushing it back into her mouth. At that moment Dorothea did exactly the same, and both of them giggled like children. Hedy took another bite, astonished at herself. She had anticipated revulsion, or at least regret; the trauma of the slaughter, the nausea she'd felt scraping the filth from the carcass under the cold tap, the imagined horror of her mother. But right now she felt as if every cell within her body was bursting into life, like a wilting plant finally taking water. Singing still swelled and faded from the other side of the party wall, adding to the sense of celebration, and the light of the paraffin lamp danced on the wall above the table. Dorothea had opened a bottle of Beaujolais she had been saving for a special occasion – it was a little vinegary, but velvety on the tongue – and by the third sip Hedy could already feel its effect.

'What should we do with the rest of it?' Hedy wondered aloud, using a small crust of bread to mop the remains of the juice from her plate.

Dorothea shrugged. 'Tomorrow we must skin it and cut it up. Then we can keep it in the attic where it's cold – sorry, I'll put it as far away from you as I can. Should last at least a week.'

'What about the backyard?'

'Too dangerous. Someone might steal it, or a dog will get to it.'

'Do you think we can get through it all in a week?'

'If we don't, we can trade it for eggs or fresh rabbits. There's still things you can get in the country parishes, if you know who to ask.'

Hedy's chewing was interrupted by a mouthful of gristle, but she happily swallowed it anyway. 'How did your cousin manage this? I thought the Germans accounted for every piglet born?'

'The farmers have their tricks. They'll sneak a sow into another pen while the Germans aren't looking, so it gets counted as a different pig – then the Jerries don't notice when one goes missing.' She snorted laughter through her nose. 'Apparently one farmer tied a bonnet on a pig and put it in his bed, told the Jerries it was his sick mother! They wouldn't even go in the room!'

Hedy burst out laughing, and they continued eating for a few more minutes until she piped up again: 'I still don't understand why your cousin agreed to help us? I thought, apart from your grandmother, none of your family spoke to you any more?'

Dorothea glanced down and hesitated a moment before replying. 'He didn't want to help me, and he made it clear it's just this once. We won't be able to ask him for anything again.'

'So why today? Because it's Christmas?'

Dorothea shook her head. 'I told them Anton was dead.'

Hedy sat back in her seat. 'You lied to your own family?'

'I don't know that it is a lie.'

'Dorothea!'

'I've heard nothing for months – Anton may very well be dead.'

Hedy felt a rush of pity. 'You can't really think that? How do you carry on?'

Dorothea looked her straight in the eye. 'I love Anton with all my heart, but we all have to face facts. God will find a path for me, for all of us, if it's his will.'

Hedy shifted uncomfortably in her chair. 'You still believe in God? After the last few years?'

Dorothea looked a little puzzled. 'Of course.' She turned her attention back to her plate, wiping the last specks of meat juice with a damp finger, wasting nothing. Hedy did the same, glancing up at Dorothea's face. There were dark rings beneath her eyes and flecks of grey at the sides of her jet-black hair. But she noticed a rigid set of her jaw and the pale lips that tightened when she was forced into an opinion or decision.

As Dorothea stood to collect the plates and take them to the sink, Hedy stopped her. 'Is that why you agreed to shelter me here?'

Dorothea turned, the plates in her hand. 'What do you mean?'

'Because you believe it's what God would want? That it's your duty?'

'I never thought about it like that.'

'But you know what you're risking,' Hedy pressed her. 'What if Anton *is* still alive? He could be back in less than a year! You're both young, you'd have the rest of your lives together. Yet you've chosen to jeopardise all that for me.'

Dorothea thought for a moment, then sat back down, placing the crockery on the table. 'I didn't really think about any of that, to be honest. You're Anton's closest friend here, and you were in trouble. It was just the right thing to do.'

Hedy shook her head. 'I don't want to be responsible for anything happening to you. Kurt could find me another place.'

'Don't talk daft.' Dorothea put her arms around her. 'You're far safer here. And I like the company.' She began to pull away, anticipating Hedy's usual reluctance, but this time Hedy reached up and held her in the embrace.

'Thank you.'

They stayed like that for a moment until the coded tap at the back door made them both jump. Dorothea hurried to open it, and Kurt, his collar turned up high for warmth and concealment, stepped lightly inside. Hedy, warmed by the wine and events of the day, ran to him and kissed him passionately, right in front of Dorothea. Both women gabbled at him for several minutes, talking over each other in their enthusiasm to tell the story of the pig's arrival, the drama of the slaughter, the wonderful meal.

Kurt listened to all of it before pushing back his hair with one hand and looking at both of them with a combination of admiration and horror. 'If that cart had been stopped on the way over here, you'd have been arrested along with your cousin. Within a couple of days we'd all be in jail.'

Dorothea nodded. 'I know.'

Kurt looked to Hedy for agreement, but Hedy shrugged. 'Dorothea did this for us, Kurt. I think she's been incredibly brave.'

Kurt raised the small glass of wine that Dorothea had poured for him. 'You're right. To a merry Christmas, and a better one next year.' Then he glanced awkwardly at Dorothea and back to Hedy, too embarrassed to be specific. 'I won't be missed at my billet for a couple of hours . . .'

Without waiting to be asked, Dorothea gestured towards the hallway. 'Use my bedroom – I need to clean the kitchen up anyway.' Hedy blushed. But Dorothea made a shooing movement with her hands. 'Go on, make the most of it. It's Christmas, after all.'

Kurt nodded his thanks and took Hedy by the hand, leading her towards the stairs. Halfway up, Hedy stopped and leaned over the banisters. 'Thank you. You're a good friend, Dory.' She hesitated. 'I believe Anton is still alive. And he'd be really proud of you.' Then she followed Kurt up the stairs, feeling her body grow warm at the thought of him.

June 1944

'Hedy! Hedy, wake up!'

Hedy sat bolt upright on her mattress, almost banging her head on the rafter above, filled with panic before she was even properly conscious. In the slivers of morning light rising through the floor hatch, she could just make out Dorothea's features, and saw that she was smiling.

'What? What is it?'

'Listen. Can you hear them?'

Hedy sat perfectly still. The sound was outside – far way, but loud enough to penetrate the walls and windows. It was indisputably the throbbing drone of aeroplane engines. Not in ones and twos, as they were used to, but in dozens, perhaps scores. The noise was followed by another, louder and intermittent – the rat-a-tat-tat of anti-aircraft fire. Hedy pushed the blankets off her legs and clambered across the rafters towards the hatch. 'I want to see them.'

Dorothea nodded and let herself down the ladder into the bedroom below, with Hedy following behind. They hurried to the window. Dorothea pulled back the blackout and the thin fabric curtain, and pressed her face to the window, her eyes skipping about to detect the movement of neighbours. Finding the backyards deserted, she beckoned Hedy towards her.

'Here . . .' She grabbed a small towel from her bed and handed it over. 'Wrap this around your hair, as if you'd washed it. Then, if someone sees you, I can say it was me, and they made a mistake.'

Hedy did as she was told, then, kneeling on the bed, pushed her face towards the window, looking out across the yard and onto the backs of the houses beyond. The long-forgotten colours of the outside world, even on this unseasonably cloudy day, set her senses alight – the emerald of the scrubby grass, the subtle blues and lilacs of the rain clouds! But the real excitement was in the distant sky. A squadron of planes, like a cluster of disciplined insects in rigid formation, was heading towards the French coast, followed by another, then another. She sat motionless for a moment, enthralled by the light, pattern and complexity, then dropped the curtains back.

'What time did this start?'

'A little while ago, and there's no sign of it stopping.'

'So this is it? The Allied invasion?'

'I don't see how it can be anything else.'

Hedy involuntarily clenched both fists and her teeth, emitting an impassioned growl. 'Come on, come on! Let those bastards have it!' Then she saw the wince on Dorothea's face, and instantly regretted it. 'Oh, Dory, I'm sorry.'

Dorothea shook her head. 'Don't worry. I know what you meant.' She hastily buttoned her cardigan, and Hedy saw that her hands were trembling. 'I'm going down to the market, see what I can find out.'

'Be careful!' Hedy called after her. 'The Jerries will be on edge today.'

Hedy, washed and dressed, tried and failed to find something to distract her while she waited for Dorothea to return. The tick of the kitchen clock punctured the air as she paced the hallway; she could still hear the far-off hum of aeroplane engines and the crackle of German guns. She ached to switch on the wireless in the cupboard, but didn't dare. There was nothing for lunch, but she felt too nervous to eat.

Eventually, a little after four, Dorothea returned, flushed with excitement. Hedy immediately dragged her into the kitchen and sat her down at the table.

'It's crazy out there!' Dorothea's voice was thick with agitation, and Hedy could hear her asthma bubbling underneath. 'All the locals are smiling, some are even wearing red, white and blue rosettes! There are truckloads of Germans being driven out to man the gun emplacements and to guard billets. One man told me there are barbed-wire blockades across some roads in and out of town.'

Hedy breathed deeply, trying to take it all in, attempting to picture the scene. 'So Jerry thinks a full-scale Allied attack is on the way?'

'Must do. They were stopping lots of people, just ordinary pedestrians and cyclists, checking their papers.' Dorothea's hands fidgeted in her lap. 'There are so many rumours. Someone reported an American ship in St Aubin's bay this morning, but it's nonsense. A woman told me she thought she'd seen Churchill himself in a car with the Field Commandant. I think she may be sick in the head,' she added sadly.

Hedy reached out and patted Dorothea's hand; it was a mauve colour, and the temperature of stone. 'We need to stay calm. There will be more news on the BBC tonight.' She hesitated. 'I don't suppose you saw Kurt?'

Dorothea shook her head. 'I doubt he'll be able to visit for the next few days. They're all on high alert.'

But a little before nine, just as they had finished their dinner of boiled macaroni, and Dorothea was about to pull the radio from its hiding place, Hedy heard Kurt's tap on the door. Grey-faced with dark rings beneath his eyes, he slumped at the kitchen table, throwing his cap onto the neighbouring chair, while the two women stood around him, too nervous to settle.

'It's huge – I mean, massive. Thousands landing on the beaches in Normandy, vast air support. It's got to be the start of the end.'

'So what happens now, I mean, here on the island?' Dorothea, beside the sink, was pushing up and down on her toes with excitement.

Kurt pulled a copy of the local evening paper from his inside pocket. 'Read for yourself.'

Hedy picked up the paper, and read aloud the proclamation dominating the front page: '"Germany's enemy is on the point of attacking French soil. I expect the population of Jersey to keep its head, to remain calm, and to refrain from any acts of sabotage, and from hostile acts against the German forces, even should the fighting spread to Jersey. At the first sign of unrest or trouble, I will close the streets to every traffic and will secure hostages. Attacks against the German forces will be punished by death. Signed, the Commandant."' Hedy shivered. 'They sound scared. They really expect the locals to rebel?'

'God knows,' Kurt replied. 'They're taking some precautions – shipping out non-essential workers like nurses and canteen staff. And College House staff are sleeping on the premises in case of a night attack, though I don't see what good that will do.'

'So they don't intend to surrender?'

'Most of the ordinary soldiers here would happily surrender, but the high-ups won't stand for it. With the defences we've put up in the last two years, it could be a bloodbath.' He rubbed his eyes, as if trying to press the images away. 'But I suspect the Allies know that. Which is why I don't think—' He stopped abruptly.

Hedy felt her surge of hope ebbing away. 'You don't think what?'

Kurt sighed deeply, from the gut. 'The Allies will be looking to limit their losses. If I were them, I would press on, try to gain ground on the Continent. The Channel Islands are tiny, after all. Plenty of time to come back for them later, when they've pushed the enemy line further.'

Hedy, suddenly feeling a little unsteady, sank down onto the remaining chair. 'You're saying they'll just . . . go around us?'

'Quite possibly.'

'But if that happens, the islands will be completely cut off. There'll be no food or fuel from France or England. How will we survive?' She felt a painful lump form in her throat. 'We'll all starve together.'

Kurt squeezed her hand, but it brought no comfort. 'Exactly.'

★

'The public telephone system will remain suspended. A section of Gloucester Street jail is being set aside for casualties, and a Red Cross flag will be placed above it. Food stocks are to be removed from out-of-town depots and brought into stores in town . . .'

Baron von Aufsess paused, reading ahead down his list as if mentally sifting out some of the items. Kurt, standing a good six metres from him, swore he could hear the new chief administrator emit a small sigh. Then the baron coughed and continued, his clipped, aristocratic voice booming out across the hall. Something about potato supplies, and locals being warned away from the beaches. It was all the usual business: protect the garrison, override the populace, no surrender.

Kurt let his gaze wander. Beyond the windows of College House the sun was blazing, gulls were gliding on the summer breeze, and far above Allied planes continued to stream across the azure sky. Now and then came the dull boom of one of the giant cannons across the Channel; last night anti-aircraft guns had brought down a British pilot at Les Landes, destroying two houses.

The baron continued to list instructions and priorities: all military were to use discretion, but come down hard on the smallest dissent; the deportation of all civilians to France could not be ruled out at this stage. Kurt looked at the haggard faces around the room, rigid with tension beneath a stoical veneer, and wondered who they believed they were fooling. It was just like the picturehouses where he'd watched Bela Lugosi films as a youth, when all the boys jutted out their chins and pretended not to be scared. Kurt's own stomach had been churning for days now, and the acrid scent of sweat and sulphur in this room told him he was not alone.

Von Aufsess reached the end of his list and instructed his deputy to hand out new sectional orders. Kurt was charged with checking the working condition of every truck within his compound, maximising transport potential should the need arise. Turning to leave, Kurt spotted Wildgrube at the back of the room. Like all the secret police, he was today dressed in military uniform, the first time Kurt had ever seen him so attired. From his strutting gait and the gleam in his eye, Kurt saw that the spy relished the opportunity to appear in public as a real soldier, and was forced to admit that it gave the little oik a genuine sense of authority. Hoping to avoid him in the crowd, Kurt pressed towards the door, but within a minute found Wildgrube at his shoulder.

'Kurt, my friend. How are you?'

'Just fine, Erich. Looking very smart today.'

Wildgrube played with his cuffs. 'We must all be on our best game to face what is before us.' Kurt nodded, hoping that might be the end of the conversation. He'd seen little of Wildgrube since his attempt to intimidate him at the compound; Kurt had long hoped that a cold trail, combined with simple lack of manpower, had caused the investigation to be abandoned. Kurt had spotted the odd secret police minion outside his billet, and had twice curtailed a visit to West Park Avenue on the suspicion that he was being followed, but overall it seemed that Wildgrube had found other fish to fry. Kurt threw the spy a polite smile and went to move on, but felt a tug at his elbow. 'Of course, recent events will necessitate a little . . . housekeeping.'

'Housekeeping?'

'Old cases, unsolved problems. We need to reduce the burden of excess feeders on the island.'

What kind of mind, Kurt thought, divided the human population up into such categories? 'So?'

'So, we must make sure there are no ancient parasites lurking. One thing about me, Kurt . . .' He smirked, a cobra that had spotted a wounded mouse. 'I am often commended for my scrupulous cleanliness.' He patted Kurt on the shoulder then disappeared through the doorway and down the corridor, his blond head bobbing through the crowd.

Kurt watched him go with an indifferent sniff. Wildgrube had no more information about Hedy eight months on than he had in the week of her disappearance – he merely enjoyed the power of menace. If he had discovered anything new he'd have taken great delight in hauling Kurt into the notorious Silvertide building for questioning. Kurt decided there was enough to worry about this week – real, imminent dangers that far outweighed the niggling irritation of this idiot.

Kurt forced his way into the grey flannel mass of the corridor, pushing past the other officers, watching their reactions to the morning's briefing. Some were grimly silent; others opted for fake bravado, braying about finally seeing some action. He stuffed his hands into his pockets to imply endeavour and urgency, and instantly felt the lining of the right pocket, loose for some time, give way under the weight, allowing his hand to slip through to the inner layer. Glancing at the large mirror in the reception hallway to see if it was noticeable, he took in his whole reflection. Weight loss was causing the uniform to hang off him, like a schoolboy in his father's clothes. There was a grass stain on the knee of his trousers, picked up on an awkward repair job last week, which Mrs Mezec's half-hearted laundering had not removed. And now he noticed a button missing from the front of his tunic, causing the fabric to gape instead of giving a crisp, smart line.

The thousand-year Reich, he reflected with irony, was literally starting to fall apart at the seams.

★

'But my absolute favourite part . . .' Dorothea's eyes shone with excitement as she recalled the moment. Her palms ironed flat the open pages of the scrapbook on the table. ' . . . is where she dumps Westley at the altar and rushes for her car. It's Peter she really loves, you see, and she realises that true love is more important than anything.'

'And her father approves?' Hedy traced the outline of Claudette Colbert's face with her finger. The edges were starting to curl for want of fresh paste, and her right ear had already disappeared.

'Her father is the one who tells her to go! He knows she doesn't really love Westley, you see, and he wants her to be happy.' Dorothea turned the page. Shafts of golden-pink evening light slanted through the kitchen window and onto the table, creating patterns on the frayed paper and highlighting every line of Dorothea's face. 'When all this is over, I'll take you to see it. It's my favourite movie.'

'I'd like that. It sounds wonderful.'

Hedy slowly gathered up the two plates and spoons they had used for their evening meal of unsalted potatoes, and carried them across to the draining board. The potatoes had been hard in the centre, and sat heavy in her stomach; now that the gas supply was shut off and they were forced to rely on the communal bakehouse, it was pot luck whether what Dorothea picked up at the end of the day was cooked through at all.

'Dorothea, do you ever think about your own parents?' The question was out of her mouth before she'd had time to weigh it, and she instantly regretted it. Dorothea always neatly sidestepped any reference to her family, making it clear that the subject was out of bounds. But Hedy had noticed, in recent weeks, they had both been voicing more direct, personal questions than they would have dreamed of asking six months ago. Perhaps it was the sense that the end to this bizarre, enforced marriage might not be far away, though neither of them dared to venture what that end might look like.

Dorothea kept her eyes on the scrapbook. 'Sometimes.'

'You ever think about going to see them?'

'Waste of time. My stepfather wouldn't allow it.'

'Are you sure? It's been so long.' A long silence. Dorothea slowly turned another page. Claudette Colbert gave way to Katharine Hepburn posing with a besuited Cary Grant. 'Kurt says lots of older people are starting to get sick, with the shortage of food and medicines.'

'I know.' A strip of paper bearing the words *Bringing Up Baby* in curly, romantic lettering escaped completely from its ancient paste and fell to the bottom of the page. Dorothea caught it and stubbornly tried to force it back into position, to no avail.

Hedy returned to her chair. 'Only. . . I know if I had the opportunity to see my parents just once more, no matter how painful—'

'Hedy, I tried, okay?' Dorothea slammed the book shut, her voice uncharacteristically loud. 'I went up there in February, on my mother's birthday. My stepdad wouldn't come to the door, said if my mother didn't come back into the house he was done with her too.' She shrank back, ashamed of her outburst. 'My grandmother wrote to them, he tore the letter up. Like he said – I'm dead to them.'

Hedy placed a hand on Dorothea's arm. 'I'm sorry. You never said.'

'You have enough problems of your own.'

'It was brave to try.'

Dorothea raised her finely plucked eyebrows, held the thought for a moment, and let them fall again. 'I loved Anton so much, and I really believed that was all that mattered. But now . . .' She looked towards the window, and the last tips of the sun's rays coloured her eyes an extraordinary blue. 'Now I'm not so sure. Even if he does come back. At least you and Kurt have each other now. Sometimes, when I see the two of you together . . .'

'I'm sorry. We're not trying to—'

'Don't be silly. I know. You would never try to hurt me.'

Hedy felt a flush of shame as a dozen memories rushed in: her resentment and dismissal of Dorothea at the start, her hope that she and Anton would cancel the wedding. Dorothea must have sensed at least some of it, yet in those wide, trusting eyes there was not a speck of resentment. Hedy had just begun to phrase some kind of apology in her head when Dorothea leaned back in her chair and began to cough.

'Do we have any mustard powder left?'

'I don't know, why?'

'I'm having trouble breathing.'

Hedy rushed to the larder and scrabbled through the shelves looking for the bottle. Sure enough, at the back was a small tin with a spoonful of mustard powder inside – she grabbed it and returned to Dorothea's side. 'I've got it. Give me one minute.'

Hedy shook out some of the powder onto a saucer. From the tap she added a few drops of water, dripping it in with her fingers, and stirred it into a yellow paste. Dorothea was by now leaning back in her chair, the wheezing of her breaths coming in short, strained gasps. Hedy pulled Dorothea's blouse open and smeared the paste onto her chest. Dorothea recoiled a little and began to whimper. 'Burns!'

'I know.' Hedy deliberately kept her voice low and steady. 'But it will help. Try to keep your breaths regular. Count with me – in for five and out for five. One, two . . .' Her mind raced ahead. If Dorothea turned blue or began to lose consciousness, what was she to do? Kurt would not call till tomorrow at the earliest. Asking the neighbours was impossible – Hedy had never even seen them, far less judged whether they could be trusted with the sudden appearance of a foreigner on their street. '. . . And five. Now the same, going out. Come on, Dory, you can do it.' She scrabbled for a plan. Perhaps she could drag Dorothea onto a neighbour's path, bang on the door then run back to the house before anyone saw her? The hospital was less than ten minutes away, surely someone would go for help? Though even there, the chances of them having any medication to help her were almost zero. 'And again. You're doing well.'

The breaths grew shorter and more tortuous. In the fading light of the kitchen, Hedy peered at Dorothea's features, and saw that the shade of lilac ash she most feared was now blooming on her lips. Her eyelids were drooping a little and she was starting to slump down on the tabletop. Hedy sat her back in her chair and held her upright to keep the airways open, all the while stroking her hair and keeping up a constant muttering of encouragement. But as the minutes crawled by and the hissing breaths grew weaker, Hedy knew she had to make a decision.

'Dory, I'm going to have to go for help. Just try to hang on.' She turned to go, but felt a sudden clamp on her wrist. For a moment she barely believed it was Dorothea, so strong was the grip, but it pinned her where she stood. Then Dorothea, clinging to the struggling outbreaths as they fought their way through the fog of her lungs, pushed out the words: 'No! Dangerous!'

'I know, but the hospital is the only place we have any chance of help.'

Dorothea's hold, using only her thumb and forefinger, actually increased. 'No! Not worth it!' She extended the fingers of her right hand and held it towards Hedy's face. 'Five minutes.'

Seeing that the suggestion was simply causing more stress, and afraid that Dorothea wouldn't survive her absence for longer than a few minutes, Hedy dropped back into her seat, dreading that she was making the wrong choice. Dorothea hauled in breath after breath, her face scrunched with concentration, each inhalation a private war with herself. The moments crawled by, the golden rays replaced with dim blue haze and purple shadows, and still Dorothea sat there, clay-faced, battling, until at last Hedy sensed the breaths grow fractionally looser, and the grip on her wrist released a little. Dorothea raised a finger from her limp hand on the table to indicate that change was afoot, and within a few minutes a little colour returned to her lips and forehead.

'It's okay.'

Relief bubbled up until it hurt Hedy's throat. 'Thank God. But next time . . .'

Dorothea shook her head. 'No! Never! We've come this far. We must reach the end now.' Then it was Dorothea's turn to comfort Hedy, as she dropped her chin to her chest and sobbed like a baby.

★

The spider crab, wrapped in newspaper and then in a torn pillowcase, was pressed so hard against the side of his body that Kurt could feel it wriggling. He had watched the fishmonger bind the claws tight with string, but it was still an unnerving experience to feel the creature strain and fight against the confines of its human prison. It had cost him a huge chunk of his wages and a proportion of his pitiful tobacco allowance, but none of that mattered. Kurt kept his arm firmly in place as he walked up Cheapside, imagining how Hedy's face would look when he presented her with it. There'd be no mayonnaise, of course, probably no bread either. But the ingenious contraption Kurt had set up on a recent visit, involving an old metal paint tin suspended over the fireplace, would enable them to boil the crab at home, provided they had enough wood, and eat it fresh from the shell. He thought about the two women cracking the claws, licking the delicious meat off their fingers, and smiled.

At the corner of the road, Kurt was forced to admit to himself the suspicion that had been nibbling at the edge of his consciousness for several minutes. He was being followed. Glancing around as if checking for traffic, he scanned for a visible figure engaged in any kind of suspicious activity, and caught a glimpse of a man in a mac and trilby-style hat, fiddling pointlessly with a newspaper in a doorway. He couldn't tell from here whether or not it was Wildgrube – the hat suggested otherwise – but the behaviour certainly suggested one of his henchmen. Either way, heading straight for West Park Avenue at this point was clearly out of the question. Kurt doubled back into the little park, following the tarmac path towards its centre then suddenly swerving back towards the north end of Elizabeth Place. If this guy was following him, these twists and turns would surely force him out into the open. Kurt knew that he was clean – the crab had been legitimately bought and there was nothing about his person that couldn't be explained – and on that basis he felt confident about tackling the spy head on. He began to prepare a stinging rebuke in his head, a righteous indignation at the waste of resources, snooping on German officers in their precious free time.

As he cleared the park and headed up the street, he turned to look behind him. The man was still following, some distance away, but now making little attempt to hide his intent. He was moving slowly, and it occurred to Kurt that this might be a consequence of poor fitness, rather than incompetent subterfuge. Recent rations had been atrocious; perhaps the TB currently running rife through the local population was starting to infiltrate the sanctity of the secret police. Serve the bastards right, Kurt thought. But the thought gave him another option: to pick up his pace and make a clean getaway.

Kurt accelerated his stride until he was in a rapid march, his long legs moving like pistons across the paving stones. Reaching the corner of Parade Road, he took a speedy left and jogged past the terraced houses. He knew that coming up on the left was the entrance to the alley that ran parallel with the backyards of West Park Avenue. If he managed to put enough distance between them, he might be able to slip down there before his pursuer figured out where he'd gone. But as he was about to do just that, he glanced behind him and saw that the figure was still on his tail.

Kurt recalibrated. He was too close to the house now to take any chances. It wasn't beyond the power or will of Wildgrube's cronies to turn a whole street over, if they thought they might find something that would earn them credit or promotion. Kurt decided to return to his original plan and confront the spy – from here, he looked exhausted, giving Kurt an additional advantage. Pushing back his shoulders and stretching himself to his full height, Kurt walked back to where the man was now standing quite openly on the public pavement, his arm outstretched to the nearby wall for support, breathing heavily. His head was dropped in an attempt to recover, his face obscured beneath his hat.

Kurt assumed his most officious tone. 'What the hell do you think you're playing at?' As the man raised his head, Kurt gasped. It was more than two years since he'd seen those craggy features, but even with the man's weight loss and significant ageing, he recognised him instantly. 'Doctor Maine!'

'I'm sorry . . .' The doctor waved his hand to indicate he needed an additional moment, then pulled himself upright. 'I would have gone straight to Miss Le Brocq's – I mean Mrs Weber's – house, but I was uncertain of the situation. One doesn't want to draw unnecessary attention to delicate circumstances, you understand?' Kurt nodded. 'Then I recognised you walking up Cheapside, and suspected you might be on your way there.'

'Has something happened?' Kurt glanced around, anxious; there was no one on the street, though he feared any number of eyes might be peering through twitching curtains at this very moment.

Maine nodded. 'I'm afraid so.' His exhausted brown eyes stared up at Kurt from beneath the brim of his hat. 'Something very serious.'

★

'But I don't know this man. I don't understand?'

Dorothea was on the edge of her seat, her fingers in her mouth, chewing at what was left of the fingernails. Hedy looked from her to Kurt, trying to control the violent thumping of her heart. The spider crab he'd donated lay forgotten in the kitchen sink, twitching and squirming through its stay of execution.

'Fintan Quinn was pulled in by the secret police last week for further questioning – part of Wildgrube's "housekeeping" policy,' Kurt explained. 'They must have found a way to put pressure on him, because this time he offered up the doctor's name, linking him to the coupon theft. Next day they pulled Maine in for questioning too.' Hedy thought of the gentle, exhausted doctor in an interrogation cell, and closed her eyes in horror. 'Maine told them nothing, of course,' Kurt went on, 'and they have no evidence, so he's in the clear. But they checked his list of patients and found Dorothea's name. Now they're trying to join the dots, hoping it leads them to Hedy.'

Hedy swallowed. 'So they plan to search here?'

'Maine couldn't be sure – what he overheard was through a doorway into the corridor, and his German isn't that strong. But he thinks he heard the word "*Freitag*".'

'Friday! That's tonight!' Dorothea's eyes were liquid with panic.

'That's why there's no time to waste.'

'Should we move Hedy into the attic?'

Hedy felt sick. The room was spinning a little. A cold toxicity seemed to be building in her veins. The moment had finally come. She had ceased to be a person; she was now a problem, a living liability to be discussed and hidden away like an illegal

216

wireless or a pistol. She opened her mouth to speak, but nothing came out.

'The attic's far too dangerous for a targeted search,' Kurt was saying. 'It'll be the first place they look.'

'But where else can she go? If Maine is under suspicion too—'

'I think I've got an idea,' Kurt cut in. 'First, we need to get the wireless set out of the house. Is there anyone you could leave it with?'

Dorothea nodded. 'My grandmother. I could hide it in her garden shed.'

Kurt nodded. 'Take it round there now in the wheelbarrow. Make sure you cover it – leaves, an old blanket, anything. Go now, while the early shift is changing; the streets will be quiet.' Then Kurt turned to Hedy and looked her dead in the eye. 'And you – you, we need to get dressed.'

'Dressed?'

'It's dangerous, but it's the best I can come up with. And it might work.' He bent down and revealed a canvas satchel he had brought with him, undoing the straps as he spoke. 'I want you to put this on.'

Hedy watched as Kurt pulled out the bag's contents and laid the garments on the kitchen table. She heard Dorothea gasp, and felt her own legs grow weak.

'Kurt, you can't be serious? Have you lost your mind?'

On the table lay the drab grey woollen uniform of a Wehrmacht staff sergeant.

'What do you think?'

Hedy glanced at Kurt, then at the jagged section of mirrored glass in front of her. It sat propped up on a stool, leaning against Dorothea's bedroom wall, and the angle made her look even shorter. She took in her new outfit – the heavy tunic with its neat metal buttons, the loose trousers with the tapered ankles and reinforced seat – and marvelled at the imagined power that could be gleaned from a suit of clothes. She thought of the soldiers in the concentration camps, pulling on the same garments, believing themselves to be supermen, a superior species. All she saw was a stick-thin Jewish girl playing a tasteless game of dress-up. She pulled a face.

'It was the only one I could get – left behind by a sergeant at our billet a few months back. Luckily he was a small guy.'

'Not small enough! No one is going to take me for a soldier.' She turned to him, choking back the simmering terror. 'Kurt, this will never work.'

He took her face in his hands. 'It's our best chance. This administration becomes trapped by its own logic – if it decides something is impossible, it no longer views it as a threat. Hiding in plain sight is the one thing they won't be looking for.' He kissed her lightly on the lips. 'Put the field cap on, that will make all the difference.'

Hedy took the cap and placed it on her head, tucking her hair up around the sides. 'Better?'

'Still too much hair showing. Sorry, my love, but it's going to have to come off.'

Hedy nodded without speaking. It was no occasion for

time-wasting arguments. Within minutes Kurt returned with Dorothea's kitchen scissors, the only ones in the house, and began to chop. Hedy kept her eyes on his face as he worked, knowing his calm expression to be a lie. He worked his way methodically around her skull, occasionally giving her little smiles of reassurance. She thought back to this morning, when she had spent an hour over the kitchen sink, washing her beloved locks with a sliver of low-grade soap that lathered no more than pumice stone. How long ago that seemed. Even the frantic scrabble around the house a mere two hours ago, trying to eliminate every sign of her presence by stuffing her remaining clothes into Dorothea's wardrobe and moving the mattress from the attic into the back bedroom, seemed like days away. Life could no longer be measured in days or weeks, but in minutes. It made her hypersensitive to every sight, sound and colour, yet at the same time strangely numb.

She felt her tawny curls fall to her shoulders and slide to the floor, while Dorothea, still breathless from the sprint to her grandmother's house with the wireless, scurried around her feet, sweeping up the evidence into an old metal dustpan. Then Kurt wetted his razor from a bowl of cold water, and Hedy stood perfectly still as he scratched away at the nape of her neck and around her ears, until there was nothing left there but raw, prickly skin. Once or twice the razor nicked her and she flinched, but she never made a sound; Kurt pressed on the tiny wounds with his handkerchief until the bleeding stopped. When he was done, he tenderly kissed her forehead, placed the cap back on her head and turned her towards the mirror. Hedy took a sharp intake of breath. He was right: the loss of hair made all the difference. Before her stood a slight, undernourished boy soldier of the German army. The uniform was thick and warm, but she could feel her entire body trembling.

Kurt, standing behind her, wrapped his arms around her. 'Good job you're so pretty to begin with, huh?'

Hedy forced a smile. 'We should go.'

Kurt placed a comforting hand on Dorothea's shoulder. 'Leave us a sign by the back door. If it's open, we'll know they've not yet been, or are still in the house.'

Dorothea nodded without flinching. 'Good luck.'

Stepping out into the yard, Hedy felt a sensory rush. The freshness of the late summer breeze, the luminosity of the approaching dusk and the smells drifting in from the street were overwhelming. Asphalt, horse droppings, distant pine, sea salt, diesel . . . They walked briskly down to the end of the alley and out onto the street. Immediately her head began to spin. The vastness of the sky, the seemingly endless length of the road – how had she ever coped with this degree of exposure? In the distance, barely visible, was St Aubin's bay and the immense openness of the Channel. She thought about the depth of it, filled with rocks and creatures and armed ships. How did anyone navigate all this space, handle this amount of vulnerability? Her feet seemed planted where she stood, but Kurt gave her a firm push in the back, propelling her away from the house, and at that moment she gave in to the situation and allowed him to take control. The one thing she vowed was that, whatever happened, she would not let him down.

They walked down Parade Road. It felt exhilarating but exhausting to walk so far in a straight line, to feel her feet covering distance on a pavement again, especially in unfamiliar German boots. She had never worn trousers before, and the sensation of fabric between her legs was peculiar. She tried to relax into the uniform, to walk with weight and purpose, like a man. But now she was becoming aware of the sensations of noise around her, even though the evening was quiet. A distant engine, someone shouting from a window, birds in the trees, a far-off plane. What permanent damage had been done to her sensory organs, she wondered, by all those months shut away from the world? Would she ever be the same again?

'Where are we going?'

'We'll stick to the side roads,' Kurt replied, 'where it's quiet.'

She yearned to look around her but kept her eyes down and let Kurt make the decisions. One or two locals returning home in time for curfew crossed the road in order not to get too close. Hedy fought her desire to peer at them, to take in the contours of a human face that did not belong to Kurt or Dorothea. Instead, she tried to focus on the effort of putting one foot in front of the other. Within a minute she was panting heavily.

'Kurt? I'm so tired.' She sensed his tension straight away, a mixture of sympathy and frustration.

'I know. We're going to walk into the park, then we can sit down for a minute, but only a minute. All right?'

She glanced up at him from beneath her cap. His focus was firmly on the middle distance, his eyes noting every potential hazard.

'Kurt? You know that I love you?' A sense of dread was building inside her. If this plan were to fall apart, one thing was certain: it would happen in seconds, and she would never see Kurt again.

'I love you too, sweetheart. Now, no more talking.'

They reached the Parade Park and found a bench. The sun had set, and the wind sent the first yellowing leaves bundling across the lawns. On the road opposite, German uniforms appeared round corners in twos and threes then disappeared, to be replaced by fresh ones. When Kurt spotted two young privates heading towards the park, he stood, indicating to Hedy that she must follow.

'Sitting down is an invitation to conversation,' Kurt muttered. 'We need to keep on the move.'

'What if someone addresses me directly?'

'There's no reason why they should. Come on.'

They set off down the Parade and turned into the little network of streets that crisscrossed this section of the town.

Here, the front doors of the cottages opened directly onto the narrow pavement, so that they were no more than a couple of metres away from anyone sitting in their front room who chose to look out of the window. Their proximity was disturbing, and Hedy kept her chin pressed to her chest, but at least there was no one on the street itself. When they had completed a couple of circuits, Kurt looked anxiously about him.

'We need to move on. People will become suspicious if they see the same two soldiers walking by over and over again.'

They marched purposelessly onwards. As darkness fell, they cut through to Val Plaisant, crossed Rouge Bouillon and started up Trinity Hill, where the town petered out and gave way to winding, tree-lined roads.

Kurt brought them to a halt. 'There's nothing up there – going on would look suspicious. We'll go back along the north side of the town.'

Hedy's feet were throbbing. 'How much longer?'

'They're likely to send the search party soon after curfew. Couple more hours at least.'

Hedy sunk her teeth into her bottom lip. Don't let him down, she told herself over and over.

They walked on, over St Saviours Hill, then back south towards the Howard Davis Park. The last glimmers of light had vanished now, and as the sky turned black the sound of planes in the sky grew louder and more numerous – night-bombing raids by the Allies, Hedy supposed. She strained to listen for return fire but heard none, just the distant sound of groups of Germans on exercises, practising for a land assault. Her legs seemed to be moving independently, swinging below her like the string legs of a wooden doll. It will be all right, she told herself. Just a little longer.

As soon as they turned the corner of Colomberie, she saw them. Three NCOs, all in uniform, jostling each other on the pavement. She felt Kurt try to steer her to the other side, but just as he did so, one German's voice rang out across the quiet street.

'*Haben Sie Feuer, Leutnant?*'

They were close enough to sense that the men had been drinking. Hedy saw Kurt's shoulders stiffen inside his uniform, and absorbed every thought as if by osmosis. If he said no, no matter how cheerily, and walked on, the men were just drunk enough to make something of it. If he said yes and gave them a precious match, it would be impossible to avoid a conversation. She saw a flick of Kurt's fingers, indicating she should stay where she was, and watched him step forward, feeling in his pocket for his matches.

'These cost me three marks – better light it first time!' Kurt's relaxed smile and easy manner astonished her. He could be in any bar, on a night out with friends. She watched him strike the match and the three of them lean towards it with their roll-ups, shielding the flame from the breeze. Wisps of blue smoke rose into the air and they smiled their thanks. Then, as Kurt was about to pull away, it came.

'What you and your pal up to tonight, sir?'

Kurt's answer was clear and confident. 'Just out for a drink.'

'Take us with you, would you, sir? We've finished our bottle, and all our usual places are closed.'

Kurt faked a laugh. 'Sorry, soldier! Can't help you there.'

Hedy kept her eyes downwards and distant, as if distracted by something more significant than the current conversation. But then the tallest of the three, a corporal, turned towards her. 'How about you, Sergeant? Buy us a beer?'

Panic bubbled and spat in her stomach. She still had sufficient distance, perhaps five metres, to maintain the illusion in the darkness, but she knew that if she opened her mouth she was done for. They had had no time to prepare for this eventuality – now it was up to her to get them out of it. Her brain was spinning, a fruit machine with no controls. She thought of Roda. The smiles at the border, the confidence, the charm. It was all about creating a story and convincing others of its truth. At that second an idea popped into her head. She leaned to her right, hard enough to unbalance herself, and stumbled a little, praying to any god that might be watching that Kurt would take the hint. For a long, terrible moment she thought he'd missed it. Then she heard his voice. 'I'm afraid the sergeant's already had quite enough. Can't take his drink.'

Recalling images of her drunken cousin at old family parties, Hedy raised a hand towards the group as if in apology, then let it flop down by her side, allowing herself another sway and side-step as she did so. The ensuing silence seemed to last eternally, hovering in the night air, and Hedy feared she'd overplayed it.

Then Kurt must have somehow given them permission to react, because the laughter came thick and fast, peppered with cackling remarks.

'Sarge, you look rough!'

'Going to feel bad tomorrow, Sarge!'

'Got the spins yet?'

Now the corporal was slapping his compatriots on their shoulders, the others returning with shoulder punches, throwing back their heads in enjoyment of the joke. Kurt marched back over to Hedy and gave her a hard thump on the shoulder. Maintaining character, Hedy stumbled again. This time Kurt grabbed hold of her upper arm as if to support her, and steered her away down the road, calling over his shoulder as he went, 'Have a good evening, gentlemen.'

The punchy shouts of the soldiers' laughter, rising into the night sky, sang in her ears as they moved away. Kurt kept a vice-like grip of her arm, and as the adrenaline drained from her and the realisation of what had just happened began to sink in, Hedy knew that this buttressing was no longer part of the performance, but a physical necessity. They continued, past the shuttered shops and darkened windows of the town. Hedy's breath was coming in thick, irregular pants, Kurt's nervous energy fizzing through the layers of his uniform. It was several minutes before he spoke, making sure that no words would carry on the night breeze. When he did, they were the most thrilling words she had ever heard.

'Oh my God, sweetheart. Well done!'

By the time they reached the corner of West Park Avenue, it was gone midnight. Kurt signalled to her to stay back in the shadows of a shop doorway while he went into the alley to check ahead. A moment later, he returned and beckoned to her, and the two of them scampered up the passage and in through the back of the house.

Dorothea was standing in the front room, tears of frustration in her eyes. The house was a wreck. Chairs had been overturned, the contents of the attic and its hatch cover lay in a heap at the bottom of the stairs. Broken glass glittered everywhere.

Kurt put his arm around her. 'How many of them were there? Did they do much damage?'

Dorothea nodded. 'Four soldiers. They pulled everything out the cupboards, upturned the beds. They broke my last teapot – I'll never be able to replace it.'

Hedy held Dorothea close. 'I'm so sorry, you must have been terrified. But we'll help you put everything back as it was. What matters is they didn't find anything.' She felt Dorothea shrink, and pulled back. 'They didn't, did they?'

Dorothea's fingers fluttered to her face, patting her skin to comfort herself. 'I'm so sorry . . . I thought I'd swept everywhere, I thought I'd been so careful . . . It's my fault.' Her words began to sputter as the tears quickened, choking her.

Hedy's bowels twisted and she felt an urgent need to use the lavatory. 'What did they find?'

'A button, underneath the kitchen table. A button from a German uniform tunic.'

Hedy looked towards Kurt, whose face had lost all its colour.

'It's not your fault, Dorothea, it's mine. I knew that button was missing, but I never thought it would be here. *Scheisse!*'

Hedy pulled the field cap from her head, stroking her shaven neck. 'Would they not think it was Anton's?'

'That's what I told them, but I don't think they believed me. He's been gone for too long.' She blinked up at him, grasping at straws. 'It doesn't prove anything, though?'

Kurt pushed stray hair from his face. 'No, but Wildgrube will be onto that in a flash. He's been searching for months for something connecting me to Hedy.'

'You think they'll come back? Should we go back out?'

To her relief Kurt shook his head. 'Not tonight, but they will be back – tomorrow, or the day after, or next week. And next time we'll get no warning. What we need is something to put the bastards off the scent for good. But I'm damned if I know how.'

Hedy reached out and touched his arm. 'There is one thing that might work.'

★

The girl serving behind the bar was young, probably no more than seventeen, but she had the careworn face of a woman fifteen years older. Kurt, swirling the last drops of his brandy round the bottom of a grubby glass, wondered what the circumstances were that had forced her to take this job. Perhaps her father was out of work like so many local men, the family scraping together every penny to pay for black market food. Perhaps her parents were dead and she was trying to support herself and her siblings. Whatever it was, the girl was struggling to hide her contempt for the louche, loud officers who lounged around in here tonight, scraping their chair legs on the parquet floor and letting their cigarettes butts burn holes in the soft furnishings. What was the French expression? *Fin de siècle*. Kurt watched them as they drank and laughed together at jokes they had repeated a hundred times before. The master race, he thought bitterly as he knocked back the remains of the brandy. What a joke.

Kurt surveyed the scene. Fischer was perched in a tub chair in the darkest corner, deep in conversation with two high-ranking officers from College House; their voices had dropped even lower once Fischer realised that Kurt was trying to catch snippets of their conversation. But those guys were not his focus tonight. Kurt's target was over by the window, drinking with some secret police cronies. Wildgrube had long ago given up any pretence about the true nature of his job, and now seemed to enjoy flaunting it. The presence of the other spies gave Kurt the confidence he needed – it would make his task that much easier.

Everyone was in this evening. This was the last remaining club for officers and 'approved' clientele that still had a regular supply of French brandy, partly because the boss of the secret police, a notorious black marketeer, frequented the place. It was even still possible to get a crust of bread and a little cheese here sometimes, though the portions had more than halved. Kurt watched Wildgrube help himself to another drink, but noticed that he was displaying an unusual degree of decorum and control tonight, sipping instead of gulping, and occasionally throwing Kurt what he clearly considered to be subtle, scrutinising glances. Kurt banged the glass down on the bar loud enough for Wildgrube to hear, edged his way across the room to the area where the spy was standing, and glared at him.

'Well, if it's not the big man himself.'

Wildgrube looked Kurt up and down, getting the measure of his mood. 'Lieutenant . . .'

'Made any good arrests lately?'

Wildgrube glanced around, already seething at this disrespect. 'I beg your pardon?'

Kurt stepped closer, using the height difference to intimidate the spy. 'Don't be coy, Erich. I thought you were proud of your work?'

Wildgrube delicately stepped backwards a little, trying to gain some distance. 'I'm sure we are all proud of how we serve the Reich.'

'So, spit it out. Turned over any good houses? Smashed up anything? Because I know how much you guys love doing that.'

Wildgrube's mouth set in a tight, thin line. His lips were too rosy pink for his pale face – it gave the impression he was wearing lipstick. 'If you have some issue with my department, Lieutenant, I suggest you go through the proper channels.'

'No, I think I'd rather say it to your face. Must be an exciting time for you, now that we're shut off from the rest of the world. Chance to get properly stuck into the locals. Doesn't really matter whether they've done anything, does it? We've got to show them who's boss, isn't that right?'

'I mean it, Kurt. This is not the time nor the place. I suggest you go home before you get yourself into real trouble.'

Kurt leaned into his face, so close he could smell the man's pungent breath. 'I'm going. Don't much like the atmosphere round here. But I'll be watching you, Erich – very, very closely.' And with that, Kurt spun on his heel and marched from the room, pushing a young officer out of the way as went.

Once outside, Kurt took a deep breath of night air, then sneaked into a nearby doorway to light a cigarette. He waited another thirty seconds, then set off down the road at a moderate pace. At the corner, he looked both ways for traffic – there would be few official vehicles out at this time, but it gave him an excuse to glance backwards. There, exactly where he knew he would be, was Wildgrube, cap jammed neatly under his arm, staying close to the shadow of the buildings to keep himself hidden. At his side were two heavily-built junior officers, all of them waiting for Kurt to get a little further down the road.

Kurt set off in the direction of Cheapside, resisting the temptation to look back again. His heart was hammering. Beneath his tunic, sweat was prickling his skin and running in itchy rivulets down his back. In his mind he felt calm and precise, but his body was taking delight in reminding him that when it came to abject fear, the body always gets the upper hand. He thought of Hedy, and allowed himself a small, black chuckle. Love. The insanity it pushed you to. For this, without doubt, was true insanity.

★

Hedy closed her eyes, breathed in deeply, and tried to focus on a comforting thought. But choosing one was harder than she'd anticipated. The warm kitchen at her old family house was too painful a picture . . . the coastal walks she'd taken with Anton too harsh a reminder of what was lost. In the end she settled for her and Kurt tucked up together in a warm bed, in some vague, undefined room, sometime in the future, the smell of him in her nostrils, his arms scooping her into his body. If she could focus on that, she told herself, perhaps the physical pain and horror might fade into her subconscious.

She twisted her body a little, trying to ease the pressure. The space was cold and damp. There was little more than five centimetres above her head, the boards trapping her, coffin-like, in one position. Even the slightest movement caused a joist to press into her flesh, or a sharp splinter to push through her clothes into her skin; it also increased the risk of her falling straight through the plaster of the ceiling below. Stretching out a leg, or her spine even a little, was impossible. When Dorothea had announced that it was time, and had screwed the last floorboard into place over her head, the pitch black and confinement sent her into such a panic that for several moments Hedy truly thought she might die of fright. But she told herself over and over that it wasn't really that different from the darkness in the attic she'd learned to contend with for the last ten months; if she could control her breathing and keep the dust out of her nostrils, she would be all right.

There was one salvation: the tiny gaps between the floorboards allowed her to hear some of what was going on in the bedroom above. It gave her a sense of connection to the world, and calmed her claustrophobia. And she knew she would not have long to wait. Somewhere down on the ground floor, she heard the opening and closing of the front door. Then there were footsteps on the stairs, followed by the indistinguishable sounds of people moving around a room. A moment later, she heard the ancient springs of Dorothea's bed creak and groan as they contracted under the weight of a human body. There was some whispering – short nervous sentences exchanged in pops and crackles – then all went quiet again. Everyone, it seemed, was listening.

Hedy closed her eyes, trying to guess how much time had passed. She used to play this game as a child in her schoolroom, forcing herself not to turn and look at the clock on the wall, betting with herself. If she guessed the right time within a five-minute margin, then Papa would take her for ice cream on Sunday; if she got it wrong by more than ten, she'd have to walk home through the nettle patch at the side of the school road. She'd got pretty good at it. Now she calculated that a good half-hour had passed since the last discernible noise. Surely it couldn't be much longer? If this idea was going to work then they . . .

CRASH.

The sound was so shocking it caused Hedy to jump, jarring her body against the joists. Her heart pounding like a kettle drum, she squeezed her eyes even tighter shut. They were here.

★

The noise of the door being forced must have been audible four houses away. Kurt propped himself onto his elbows, his head against the bars at the top of the bedstead, and glanced across at Dorothea, whose ashen face was almost indistinguishable in colour from the pillow behind it. Instinctively she pulled the blankets higher and tighter around her upper body, horrified at her own nakedness, her eyes huge with terror. Kurt checked that his trousers were correctly heaped in the centre of the floor, then glanced down at the space between them. With an apologetic twist of his mouth he eased himself a little closer to her body, and Dorothea nodded her understanding. No point going this far and not making the final image realistic.

They lay perfectly still, listening to the thumping footsteps running through the downstairs then bounding up the staircase. Kurt closed his eyes for a second, and took a deep breath as the bedroom door burst open. Wildgrube was standing in the doorway, the shadows of his two huge assistants falling behind him. His cheeks, pink from the night air, highlighted the twinkling triumph in his eyes. How long had he dreamed of this moment, Kurt wondered – fantasised about clicking the cuffs around Kurt's wrists and dropping the completed file on his boss's desk. But even now those eyes were zooming in on Dorothea, comparing her to the photograph of Hedy that the spy carried in his head, and sensing that something had gone terribly wrong. His face reminded Kurt of a flick book he'd had as a child, where a visual story magically emerged by running the pictures together quickly with one's thumb; in the space of three seconds Kurt saw the shift from delight, to confusion, to disappointment, and finally, plain anger.

'You, whore! Where are your papers?' Dorothea, in a panic that Kurt knew was no act, whimpered and pointed to the chest of drawers in the bedroom alcove. 'Get up and bring them to me.' Dorothea obeyed, dragging the blanket from the bed to hold around herself, leaving Kurt naked on the mattress. Wildgrube made a performance of scanning Dorothea's identity card, but there was no doubt in Kurt's mind that the spy's subtle, involuntary peek at Kurt's exposed genitals, when he thought no one was looking, lasted a fraction longer than natural curiosity demanded.

'You, Lieutenant – put your clothes on!' Kurt silently did as he was told. 'So, this is how you honour a fellow servant of the Reich, a soldier fighting for our country? You come into his house and screw his wife?' Kurt looked as ashamed as possible. 'How long has this business been going on?'

Kurt sighed, as if reluctant to confess this final indignity. 'Since her husband left.' He risked a glance into Wildgrube's eyes, and knew that the spy was calculating backwards, remembering some of Kurt's suspicious behaviour, believing he was piecing it together. The man's face contorted into a sneer of repugnance, but not before Kurt had caught one more brief emotion upon it – admiration.

'If there were any law available to me,' Wildgrube opined, 'I would arrest you both now. As it stands, you will be amply judged when this war is won. You both disgust me,' he added, before turning with what he clearly imagined to be dramatic effect and sweeping from the room. Kurt, wearing only his trousers, and Dorothea, still wrapped only in a blanket, remained motionless in the centre of the room until the footsteps reached the front door, listening to it open and bang shut. Even then, it was another full minute before either of them dare make a sound.

Eventually Dorothea let out a nervous giggle. 'I think it worked!'

Kurt nodded. 'I think it did.' Suddenly embarrassed, he took her dress from the bottom of the bed and passed it to her. 'Put this on quickly, you must be freezing. I need to get this floorboard up quickly.'

★

Hedy stooped over the bowl, soaking then squeezing the cloth, moving it carefully over her body. Trickles of water ran down her arms, her chest and in between her breasts, making tiny pathways through the dust and grime then vanishing beneath her slip. She was painfully aware of Kurt watching her, especially conscious of her scalp with its uneven tufts sprouting where her hair had once been and her body so thin she looked like a young boy. But when she looked across at him he was gazing at her with adoration.

'How are you feeling now?' he asked. She nodded, trying to indicate an improvement, though every joint in her body still ached, and it had taken her a full half-hour to stop shaking after they'd pulled her out. 'You were so brave, you know.'

'You must have put on a pretty good show yourself. Tell me again what happened in the club?' He had already described the whole event to her twice over, but she felt like a child with a bedtime story.

He sat down on the chair opposite. 'I knew it was the perfect night. He'd had a little to drink, but not too much, and he was virtually pawing the ground, desperate for a chance to catch us together, prove his theory. Like you said, all I had to do was convince him this was the perfect opportunity.'

She smiled at the thought. 'You really shouted at him?'

'Just enough to humiliate him a little, stir his instinct for revenge. Not hard with men like that.' The door clicked open, and Dorothea slipped in like a ghost. Hedy noticed that she avoided Kurt's eyes and kept her body turned away from him as she fussed around the kitchen, tipping more hot water into the bowl. Hedy threw Kurt a meaningful stare – it was going to be up to him to repair the damage. 'And as for Dory,' Kurt continued seamlessly, 'that performance deserved an Oscar! I started to believe it myself!'

Dorothea blushed pink to her roots. 'I just knew that it had to look good.'

'I really didn't see anything, you know,' Kurt assured her. 'I kept my eyes shut as you were getting into bed.'

Dorothea's cheeks were still flushed, but she managed a smile.

'It's fine, honestly. I know that Anton would understand if he were here.'

'More than that,' Hedy assured her, 'he'd be proud of what you did. Of all of us.' Taking a small towel to dry herself, she turned to Kurt. 'But is it enough to put the authorities permanently off the scent?'

Kurt nodded with genuine confidence. 'It would seem like a personal grudge for Wildgrube to continue pursuing me for such a private matter. He'd be made to look a fool. God knows there's enough going on in this island to keep him busy.'

'So we're safer now?'

He pressed his lips together. 'Safer, but not safe. We still need to be careful. Though to be honest, I don't think the secret police are our biggest problem any more.' Hedy and Dorothea both looked at him, willing him on. 'The islands could face starvation in the next few months. Fischer was at the club with some officers, and I overheard them say that Churchill is refusing to permit the Red Cross to send relief.'

Dorothea's eyes widened in horror. 'But why?'

'Probably thinks the Germans would take the parcels for themselves. But from what they were saying, it might be revenge – a payback for what Churchill sees as collaboration.'

'Collaboration?' Hedy stopped drying herself and threw the towel onto the back of a chair. 'Why would he think that? Churchill has no idea what's gone on here!'

'Apparently the British Government are under the impression that we've all been rubbing along, and that things haven't been too bad till now.'

Hedy looked back towards Dorothea and watched the now familiar fury begin to rise.

'What were we islanders meant to do, fight the German army with our bare hands?'

'Just telling you what I heard.'

Hedy's eyes slid automatically to the larder, calculating

exactly what was in there to last her and Dorothea the rest of the week.

'How are we expected to survive, with no supplies and no outside help?'

'The garrison reckons it can hang on till January,' Kurt replied, 'if it takes control of all provisions. But it's going to be harder for me to get hold of anything for you. And if the Allies don't push across France quickly, then . . .'

Hedy went to the kitchen window, touching the blackout blind with her fingers, remembering the sights and smells of the outside world that she had tasted the other night. The kitchen suddenly seemed a great deal smaller.

Kurt rose and slipped his arms around her waist. 'Don't worry, sweetheart. Churchill will have to relent if things get bad. We'll all get through this.' But there was little conviction in his voice.

Hedy sighed with a deep resignation. 'Who knows? Secret police or not – this winter may kill us after all.'

The three of them sat down at the kitchen table, and after a while Dorothea brought out a packet of playing cards. They played for tiny pebbles from the back garden, sitting in silence, unable to think of anything else to say. Summer was over. The nights were cooling fast, and the sunsets were slowly creeping their way towards the afternoon. Far away across the Channel, the rumble of distant guns could be heard, occasionally rattling the windows in their ancient frames.

★

Tick, tick, tick. The kitchen clock ran on its hypnotic rhythm in the darkness. It would be another hour before the electricity supply returned, and the last candle had been used days ago. Now even reading, the last pleasurable activity left, was impossible after late afternoon. Rumours in town suggested that within two months there would be no electricity at all.

Hedy huddled by the kitchen fireplace, holding out her hands towards the warm ashes to extract the last heat. Next to the hearth, the log basket sat empty, nothing but tiny remnants of twigs and dried-up leaves scattered at the bottom. Dorothea had spent all the previous day 'wooding' on Westmount, collecting any small sticks and kindling she could find, but every able-bodied person in town was doing the same, and the ones with proper, sharp saws were walking away with the lion's share. It didn't help that even the paltry bundle of twigs Dorothea did manage to bring back was soaking wet, and would take days to dry out in the cold, damp house.

Hedy sat back and listened to the rain beating on the windows and bouncing off the concrete in the yard. It had been raining for days, weeks. The wettest November for ten years, the locals were saying. She felt her stomach growl again, and the twinge of pain that she suspected was the start of an ulcer. Kurt had recently complained of the same thing – even officers were going hungry now. Last week he'd told her that a number of ordinary soldiers had been arrested for violent outbursts and theft from domestic properties. Hedy had wanted to put an additional bolt on the kitchen door, but Dorothea tried every hardware supplier in town and could find nothing. Perhaps, they reflected, it didn't matter that much – any burglar looking for food was far more likely to target the farmhouses of the country parishes, which sometimes still contained the carcasses of rabbits or a few home-grown vegetables. No point in breaking into a town property that had nothing in it.

Kurt's predictions had turned out to be true. Wildgrube and his cohorts had lost all interest in Kurt since the abortive house raid, and had evidently given up on finding Hedy too. The three of them had slowly gained confidence that the soldiers would not return, and in recent weeks Hedy had started sleeping in the spare room at the back of the house. It was wonderful to lie in a proper bed and be able to get up in the night if she needed to, though bizarrely she slept more fitfully there, having adapted over the months to the life of a bat in the attic. Truthfully, no one was sleeping well any more. Who could sleep with a hunger so extreme it gnawed at your organs and pushed acid up your throat as soon as you lay down? Last night they had had absolutely nothing in the house to eat until Kurt had arrived with a tiny portion of German sausage and a crust of something no one would describe as bread. Two days before, Dorothea had fainted at the bottom of the stairs.

Hedy heard the latch turn on the front door and Dorothea hurry in, slamming it behind her. Scrambling to her feet, Hedy went to meet her. They were so attuned to each other's sounds and movements now that any tiny change of mood was immediately obvious. Hedy watched her fold down her umbrella with the two broken spokes, spattering raindrops all over the floor, and stand dripping in the hallway. Dorothea's eyes were red and her mouth was pulled tight in a poor attempt to stem an outburst.

'What's happened?'

'I just saw Mrs Le Cornu, the old lady down the road, crying in the street. Her cat's gone missing. She thinks the Germans took it.'

'No!' Hedy's hand flew to her mouth.

'She says the same thing happened to her neighbour. They trap them and shoot them, apparently, then cook them at their barracks. I've noticed there are no dogs around lately, either.'

'But that's horrible!' She remembered Hemingway's fluffy grey face nuzzling her cheek and prayed that he had escaped that fate.

'It's all horrible. Everything's horrible. I'm so sick of it.' The tears began to run down her cheeks. 'I was queuing outside the butcher's – there was a rumour that they had some rabbit, but it wasn't true – when this fight broke out between two women. A proper fight, they were hitting each other – all over a couple of rotten apples in the market.'

She let out a strange little moan then slid down the wall until she was crouched on the floor, sobbing into her hands. Rainwater from her coat and hair pooled around her on the linoleum.

Hedy crouched down beside her and put an arm around her. 'It's all right.'

'No, it's not all right. It's happening all over,' Dorothea wailed. 'Everyone's so hungry and angry! There's nothing in any of the shops, and we can't even forage for limpets and winkles till the next low tide, and then everyone else will be doing the same.'

'What about your cousin?' Hedy bit her lip. They both knew it was a stupid pointless question, but Dorothea pretended it was reasonable.

'The Germans are taking everything from the farms. I doubt he could feed his own children, never mind us.' Words failed her for a while, crushed by the weight of her misery, then she took a deep breath. 'I'm so stupid. You know, when Kurt said back in June that the Allies might not come for us, I didn't believe him. I pretended I did, but I was sure they'd come. My mother always loved King George – we always stood for the national anthem – but I never thought he'd let this happen. I thought they would send a ship, something . . .'

Hedy hugged her close. 'If they had, the Germans would have fought back – it would have been a bloodbath. We might all be dead now.'

'Perhaps that would be better!' In the darkness of the hallway, her pale skin was almost translucent, and Hedy could clearly see the blue veins beneath the surface. 'Perhaps it's better to die quickly, fighting, than to sit around helpless, waiting for it.'

'But we're still here.' Hedy drew her closer. 'We've survived so long, Dory, against the worst odds. We've fought back in the only way we could. We can't give up now.'

Dorothea was still crying, but it was a different kind of weeping now, quiet, resigned. 'I'm not sure I have the strength, Hedy. I'm so tired, and everything hurts all the time. Sometimes'

– she wiped a dollop of snot from her nose – 'sometimes I wish I'd just have an asthma attack in the night and not wake up.'

'Don't say that!' Hedy heard her voice, shrill and desperate. 'I need you, and so will Anton. We just have to hang on. Kurt will always bring us whatever he can. And it can't be much longer. It just can't.'

Dorothea shook her head. 'I don't know . . .'

'*I* know! Belgium is liberated now. The Americans are already crossing parts of the Rhine. The Allies will win, Dory, everyone knows it. We just have to get through the next few' – she couldn't bring herself to say months, though that was what she was thinking – 'weeks.'

'I'm just so tired. So, so tired.'

Hedy pressed her face against Dorothea's downturned head and closed her eyes. The rainwater on the floor was soaking up through the hem of her dress, adding a new layer of cold, but she took no notice. There was nowhere to go and nothing to do, but sit there, rocking gently on the hall floor, watching their own breath steam in the cold air, and listening to the relentless tick-tick-tick of the kitchen clock.

12

1945

Evening Post
8th May, 1945

I appeal to you to maintain your calm and dignity in the hours that lie ahead, and to refrain from all forms of demonstration.

. . .

I feel that the conclusion of the Prime Minister's speech this afternoon will be the appropriate moment for the hoisting of flags, and I make the strongest appeal to you, in the interests of public order, not to fly flags before that time.

I was present last evening at the release from custody of the majority of political prisoners, and I am doing all in my power to obtain the immediate release of the remainder of them.

I shall make known to you immediately any further developments.

A. M. Coutanche, Bailiff

This was a new smell, Kurt thought, as he shuffled into the main hall of College House with the other officers. Not the usual mixed scents of damp uniforms, body odour and leather. Not even the stink of fear that had pervaded in the early days of the land invasion. He couldn't place it at first, but the answer lay in the expressions on his colleagues' faces, the dejected slope of their shoulders, and especially in the undisguised curses and questions skimming through the room. Questions no longer muttered in corners or the silent corridors of officers' clubs, but spat forcefully with rage and resentment. It was defeat.

He gazed through the same leaded window he had looked through so often before, struck by the precious blue sky and bouncing white clouds, and mentally repeated some phrases on a loop, trying to make the news real to himself. It was all over. Hitler was dead, Germany was finished, the great dream of the Fatherland was no more. Millions of lives lost or wrecked, all for the fever dream of a nation too consumed with fury and ideology to see its own reflection. All for a mirage. All for nothing. Kurt tried to figure out what he was feeling, but all he could identify was a sense of relief.

The day of reckoning was no longer a possibility somewhere in the future. Within days – perhaps hours – British troops would be landing on these shores, and every man in this room would be going to jail. Some of them would be put to death. With a strange detachment, Kurt wondered if he would be one of them. How tragic, he thought, to have survived this long, to have kept alive the woman he loved, only to be snatched from the earth now, when happiness was finally possible. But he felt no fear or self-pity, just an eerie calmness. Nothing was any longer within his control – all his responsibilities were in the past. Perhaps that was part of the odd aroma in this room today – the passive pleasure of release from duty. The future was out of their hands.

Baron von Aufsess, standing on a desk at the end of the room, spoke in a confident voice as if dispatching notices for any normal day. 'I have been informed,' he said, 'that Mr Churchill will address the British nation via the BBC at three o'clock this afternoon. I have received orders that we are to prevent the public from hearing any such illegal broadcast . . .' He hesitated here, and gave a little cough that seemed to Kurt more about punctuation than clearing his throat. 'However, as we also have it on good authority that British naval ships are already on their way to the islands carrying orders for our immediate surrender, I have given permission for the broadcast to be available to any of the local population in possession of a wireless.' A soft murmur went quickly around the room. Everyone knew that at least half the locals on the island either had their original radios or an illegal crystal set. 'Meanwhile,' von Aufsess continued, 'you will be aware that I will be speaking with the Bailiff today regarding the release of ration stores, and that the Bailiff has urged the islanders to act with restraint, and not get any foolish ideas of retribution.'

Kurt grimaced, on the edge of laughter. Even now, they couldn't shake off that underlying assumption of superiority! What a shock the coming days would be.

The baron dismissed his officers, and minions passed around instructions on hastily handwritten cards. Kurt skim-read his orders and tucked them into his breast pocket. Moving slowly through the crush towards the door, he managed a quick glance at some of the other orders handed out. *Remove . . . destroy . . . dismantle.* It was clear that the Area Command's priority now was an island-wide concealment of what had been going on here for the last five years. Mountains of paperwork, private German food stores, anything that could be viewed by the Allies as contrary to the Hague Convention. Kurt buttoned his tunic and set off from College House with the rest, but instead of heading to the compound to bonfire stock lists as instructed, he turned at the bottom of the hill and headed for West Park Avenue. To hell with them – what could they do to him now? And at this moment he needed to see Hedy more than anything.

The streets were buzzing with locals, many of whom had clearly abandoned work for the day. Some grinned at him as he passed, filled with vengeful glee. Others shouted insults. Several women had gathered to watch four German privates desperately whitewashing over the giant red cross that had been painted on the wall of the officers' club nine months earlier, in a desperate attempt to save it from bombing. The whitewash turned the cross pink, but its outline remained stubbornly visible, to the growing panic of the paint-spattered soldiers. Kurt snorted at the pertinence of the image. Not enough whitewash in the world, he thought to himself.

In defiance of the appeal, many Union Jacks and Jersey flags were already being openly displayed in private windows. They had appeared from nowhere, after years stashed away in attics and cellars, or hidden in the storage rooms of shops. Crossing Val Plaisant, he spotted a beaming old gentleman placing speakers on his windowsill, ready to broadcast further news to all and sundry that afternoon. Kurt felt the man's joy and couldn't help smiling. It felt strange to be surrounded by so much happiness and to know that your own demise was the cause of it.

At Dorothea's house, he tapped his usual coded knock and was quickly shown inside. Dorothea was resplendent in the dress she had worn for her wedding but rarely worn since. Hedy was wearing the grey floral cotton frock and ancient cardigan she had been in most days for the last eighteen months, but Kurt's heart dissolved when he looked at her. There was a gleam in her eye he hadn't seen in months, and the featheriness of her movements as she skipped around the house reminded him of illustrations in fairy stories. Her hair, though still not back to its original length, was now curling around her jawline, its rich tawny colour as beguiling as ever.

'We had a whole tin of salmon between us for dinner last night!' Hedy bubbled. 'It was the last thing left in the April Red Cross box, but apparently the British ships are bringing relief parcels, so we decided to give ourselves a treat!'

'Quite right too.' Kurt reached out and touched that hair, marvelling at its softness. 'Do you have somewhere to listen to the speech at three o'clock?'

'Dory fetched the wireless back from her grandmother's house. She walked right by a German soldier at the top of the road, pushing it in the wheelbarrow, and he didn't even ask to look under the blanket! That's when we knew, when we really understood that it was all over.'

He wound her tresses around his fingers. 'The British boats will be here tomorrow. You should go down to the harbour to greet the Tommies – it'll be a quite a day.'

'Come with us?' Dorothea suggested, peering at her reflection in the mirror of her empty powder compact.

Kurt glanced towards Hedy. The look between them said everything.

'I think I may be required elsewhere.'

Hedy took his hand from her hair and led him into the privacy of the front room. 'I've got a plan. As soon as I'm certain it's safe, I'm going to go to the Jersey States offices to tell them everything. I'm going to tell them about you, and how you helped me.'

Kurt tried to look pleased and grateful. 'Well, I appreciate that—'

'I'm sure that the British will have to round you all up initially. But they can't treat you all the same. They'll want to identify the leaders. But I'm living proof that you're in a different category.'

'Hedy, I'm an officer.' He tried to speak gently. 'That has certain implications.'

'At first, yes, but the British judicial system is very fair. Once they know the whole story, I'm certain they'll make exceptions. I mean, they might decide not to imprison you at all.'

Unwilling to snatch this moment from her, Kurt indulged himself, falling into those sea-green eyes one more time. As sunlight poured in from the window, bathing them both, he pulled her towards him and held her, relishing the warmth of her body, the softness of her breasts through his tunic, the security of those skinny arms around his neck. Then he kissed her, long and deep, and took a deep sniff of her neck, breathing in the natural perfume of her skin. Finally, he pulled back and forced a beaming smile.

'I need to go, sweetheart. I have so much to do. Enjoy Churchill's speech.' And with that, he set off towards the east and his billet.

*

Hedy and Dorothea gazed at the crowds around the harbour in astonishment. The shouting, singing and cheering seemed to fill the sky. Like a giant, chaotic whirlpool of humanity, eddies and swirls of faces circled in different directions, all trying to reach the next vantage point, or reach a friend lost in the melee. The greatest surge of people was on the West Park side, where streams of British soldiers were now pouring off the troop carriers in the bay and trudging their slow, shambolic path through the thousands of well-wishers. Old farmers stretched out their arms to shake hands with them, women young and old threw themselves at the newcomers, showering them with kisses. Eager fingers reached across every gap, begging for the cigarettes and sweets in every soldier's pocket.

Hedy's eyes darted from one extraordinary sight to another. 'Look, Dory – the hotel!'

The Pomme d'Or, home of the German Naval headquarters for the duration of the war, was now filled with British uniforms, military men brimming over its front balcony. The raising of the Union Jack from its flagpole drew another roar from the crowd, and a spontaneous chorus of 'God Save The King' burst out and spread right down to the quayside. Everywhere she looked, Hedy saw faces creased with emotion – women cuddling children, husbands kissing wives, old men wiping tears of joy.

'Isn't it wonderful?' Dorothea's voice was high and bright, but when Hedy turned to her she saw only a fixed mask of theatrical joy. She knew that her own face projected the same lie. In fact she was finding the whole experience terrifying. The closeness of strangers pressed against her, the dozens of unknown hands touching her arms and back – it felt revolting. Less like celebration, more like defilement. Her breath was coming in uneven bursts, and she wondered how Dorothea's asthma would fare with the emotion of the day.

At that moment, as if conjured by her own thoughts, she spotted a familiar figure on the far side of the Weighbridge, a man in an old brown mackintosh being carried along by a river of people towards the landing area. As Hedy looked towards him, Oliver Maine turned his head and miraculously caught sight of her, immediately taking the hat from his head and waving frantically in affection and triumph. Hedy waved back, gesticulating that to try and reach him now would be hopeless, and the doctor laughed in agreement before disappearing into the crowd. Hedy felt her heart swell, and promised herself that her first visit when this madness was over would be to the hospital. Perhaps, she considered, in a week or two she might be able to get hold of a few eggs and a little sugar. If so, she would make him an apple cake to take home for his wife.

Hedy realised that Dorothea was pulling her by the arm.

'There's two soldiers over there. I want to find out what they know about the war in Europe.'

'What do you mean? Know what?'

But Dorothea was already pulling her towards two young Tommies, shouting at them for attention. As they reached the men Dorothea reached out and grabbed one of them by the arm. He was little more than twenty, pasty-faced and chubby by island standards. Dorothea pressed her face close to his. 'Could I ask you something? I'm trying to get news of my husband. Last I heard he was fighting in East Prussia. Don't suppose you know what happened to the soldiers out there?'

The Tommy looked at her with confusion. Hedy pulled at her dress, but Dorothea's eyes were fixed on the young man and she refused to budge.

'No Brits out there, love. Ruskies pushed Jerry back over that side. Which regiment was your old man with?'

Again, Hedy pulled; again Dorothea resisted.

'He's Austrian, he was forced to fight with the Germans. Do you know if the Russians took many prisoners? How do I find out if he's alive?'

The Tommy was now backing away from them, as was his friend. 'Your husband fought for the Jerries?'

'He didn't want to, he was conscripted. I just wondered if you could tell me how to find out what happened to him?'

'Dory,' Hedy muttered, 'let's go. This isn't the right time.'

Hearing Hedy's voice, the Tommy whipped round to look at her. 'Here, that accent! You a Jerry too?'

'No, I'm not German.' Hedy felt her heart bang in her chest. 'I'm . . . I've been . . .'

The Tommies looked them both up and down, then pushed onwards through the crowd.

Hedy watched their uniforms disappear into the throng, then turned to a deflated Dorothea. 'It's just not the right day, Dory. Those men aren't from here, they don't understand. Why don't we go up to Fort Regent? That must be where they're going to hoist the Union Jack.'

But Dorothea was no longer looking at Hedy, or at the departing soldiers. Her eyes were focused on a fast-moving rabble on the Esplanade side of the crowd. A pack of half a dozen men, young and in shirtsleeves, was moving at speed, running as fast as the crowd allowed, apparently chasing something or someone. The rumble of their collective feet parted the hordes, and as a space appeared, the object of their pursuit suddenly became visible. For a moment Hedy thought it was a youth wearing some kind of pale, tight-fitting overall, then to her horror she realised that it was actually a young girl. Her hair had been roughly cut down to the skull and she was entirely naked. The girl was running as fast as she could in desperation to escape her pursuers, and her intermittent squeals of terror carried across the heads of the throng, causing everyone to turn and stare. A second later, the girl escaped up a side street and two of her hunters were stopped by a local policeman.

Hedy turned to look at Dorothea, whose face was now completely colourless.

'Oh my God, Hedy . . . was that what I think it is?'

Hedy scrabbled for words, but found none. She nodded.

'Is this what it's going to be like? Is this how they're going to treat us? What was it all for?'

Hedy took Dorothea's hand in her own. 'Come on. Let's get down to the collection depot, pick up our Red Cross parcels. Then we'll just go home.'

Dorothea meekly followed Hedy through the heaving streets, the collective frenzy of the day still ringing in their ears. As they forced their way against the current of revellers, Hedy watched Dorothea's eyes constantly flick back to the lengthening line of Tommies snaking into the town centre, redrawing each face with Anton's thick dark hair and smiling eyes. They had talked so often of this day, dreamed about it, pinned a picture of it in their minds for years. Now all Hedy could think about was returning to the peace and sanity of Dorothea's little kitchen and keeping this feverish world at a safe, manageable distance.

★

'Neumann, his name is Lieutenant Kurt Neumann. He's an engineer. He's been based at the Lager Hühnlein compound since 1941.'

Hedy crossed her legs and deliberately added a touch of iron to her gaze. This office hadn't changed an iota in five years. The same leather-topped desk, the same oversized chandelier, same neatly stacked files on the shelves. She remembered every detail, of both the room and the conversation, and she wanted Clifford Orange to know that she did. Given the expression on his face, she was pretty confident that he knew what she was thinking.

She peered at him as he made his notes with agonising slowness, holding his fountain pen in red flaky fingers. He had lost weight, of course, and more of his hair. The crimson flush that once bloomed across his cheeks, presumably the result of too much drink, had now been replaced by malnourishment eczema.

But the biggest difference, evident to Hedy as soon as she entered the office, was a visible loss of authority. He seemed smaller, not merely in bulk but in character, as if someone had scooped out all his arrogance with a spoon, leaving only a husk of desiccated obedience. Hedy wanted to leer, to let him know that she saw his decline and was glad. But she thought of Kurt, and kept her face expressionless.

The news was out now. Photographs of the liberation of Bergen-Belsen, where a Jerseyman had miraculously been found alive, had been placed in the window of the town post office. News reels had been shown in the local cinema, to the audible screams and tears of the audience. No one, not even Orange, could now pretend that the consequence of classing any person a Jew was not fully understood. Hedy wondered if it was guilt that had shrunk this man so much, whether he acknowledged any aspect of his wretched role in history. But Orange gave no hint of it as he finished his notes and raised his face to her. He focused, she noted, not on her eyes but on a space a little lower, around her top lip.

'Well, Miss Bercu, it seems that, thanks to your clever concealment at the home of Mrs Weber, you have had an extraordinary escape. Might I offer you my congratulations, and express relief that you have emerged from this experience no worse for wear. No harm done, it seems.'

Hedy thought of her parents behind fences of barbed wire, being herded towards gas chambers. She wondered how many other people had sat in this chair, listening to Orange's trite, mindless phrases, taut with perfect grammar and devoid of meaning. But the truth was, even now, the power still lay with these grey-suited men, and she was still required to beg for favours at their door.

'And Lieutenant Neumann?'

Orange replaced the cap of his pen with precision. 'I will pass this information on to the appropriate department, of course. But in all honesty, I doubt it will make any difference.'

Hedy shifted in her seat. 'He saved my life. He risked his own to keep me safe and bring me food. Do you understand what the Germans would have done to him if they'd discovered he was protecting a Jew? An officer of his rank?' She heard her volume increase and tried to rein herself back. 'What I'm saying is, he's not a Nazi. He hated the German authorities here as much as' – she paused, knowing her meaning would not be missed, but no longer caring – 'any decent person. And to my mind, that should be taken into account.'

Orange smoothed down his spiky grey moustache with two fingers. 'As I've said, Miss Bercu, the information will be forwarded. But Lieutenant Neumann was – indeed is – a serving officer of the German military and, as such, will be subject to the laws and decisions of the British legal system. I'm sorry that I can't help you further.'

The door swung open. Hedy looked up, surprised to see two British officers enter the room without waiting for permission. The senior of the two, a captain, jerked his head towards Orange. 'The major would like to see you in his office, please, sir.'

Orange's hand went instantly to his collar, pulling it away from his throat. 'I am, as you can see, in the middle of an interview.'

Hedy stood up and addressed the captain directly. 'Actually, Mr Orange has just informed me that he's unable to help me further. So I think this interview is over.'

'Thank you, ma'am'. The captain turned back to Orange. 'After you, sir.'

Orange rose slowly from his desk chair, hoping to give the impression of moving at his own speed, though Hedy suspected it was more that he was feeling a little faint. He walked deliberately to the door and allowed the officers to escort him out.

Hedy picked up her bag and turned to leave the office when another Jersey official entered the room, bustling in a way that suggested frantic activity. Hedy recognised him at once. 'Excuse me, Deputy Le Quesne?'

The man turned to her with a weary smile. 'May I help you?'

'I just wondered . . .' Hedy hesitated; this was probably a waste of time. But there was something about this tired old politician that she trusted. 'Why do those officers want to speak to Mr Orange?'

'All local representatives are being interviewed by British intelligence,' Le Quesne replied, 'for debriefing and assessment.'

'Assessment?'

'To make sure that we exercised our duties correctly. It's been asserted that certain public servants' – he hesitated just long enough to make his inference clear to her – 'were somewhat overzealous in the execution of German orders. Should that be proven, there will be consequences.'

Hedy gave him the smallest smile, then nodded. 'Thank you, Deputy. Good day to you.'

★

Kurt stuffed his toothbrush into the pocket of his rucksack and buckled it up. It had taken him all of five minutes to pack. Five minutes for five years. He looked around the pretty room that had been his bedroom for so long. The little casement window, the Edwardian washstand in the corner, with its china washbowl and jug. That cream-painted plaster ceiling with the hundred little cracks he knew by heart. How many nights had he lain awake till dawn, staring at them and fretting about Hedy – if she was safe, if she had enough to eat, when he would be able to see her again. Now the tables would be turned, and it would be Hedy's turn to lie in a comfortable bed, her mind twisting with imagined nightmares. He threw the rucksack over his shoulder and was preparing to go downstairs when he heard Hedy's voice from the hallway.

By the time he was halfway down, Kurt could see Hedy remonstrating with the harassed British sergeant who had been standing in the billet hallway since early that morning, ticking off names and serial numbers of German officers on his clipboard.

'You don't understand,' Hedy was shouting. 'I am not trying to prevent you doing anything. I just want a private moment with Lieutenant Neumann.'

'I'm sorry, ma'am,' the sergeant replied, 'but these men are now prisoners of war. There is an armoured truck outside that needs to leave in five minutes to deliver them to their assembly point.'

Another five minutes, Kurt thought. Years of clock-watching and waiting, and now everything is happening in five minutes.

'It's all right, Sergeant.' Kurt used his most polished English accent for maximum impact. 'I'm aware of your schedule and I give you my personal guarantee that all officers from this billet will be on that truck at the correct time. If you could just give me a moment?'

The sergeant gave Kurt a doubtful look, and Hedy an even more doubtful one, then stepped out onto the porch to give them privacy. Kurt dumped his rucksack on the parquet floor and looked at her. She looked as lovely as ever, but there was a look about her that startled him, a determination. It was the same look he'd seen the day she'd first arrived at the compound to apply for the translator's job. He stood before her, waiting.

'I saw them lining the soldiers up on the beach. I didn't know if you'd already been taken away.'

'You heard the man. Five minutes.'

'Were you not going to come and say goodbye?'

'I've not been allowed to leave this house since yesterday. And to be honest I wasn't sure . . .' To his horror, he felt a lump in his throat and had to swallow hard. 'I wasn't sure either of us could stand it.'

Hedy nodded. 'But you've forgotten something.'

'Have I?'

'You told me you were with the Jungenschaft. You're meant to remember your manners.'

'Have I offended you?' He sensed laughter building inside,

but he couldn't be certain it wouldn't convert to tears on its way out, and swallowed again.

'A little. I'm still waiting, you see.'

That jutting little chin, that stubbornness. He wanted to tear her clothes from her and take her right then and there on the parquet floor. 'Waiting for what?'

'For my engagement ring.'

A little snort escaped from his nose. 'You're right. Forgive me. These last few days, there hasn't been much opportunity for shopping.' They both giggled a little at this. Then Kurt had an idea. 'Wait there.'

Kurt hurried out to the porch and approached the British sergeant, who was still clutching the clipboard and glancing repeatedly at his watch as if he couldn't make its information stick.

'Excuse me, Sergeant, may I ask you one more favour? That rubber band holding together your notes – may I have it?' The sergeant leaned back a little, anticipating some kind of trickery. 'I need to give it to my girlfriend.' The man looked puzzled for a moment, then seemed to understand. Without a word, he removed the thick brown band from his clipboard and gave it to Kurt, who smiled his gratitude then hurried back to the hallway.

Taking Hedy's left hand, he gently placed the rubber band on her third finger, doubling it over until it fitted. 'It's not exactly what I had in mind, but it's something until I can get to a jeweller's. Which might be a while,' he added.

Hedy splayed out her hand and touched the rubber band with affection. 'I don't mind waiting. This one will always be my favourite.'

He stared at her, still clinging to the tips of her fingers. He wanted to hold her, but was frightened that if he did, he would be unable to let go. He saw himself being dragged from the room like a screaming toddler, wailing and flailing. The humiliation was almost as unbearable as the sense of loss. He groped for some-thing to say, and opted for a lousy joke. 'Summer or winter wedding?'

'The day after you're released.'

'You know that could be years?'

'Of course I know.'

'There's a public outcry over the concentration camps. People will want revenge, and the politicians may provide it.'

'I know that too.'

He continued to massage the ends of her fingers, as if trying to press all the emotions of his body into the smallest possible area. 'What are you going to do now?'

Hedy shrugged. 'Stay here for a while, try to find out what happened to my parents, to Roda and my other siblings. Europe is a mess; it will probably take a while.'

'How will you live?'

'I'll get another job. I hear lots of evacuees are planning to return – perhaps the Mitchells will come back.' She smiled with sadness. 'Of course, they might not need me any more.'

'I can't see anyone not needing you any more.'

'I'll be fine. I'm tougher than I look.'

'That I know.'

'I'll be like King Canute – letting the waves roll over me, knowing there's nothing I can do to stop them.'

He grabbed her and kissed her, then he pulled back and threw his rucksack back over his shoulder. 'I have to go. Don't wait to watch the boat. Go home and see Dorothea.'

She blinked her agreement and bit her lip.

'*Auf Wiedersehen.*'

She shook her head. '*Bis bald.*'

He nodded, walked quickly out through the porch to the waiting armoured truck, and slumped down onto the bench without waiting to be asked. He knew the dam was about to burst, and that when it did, he would be out of control for some time. It was almost a relief when the door crunched shut and delivered him to the dark, chill metal interior of his future.

She waited to watch the boat, of course. She knew that she would, even when she promised not to. Standing by the sea wall, shivering in the stiff spring breeze for two hours, even though she knew full well that even if Kurt was one of those on the beach below, she would never be able to make him out. Not among those vast snakes of tiny toy soldiers that stretched across the West Park sand, some in straight lines and some in odd curled shapes, as though the hundreds of figures down there were attempting to spell out a giant message across the shore. The men were peaceful, as far as she could make out – sitting or standing, muttering to their neighbours, smoking if they had any tobacco, or simply staring at the horizon.

Strange, Hedy contemplated, what terror these figures had once stirred in her. Today they were nothing but numb, exhausted boys in grubby wool tunics, all longing to go home, yet knowing that that dream, too, had vanished, along with all the others. She almost felt sorry for them. There must have been others like Kurt, youngsters forced into a movement they never believed in. But perhaps there were just as many who still believed, who still held that filthy doctrine dear. Right now, she didn't have the energy to figure it out, or even to care. An exhaustion of monstrous proportion was slowly gripping her, and had it not been for the cold and the freshness of the air, she felt she might fall asleep on her feet.

Out in the bay, the landing craft sat waiting on the flat silver sea for their human cargo. By evening they would all be gone, and only the low silhouette of Elizabeth Castle would be left against the pearly sky. Normality was rapidly returning to the island. Trucks filled with coal rumbled through the streets, shops made window displays of goods that would be available to buy in a matter of days – shoes, children's clothes, cooking pots. Last night's *Evening Post* had announced that the postal service would be operational again from today. Tonight, Hedy and Dorothea would sit down to a delicious tuna hotpot that would swell their bellies to bursting, while Kurt would be halfway across a rolling English Channel, on a share of prisoners' rations.

Hedy stood watching the landing craft swallow load after load, until the wind bit through her thin coat and into her bones, and she finally accepted it was time to go. Slowly she made her way along the Esplanade through crowds of smiling locals, trying to respond to each joyful greeting with something appropriate. But as she grew closer to West Park Avenue, a sense of foreboding grew in her. She told herself it was just the misery of losing Kurt and the massive emotional adjustment of returning to a forgotten life. But by the time she reached the house she knew that something bad was going to happen. Pushing open the front door – everyone had now stopped locking their doors, as they had before the Occupation – she heard voices in the kitchen and hurried through to investigate.

Dorothea was standing with her back to the kitchen sink. At the table sat a man of about forty, wearing a British uniform with the two white stripes of a corporal.

Hedy stared from one to the other. 'What's going on?'

Dorothea's voice was tight and croaky. 'This gentleman has brought a message from the German War Office. Apparently it arrived a week ago, but with all the mayhem, nothing was sent on. So the British Commander ordered it to be delivered by hand.' She held up a small piece of creamy-brown paper. It was years since Hedy had seen one, but she instantly recognised it as a telegram, and froze. 'Anton?'

Dorothea nodded, and handed the paper to her. 'It's in German, but the meaning's pretty clear.'

Hedy read the typewritten words on the white strips of paper several times before they made any sense: 'Regret to inform you Lance Corporal Anton Weber 734659 24th Infantry Division died in service of his country 14th October, 1944.'

Hedy rushed to Dorothea and put her arms around her, waiting for the outpouring, but nothing happened. They both just stood silently together in the kitchen for what felt like a long time, holding each other. Perhaps the probability of Anton's death had lived with them for so long that its reality no longer shocked them. Or perhaps neither of them had any emotion left to expend. In her mind, Hedy reached out for Anton's face: the day outside the cinema when he had first introduced to her to Dorothea; the day they had searched for limpets down at Seymour Tower. But all she felt was a hollowness. Only when the corporal awkwardly scraped his chair on the kitchen floor did she recall there was anyone else in the room.

'Sorry to interrupt,' he broke in, embarrassed, 'but is there anything else I can do?'

Hedy went across to shake the man's hand. 'No, thank you. It was good of you to come.'

He nodded. 'They're never good news. I got a similar one last year – sister and her family all killed by a V2. Nothing prepares you.'

'I'm so sorry.' Hedy noticed that his eyes, which were warm and hazel, were set against a tan, leathery skin, suggesting he'd spent part of the war in North Africa. 'The Occupation has been very hard . . . but at least we didn't suffer the Blitz.'

'We all fought our own war,' the corporal replied. 'I'm very sorry for your loss, Mrs Weber.'

'Are you?' Dorothea spat. Hedy held up her hand, indicating this was the wrong moment and target for bitterness, but Dorothea couldn't stop herself. 'He died fighting for Hitler. I wouldn't want you to waste your precious sympathy.'

The corporal turned to her. 'I mean it. I came across a ton of different nationalities fighting on both sides. Only thing they had in common was not one bugger actually wanted to be there – pardon my French.'

Dorothea's scowl faded. 'Thank you for saying that, sir.'

'Please' – he held up a palm – 'Frank, Frank Flanagan. Sick to death of being a number, to be honest. Just want to get back to Cheshire.'

Hedy caught the affection in his voice and felt sick with envy; to have a home to return to, a community still filled with familiar faces.

Flanagan picked up his cap from the table, then turned back to Dorothea. 'Anyway, you've had a shock, so I'll leave you to it, now your friend's here.'

He slipped quietly down the hall and let himself out, leaving Hedy still holding the telegram in her hand and Dorothea standing in the middle of the kitchen as if she had no idea what to do next.

'Is Kurt gone?'

Hedy nodded.

'So that's that.' Dorothea pushed the hair from her eyes and gave herself a tiny shake. 'I suppose I should make dinner.'

'Let me.'

'No, I'd rather have something to do.'

Dorothea busied herself in the kitchen, and at six o'clock the women sat down at a kitchen table laid for two, spooning out generous portions of tuna hotpot. In the corner stood the wireless; human voices and music filled the room, connecting them to a distant, rejoicing world. While they ate, the newscaster informed them that the last unrepentant Axis forces had been beaten back in Yugoslavia by local partisans, supported by British troops, and that Nagoya had been bombed heavily, bringing victory in Japan ever closer. Then Tommy Handley evoked gales of laughter from his audience by his rendition of the Minister of Aggravation and Mysteries at the Office of Twerps. Dorothea offered Hedy another portion of hotpot, but she declined. Neither of them had yet eaten half of what was on their plate.

The delivery of the evening paper caused a brief hiatus. Hedy flicked through the proclamations of the Bailiff and notices about the restoration of sterling, until her eye was caught by a smaller headline on an inside page. The report described attempts by some senior Germans to escape capture by dressing as civilians and trying to pass as locals. British army officials, it reported, had discovered one such coward on an abandoned farm property, hiding in an outhouse. He had 'offered no resistance', but had wept 'hysterically' on his arrest. He was named as Erich Gerhard Wildgrube, formerly of the Geheime Feldpolizei.

After dinner the women washed up together, using baking soda and vinegar. From the open window, they could hear the shouting and singing of a party going on next door; children were running in and out of the garden wearing cooking pots for German helmets and firing finger guns at each other, while the adults inside were belting out rousing choruses of 'All The Nice Girls Love A Sailor' and 'Bill Bailey'. As the songs came to their loud, chaotic climaxes, Hedy and Dorothea couldn't help smiling at each other.

The plates were put away. The sun was dipping, and shafts of golden light peeped down the hallway. Dorothea switched off the radio and lit a small coal fire as the chill of the evening began to bite. They sat back down at the table; Dorothea with some mending, Hedy with a book. Over two hours, Dorothea sewed one button, while Hedy read two pages. Neither of them spoke. The party next door gradually fizzled to an end and they heard the door bang as people left. The clock ticked on the wall and the light dimmed. There were two new candles in the larder but neither of them suggested lighting one. Night fell, and Dorothea went to bed.

It was the end of the Occupation. It was over. They were both alive and free.

Hedy sat for another hour in the dark kitchen, staring at nothing. Then she, too, went to bed.

Epilogue

1946

The suitcase was simply not going to close. She tried sitting on it, bouncing her bottom on it, then leaning heavily on one end while trying to push one of the chrome hasps into its slot. Eventually Hedy gave in to the inevitable and removed one cardigan and the slippers she'd been given at Christmas. She had other woollens, she told herself, and she could buy another pair of slippers with her first wages, once her ration card had been reissued. The case instantly closed without difficulty, and satisfied that it wasn't going to pop open again, she dragged it off the bed and down the stairs, being careful not to scratch the polished wood at the side of the runner carpet. Mrs Mitchell was extremely proud of her staircase.

She was glad that the family were all out at this hour. The thought of another goodbye was more than she could take. The farewell party they'd given her last night had been sweet and moving, with thoughtful gifts of handkerchiefs and lavender soap, and a handmade card from their daughter. She knew that she would miss them horribly, and had made them promise to write every week. All that supervised homework and the trips to the beach hadn't felt like work at all; even the housework had been no burden, as she revelled in the scent of freshly laundered sheets and furniture polish, and she'd taken great pleasure in lining up the family's wellies in order of size in the hall. But at other times, walking alone on her day off or lying in her solitary bed, the gap between the family's cosiness and her personal situation tugged at her soul, and in recent weeks she'd known for certain that it was time to go.

She pulled on her thick brown winter coat and its matching hat with the pink trim; it was mid-December, and the frost was already thick on the grass. At the hall mirror she had only time to apply some lipstick and dab a little extra powder on her nose before she heard the honk of the car horn outside. Taking a last look around the elegant, gleaming hallway, she picked up her case and walked out into the winter afternoon.

Dorothea waved at her from the passenger seat of the old Austin. Frank Flanagan, after heaving himself out of the driver's seat, helped her with the suitcase, making a joke about how light it was.

'This all you've got?'

'My worldly possessions,' Hedy confessed with a wry smile. 'Do you think I need to start making a trousseau?'

'Well, Dory never had one, and I weren't bothered. And I don't imagine it's your linens your fiancé will be interested in when he gets out.'

Hedy laughed and climbed into the back seat while Frank restarted the car. Soon they were heading down St Saviours Road towards the harbour. Dorothea stretched her hand over the back of her seat towards Hedy, twisted round in her seat like a schoolgirl. 'Oh, Hedy, I'm so excited for you! What time does the boat get to Weymouth?'

'We dock at six tomorrow morning. Then I have to catch a train – three trains actually – to get to Plumpton.'

Dorothea raised her hand to her cheek. 'Goodness! You'll be exhausted. I should have brought some sandwiches for you. Didn't I say, Frank, I should have made her some sandwiches?'

'Certainly did – woke me up to say it too.' Frank grinned at Hedy in the mirror and gave her a wink.

'And when will you get to see Kurt?'

'If the paperwork comes through, next Thursday. He looks

good in the photo he sent me – he's been working outside most days since he was moved again.'

'You'll give him my love, won't you? You two are going to be so happy.' She turned to face the front, and Hedy sat back to take in her last views of the island. The roads where Kurt had walked her weak, failing body in German uniform ... Mr Reis's bakery, now owned by someone else . . . the jail where Kurt served his time. Memories galloped in, images forming and evaporating. By the time the car pulled up at the end of the quay, her head was spinning.

Frank went off to park the car, while Dorothea stood at Hedy's side, looking up at the ship. The stripes of its giant funnel stood sharp against the darkening sky, and shiny blue cranes swung cargo across its bows to the hold. Far below, the water, closing in on its high-tide mark, slapped against the ancient blackened stone of the quay and hinted at the swell beyond. Hedy looked at Dorothea, remembering the last time they had both stood in this spot.

'Anton would be happy for you, you know,' Hedy said, reading her thoughts.

Dorothea nodded. 'I know. Frank's been so kind, and it's made such a difference. Everyone at my new office only knows me as Mrs Flanagan. Sometimes I wish I could tell them about Anton – tell them how wonderful he was – but . . .'

Hedy nodded. 'Sometimes it's best to let things be.'

'Anyway, we're moving to Cheshire in the summer. Frank wants to start a new business – all his contacts are there. Be a fresh start for us both.'

'Don't forget to write.'

'Silly! Why would I not write to my best friend?'

Hedy held her close for a moment, the brims of their hats rubbing against each other. Frank arrived with Hedy's suitcase, and the three of them huddled together in the cold, speaking over each other with their wishes of good luck and promises to visit each other soon. When there was no more to say, Hedy gave them both a final kiss and made her way up the gangplank, turning twice to wave until she saw them turn and head back to their car. She walked down two enclosed staircases to her reserved seat where she stowed her case, then returned to the stern of the top deck and found a quiet section of rail to wait for departure. Soon the engines were thundering beneath her, sending vibrations pulsating up through her feet and knees. The water below fizzed white and foamy, and with creaking slowness, the ship pulled away from the quayside and headed for the harbour mouth.

For a while Hedy stood watching the departing shore, marvelling at the light reflections skipping across the blackness of the water. Then she reached into her bag and took out her most precious possession – the beribboned brown envelope containing all her recent letters. She took the one from the top, smiling at Roda's curly, girlish hand; she thought about the day it had flopped onto the doormat of the Mitchells' hallway and her employers' excitement when they saw her reaction. Now her eyes, as always, jumped to her favourite section:

> . . . and now find myself living by the sea in Hadera. So can you imagine my delight when I found out that our darling baby brother was less than fifty kilometres away in Tel Aviv? Daniel is doing so well, and writes regularly to Golda in London now the post is working again. Chana and her husband love Australia and plan to stay. We are all agreed, and very determined, that no matter how long it takes, we will find out what happened to Mama and Papa. We believe the Red Cross may be able to help.

Hedy tucked the letter back into place with a sigh. In truth, she knew there would be little to discover. Dates and precise locations wouldn't change what they already knew. Perhaps, though, the information would bring a little closure, maybe eventually acceptance, after all the years of uncertainty. Her fingers slid back into the envelope, this time drawing out the sheet with the words *HMP Ford* printed at the top.

> Sweetheart, I can't believe this new job means you will be only a few miles from my new placement. I'm enjoying farm work, and there's talk of release within the next six months. As soon as I have a date, you must choose a wedding ring, and start saving for your ticket to Germany! Being without you has been the only unbearable part of this. Can't wait to see you. All my love, K.

She pressed the thin, translucent paper to her chest before placing it carefully back in her bag. And at the same time, she smiled at the brown rubber band on her third finger and kissed it.

The harbour began to fade, and the sea grew choppier as the ship chugged towards the open sea. It looked so small from here, this tiny prison of an island. She knew she was one of the lucky ones. So many had perished here at the invaders' hands, so many others would never see these shores again. It was hard to think about them without a furious desire for revenge. How easy it was to access hate, Hedy pondered. How close to the surface that putrid emotion always floated, waiting for a target, biding its time to find a focus and bloom like a poisonous algae, while forgiveness lay limp and impotent at the bottom of the soul, guiltily aware that duty called, but without the energy to do its job. Would she and Kurt have the strength to resist that temptation? 'Even if you forget the past, it will remember you,' her mother had been fond of saying. Only in the years to come, Hedy supposed, would she discover if that were true.

The waves were fierce now, and the ship rolled back and forth as it ploughed across the southern bay of the island and prepared to round Noirmont Point. Hedy gripped hard to the rail, sensing the unseen forces that were pushing and pulling at the hull, battering it below the surface. The currents of the Channel would try to drag the ship west as it pressed on towards the English coast; only the strength of the steel pistons beneath would keep it true.

Hedy closed her eyes as the freezing wind sucked at her skin, and smiled into the dark. She and Kurt would be all right, she decided. They would find a way to discard their past, seek out different lands and create new adventures. Europe was broken, but already thousands were coming together with tools, ideas and laws with which to mend it. A hundred miles away at this very moment there were young, scrub-faced children being informed of Hedy's imminent arrival, and a fresh bed being made up for her in a pretty country bedroom. In a few months Kurt would be a free man. And somewhere beyond that invisible horizon lay the fresh allure of Weymouth harbour, working farms and scattered villages, firm ploughed fields of winter wheat and the crisp golden light of the morning.

Acknowledgements

In accessing the factual material on which this novel is based, I would like to thank Dr Gilly Carr, Senior Lecturer at the University of Cambridge, and author of numerous books, journals and papers on Occupation history. Her submission to the Yad Vashem World Holocaust Remembrance Center for the acceptance of Dorothea Weber (née Le Brocq) of Righteous Among the Nations status did much to bring that extraordinary piece of history to public attention, and her contribution to a wider understanding of Channel Islands history is to be applauded.

Thanks are due to Bob Le Sueur and Bruce Scott Dalgleish for sharing their personal memories; to Susannah Waters and Julie Corbin for their substantial assistance in my transition from screenwriting to prose; to Maurice Gran, Jo Briggs and Gabbie Asher for their scrutiny of Jewish issues and phrases; to the brilliant George Aboud who did more than anyone to help shape this project, all out of the kindness of her writer's heart; to my late grandmother Grace Lecoat for passing on to me the 'Beautiful Swedes' song (originally from an amateur Green Room Club production of the period).

Thanks also to Sean McTernan, my book agent John Beaton for showing faith, and to my incredibly supportive editor Alison Rae.

Finally, to my fantastic husband, who dealt with my frequent tantrums and insistence that this project was impossible to complete with his usual stoicism, humour and love.